THE POACHER'S DAUGHTER

Center Point
Large Print

Also by Michael Zimmer and available from
Center Point Large Print:

Dust and Glory

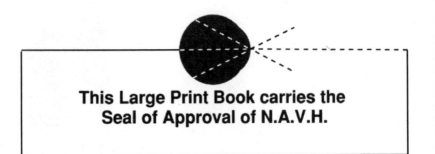

**This Large Print Book carries the
Seal of Approval of N.A.V.H.**

THE
POACHER'S
DAUGHTER

A Western Story

MICHAEL
ZIMMER

CENTER POINT LARGE PRINT
THORNDIKE, MAINE

This Center Point Large Print edition is published
in the year 2016 by arrangement with
Golden West Literary Agency.

First Edition, March 2014

The text of this Large Print edition is unabridged.
In other aspects, this book may vary
from the original edition.
Printed in the United States of America
on permanent paper.
Set in 16-point Times New Roman type.

ISBN: 978-1-62899-975-4

Library of Congress Cataloging-in-Publication Data

Names: Zimmer, Michael, 1955– author.
Title: The poacher's daughter : a western story / Michael Zimmer.
Description: Center Point Large Print edition. | Thorndike, Maine :
Center Point Large Print, 2016. | ©2014
Identifiers: LCCN 2016008254 | ISBN 9781628999754
   (hardcover : alk. paper)
Subjects: LCSH: Fathers and daughters—Fiction. | Frontier and pioneer
life—Fiction. | Yellowstone River Valley—Fiction. | Montana—Fiction.
| Large type books. | GSAFD: Western stories.
Classification: LCC PS3576.I467 P63 2016 | DDC 813/.54—dc23
LC record available at http://lccn.loc.gov/2016008254

Dedication

I would like to dedicate this novel to the many individuals who made it possible. A small sampling of those include: Cathay Williams (Buffalo Soldier); Nellie "The Angel of Tombstone" Cashman (nurse and prospector); Margaret Heffenan Borland (first woman to boss a trail herd to Kansas, 1873); Mary Fields and Miss Charley Parkhurst (stagecoach drivers); Annie Oakley and Lillian Smith (sharpshooters and rivals); Rose "The Rose of Cimarron" Dunn, Pearl Hart, Belle Starr, and Laura "Rose of the Wild Bunch" Bullion (cattle rustlers, horse thieves, bank and stagecoach robbers); Miss F.M. Miller, Miss S.M. Burche, and Mamie Fossett (deputy U.S. marshals, Oklahoma and Indian Territory); Ellen Liddy (Cattle Kate) Watson (unjustly accused of, then hanged for, cattle rustling by the local Cattlemen's Association); Martha Jane "Calamity Jane" Canary (muleskinner, stagecoach driver, sharpshooter, nurse, prospector, and, altogether, probably the most colorful of them all).

And last but not least, Vanessa Zimmer (biker, mountain woman, sharpshooter, journalist, and adventurer, who would have fit right in).

My thanks to all of these, and the thousands of others.

HORSE THIEF
1885

Chapter One

Rose Edwards spotted the horses as soon as they rounded the bend along the Yellowstone River, about a mile away. She paused in her work to watch, easing back from the edge of the bluff where she wouldn't be easily seen.

The horses were a motley bunch—paints, bays, buckskins, sorrels, and blacks. They were being driven upstream at a swift trot by four wranglers. Three of the horsemen were with the herd. The fourth rode about fifty yards in advance, a rifle balanced across the pommel of his saddle. Rose watched until they turned the horses away from the river, toward the mouth of a side cañon where a trail led through the bluffs to the short-grass country above, then returned to her shoveling.

It was a warm day, but she was shaded by an old, lightning-scarred pine, and a gentle breeze kept the sweat across her brow to a minimum. The pine stood on a knoll above the broken, yellow-gray bluffs that flanked the river and gave it its name. It commanded a spectacular vista of rolling plains, jutting buttes, and distant, snow-capped mountain peaks. Just yesterday she'd come up here with a cup of tea to sit and gaze out across the wind-swept miles and daydream, but that seemed like a lifetime ago. Behind her, down the long, easy slope to the meadow where the Edwards' homestead had stood, the charred walls of her cabin still smoldered. The barn—a small picket shed with a sod roof—had also been set ablaze, although without hay to fuel the burning brand tossed inside, the fire had soon smothered in the thick dust of the dirt floor.

The mob had been more thorough in setting fire to the house. After tearing the interior of the cabin apart in their search for Muggy's gold, they'd shoved what furniture the Edwardses owned into the center of the dwelling's single room and doused it with coal oil. Then they'd trooped outside, where one of the masked vigilantes had tossed a sputtering torch through the door. Within minutes flames were soaring sixty feet into the night sky, embers darting like fireflies. Some of the tiny cinders fell into the dry grass surrounding the cabin, and soon a prairie fire was racing toward the open county to the east, where it might have burned all the way to Junction City if a thunder-storm hadn't blown up shortly before dawn and extinguished it. The rain had been too late to save the cabin, though.

Rose kept her back to the tilted walls and collapsed roof of her home as she shoveled the final spadeful of dirt over Muggy's grave. She knew she ought to cover the site with stones, but she was exhausted after last night's ordeal, her shoulders aching from digging in the rocky soil. Nor was she feeling overly charitable toward the body she'd just interred. Muggy had been a poor husband in her estimation, and she blamed him not only for his own death at the hands of a lynch mob, but also for bringing the mob to her door.

Muggy's christened name was Robert Thomas, but Rose doubted if half a dozen people in all of Montana Territory knew that. He'd been called Muggy for as long as she'd known him, and even signed their marriage certificate that way. Not that theirs had ever been a traditional marriage. Muggy had spent the last eight months up in Helena, gambling and drinking all night, then shacking up through the day with a Jane-about-town called Daisy LaFee. In all that time he hadn't sent a single dime, not even a letter, down the trail to his wife. Rose had been contemplating a divorce for months —they'd been married a little over four years, and he'd been away for all but a few weeks of that—but she'd been afraid he might sell the homestead out from under her if she attempted it.

The place wasn't much, Rose supposed, but she was fond of it. She'd worked hard to make it a home, cultivating a fair-size garden along the creek, raising enough truck to haul a wagonload of corn and squash into Billings every fall, which she traded for staples to see her through the winter. It had been a good life, though spartan and lonely.

She was still debating how to finish the grave when she heard the clatter of hoofs on the trail leading up from the river and remembered the horses. Although alone, she wasn't particularly worried. A Sharps rifle leaned against the trunk of

11

the ancient pine, and Muggy's Smith & Wesson revolver, wrapped in its holster and cartridge belt, lay close by. She could handle both proficiently.

Rose cinched the Smith & Wesson around her waist, then went over to stand beside the Sharps. It wasn't long before a cowboy on a lathered pinto hove into sight. He acted surprised when he spied the smoking hull of the cabin. Butting a lever gun to his thigh, he came forward at a walk, but hauled up when he spotted Rose. Then he grinned and lowered the rifle. Under the sprawling limbs of the old pine, Rose also relaxed. Leaving the Sharps behind, she walked out to meet him.

The rider pulled up at the foot of the knoll. "Ye be all right, Rosie?" he called.

"Hello, Wiley. Yeah, I'm still kickin'."

Wiley Collins laughed, then lifted his gaze. His expression sobered when he saw the grave. "Muggy?" he asked.

"Uhn-huh."

"How'd it happen?"

"Vigilantes. They followed him down from Helena."

Wiley's expression darkened. "I'd heard he'd been up to the Last Chance," he said, referring to Helena's old moniker from its days as a tented mining community. "I sure never expected this."

"I doubt if he did, either," Rose replied with unexpected bluntness, sweeping a strand of blonde hair from her eyes. She was tall for a woman, but not overly so; stout without being fat.

Sturdy, Muggy used to call her when he was feeling charitable. She had an old gray dress hanging over the tailgate of a small wagon beside the barn, but was wearing the heavy duck trousers, faded blue shirt, and mule-ear boots she normally donned for gardening. A sweat-stained hat lay on the ground beside the Sharps. She'd washed her gardening clothes yesterday and hung them on the line to dry, which was why they'd escaped the fire. The Sharps and the Smith & Wesson had belonged to Muggy, and had been tossed out of the cabin's rear window by one of the vigilantes soon after the mob broke in. The rest of her clothing and household articles had perished in the flames.

"Did they say why they hung him?" Wiley asked.

"They weren't specific. There was some mention of missing gold, but . . ." She shrugged, letting the words trail off. She felt baffled by her lack of emotion, the absence of grief. There were shades of anger that came and went, but they were never overpowering. It was as if she'd found a squirrel lying dead under the old pine that morning, rather than her husband. "I reckon it was bound to happen sooner or later," she finished lamely.

They were distracted from their conversation by dust billowing above the lip of the coulée that was the head of the trail. Soon, horses were spilling out of the gulch as if from the earth itself. Rose counted twenty-seven head, but could have missed a few in the powdery confusion. The wranglers turned the herd east, away from the cabin, and let it spread out to graze. While two of the men stayed with the horses, a third loped his mount toward Rose and Wiley.

"Why, ain't that Shorty Tibbs?" Rose asked, glancing at Wiley with a trace of amusement in her light blue eyes. "Last I'd heard, you'd sworn to have his liver on a stick."

"Aw, now, Rosie, ye know how it is. Fellas get in a row from time to time, but they patch things up. Besides, I'd feel mighty bad if I shot him. His mother's an awful sweet person. I met her down in Texas once, some years back."

Reining up alongside Wiley, Shorty said: "Hello, Rose."

"How, Shorty."

He glanced at the cabin. "Was it lightning? We saw some over this way about dawn."

"It wasn't lightnin', ye dolt," Wiley Collins said. He pointed out the grave with his chin. "The vigilantes got Muggy last night. Rosie's buryin' him."

Shorty looked genuinely distressed as he removed his hat, revealing a forehead that was as white as a fish's belly and a bald, freckled pate where only a few wispy strands of curly brown hair remained. "Rose, I am truly sorry. Muggy was a fine man."

With a flash of irritation, she said: "Shorty, you're a dang' liar. You know as well as me Muggy was a scoundrel."

"That may be, but he was your husband, and

you've always treated me kindly. I had a wife myself when I was younger. She died giving birth. The boy died with her."

"Aw, hell." Rose looked away. "I didn't mean to be so snappy, and I'm sorry about your wife. I didn't know you'd ever had one."

"She's been gone almost fifteen years." He returned the hat to his head. "What'll you do now, if you don't mind my asking? If you're thinking of rebuilding, I'd be proud to help."

"Hold on, hoss," Wiley said quickly. "We've got these ponies to deliver, lest ye've forgot?"

"I ain't forgot, but I won't leave a woman in a bad fix, either. Especially Rose."

"That's all right, Shorty," Rose interjected. "To tell you the truth, I ain't decided yet what I'm gonna do."

"Why don't you ride along with us?" Shorty offered. "We could use an extra hand, and I've seen you ride. You're as good as any man."

"Naw, you boys go on." She grinned to take any sting out of her refusal. "Likely you're needin' to jingle your spurs some, anyway."

"Now, Rosie, I know what ye're thinkin', but it ain't so," Wiley protested.

"Aw, the hell it ain't," Shorty said, winking at Rose. "Wiley's right, we can't tarry, but you're welcome to ride along, if you'd like. You know me 'n' Wiley, and those two jaybirds"—he inclined his head toward the horsemen still with the herd—"they're good men. That short, skinny fella with the sombrero is Garcia. The other one is Jimmy Frakes, from the Sheridan range. They'll give you no trouble. But if you're set on rebuilding, why, I'd be glad to help with that, too. We've gotta run these horses down the Musselshell to Two-Hats's place, but I could be back inside a week."

Rose eyed the two men thoughtfully. Wiley Collins was the taller of the pair. He had an unruly mop of sandy hair that curled out from under his hat, and eyes as blue as a mountain lake. He was broad through the shoulders, lean in the hips, clean-shaven when time permitted.

Shorty Tibbs stood about five foot seven which was only a shade under average, but he was of slight build, which gave him a smallish appearance. He was quick and sure in action, and had a forward roll to his shoulders that made him look as if he was always traveling just a little faster than his bowed legs could keep up with. He had dark eyes, a black mustache, and a face weathered to a deep walnut hue.

Although the idea of traveling with them was intriguing, Rose was leery. She knew Wiley as a randy sort, and suspected not too many evenings would pass before he'd try to slip into her blankets, Muggy's recent death notwithstanding. Nor would it be the first time, if she allowed it. It had been lonely with Muggy gone so much, and Wiley had passed through on a fairly regular basis.

Still, as much as she loved this place, this little homestead above the Yellowstone, it occurred to her that it might be time to move on. A yearning for something different had been building inside of her for some time now. She knew she could raise another cabin, with or without Shorty's assistance, she just wasn't sure she wanted to.

"What do you say, Rose?" Shorty asked, leaning forward in his saddle.

She glanced at the corral, where her strawberry roan gelding, Albert, was watching the horses across the trail with high-headed interest. Yesterday there'd been a pair of mules in the corral, and Muggy's bay last night, but the vigilantes had taken everything except the roan, leaving Rose with a warning to clear out before the end of autumn.

"All right," she said impulsively. "I'll come ride the Owlhoot with you two roosters. Why not?"

"That's a girl," Shorty said, grinning.

And despite some misgivings, Rose couldn't help a smile of her own. It was about time, she thought, that she sought some adventures of her own, instead of always listening to the tales of others, told to her as they passed by her door. About damned time Rose Edwards found some tall tales of her own to spill around the hearth.

Hers was a pretty sorry outfit upon which to go see the elephant, Rose reflected, backing off for a broader view. Albert stood hipshot beside the corral, his graying muzzle drooped toward the ground. On his back was a Mother Hubbard saddle with a high, flat horn. Although solid and well-made, the rig had seen hard use over the years; web-like cracks that no amount of oiling would ever close tracked the heavy leather *mochila*, and the stitching was frayed.

The rifle scabbard under the right stirrup strap was patterned for the lever-action carbine she'd lost to the vigilantes, and was a poor fit for the long-barreled Sharps, but it would have to do. She'd folded the gray dress she'd worn last night, a chunk of lye soap, and a couple of rags for washing—all that had escaped the fire—into her saddlebags, then dug up a tin money box from the northeast corner of the cabin, having to burrow through a section of collapsed roof to reach it. The box, buried under several inches of loose soil and a twenty-gallon water keg, had survived the blaze but yielded only $6 and some change, the deed to the land, and her marriage certificate. Wrapping the money and legal documents in a rag, Rose stowed them in her saddlebags.

Her bedroll was an old Hudson's Bay blanket she'd cinched over Albert's back and hips on cold winter nights. It was worn and mouse-chewed, but, as with the rifle scabbard, it would suffice. The larger hand tools—spade, axe, hoe, and bucksaw—would be left in the barn. She'd backed the wagon inside, too, where it would be sheltered from the elements. She could return later with a team and haul everything into Billings to sell if she didn't rebuild.

She still needed a heavier bedroll, a slicker to shed the rain, and a good knife to replace the one she'd lost in the fire, but what she wanted most was ammunition for the big, single-shot Sharps. All she had was the cartridge Muggy had kept chambered—a .44-90. The Smith & Wesson revolver held a full wheel of .38-caliber rounds, plus another twenty or so in the loops of her cartridge belt, but, even with that, she'd be handicapped if they ran into trouble. And Rose had little doubt that, sooner or later, they would. Neither Wiley nor Shorty would tell her where the horses they were running up to Two-Hats's trading post had come from, but she figured they were Crow ponies, stolen off the reservation south of the Yellowstone.

The Crows, who had always been on more or less friendly terms with whites and had scouted for the cavalry during the late Sioux hostilities, ran sizable herds. It had become fairly profitable for horse thieves to slip onto the reservation and steal a few head whenever the fancy struck them. Rose had seen Indian ponies selling openly on the streets of Billings, Bozeman, and Miles City, and even though everyone knew where they came from, no one except the military seemed to care.

It took thirty minutes to ready her outfit. While she was doing that, Wiley and Shorty returned to the herd to switch mounts. By the time Rose got there, Wiley was champing at the bit.

"Let's go!" he barked. "By God, if this is what

it's like to travel with a woman, I'm regretting it already." He jerked his horse around and rode off at a gallop.

Reining alongside, Shorty said: "That's just Wiley. Don't pay him any heed."

"I didn't hear nothin' from him I ain't already heard twice from Muggy," Rose replied. "I never paid him no mind, neither."

Shorty smiled. "Slip in there between Jimmy and Garcia and bring up the rear. I'm going to ride point a while. Keep your eyes peeled, and if you see anything, even dust on the horizon, you fog it on up and let me know."

Jimmy and Garcia were already hazing the herd northward. Guiding Albert into the drag position, Rose was immediately engulfed in dust. In less than fifty yards she could feel it in her eyes and on her tongue, tickling her nostrils. She pulled one of the rags out of her saddlebags and tied it around her nose like a bandanna. She only looked back once, just as the herd dropped behind a swell of land that she knew would take them out of sight of the cabin's remains. It wasn't the cabin she found herself gazing at, though, it was the old, gnarled pine and the rocky ground under it, where Muggy's grave was already too far away to see.

"Well, that's it then," she said softly, the bandanna puffing in and out like a beating heart. Turning away, she knuckled impatiently at her eyes, which had teared up in the dust. "Serves you right," she added, although, for the life of her, she couldn't have said whether she was speaking to Muggy or herself.

They made good time, despite the woolliness of the country. Although the cavvy had been pushed hard the night before, it had enough spunk left to keep things lively that first day. It had been close to noon when they left the bluffs above the Yellowstone. By dusk they were well into the foothills of the Bull Mountains, that low range dividing the drainages of the Yellowstone and Musselshell Rivers. Wiley led them to a shallow box cañon where a dilapidated jack-leg fence made from juniper poles closed off the mouth. They drove the horses inside, and while Jimmy and Garcia rigged a gate from loose poles left lying nearby and Shorty started cutting boughs to patch gaps elsewhere, Wiley ordered Rose to gather some wood and start a fire.

"New hand does the cookin'," he told her. Then he was gone, riding back the way they'd come to look for signs of pursuit.

Rose chafed at the assignment. She couldn't help thinking it was on account of her being a woman, rather than the new hand. Still, she knew the Owlhoot well enough to know that partnerships along it dissolved faster than a spring snow. It wouldn't be long before someone quit and someone else joined up. Then they'd see who did the cooking.

By the time she'd gathered enough wood to last

21

the evening, the men were just finishing their repairs to the fence. Shorty came over, slapping dust from his chaps. "Build your fire over there," he said, nodding toward a sandy coulée with tall banks. "Keep it small, and we'll put it out before full dark. Up this high, even dying coals can been seen for miles."

"Who's chasin' us, Shorty?"

"Why, I don't know that anyone's chasing us. We're just being cautious."

Jimmy Frakes jogged his horse over, leaving Garcia with the herd. Jimmy was a lanky kid of eighteen or so, the only one in the bunch who didn't sport a sidearm, although he carried an old model Henry repeater on his saddle. Rose had known Jimmy's daddy in the old days, when the Sioux still ran wild and buffalo covered the plains. The Frakeses had homesteaded a small ranch some miles from her pap's place west of Bozeman, before moving on to a larger spread near where Sheridan, Wyoming Territory, now stood. Rose had been fourteen and Jimmy only eight or nine when the Frakeses left the Gallatin Valley; although she remembered the family well, she couldn't tell if Jimmy recognized her.

Before Jimmy could dismount, Shorty tossed him a collapsible canvas bucket. "There's a spring about three hundred yards east of here. Fetch some water. Rose, there's bacon and flour in my war bag. Use what you need. I'll bring in some more wood."

It didn't take long to fry up the bacon and make some biscuits, although even Rose had to admit it was a wanting meal—the meat too crispy, the biscuits black as coal on the bottom, and only water to wash it down. Afterward, Jimmy took a plate to Garcia, then stayed with him to talk. Wiley hadn't returned, but Shorty set aside some food for when he did. Then he settled back to roll a cigarette.

Rose lay against her saddle, her feet stretched toward the dying embers of the fire. In the west, above the rimrock and rolling hills crowned with scattered pines, the sky had turned a soft, deep purple, the higher clouds edged in gold. Although still light, the evening's chill was creeping through the hills. Rose folded her arms under her breasts and wished for a good coat. Shorty had already slipped into his sheepskin jacket, turning its broad collar up to cover the back of his neck.

"Dang' weather," Rose complained, just to make conversation. "Montana is the only place I know where the sweat on the tip of your nose can freeze into an icicle at sundown."

Shorty chuckled. "You ever been anywhere besides Montana, Rose?"

"Not really. Pap says I was born in Tennessee, but my earliest recollection is of Bannock, over on Grasshopper Creek."

"I've never been that far west, although I've heard it's a pretty country. I was born in Georgia, but my folks moved to Texas after the war. I went with 'em."

"Did you fight in the war, Shorty?"

"Some, near the end, though I was young to be toting a musket. It was in Texas that I started to drift. Ended up clerking in a hardware store in Fort Worth. That's where I met Katy, working in her father's store next door. After she died I went to Colorado, but danged if my rope didn't keep getting tangled up on other people's beeves. Hell, maybe I was looking for trouble. On the prod, you know? Anyway, the law was watching me pretty close, so when Crazy Horse surrendered and Sitting Bull ran off to Canada, I came up here. Did a little prospecting in the Black Hills, but never had much heart for that kind of work. Then I met Wiley in Deadwood." He let the story end there, as if figuring anyone who knew Wiley Collins could fill in the rest on their own.

"I didn't know you'd led such a varied life," Rose said. "How long was you married?"

"Not long enough," he replied in a tone that invited no further intrusion.

They grew silent as the light drained out of the sky and the coyotes tuned up in the hills. Far off, a wolf howled at the stars. It made Rose sad to listen to the baying of the wolf and think about Shorty and his wife, whose death still haunted him. It reminded her of Muggy, and the hopes she'd pinned on marrying him. She knew now that she'd only done it to escape her pap, the irony of the endeavor being that it hadn't been much of a swap. They'd been about the same,

Muggy and her pap, although Muggy had been a more accomplished liar.

Her pap's name was Daniel Ames and he lived in Billings now, not thirty miles from the cabin where Rose had settled after marrying Muggy. She didn't see him more than once or twice a year, though, and then only when she made the trip into Billings. Whenever anyone asked, Rose would say her pap was a market hunter, but the truth was he'd fallen into a bottle so many years ago she could barely remember his sober times.

It hadn't always been that way. In Bannock, her pap had been a respected businessman, but he'd changed after Rose's mam passed away. He'd gone on a year-long drunk, and by the time he came out of it, he'd lost both his butcher shop and his good name.

With everything gone to hell in Bannock, they'd come over to the plains, where he'd gone to work for a robe trader out of Fort Benton, but that hadn't panned out, either. He'd tried going into business for himself, hunting buffalo in the winter for hides and meat, then trading among the Indians for robes during the summer, but the isolation finally wore him down. That was when they'd moved back into the mountains near Bozeman to try homesteading.

It was in Bozeman that Rose met Muggy Edwards. She'd been nineteen at the time, a big, gangling country girl, slope-shouldered and large-breasted, and lucky, she figured, that someone with Muggy's flash would even consider a woman as dull as she. They were wed in her pap's cabin with nobody to attend the ceremony but a traveling Methodist minister, her pap, and some of the Jenkinses clan, who lived down the Gallatin River and ran sheep. Rose's brothers were already long gone by then, scattered across the Northwest. The wedding had been fitting enough, although she'd cried afterward when Muggy, her pap, the minister, and old man Jenkins got drunk on sour mash whiskey behind the barn.

It was Muggy who bartered four spans of mules and two large Mitchell freight wagons—the whole shebang won off a freighter in a poker game—for the cabin above the Yellowstone and a quit-claim deed to the spring, creek, and a six-hundred-and-forty-acre section of rangeland that ran from the pines west of the cabin to a shallow cañon that led down to the Yellowstone on the east; the southern boundary was the edge of the bluffs; a pair of stone cairns marked the northern line.

Six hundred and forty acres was a rough estimate since the land had never been surveyed. Nor was Rose certain how legal the deed might actually be, Montana's political arena being somewhat tempestuous in its earliest days, but for four good years the place had been her home, and she'd come to know every inch of it by heart, and a good deal of the surrounding country, too.

It was full dark when Wiley returned. Dismounting at the corral, he tossed his reins to Garcia, then came into the coulée. He jerked to a stop when he saw Shorty loosening the drawstring on a tobacco sack. "Sitting here comfortable as a lord in his manor, are ye?" he asked sarcastically.

"Pert near," Shorty agreed, grinning broadly but not looking up. "No point in both of us foaming at the bit."

Wiley's voice turned harsh. "Nope, none a-tall, though ye might want to save that smoke for tomorrow. We're bein' followed."

<u>Chapter Two</u>

Shorty froze with his tobacco sack poised above the shallow trough of his paper. "How many?"

"I didn't count 'em," Wiley replied, then grudgingly admitted: "They're still ten or twelve miles back. All I saw was the haze of their dust through my field glasses." He stooped for a biscuit.

Looking relieved, Shorty continued his cigarette.

"I'm telling ye, they might've sent scouts ahead," Wiley warned.

"Might've," Shorty agreed, "but I doubt it." He pulled the drawstring closed on his tobacco pouch and tucked it away.

"Ye be a damn' fool, Shorty," Wiley said, then gnawed off a chunk of biscuit.

Keeping her blanket around her, Rose said: "You figure it's cavalry?"

"If it was cavalry, they'd be bivouacked by now and have their mess fires lit," Shorty replied.

"No, they're Crows. Probably hotheads, too fired up to run back to the agency for permission to leave the reservation." He struck a match with his thumbnail and held it to his cigarette. "Or else they just got fed up with supplying us White Eyes with horses," he added through a wreath of tobacco smoke.

"Maybe they're drifters," Jimmy said. He'd returned to the coulée at dark and crawled into his bedroll, leaving Garcia to stand first watch over the horses alone. "You said yourself, Wiley, that this is a handy trail to Helena."

"Well, I may've misled ye there," Wiley said. " 'Tis one way to the Last Chance, right enough, but probably not the handiest."

"A man generally coyotes this trail when he doesn't want others to know he's around," Rose put in. Having run an informal roadhouse along the trail for the past few years, she figured she knew a thing or two about the character of the men who traveled it.

"They could be miners or drovers," Wiley allowed, "but it ain't likely. They're either Crows, like Shorty figures, or hardcases plannin' to help themselves to our horses now that we've done all the dangerous work. Either way, I want to keep as many miles between them and us as possible." He glanced at Shorty. "What do ye say, hoss? Could we make it through these mountains before first light, was we to leave now?"

"That moon'll go down a couple of hours before

dawn," Shorty replied. "We'd lose some horses in the badlands on the other side if we tried to push 'em through with just the stars to guide us."

"We've got twenty-seven head. I only promised Caldwell twenty."

"Seven head's still seven head. They'd pay most of the wages for Garcia, Jimmy, and Rose if we delivered all of them."

Wiley looked up, a slice of bacon halted halfway to his lips. "Nobody said anything about payin' Rosie. I figure feedin' her'll be pay enough."

"No, she's doing her share. She deserves some coins to jingle."

Rose remained silent, waiting for Wiley's reply. It was a long time coming, but finally he said: " 'Twasn't the deal, Shorty. We agreed on just two extra hands. If ye want to pay her something out of your own poke, that'd be your business, but I ain't kickin' in anything."

"No." Shorty's eyes narrowed above the glowing tip of his cigarette. "We'll pay her something. It's only fair."

Wiley guffawed as he pushed a strip of bacon into his mouth, folding it against his tongue like an accordion. He studied Rose thoughtfully for a moment, then said: "If it came to a shootin' scrape, girl, do ye think ye could hold ye own?"

"I'd stand my ground as long as you do."

A twinkle came into Wiley's eyes. "By damn, I bet ye would. All right, Shorty, we'll pay her. But not the same as Jimmy and Garcia."

"That's fair," Shorty agreed. "She came on late." He looked at Rose. "Let me 'n' Wiley talk it over . . . decide what's right. It's still a couple of days to Two-Hats's."

"If we make it," Wiley amended. " 'Tis a ways yet between here and that whore's son, and them Crows, if Crows they be, will be makin' better time than us."

"Then maybe we ought to saddle up right now," Shorty replied. "We could damn' near be through these hills by sunup if we didn't dally."

Wiley laughed and wiped his fingers on his chaps. "Now ye're talkin'. Rosie, get this gear stowed away. Jimmy, haul ye butt outta them blankets. By God, we ain't payin' the two of ye to sleep."

They reached the top of the Bull Mountains shortly after midnight and stopped to let their horses blow. Wiley, who'd been scouting ahead, came back to sit his mount between Shorty and Rose, the three of them staring out over their back trail.

Far to the southwest, Rose could make out the jagged peaks of the Absaroka Range, moonlight shining off the streaks of snow and ice. To the west, the mountains rode lower, slashed with cañons that looked like rivers of spilled ink in the thin light. To the east and south, however, the land was all rolling plains and flat-topped buttes, sculpted by wind and rain and spring run-off, far-flung and mostly empty nowadays.

It was a country known well to the Crows, the Blackfeet, and the Assiniboines, and to a lesser extent the Sioux, Cheyennes, and *Métis*. Others had made their homes here as well—trappers and traders, scouts and squawmen, miners and hunters. And the Army, if a person looked at it that way, making their living chasing the Indians.

Buffalo hunters, both white and red, had only recently killed off the scattered remnants of the great northern herd, the last remaining animals of the millions that had once roamed the plains from central Canada to Mexico. And even before the final bull had been skinned, the last hide hauled to market or back to the reservation, the cattle-men had started moving in. With their big Texas herds and hard-bitten, get-the-hell-out-of-my-way attitudes, they were swallowing up huge chunks of land, claiming as their own private domain what earlier inhabitants—the Indians and traders and hunters—had considered unclaimable.

Rose felt a twinge of melancholy, thinking about how everything in the territory seemed to be going to hell of late. She felt like crying, as she had a dozen times already since watching her life go up in flames not twenty-four hours before. She didn't, though. It had been a long time since she'd bawled real tears, and she'd be damned if she'd start now, with Wiley and Shorty there to see her and maybe make fun of her soggy-eyed mewlings.

But the two horse thieves seemed oblivious to

her sadness, and were all business as they scanned their back trail, Wiley through a pair of field glasses carried in a Seventh Cavalry case. It was prob-ably twenty minutes before he lowered his binoculars. " 'Tis the Crows, like ye figured, Shorty. Can't be no other, stuck to our hinders the way this bunch has been."

"We've got a jump on them now, but not enough to outrun them."

"Ye think they'll catch us, then?"

"More sooner than later, I expect. Maybe we ought to cut our losses while we're ahead. I ain't sure these horses are worth a shooting scrape."

"The hell!" Wiley retorted. "Ye cut ye own losses, hoss. I gave me word I'd deliver twenty head to Two-Hats by the end of the week, and, by damn, that's what I intend to do."

Shorty shrugged. "It was only a thought."

"Well, 'twas a damn' poor one," Wiley grumbled. "Are ye gettin' too old for this business?"

"I'll likely die with a noose around my neck, same as you," Shorty replied curtly, pulling his horse around. "Come on, we're only halfway across and the worst is still ahead of us."

Rose rode back to the herd with the boys, easing the buckskin Shorty had roped out for her over next to Jimmy, while Wiley and Shorty went ahead. Although they'd barely spoken to one another all day, she felt more comfortable around young Frakes than she did Garcia.

Garcia was maybe forty years old, a short, wiry

man with coal-black hair and a pockmarked face who, to Rose's knowledge, hadn't looked directly at her once since she'd joined the drive. She told herself he was probably shy around women, but that argument wasn't affording her much comfort. Garcia didn't handle himself like a shy man; he handled himself like a brash one.

Although Rose had talked a good bluff to Wiley and Shorty, she was beginning to regret her decision to throw in with them. She felt ill-prepared for the life of an outlaw, and had she a home left standing to go back to, she might have given up and gone.

The sun was just rising as they exited the mountains, coming into a stretch of rolling hills dotted with scrubby pines and crumbling sandstone bluffs. The Musselshell lay no more than a few hours ahead now. With daylight, Shorty called a halt, then rode to the top of a nearby ridge for a look-see. Wiley was nowhere to be found, and Rose assumed he'd dropped out to watch their back trail. While the horses rested, Garcia eased his mount over to where Rose and Jimmy were waiting.

"Twenty-three head," Garcia remarked casually. "Four horses we lost last night."

"Four?" Jimmy echoed. "Where'd they go?"

They'd followed a cañon most of the way down, and Rose hadn't seen any place to lose a horse, but Garcia only laughed and reined into the herd. Shorty returned a few minutes later and swung down. He looked annoyed when he saw Rose and Jimmy listlessly sitting their trail-worn mounts to one side. Garcia, Rose suddenly noticed, had switched his saddle to a fresh horse while waiting for Shorty's return, but she'd been too sleepy to think of it. Seeing Shorty tugging at his latigo embarrassed her, and she quickly dismounted. Jimmy also swung down and started to unsaddle his horse.

"We should've had this done already, Jimmy," she said. "If them Indians had jumped us, we'd've been a-straddle tuckered-out bronc's, while all the fresh horses ran away from us."

Jimmy gave her an ugly look. "I wish you'd quit hanging on me all the time. We ain't friends."

Rose paused with her arm under the Mother Hubbard's frame. "Sure we are," she said, taken aback. "Don't you remember me? Rose Ames, from the Gallatin Valley. Our daddies . . ."

"I know who you are," he replied curtly. "I just don't want to talk to you, all right?"

"No," Rose said stubbornly, but before she could pursue it, Shorty walked past with his lariat.

"Saddle up, Rose. I saw dust not three miles back."

"Dang it, Shorty, quit bossin' me around like I was some weak-bladdered pup."

"Then quit yapping like one," he tossed over his shoulder.

Lacking a lariat, Rose had to settle for Albert to replace the buckskin she'd ridden all night. She led the roan out of the herd by his forelock and quickly cinched the Mother Hubbard in place. Five minutes later, they were mounted and on the move, arriving at a horseshoe bend of the Musselshell by midmorning. The land inside the broad, flat curve of the river was knee-deep in grass, the sandy banks lined with trees. By now the horses had been without drink since sundown the night before, and they made a beeline for the river.

Rose guided Albert upstream, to a spot above the rest of the cavvy and the mud it churned up. There she knelt at an ankle-deep eddy to cup up handfuls of cool, clear water. After slaking their thirst, the drovers rode along the riverside of the herd and pushed it back into the tall grass of the bend.

"Let 'em eat," Shorty instructed Rose and Jimmy, "then let them have some more water if they want it. Just don't let 'em drink too much. We may have to bust out of here at a run. Me 'n' Garcia'll ride back a ways, see if we can find Wiley." He snaked his rifle from its scabbard and laid it across his saddle. Garcia rode up with a new-looking Winchester butted to his thigh.

"We go now, huh?" Garcia said.

"Let's ride," Shorty agreed. He reined his horse around, and within minutes the two men were out of sight.

Jimmy walked his mount to the far side of the bend and swung down in the shade of a cotton-wood tree, keeping his old, bronze-framed Henry rifle with him. Rose debated going over to talk to him, then decided against it. She was tired and feeling put out herself, and figured whatever was bothering Jimmy could wait.

She dismounted but hung onto her reins. Nearby, the Musselshell purred like a contented kitten, and the wind soughed in the trees. Birds chirped and locusts hummed, and the warming rays of the sun soothed her aches after nearly twenty-four hours in the saddle. She might have dozed a little. She didn't think she had, but she didn't know how else to explain the Indian who seemed to materialize out of nowhere about eighty yards away, leveling a rifle at Jimmy, who sat with his chin tucked against his chest, his hat tipped forward.

The Indian was near the top of the ridge that sloped up just south of the horseshoe bend, partially hidden in the sage. He looked young, and had thick black braids that hung forward over his shoulders. A bandoleer of cartridges and what might have been a coiled lariat criss-crossed his chest.

Rose tried to shout a warning, but she was so startled by the Indian's appearance that the words wouldn't come. It seemed an eternity that she sat there with her mouth agape, although it couldn't have been more than a second or two. Then a flurry of gunfire erupted from far up the trail and her paralysis broke. Jumping to her feet, she yanked the Sharps from its too-short scabbard and brought it to her shoulder. The Indian hesitated, then swung his rifle toward her.

"Oh Lordy," Rose murmured, earring back the big side hammer.

The Indian got his shot off first, the bullet plowing harmlessly into the dirt several feet in front of her. Then Rose touched the Sharps' trigger and the big rifle roared like a grizzly. Through the powder smoke she saw the Indian flip backward out of sight, hidden by the sage.

Jimmy jumped to his feet, clutching his rifle in both hands.

"Indians!" Rose shouted, scrambling into her saddle. Her knuckles were white where she gripped the Sharps, and it took a moment before she recalled that she'd fired her only cartridge. She returned the rifle to its scabbard, then palmed the Smith & Wesson. Jimmy loped over, owl-eyed at the sound of gunfire drifting down the trail from the south.

"What is it?" he demanded in a voice that was too loud. "What'd you shoot at?"

"A danged Indian is what I shot at," she said, her heart racing. "He was about to take your head off with a needle-gun, Jimmy."

"Where?"

She nodded toward the ridge. "Over yonder."

Jimmy looked, but there was nothing to see. "Are you sure? Maybe you dreamed it. I almost dozed off myself."

"He was there," she said darkly, staring at the sage where she knew the body still lay.

In the bend, the Crow ponies were milling

nervously, watching to the south. Then the rattle of gunfire abruptly ceased, and Rose licked her lips uneasily. "That don't sound good," she remarked. After nearly twenty minutes of straining to hear more, she eased back in her saddle. "What do you think?"

"How the hell would I know?"

"Dang it, what are you so cantankerous about?"

He gave her a withering look. "You ever . . . ?" He let whatever he was going to say die. "Just drop it." He looked back up the trail, then straightened his shoulders with relief. "Here they come."

Shorty was in the lead, his head swiveling back and forth as he surveyed the ridge lines. Garcia came next on a limping horse, while Wiley brought up the rear.

"What happened?" Shorty asked, drawing rein. "We heard a shot." He was looking at Rose, but it was Jimmy who answered.

"She says she saw an Indian, but I think she just dreamed it."

Shorty never took his eyes off of hers. "Where?"

Rose pointed out the spot with her chin. "In that patch of sage. I figure he's still there. I hit him center."

"What happened up the trail?" Jimmy asked, hogging in. "It sounded like a real battle."

"It was," Wiley gloated. "As pretty a fight as any ye'd ever want to see. Custer hisself couldn't've done any better."

"Probably not," Rose replied tartly. "Else he'd still be alive, and a lot of good boys with him."

Laughing, Wiley said: "Well, at least ye kept the horses from runnin' off, and killed an imaginary Indian, to boot."

"Ride on over and take a look if you think he's imaginary," Rose charged hotly. "I'd go myself, but I've already seen him." She didn't add that she wasn't curious to see him again, to view the results of a 450-grain lead slug ripping through human flesh and bone.

"I'll go," Shorty offered, but Wiley stopped him.

"It doesn't matter what Rosie saw or thought she saw. We cut that bunch up pretty bad, and they ain't likely to jump us again, but there's no point taking any chances. We've got a long way to go, so let's just get these ponies movin'."

While Garcia switched horses, the rest of them started the herd downriver. As they left the horseshoe bend, Rose couldn't help a backward glance. In the sage where the Indian had stood she spotted a flash of black and white, then heard the raucous call of a magpie, scavengers already homing in on a meal.

Turning away, she said in a quavery voice: "This ain't the way it was supposed to be, Albert. I reckon I made a mistake ridin' along with this bloodthirsty bunch, and drug you in with me. Likely we'll both end up dead before it's over, just more fodder for the magpies."

Chapter Three

Wiley related the details of the fight to Rose and Jimmy at noon, while Shorty watched the herd. According to Wiley, he, Shorty, and Garcia had attempted to set a trap for the pursuing Indians, but the Crows spotted them before it could be sprung and fled into the hills. The horse thieves followed, and soon the Crows turned and began a mounted attack that ranged back and forth across the side of a small hill.

Wiley counted eight braves in the Crow party, all well-armed and crack shots by his reckoning. Finally Garcia knocked a warrior off his pony and the Indians pulled back, taking the wounded brave with them. Although Wiley claimed numerous hair's-breadth escapes for the White Eyes, only the one Crow had been wounded. Garcia's horse hadn't been shot, as Rose at first suspected, but had pulled a muscle jumping a shallow coulée.

Wiley's enthusiasm as he relived the battle troubled Rose. It made her realize how much she'd come to depend upon Shorty's influence within the group, and how badly she'd miscalculated Wiley's dependability. Worse than Wiley, though, was Garcia. Yesterday he'd barely acknowledged her. Today his gaze seemed to follow her everywhere, with a boldness she understood all too well.

In her blanket that night, the image of the Indian she'd shot returned. With something of a start, she realized he hadn't been a Crow. He hadn't worn his hair the Crow way, and his clothing had been wrong, too—at least what she'd seen of it. A Blackfoot, she decided, or an Assiniboine, off by his lonesome and thinking he'd stumbled onto a trove of horses, with a woman thrown in for fun and only a dozing youth in his way. What a surprise it must have been for him, Rose thought, and what a shock for her. She'd never killed anyone before, and was distressed to discover how easily it had been accomplished, how simple it was to take a life, then just ride away. There should have been more to it, she fretted; with a human life involved, a human's soul set free to drift, there should have been more.

They left the Musselshell the next day and struck out northwest, on a line with some badlands that bordered the Missouri River. The short tan grass crackled beneath the hoofs of their horses, and in the blazing sun the scrubby junipers looked more black than green. There was no trail that Rose could discern, but Wiley led them with conspicuous confidence, riding up front with his chest out like a strutting game cock.

It was nearly sunset when they came to a bench overlooking a small creek. Two-Hats's trading post sat on the opposite bank, under a cliff. Maybe half a mile to the north, Rose could make out a stretch of the Missouri through a gap in the hills.

While Garcia and Jimmy held the cavvy out of sight, Rose, Shorty, and Wiley drew up on the rim of the bench. Rose pulled down her bandanna and wiped her lips with the back of her hand. "I hope Two-Hats has got something cool to drink," she said thickly. "My tongue keeps stickin' to the roof of my mouth."

"We'll save ye a sip," Wiley promised, "but right now I need ye to stay put. Me 'n' Shorty'll mosey on down for a look-see. If something goes wrong, get the horses outta here quick. Keep 'em movin' until me or Shorty catches up."

A frown creased Rose's brow. "You expectin' trouble, Wiley?"

"Ye never know, darlin', ye never know. I've not dealt with this jasper before. For all I know he could be a marshal, or a Regulator."

"Or a horse thief," she commented dryly.

Laughing, Wiley said: "Horse thieves don't worry me, but government agents and Regulators can sour a man's milk mighty fast." He lifted his reins. "Keep ye eyes peeled, now."

"Just see you don't get to palaverin' and forget about us wranglers!" she called as the two men began their descent.

Rose narrowed her eyes against the glare of the setting sun. The trading post looked like a slovenly affair, to her thinking. There was a single log building with a gullied sod roof, and an empty corral to the north. The cabin's front door was thrown open as if expecting a breeze for company, and there was a bench under the lone window but no glass in the dark, square opening, or smoke from the chimney. Several ribby hounds lolled in the shade nearby, but only a couple raised their heads as Wiley and Shorty approached.

It was a lonely, desolate place, and not rightly a trading post at all, but a kind of watering hole and overnight stop along the vaguely defined Outlaw Trail that ran south from Canada all the way through Montana and Wyoming, before peeling off a corner of Colorado and plunging into the cañon lands of southern Utah. Having lived along a branch of the trail for some years, Rose had often heard of Two-Hats, but this was her first view of the place.

Her gaze kept wandering back to the corral. For some reason the vacant enclosure nagged at her. With the cabin's door and window hanging open, it gave the place an eerie, unfriendly feel. It called to mind the fear and uncertainty she'd experienced last summer, during the Stranglers' sweeping raid.

To this day, neither Rose nor any of her acquaintances knew the identities of the men involved in the hangings, but there was little doubt that they'd had some powerful backing. Some even went so far as to suggest old Granville Stuart himself, one of Montana's earliest pioneers and a leader in the cattle trade, had led the raid personally, riding a big white horse with a pair of hangman's ropes tied off either side of his pommel. It was possible, Rose thought. Granville Stuart was a tough old bird.

Vigilante style, the Stranglers had swept across southeastern Montana like a bloody scythe, and when they vanished a few weeks later, more than sixty men had either been strung up or shot.

The Eastern newspapers had had a field day condemning the Stranglers' blatant disregard of due process, as well as their attacks upon the workingman. Collaboration had been implied as high as the territorial governor's office, and the story—widely believed—was that not everyone dispatched by the Stranglers had been rustlers. More than a few, it was rumored, had been guilty of nothing more sinister than holding title to some choice piece of rangeland coveted by a wealthy cattle baron.

Yet the Stranglers had their defenders, too, men who considered the determination of the hangmen to rid the region of its outlaw elements essential to the salvation of the cattle industry. These champions of the noose, many of whom were long-time residents of the frontier, pointed out that the Stranglers had accomplished only what the law had failed to do, and that the men they'd hung had been confirmed thieves and hardcases.

Rose considered both sides of the issue to be filled with about as much hot air as solid substance. All she knew for sure was that the Stranglers had started their raid among the breaks of the Missouri River, concentrating on the hideouts and rendezvous sites within the badlands between the mouths of the Judith and Musselshell Rivers. Then they'd come south to employ a private train at Billings, with slatted cars for the horses and coaches furnished with bourbon and champagne for the men. The train had traveled east from Billings, paralleling the Yellowstone and making frequent stops along the way to complete another of its grisly tasks.

The thought of that much power—to be able to rent a train incognito—had frightened Rose almost as much as the possibility of being hung. For weeks she'd slept in the trees along the creek behind the cabin, keeping her carbine with her constantly. But no one came, and in time she'd learned that a lot of the smaller outfits, some of the more isolated hide-outs and individuals like Wiley and Shorty, had escaped the Stranglers' net.

Although nothing had been heard of the Stranglers since their breakup last year, Rose knew their shadow lingered on the high plains. It made her wonder what Wiley and Shorty were thinking as they approached Two-Hats's.

The boys hauled up on the near side of the creek, and Wiley hailed the cabin. After a couple of minutes a figure appeared at the door, calling out a question that Wiley answered. Their words were indistinct to Rose, but apparently satisfying, for soon Wiley and Shorty were splashing their horses across the creek and riding up to the post.

It seemed to Rose that she waited there a good long while. She passed the time by running her fingers through her hair, teasing out as many of the tangles as she could. From time to time she would glance behind her to where Jimmy and Garcia were grazing the herd about a quarter of a mile away. Garcia sat his mount off to one side, and although his face was hidden beneath the broad, curled brim of his sombrero, Rose knew he was watching her.

Jimmy had dismounted and was sitting in the skimpy shade of his horse. Even from here, Rose could tell he was half asleep.

A cooling breeze began to stir when the sun went down. Rose pulled off her hat and turned her face to the stirring zephyrs, closing her eyes to savor the moment. When she opened them, the first thing she saw was a cloud of dust rising in the south. After a startled exclamation, she froze in indecision. Before she could make up her mind whether to ride down and warn the boys or get the cavvy started for the Musselshell, Shorty appeared at the trading post door and waved her in. Rose pointed south, toward the dust. Shorty looked but seemed indifferent. He waved again, making a broad gesture of it so that she knew he wanted her to bring the herd down, too. She glanced once more at the dust, at least a mile off and advancing slowly, then reined away.

"I reckon I'm just gettin' jumpy," she told her horse, a short-coupled Grulla Shorty had roped for her that morning. "I ought to've known better than be thinkin' about Stranglers today."

It was a little dicey going down—the Crow ponies wanted to scatter on the steep slope—but they made it without mishap and bunched the herd on the east bank of the creek, where Shorty met them.

"Wiley's man is here," Shorty informed them, "but he's playing it close to his vest, trying to get the price down."

"Shoot, he ain't even seen what he's buyin'," Rose said. "He ought at least to eyeball 'em before he starts dickerin'."

"He ain't that kind of trader," Shorty replied.

"Here they come," Jimmy said, nodding toward the post.

Wiley was heading for his horse. A second man had followed him outside but was angling toward the herd on foot. He was tall and lean, dressed in a black broadcloth suit powdered with dust. His hat was black and flat-brimmed, and he wore his blond hair long, combed behind his ears and over his shoulders like an old-time plainsman—or a pistoleer.

"Who is this jaybird?" Rose asked quietly. "I don't much like the cut of his outfit." She meant the arrogant way he carried himself, rather than his clothes.

"His name's Frank Caldwell, and you don't have to like him," Shorty said. "Hush, now. This deal ain't done by a long chalk."

Caldwell paused on the far bank, paying more attention to Rose, Jimmy, and Garcia than he did the horses. Wiley rode up beside him, his face flushed as if he'd already been at a bottle.

"Yonder they be," Wiley said loudly, gesturing toward the herd with a reckless swing of his arm. "Twenty-three of the prettiest ponies this side o' the Yellowstone."

Caldwell, though, was studying Garcia. "Hello, Billy," he said.

Garcia gave him a sullen look. "Do I know you, *señor*?" he replied pointedly.

Caldwell's expression went blank. "My mistake," he said, then crossed the shallow creek to where he had a clear view of everyone. "That's a pretty scrawny bunch, Collins. You should thank me for taking the whole lot, and not making you cull the scrubs."

"The hell!" Wiley snorted. "There's not a dime's worth of difference between 'em. By God, ye said twenty dollars a head, Caldwell, and I'll hold ye to that."

Smiling thinly, Caldwell brushed back the tails of his coat to reveal a brace of Colt revolvers. Rose swallowed hard at a lump that formed suddenly in her throat. Tension sparked among the horse thieves like static electricity frictioned off a fancy hotel carpet. Only Caldwell seemed unaffected. "My offer was four hundred dollars for a lot of no less than twenty head," he said coolly. "You have twenty-three horses here. Four hundred is still a fair price."

Wiley's knuckles were as white as tiny, round-headed ghosts where he gripped his reins. "I won't let ye cheat me, Caldwell."

But Shorty was of a different notion. "Take the money, Wiley," he urged, keeping his eyes on Caldwell.

"God damn, he's just one bleedin' man, Shorty. Are we gonna let 'im rob us like we was a bunch of kids with candy?"

"There'll be other deals."

Caldwell mugged a smile. "Sure, Collins, I'm always on the look-out for good horseflesh. Maybe we can contract for another bunch before you boys pull out."

To Rose, Wiley looked like a boiler about to blow, but then the anger seemed to drain out of him. Flashing a conceding grin, he said: "What the hell, huh, Caldwell? Four hundred, then . . . in cash."

"In cash," Caldwell agreed cheerfully. "I'll count it out while you run those horses into the corral."

Wiley turned to Rose, Jimmy, and Garcia. "You heard him. Run 'em into yon corral, there. Me 'n' Shorty'll stay and help with the countin'."

Chapter Four

Garcia handled the gate while Rose and Jimmy drove the horses inside. As the gate swung shut, she heard the sound of hoofs from the south and remembered the dust she'd seen from the bench.

Wiley, Shorty, and Frank Caldwell were still down by the creek, but they looked up when a band of horses came jogging around the nearest bend of the creek, kicking up a spray of water that sparkled like liquid light in the dusk. Caldwell shouted for Garcia to open the gate, and Rose and Jimmy spread out to help turn the herd into the corral with their own stock. Rose counted roughly thirty horses, driven by a trio of dusty wranglers.

With over fifty head inside, the little pole corral seemed to bulge. Garcia latched the gate and two of the wranglers—mixed-bloods wearing a combi-nation of Indian and white clothing—hitched their mounts to a corral rail, then trooped inside the trading post.

The third wrangler was a loose-jointed white man who must have been pushing sixty. He was as stubbled and gnarled as an old cedar stump, and looked about as tough. He remained mounted, exchanging a long look with Garcia. Finally he leaned to one side and spat past the toe of his boot. When he straightened, he said: "Hello, Billy. I see they ain't hung you yet."

"Is that my name?" Garcia asked in annoyance. It was considered rude to blurt out the name of a man you hadn't seen in a while, not without giving him an opportunity to declare a new alias. That was especially important along the Outlaw Trail, where a fresh sobriquet might be all that stood between a man and the gallows. Yet that simple courtesy had been denied Garcia twice in the space of half an hour, and Rose could tell it was gnawing at him.

The old man seemed unimpressed with Garcia's ire, though, and with a snorting dismissal he said: "It makes no never mind to me, boy."

"Call me Garcia, old man, or Billy. Call me *boy* again, I'll cut your balls off."

"That'll be the day . . . boy."

Rose figured Garcia would go for his pistol then, but he didn't. "Web, you are a hard-headed son-of-a-whore. I ought to shoot you for being so ignorant."

"That'll be the day, too," Web replied. He glanced toward the creek where Wiley and Shorty were dividing the money between them, then at Rose and Jimmy. "Damn, Billy-Boy, you've run onto hard luck, riding with an Irishman, an elf, a woman, and a kid."

"The hell with you," Garcia replied, then heeled his mount closer, making any further conversation inaudible.

Rose rode over to Jimmy's side. "That Mexican worries me," she confided. "I figured he'd pull his shooter, for sure. Instead, he turns around all chummy. What if he's been spyin' for Caldwell?"

"Wiley and Shorty know what they're doing." Jimmy lifted his reins as if to ride away, but Rose put a hand on his arm, stopping him.

"What's the matter, Jimmy? We was friends once, remember?"

He looked at her, then away. "Not as good as you and my daddy were, I guess."

She lowered her hand. "What are you talking about?"

"You'd know better than me," he flared loud enough to draw a glance from Garcia and Web.

Tears filled Rose's eyes; she blinked them away. "Yeah, I reckon I do, but it ain't what you think. Not between me 'n' your daddy, nor any of them Bozeman chuckleheads who . . . said things. They was all a pack of lies."

"You're the liar. Everyone knows that. Why do you think we left the Gallatin Valley? Because we wanted to be closer to the Sioux?"

"Aw, Jimmy, no!" But even as she protested, she knew it must be true. She remembered Jimmy's ma, and the hateful way she'd looked at her every time Rose attempted a conversation. At fourteen, she'd been too young to know how to handle the rumors floating over the Gallatin Valley about her, or how to respond to the leers of men as she sat alone in her pap's wagon while he ducked inside some saloon for a last drink before heading home. She hadn't known then how it was for the daughter of an alcoholic, but she'd learned. God damn them, she'd learned.

"It weren't true, Jimmy," she whispered. "None of it."

"Sure it was. Mama died less than a year after we moved. Died with the shame of what you and my daddy did, back there on the Gallatin."

Rose shook her head even as she recognized the futility of denial. After a while, gossip became its own truth. "They said a lot of mean things about me back then, mostly because of my pap and the way he was."

"The way he still is, from what I hear."

Her face tightened. "Yeah, I reckon so."

"I've hated you for years," he said, his voice taut with anger. "I swore that someday I'd tell you that, make you see how you ruined my family. I'm glad now that I did, you . . . whore, you stinking, worthless . . ." Tears streamed down his face, cutting muddy channels through the dust that clung to the downy fuzz on his cheeks. His throat worked a time or two more, as if he wanted to go on, then he wheeled his horse and spurred hard for the Missouri.

Rose felt an unfamiliar coldness creep over her. It took all of her will to kick the memories away, to slam the door on that deep, painful shaft where so much of her early life resided. Shivering, she turned away. Wiley, Shorty, and Caldwell were returning from the creek, their transaction completed. Wiley walked beside Shorty, leading his horse, while Caldwell angled toward the trading post.

Stopping beside the Grulla, Wiley said: "Where'd the kid take off to?"

"He got a bug in his eye," Rose answered dully. "I reckon he went down to the river to wash it out."

"Dumb little shit," Wiley said. " 'Twas a creek right behind him." Then he glanced over his shoulder and bellowed: "Garcia, come get ye pay!"

Shorty was watching Rose as if he'd already guessed there was more to her story than bugs, but he didn't pry.

"Forty dollars, huh?" Garcia said, coming over.

"A month's pay for a week's work," Wiley agreed. "That ain't too bad, is it?"

Garcia shrugged without taking his eyes off the greenbacks Wiley was dropping one at a time into his outstretched palm. When they were done, Garcia folded the bills and shoved them into his pocket. "We are finished then, no?"

"Unless ye be interested in another job?"

"I already got another job."

Wiley's gaze hardened. "Partnerin' with Caldwell, are ye?"

Garcia gave him the same look a man might give a dung beetle, crawling across his boot, then walked away.

"Cocky little bastard," Wiley muttered.

"We don't need him," Shorty said. "I never cottoned to him, and I don't think Rose did, either." He glanced up with an easy smile. "Unless I missed my guess."

"It wouldn't hurt my feelin's if I never saw him again," she admitted.

"Mine, neither," Wiley agreed. He began thumbing bills from the pile in his hand. "Me 'n' Shorty decided on twenty bucks for ye, Rosie. We figure that's fair, no more'n ye did."

"You did real good, Rose," Shorty quickly

amended, "but you joined up late, and it wouldn't be fair to the others to give you full pay."

Accepting the cash, Rose said: "That's all right, Shorty. I'm satisfied." She walked the Grulla to the corral and hitched it next to Shorty's sorrel, then made her way to the cabin. Although it was her first visit, the place was so similar to every other trading post she'd ever been in, she barely paused at the door.

A plank counter running down the center of the room served as a barrier between the merchandise stacked on wooden shelves against the rear wall and the dirt-floored trade area where customers bartered for the items they wanted. A squatty Indian with an ample belly and collar-length gray hair stood impassively behind the counter. He wore a Hudson's Bay Company medallion from a leather thong around his neck, and pierced through the lobe of his right ear was a pair of twelve-inch long watch chains—*sans* timepieces or fobs—that served as earrings, the flat silver links draped over his shoulder like pet snakes.

The two half-breeds who'd helped Web bring in the second herd were sitting at a table, wolfing down a greasy-looking stew. Caldwell and Web stood at the far end of the counter, where Caldwell was adding figures in a column on a piece of butcher's paper. Garcia was also at the counter, about halfway between Caldwell and the dumpy Indian who, Rose figured, had to be Two-Hats. He was working on a cup of whiskey, but looked up when Rose walked in. His dark eyes followed her all the way to the counter.

If Two-Hats was surprised to see a woman in man's clothing sauntering up, he didn't show it. Scanning the shelves behind him, Rose said: "You got cartridges for a Sharps Forty-Four-Ninety?"

Two-Hats neither moved nor spoke, and after a moment Rose flushed and showed him the money Wiley had given her. Holding up two fingers, Two-Hats pulled a box of factory loads off a shelf and set it in front of her. Meeting the chunky Indian's stare, Rose's anger started to boil.

"You're charging me two dollars for a box of cartridges? That's ten cents a gol-darned shell!"

Garcia chuckled. "There are all kinds of thieves, no?" He tapped the side of his tin mug with a blunted finger. "One dollar he charges for this snake piss. I would cut his throat, except he keeps a twelve-gauge under the counter. Ain't that right, *chico*?"

Two-Hats's expression remained unchanged, his gaze unyielding.

"Son-of-a-bitch," Rose grated, then slid $4 across the counter. Silently Two-Hats placed another box of .44-90s beside the first.

In the next ten minutes, Rose purchased cartridges for the Smith & Wesson and a used butcher knife in a plain leather sheath. The knife set her back $5 and had a split handle mended with copper wire. She also bought matches, a tin billy for meals, a cup, fork, and spoon, a pair of used socks, and a picket rope for Albert. Although in dire need of a better blanket and a heavy coat, she'd nearly lost her rifle three times since leaving the Yellowstone, and decided a scabbard large enough to accommodate the hefty Sharps might be a wiser investment. Counting out what remained of her cash, she shook her head woefully. "Looks like I ain't gonna get no coat, for sure," she said to Two-Hats. "Not unless you got one for under two bucks."

"Has blood on it," Two-Hats replied, speaking for the first time.

"How much?"

"Two dollars."

"I mean how much blood, dang it?"

At the far end of the counter, Caldwell chuckled. "Quite a bit, isn't there, Two-Hats?" The Indian shrugged, and the smile vanished from Caldwell's face. "That redskin's stealing you blind, girl. Are you so dumb you can't see he's charging you double for everything?"

"I know what he's doin'," Rose snapped, "but this ain't Billings, and Herman Sutherland ain't got a store nearby where I can get my stuff for a fair price. If he did, that's where I'd be."

"Well, the competition's limited, that's true, but I still hate to see a pretty girl being cheated out of her hard-earned money. What would you say if I got Two-Hats to lower his prices? You'd do that for an old friend like me, wouldn't you, Two-Hats?" What passed for a smile returned to Caldwell's lips, but Rose saw the threat of violence in the gunman's eyes. Two-Hats must've seen it, too. He looked at Rose like he wanted to strangle her, but could only nod in compliance.

"Of course, I'd want something in return," Caldwell added.

"What's that?" Rose asked, thinking of Albert and how she'd be damned if she let Caldwell have *him*—not for all the rifle cartridges in Montana. Then Web laughed and Garcia guffawed; even the two half-breeds grinned. Rose's face turned hot as a banked fire. "You ain't no gentleman," she said to Caldwell, "and I'd rather sleep with a pig in a pig sty than share the fanciest bed in Billings with you."

"Well, there's no accounting for taste," Caldwell replied blandly, "although I might have expected different from a woman who wears trousers and rides her horse clothespin style."

Teeth grinding, Rose gathered her purchases and walked outside. Laughter from everyone except Two-Hats followed her through the door.

Coming from the corral, Wiley flashed a grin. "Where ye headin', darlin'?" he asked in that old, easy-going manner she remembered from earlier days.

"Get outta my way, Wiley," she answered testily. "I ain't in no mood to bandy words with you." She stalked to the Grulla, leaving Wiley standing outside the trading post with a startled expression on his face.

After stowing her merchandise on the horse, she

led it over to where Shorty had picketed his sorrel and rigged it out the same way. Then she lugged her gear to the fire Shorty had kindled beside the creek. He looked up as she approached, noting her cloudy mood.

"Two-Hats give you a skinning, did he?"

"Scalped me to my ears is more like it." She spiraled down opposite him, sitting cross-legged with her chin cupped in her hand.

"Some food in your belly will brighten your outlook," Shorty promised. "Bacon'll be ready in another minute."

"You don't have to feed me, Shorty. I ain't workin' for you boys no more."

"Shoo, how many times have you fed us? I bet you could eat free in this territory for ten years, just on the hospitality you've shown others."

She looked up with a grateful smile. "Thanks, Shorty."

He handed her an empty cup. "We still don't have any coffee, but that crick water's free, and it ain't too alky. I guess Two-Hats ain't figured out a way to charge for it yet."

Rose laughed and accepted the mug. She drank two cups straight down at the creek, then filled a third and brought it back to the fire.

Night had fallen over the narrow cañon, and the chill had deepened. Shorty set his skillet on the ground between them, then dug out some biscuits from the previous evening and tossed one to Rose. "I'd soak that in bacon grease first," he advised wryly. "You're liable to chip a tooth, otherwise."

"I ought to take exception to that, considerin' I was the one who baked 'em."

"Oh, they're tasty enough," he assured her. "Just a tad leathery."

Rose started to relax. "Where are you and Wiley headin' after this?" she asked, nibbling on a piece of bacon. "I got the notion from Wiley that you was boilin' up another scheme."

"I guess Wiley and I are always percolating on something or the other." He looked up, cocking a brow. "You interested?"

"It would depend on what you had in mind. I was feelin' mighty unconvinced about ridin' with you two roosters a couple of days ago, but I reckon I'm startin to get used to it. I ain't partial to schemes that might get me shot, though."

"Me neither," Shorty replied soberly. "I've run with a fair number of fools over the years, but I try to avoid them when I can. To tell you the truth, Wiley and I haven't discussed what we're going to do next. Likely we'll head for some town big enough to spend our money in first. After that . . ." He shrugged. "It's late in the season for anything big, but we might consider something small and quick."

"You got a buyer in mind? I'm thinkin' Caldwell didn't pan out the way you'd hoped he would."

"He didn't, for a fact. Caldwell promised us twenty dollars apiece for a minimum of twenty head, and he knows it. As far as I'm concerned, he stole those three extra horses. It ain't worth getting shot over, but I won't deal with him again, and neither will Wiley. But, hell, you can always find someone willing to dicker for a horse. Caldwell's an Alberta boy who's been collecting ponies to run back into Canada, but there're closer markets, especially if we're careful about where we find our herd."

"It ain't never *stealin'*, is it?" Rose mused. "I've knowed you 'n' Wiley for almost four years now, and I ain't yet heard either one of you call it what it is. It's always 'we found 'em,' or 'they followed us.' It's never . . . 'I stole these here horses off some hard-working . . .' "

"Shut up, Rose!" Shorty said harshly.

Her jaw dropped in surprise.

"Do you think we don't . . . shit." He threw what remained of his biscuit into the fire. "I figured you knew the way of it, being married to Muggy and all."

Rose had never seen Shorty so upset. Not even last summer when he and Wiley had sworn to kill one another. Coming on top of everything else, it made her want to bawl in the worst way, and for a moment she just sat there sucking in air, her fists knotted on her knees.

"Aw, hell," he said abruptly, drawing a deep breath. "I didn't mean that. I guess you just rubbed a sore spot, is all."

"It weren't your fault. I had no business . . ."

"No, don't go taking any blame for my short fuse."

Her voice lowered. "You're a good man, Shorty. I reckon your wife must've been mighty proud of you."

"Maybe that's what rankles me," he replied, staring into the fire. "I'm not sure she would've, the way things turned out. She was the church-going kind, and mighty forgiving, considering that, but I'm not sure she could've overlooked thievery."

"She would've. If she knew you half as well as I do, she would've."

"Well, it's the truth she wouldn't have had to, had she lived. We had a nice little house on the edge of Fort Worth, and I had dreams of raising horses, maybe even getting a small ranch close to town." He shook his head. "It makes a man wonder where it all went screwy, doesn't it? I've told myself a hundred times it was Kate's dying that turned me wrong side to the law, but I'm not so sure any more."

"I reckon some scabs is best left unscratched," Rose said. "There ain't a day goes by I don't think of Muggy and the mistake I made marryin' him but what's done is done, and there ain't no goin' back."

"Amen to that," Shorty replied, his voice a whisper. Before either of them could say more, a pebble landed in the dirt at Shorty's knee. Rose started to rise, but Shorty made a motion with his hand and said: "Stay put. It's only Wiley."

"Damn' tootin' 'tis me." Wiley's voice came

from the shadows behind them. "Caldwell's up to something. We gotta skedaddle."

Shorty kept his head down. "What do you have in mind?"

"Jimmy's back and we've got the horses ready to go. One at a time, I want ye to get up and mosey on over here with ye saddles, like ye was fixin' to bed down. Don't dawdle, and keep that light in Two-Hats's window in the corner of ye eye. When that goes out, we gotta shake a leg."

Rose's throat was dry as the bottom of a busted bucket. Glancing at the light in the trader's window, she tried to recall if there was a back way out, but her mind drew a blank.

"You go first," Shorty told her.

Nodding tautly, she stood and ambled out of the firelight with her saddle and rifle. Wiley grabbed her arm as soon as she was clear of the light.

"This way," he whispered, propelling her toward the creek. "Jimmy's waitin' downstream. Go on and saddle up."

Rose glanced at the Grulla, foraging at the end of its picket rope.

"Don't worry about that one," Wiley said grimly. "We'll bring 'im."

Rose nodded and started downstream. She was almost around the first bend when she heard Jimmy's low call. Following the sound of his voice, she discovered him behind some scrub, deep in the shadows of the bench. He had to guide her to the horses with a hand on her arm, as if she were blind.

She smelled the animal he led her to before she could make out its shape in the darkness, and a rush of relief surged through her. "Albert!" she breathed, running her hand along the gelding's neck.

"It's that worthless roan you started with," Jimmy said scornfully. "I'd have left him and taken a better one, but Wiley said you'd raise a fuss if we did."

"How'd you find him in that mob of horseflesh?"

"Wiley knows what he's doing," was Jimmy's curt reply.

Rose laughed softly and didn't argue. Jimmy's respect for Wiley's skills as a horse thief was well-founded. Even Shorty admitted he was almost as good as a Crow, which was indeed high praise in those parts.

She saddled the old gelding by feel, then strapped the new scabbard in place before going over to stand beside Jimmy. Away from the fire, it didn't take long for her eyes to adjust to the darkness. With Albert, there were five horses waiting behind her, and remembering what Wiley had said about getting the Grulla, Rose understood his motive in backing away from Caldwell earlier. Wiley intended to steal back the three horses he hadn't been paid for.

At the fire, Shorty continued to lounge against his saddle while Wiley struggled with the Grulla's picket pin. Shorty's sorrel had already been freed and was standing close to the Grulla. Rose glanced at the trading post, but there was no one in sight through the open window. Not even Two-Hats, behind the counter. "I don't like this," she said to Jimmy. "I can't see a soul in there."

"Just keep quiet and be ready when Wiley gives the word."

Little pin pricks of nervousness were playing up and down Rose's arms, and she unconsciously wrapped her fingers around the Smith & Wesson's butt. The breeze that had picked up at sundown continued to nose along the creek, cool off the distant mountains, but her palm was sweating around the Smith & Wesson's hard rubber grips. Something was amiss; she could feel it, as if the air itself had turned evil.

It was at that instant that Rose heard the brisk ratcheting of a pistol being cocked behind her. Jimmy swore and started to turn, but a shot exploded from the nearby brush, slamming him to the ground. More shots sounded from upstream; muzzle flashes lanced the darkness. Wiley was shouting for Rose and Jimmy to bring up the horses, but there was nothing she could do. Jimmy lay curled at her feet, gasping for breath, while Rose stared wordlessly into the maw of Billy Garcia's revolver.

Chapter Five

Garcia edged closer, his old, run-down boots gliding silently over the creek's gravel bed. His stealth surprised Rose. She wouldn't have believed anyone could move so quietly over loose stones. A thread of powder smoke, barely visible in the thin star shine, curled from the muzzle of his pistol, but the scarred brown hand remained unwavering. In the dim light his eyes reminded her of a mouse's, shiny as glass beads.

"Rose!" Wiley screeched. "God dammit, Jimmy!"

Garcia licked his lips. "Frank says I got to shoot you, but I think maybe we got a little business first, you and me, huh?"

"Damn," Rose breathed, then instinctively drew the Smith & Wesson and fired from the hip.

Garcia could have dropped her easily if he hadn't been so intent upon his "little business." Instead he hollered and spun away, dropping his pistol in the creek. He stumbled into the deeper shadows downstream, clutching the side of his head with both hands. He was making a lot of noise leaving, Rose noted wryly. Then another gunshot hammered the night from somewhere upstream, and she grabbed Jimmy by the collar of his jacket and hauled him to his feet. "Come on," she said. "We gotta ride."

Even gut shot, Jimmy had managed to hold onto the horses. He cried out as Rose pulled him off the ground, but kept his grip on the reins and lead ropes. Pushing him against his horse, she got a shoulder under his skinny buttocks and shoved.

"Ohhh, God," he moaned, "you're killing me."

"Quit complaining and take these," she said, jamming the horse's reins into his hand even as she pried the others loose. "And hang onto 'em, hear?"

Grabbing Albert's reins, Rose swung into the saddle. Running boots crunched gravel along the creekbed, and she wheeled her horse with the Smith & Wesson leveled.

"Where the devil were ye?" Wiley shouted, then grabbed his horse without waiting for a reply. Shorty appeared a few seconds later, lugging his saddle in his free hand, his pistol drawn and pointed upstream.

"Gimme that thing," Wiley demanded, riding close.

Shorty tossed him the saddle, then jerked a lead rope from Rose's hand and flung himself bareback atop the lunging, frightened horse. Raking his spurs along the animal's ribs, he raced north toward the Missouri, the others pounding at his side. The extra horses fled with them. Rose's scalp crawled as they sprinted across the open patches. She kept expecting more bullets to come buzzing after them, but only the echo of their ponies' hoofs followed them away from Two-Hats's post.

● ● ●

Rose sat alone on top of a bluff overlooking the Missouri. In the east the sun was already up, but it was cold yet. Her breath puffed little clouds of vapor every time she exhaled, and her fingers were numb where she clutched the ratty old Hudson's Bay blanket around her shoulders. When they'd stopped at first light, Shorty had kindled a fire from the branches of a dead juniper standing nearby, but Rose had shunned its warmth in favor of solitude.

Across the river, bighorn sheep were browsing along the broken scarp. She could see a ewe and two kids now, and had earlier watched an entire band scamper up the cliffs from the river's edge. She could have shot one easily, but killing a sheep on the far side of the river would have been akin to murder since they had no way to retrieve the meat.

Still, it was easier to think about wild mutton and how good it would taste than it was to think about Jimmy, who they'd buried at dawn. Rose had been holding his hand when he died, hoping to tell him once more that the stories he'd heard about her and his pap had been lies, but she never got the chance. Jimmy had lapsed into uncon-sciousness at some point during their flight down the Missouri, still stubbornly clinging to his saddle, and had passed away without coming to.

Rose was still watching the sheep when Shorty came over. He halted just out of arm's reach and held up a piece of jerky, like he would to a growly dog he wasn't yet familiar with. "You'd best eat something, Rose," he said gently. "Wiley'll want to move on soon."

She ignored the strip of dried beef and kept her eyes on the cliffs across the river, admiring the way the strengthening light seemed to change the shapes of the crags.

"A man's time comes to die, it just comes," Shorty said. "There ain't a thing you can do about it."

"He wasn't a man, Shorty, he was a kid. He didn't even shave."

"He died young, for a fact."

She remembered Shorty's wife, and the son who'd perished with her, and felt a stab of sadness for the bowlegged cowboy. Looking at him, she forced a smile. "Shorty, I'd give a silver dollar for that sheepskin coat you're wearing."

He chuckled and pushed the jerky closer. Rose hesitated, then accepted it.

"Wiley and I are going to Miles City," he said, hunkering down nearby. "You're welcome to ride along if the direction suits. I talked to Wiley, and he says you can throw in with us for a spell, too, if you want."

"Miles City," she replied, tearing off her first bite. "It's been a long time since I've seen ol' Milestown."

"It's growed," he acknowledged. "It's a right pert town now, and not at all like it was a few years ago."

"All right, I'll ride with you that far." She stood, brushing off the seat of her trousers. Across the river the ewe and kids had disappeared. Rose paused to scan the bluffs more closely, but the little family was gone.

"See something?" Shorty asked.

"Naw." She turned away. "There ain't nothin' over there but busted dreams."

Pushing past him, she began kicking dirt over the fire while Wiley and Shorty lined out the extra horses on lead ropes. Wiley wanted to keep the four riderless horses close, and he'd decided it would be easier to lead them than drive them.

Although they saw no sign of pursuit, it was obvious from the way Wiley and Shorty traveled that they expected it. They stayed off the main trail along the Missouri, and swung wide around Billy Downs's old trading post at the mouth of the Musselshell. Rose would have liked to have seen what was left of the place—the Stranglers had hung Billy the year before, in their sweep along the Missouri—but she was feeling melancholy, so didn't mention it.

They rode almost due east for two days, until they reached the divide that separated the drainages of the Musselshell and Big Dry Creek. There they turned southeast toward Miles City and began to make better time. The fear that Frank Caldwell and his men might be following them was put to rest by Wiley, who said he reckoned even a snake in the grass like Caldwell wouldn't trail them halfway across Montana just for three scrawny Indian ponies.

Two days later they pulled up on a bluff overlooking the Yellowstone River. Miles City lay below them, with Fort Keogh visible a couple of miles to the west, across the Tongue River that flowed in from the south. Rose had never been to Fort Keogh—soldiers always made her nervous—but she'd visited Miles City with her pap a number of times, back when its biggest export had been buffalo hides rather than cattle.

Wiley and Shorty were clearly excited. It was a trait of men Rose had never understood, their need to spend whatever money they acquired as quickly as possible. Muggy had been the same way, and her pap still was. She figured Wiley and Shorty had around $150 apiece from the sale of the Crow ponies, but sure as hawks flew, by the end of the week, two at the most, they'd be broke again and looking for another stake.

Wiley reined toward the trail that led down to the ferry, but Shorty held back. "What will you do now?" he asked.

"I don't know." She hadn't trailed along to Miles City for the same reasons as Wiley and Shorty. Even if she had, entertainment opportunities for women were few. "Maybe I'll look up some old friends," she said. "You know Charley Schuyler?"

"Wahoo Charley? Used to be a buffalo runner?"

"Yeah." She perked up. "Him and my pap used to hunt the same ranges, and sometimes he'd come over or we'd visit him. He was based out of Miles City, there toward the end."

"Rose, Charley Schuyler got himself killed in a bar fight about three years ago."

"Aw, no, not Charley." Her shoulders slumped. "This land is changin', Shorty. I swear it's changin' so fast a body can't hardly keep track of it."

She was thinking of the trip down from the Missouri. In two days, they'd seen antelope, a few whitetail deer in the draws, and more wolves than she would have thought possible, but not one buffalo. She'd heard that the herds had been shot out, but it had taken traveling through what had once been the heart of the buffalo's range to really comprehend the loss. The shaggies were gone, and in a sad kind of way, so were the people who'd lived off them—Wahoo Charley killed and her pap wed to a bottle over in Billings, and who knew what had become of the rest—Jim White and Doc Zahl and Hi Bickerdyke, whose mother had been so loved during the late hostilities back East—plus a host of others.

And the Indians, too—penned on reservations like sheep in a corral, all except for a few old goats like Two-Hats, who hardly seemed to count in Rose's mind. At least not when compared to the wild and woolly types she remembered from her childhood. Lord, but it was sad—the buffalo and Jimmy, and the whole damned mess that was her life right now. . . .

"Rose?"

She looked up. "Charley was a good ol' boy, Shorty. He could tell a story that would make you laugh till you dang' near fell over. Those were good days."

"These days aren't so bad. Some of the old-timers are gone, but me and Wiley are still around. And you. Shoot, you ain't old enough to be thinking so glum."

"I might be tender in years, but I was out here before it changed and I remember what it used to be. I reckon that makes me as much an old-timer as Charley Schuyler."

"Come on down to Miles and have a drink. I'm thinking you could use it."

"Maybe I could." She sniffed. "You reckon they'll let me in a saloon, Shorty, bein' a woman and all?"

"Being a woman never stopped Calamity Jane." He smiled. "You're feeling under the weather on account of Muggy and Jimmy, but you'll chipper up again. Come on down to the Silver Star. Let's have a toot."

Rose straightened, firming her grip on the reins. "I reckon that sounds fine. It's been a while since I've done any serious tootin'."

She gave Albert a nudge with her heels and they turned onto the Miles City trail. At the river, Wiley was already boarding the ferry. Rose knew he wouldn't wait. The Silver Star Saloon was only a short ride away, and Wiley Collins had become a man with a purpose.

Chapter Six

The Silver Star was new since Rose's last visit to Miles City. It was a long, narrow building with a steep-pitched tin roof and a wide verandah. There was a corral out back where thirsty drovers could turn their horses loose, and an open-faced shed where they could sling their saddles over racks made for that purpose. Hay was provided in mangers along one side of the shed, and a wooden trough assured the boozy cowpokes that their mounts wouldn't suffer for water. All this for a nickel a night, payable on the honor system to the barkeep inside.

After Rose and Shorty had seen to their horses, they entered the saloon through the rear door. Although not as stylish as some of the larger establishments along Main and Fifth, it didn't take Rose long to discover the Silver Star's allure for men like Wiley and Shorty. She'd hardly bellied up to the bar when a long-legged man in a black frock coat and sporting a wax-tipped mustache hooked the heel of his drover's boot over the brass foot rail at her side. He propped an elbow on the bar and smiled broadly, the wind-tanned flesh around his blue eyes crinkling into a maze of tiny crevices. "Howdy, Rose," he said, touching the broad, stiff brim of his hat with the fingers of his left hand.

"Sam!" Rose squawked.

The needle-like tips of the tall man's mustache curled upward like scorpion tails. "I didn't expect to see you in these parts."

She stammered some comment about business bringing her east, knowing he wouldn't take offense at the vagueness of her reply. She'd fed Sam Matthews many a time on his forays up and down the trail, and knew him as a pistoleer, a gambler, an occasional horse thief, and a full-time gentleman. Glancing around the saloon, she saw no fewer than half a dozen others who fit a similar description—all of them friends she'd fed or let sleep in the barn with Albert and the mules. But only Sam, like Wiley, had she occasionally allowed to share her bed.

"I heard about Muggy," Sam said, motioning for the bartender. "I'm awfully sorry."

"Well, I reckon he had it comin' if anyone did," she replied. She knew Sam meant well, but it was beginning to irritate her that people kept thinking she required consolation over Muggy's death just because he was her husband. She wondered who would share her grief when Albert died, yet the strawberry roan had proved a far more loyal companion than Muggy ever had.

The bartender appeared opposite them, and, feeling suddenly awkward, Rose ordered a whiskey.

"I'll have another beer," Sam said, "but get Rose's drink first."

On her left, Shorty also ordered a whiskey. Then

he leaned forward to nod at Sam. "*Qué es*, stranger?"

"Howdy, Shorty. I figure you know Wiley Collins walked in not twenty minutes ago."

"Me 'n' Wiley have patched up our differences," Shorty assured him. "Besides, he knows I can shade him in a pistol fight."

Sam seemed to relax. "I am glad to hear that. It's a sad business when friends fall out."

"Hell, I couldn't shoot Wiley," Shorty confided. "I know his ma, and it'd break her old heart if something happened to her boy."

Grinning, Sam said: "I was told by Wiley that he didn't have a ma, that he was foaled from a thoroughbred mare out of a grizzly for a daddy."

"Well, that's Wiley. If he wasn't born a liar, he picked up the habit soon afterward. If he was foaled from anything, it was some wormy, knock-kneed mustang."

The bartender returned with their drinks, collected his coins, then moved on. Sam paid for Rose's whiskey despite her protests. "I've got it," he insisted, tossing an extra dime onto the bar.

Rose let it slide, although so much chivalry was starting to make her uncomfortable. "What brings you to these parts, Sam?" she asked.

"Business. Probably the same as yours, if you're riding with this yahoo."

"Shoot," Rose said, unable to suppress a grin. She took a sip of whiskey, letting the liquor burn a path through the trail dust in her throat. It felt odd to be in a saloon, standing up to the bar like one of the boys, but damn if it didn't feel kind of nice, too. Like coming home after a long journey away.

"You keeping up on those tricks I taught you?" Sam asked.

"What tricks are those?" Shorty inquired, cocking a brow.

"Gun tricks," Rose said quickly. "Dang it, Shorty, you got an ornery mind." She put her hand on the Smith & Wesson, saying to Sam: "I ain't kept up recent-like, what with summer and all the chores that's needed doin'. Plus I got this new pistol, and ain't tried it a-tall with this. But I practiced last winter with my Colt and got pretty good for a while."

"This isn't the place, but sometime you ought to show Shorty your road agent spin," Sam suggested.

"She good at it, is she?" Shorty asked.

"One of the best."

The road agent spin was a trick Sam had picked up from an old-time Kansas pistoleer. It worked on the assumption that an assailant had gotten the drop on the shooter and was demanding his firearms. Sam, who carried a brace of revolvers when on the tramp, had demonstrated the technique to Rose after a supper she'd fed him the previous year, holding both his revolvers toward her, butt first, as if to surrender them. But when Rose reached for the pistols, Sam had flipped them back into his own hands so fast it had been a blur.

It was only when he'd showed her how to do it in slow motion—keeping a trigger finger inside each trigger guard as the pistols were proffered, then letting them tip out and down while simultaneously spinning them back into his hands—that Rose had finally understood the trick.

Although she'd never taken displays of gunmanship as seriously as a lot of the men who rode the Owlhoot, she'd been impressed with the road agent spin, and had practiced it diligently with her old cap-and-ball Colt after Sam left.

Rose finished her whiskey, then switched to beer. Sam stayed a while to talk horses with Shorty, then ambled off to join a card game. Toward evening, Rose and Shorty went out in search of a meal. She'd forgotten about the Bull's Head Restaurant until they passed it on the boardwalk. Grabbing Shorty's arm, she hauled him back. "Let's eat here," she said.

"Naw, let's go to the Yellowstone Café. It serves a better steak."

"I got my mind set on eatin' here, Shorty. My pap and I ate here once, a long time ago." She walked over to peer through the open door. The place was shabbier than she remembered, but there was still a mounted buffalo head on the wall, red and white checked cloths on the tables. "Come on, gol-darn it. I been trailin' you boys all over creation the last couple of weeks. You can trail me this once."

Laughing, Shorty followed her inside, where they ordered steaks with boiled potatoes, beets, and fried corn. The coffee was stout enough to float a nail, but the stewed apples sprinkled with cinnamon they had for dessert more than made up for it.

"I could get used to ridin' with you two roosters if we ate like this every once in a while," Rose said, cleaning out the dessert bowl with her finger.

"That'd suit me," Shorty said, leaning back to start a cigarette. "You'd better talk to Wiley, though. He's under the impression he's ramrodding the outfit."

"I'll do that, soon as we get back."

He gave her a sheepish look. "I won't be going straight back, Rose. I've got some business to attend to on the other side of town."

"I'll give you a hand."

Shorty swallowed hard and nearly choked. Then he started to laugh. He laughed so hard he spilled his tobacco, then tore the paper. Finally he shook his head and started another. "I think I'd better handle this myself," he said, eyes sparkling.

Rose felt the blood rush to her cheeks. "You're gonna visit one of them dance halls, ain't you?"

"Naw, but there's a widow woman I keep company with when I'm in town. She's a nice girl, but does a little red-light work on the side. Nothing serious, and only with drovers she likes." He shrugged self-consciously. "We get along, her 'n' me."

"You don't have to explain, Shorty. I ain't no pampered gal that don't know the ways of Nature. Men has got their needs, that's all there is to it."

"It ain't that so much," he replied, looking kind of perplexed. "It's just that every time I come into Miles, I half expect to find her married off to some local rancher. She could have her pick of the local bachelors. I can't figure out why she hasn't done it yet."

"I'll bet she's got her cap set for you, and is just waitin' for you to get the urge to settle down."

"She'll have a good long wait. I settled down once. It's too painful for my taste."

Shorty's words pierced Rose's heart. It was the truth, she knew, and something a fiddle-footed person like Wiley Collins or Sam Matthews would never understand. But Shorty knew about the pain. So did Rose. For a moment she tried to imagine what it would be like if she and Shorty threw in together as husband and wife, then tucked the thought away as impractical.

Shorty paid for the meal out of his own poke and they went outside, stopping on the boardwalk in the softening twilight. The chill on the breeze seemed earlier than usual, and, looking off to the northwest, Rose saw a familiar blue haze on the horizon. It surprised her a little to realize a winter storm was brewing, after so many days of sweating on the trail, but it was time for it, she supposed. October now, and maybe the downhill side of it at that. She'd have to find a calendar while she was in Miles City and figure out what the date was. It was something she hadn't paid much attention to at the cabin, but she'd need to keep better track of the months if she was going to hang around a town.

Making his amends, Shorty headed off in search of a shave and a bath. Alone, Rose suddenly felt big and awkward in her shabby male attire. She wished she could go with him, at least as far as a barbershop. The thought of scrubbing up with hot water and maybe getting her hair trimmed—it was bothersome, being so long—was appealing, but she was short of funds after the skinning Two-Hats had given her, and she knew she'd have to make do, dirty, until she could slip down to the river and sneak a bath after dark.

With nowhere else to go, she returned to the Silver Star. Wiley would be there, and maybe Sam and some of the boys. They'd be poor company compared with Shorty, but better than standing alone on a street corner like some addle-brained child of the wilderness, watching the lights come on in homes and businesses around town.

The bartender, Tom, was making the rounds of the saloon, lighting the dozen or so hurricane lamps along the walls with a long taper, when Rose paused at the front door. She saw Wiley playing cards at the back of the room, but he was so intent on his game she doubted if he'd even been aware that she'd left. Sam Matthews was bucking the tiger at faro, and the others she knew were likewise occupied.

Even with so many familiar faces on hand, Rose almost didn't go in. The working girls had returned while she and Shorty had supper—seven of them that she could see. They'd been away that afternoon attending the funeral of a whore who'd been found beaten and drowned in the Yellowstone the day before. According to Tom, the dead girl was new in town and had worked in a different saloon, but even though none of the Silver Star hookers had known her, they'd all experienced a certain kinship with her fate.

The whores intimidated Rose, and if it hadn't been so cold she might have gone elsewhere, but she didn't know a soul in Miles City, or own an outfit warm enough to withstand an early winter storm. Grimly she pushed inside, sidling up to the end of the bar and trying to be as inconspicuous as possible.

Although the soiled doves spotted her right away, they gave her a wide berth. No doubt they were as curious about her as she was about them. Even Calamity Jane, they said, generally wore a dress when in town, although Rose knew that wasn't something a smart man would bet on.

Rose was grateful when Tom brought her a beer. The first one gave her something to concentrate on, and the second one sparked a goal of sorts. She'd been drunk a few times in her life, so she knew what she was doing when she picked up the pace of her drinking.

It was a few minutes past 8:00 when the batwing doors swung open and her old friend, Joe Bean, walked in. The room went immediately silent, although by then Rose was too far along in her drinking to notice. She swiveled on her elbows to squint toward the doors. "Joe!" she exclaimed, and in the deep quiet the name seemed to echo cavernously.

Joe's attention had been riveted to the back of the room, his gray eyes glittering like slivers of polished flint. A muscle in his cheek twitched when Rose called his name, but otherwise he didn't move. No one did, until Joe heaved a sigh and looked her way.

"Hello, Rose."

She glanced toward the rear of the saloon, where a couple of the boys were ducking out the back door. "Dang," she said, puzzled. But Joe seemed unperturbed. He walked to the bar as if on an evening's stroll.

"Joe, I'm sorry as all get-out if I messed up some of your business. I didn't expect to see you here."

"I'll admit to a modicum of surprise myself," he replied amiably.

Joe Bean was a handsome man in his early thirties, of average height and weight, although stoutly framed. He wore his brown hair cropped short and sported a neatly trimmed mustache. His eyes were deep-set, his jaw square and solid. He wore a new-looking suit in black, a brocade vest, a string tie over a white shirt, and boots that were nearly dustless. He looked, in fact, as if he was on his way to a funeral, or had just come from one, and Rose was tempted to ask if he'd known the whore they'd buried that afternoon. Then Sam Matthews stepped away from the faro table, and Joe swung quickly to face him. "Have a loose rein there, friend Matthews," Joe advised tersely.

"You two-bit traitor," Sam snarled. "Why don't you crawl back under a rock where you belong?"

Joe's gaze narrowed. "I'll not suffer that kind of abuse for long," he replied evenly. "If you wish to press your luck, I'll oblige you right here." He moved away from the bar, flipping his coat-tails back to reveal a short-barreled Colt in a cut-down holster.

Sam teetered a moment over the line of indecision, then abruptly pulled in his horns. "Not today, but we'll meet again."

Joe smiled his friendly smile, but kept his hand poised over his revolver. Sam turned and pushed through the throng, exiting the rear door as the two waddies before him had done. Joe eyed the remaining crowd speculatively, but no one seemed inclined to take up Sam's cause.

"What was that about?" Rose asked when Joe returned to her side. "Are you two on the warpath?"

"I've taken a position with the Yellowstone Basin Cattlemen's Association," Joe answered in oddly precise tones. "That seems to have put me on the warpath with quite a number of men in here tonight."

Tom brought a whiskey poured from one of the fancier bottles behind the bar, then scooped up the change Joe carelessly tossed onto the counter.

Lifting his glass, Joe said: "Some might call you a brave woman, Rose, to stand beside a man surrounded by so many enemies. I suspect it's just innocence, however."

"Shoot, we been friends since 'way back," she reminded him. "I remember when you wintered with us up in the Frozen Dog Hills, hunting buffalo. When was that . . . 'Seventy-Nine? 'Eighty?"

" 'Seventy-Seven, I believe. I'm no longer a hunter, Rose, although some call me that." He took a sip of whiskey, rolling it over his tongue as if to savor the taste.

Understanding dawned at last, and Rose reared back in disbelief. "Joe, you ain't become a Regulator, have you?"

"That word has picked up some ugly connotations recently," he replied carefully. "We call ourselves range detectives."

"Range detectives?" Her expression crumbled. "Hell's bells, Joe. Range detective . . . Regulator . . . Strangler? What's the difference? You might as well have fought with Crazy Horse against Custer."

"There is a difference, although I doubt if you could grasp it in your present condition. I didn't know you imbibed. I hope it's only a temporary response to Muggy's death, and not a permanent affliction. By the way, my condolences on your loss."

"Condolences, Joe? Imbibed? *Affliction?* What's

got into you? You never used to use that kind of language."

He ducked his head, then lifted it doggedly. "You're right, of course. I've spend considerable time in the company of educated men recently, and picked up some of their worst habits. But it's not simply a question of conceit. I needed change in my life. I needed to wipe the stink of dead buffalo off of me for good. This job has done that. It's given me respectability. I'll not jeopardize that for the likes of Sam Matthews or Wiley Collins." He paused as if weighing an issue, then said softly: "There is a list. Have you heard of it?"

"I've heard of it," she replied tautly.

"Your name is on it. It's near the bottom yet, but it's there."

Anger stirred within her. "Why are you telling me this?"

"The fact that you're a woman means nothing to the men I work for. When the time is right, they will come for you, unless you change your ways. You rode into Miles City with Wiley Collins and Shorty Tibbs. That's bad company to be keeping right now."

"Wiley 'n' Shorty are my friends, like you used to be."

"I'm still your friend. You may not believe it, but it's true."

"I reckon you're right, I don't believe it. Not of someone who'd ride with . . ." She clamped her lips shut.

"I didn't ride with the Stranglers, if that's what you're thinking. I don't even know their identities." He paused, then said: "We aren't mercenaries, Rose. We only wish to bring justice to a lawless land."

"You keep on tellin' yourself that," she said thickly, turning her gaze to the row of bottles along the backbar. "Maybe it'll help you sleep at night."

Joe sighed, then finished his whiskey. He was turning to leave when Rose stopped him.

"Joe, you tell me one thing."

"If I can."

"Were you with that bunch that hanged Muggy?"

"No. I've heard that was the work of vigilantes out of Helena, but I couldn't state that as a fact. Muggy wasn't a threat to the cattle trade, Rose."

She nodded stiffly. "That's good. I'm . . . I'm glad it wasn't you."

"It wasn't me," he reassured her, then walked out of the Silver Star.

Chapter Seven

It was almost 10:00 when the storm Rose had seen from the boardwalk in front of the Bull's Head Restaurant made its debut in Miles City. She was still standing at the bar, although she'd given up her earlier goal of intoxication. The crowd had thinned out noticeably in the wake of Joe's visit, and it was the subdued spirit of the room that allowed her to hear the wind coming off the plains several minutes before it actually arrived.

The wind struck the side of the saloon like a giant fist, and several of the boys jumped. Tom, standing at the far end of the bar reading a recent issue of the *Yellowstone Journal*, put the newspaper aside and walked over to the doors. A porch lamp hanging on the verandah was swinging wildly, but before he could slip outside to extinguish the flame, the wind snuffed it for him.

Tom swung the batwings back and fastened them to the wall, then pulled the big front doors closed. When he returned to the bar, he was shivering in his light shirt. "Dig out your mufflers, boys," he advised the room. "There'll be ice in the water buckets by morning."

In the next two hours, the temperature outside plummeted nearly forty degrees. Rose felt the storm's frigid breath every time a door opened for a departing customer. It made her glad she was inside, and not still out on the prairies.

With the temperature inside also dropping, the crowd began to drift away. Finally only Rose, Tom, Wiley, and a trio of hookers who sat with him at the back of the room remained. Shivering, Tom tossed the *Journal* on top of the bar. "I'm calling it quits, Alice," he said to one of the whores. "Lock up when you're through, would you?"

"Sure, Tommy," Alice replied.

With the heel of his boot, Wiley shoved an empty chair part way around, calling: "Come on over here, Rosie! You look like a colicky mule, standing there all by yourself."

She gave him a dark look, annoyed that he'd ignored her all evening. But Wiley had something up his sleeve, and wouldn't be put off.

"Come on, darlin'. Be sociable."

She swung around to give his table the once-over. Alice was sitting on his lap, leaning against his shoulder and looking bored, sleepy, and amused all at the same time. The other two hookers sat opposite them, sharing a short Durango cigar; they'd been talking quietly between themselves until Wiley drew their attention to Rose.

"Dammit, Rosie, are ye gonna make me come get ye?"

"You ain't had a word for me all night, Wiley Collins. I don't figure you got anything to say now that I'd want to hear."

Laughing, he replied: "Come on, don't sulk. Me 'n' Alice want to talk to ye."

"Leave her be," one of the cigar-smoking whores said. She was a dark-haired woman in a black dress cut to expose her slim, white shoulders—a fashion statement she was no doubt regretting tonight, Rose thought. Then Alice spoke sharply and the dark-haired woman flushed and dropped her gaze.

"Rosie!" Wiley bellowed, startling everyone. "Come 'ere, gawd dammit."

Rose stilled the tart reply that came to her tongue, reminding herself of the long journey she and Wiley had just completed together, and of the grub she'd eaten at his and Shorty's expense. Clutching her beer in one hand, she walked sullenly over to the table. Wiley watched with a widening grin that Rose had come to expect whenever he was forcing his will over another human being. Stopping several feet away, she hooked a thumb in her gun belt. "What do you want?" she asked crossly.

"Ye feelin' pretty good, are ye?" Wiley asked.

"I'm feelin' like a she griz' in heat, if it's any of your dang' business," Rose retorted. It was an expression she'd heard Calamity Jane use once in Billings, but, as soon as the words were uttered, Rose felt an immense embarrassment. It was the whiskey talking, she knew, and damn if it wasn't going to get her in trouble if she wasn't careful.

Wiley roared gleefully, causing Alice to grab the edge of the table, but she was also laughing, as was one of the other whores. Only the dark-haired woman with the bare shoulders seemed unamused. She was staring at Rose with a mixture of anger and disgust that only increased Rose's shame.

"By God, I believe you're right about her," Alice said.

"Damn right I'm right," Wiley replied.

"Why don't you go to hell?" Rose muttered.

"You tell 'em, honey," the dark-haired whore said.

"Shut up, Nora," Alice said without looking around.

"Where ye gonna sleep tonight?" Wiley asked.

"That skinny ol' blanket of yours ain't gonna cut this kind of cold."

"I figured I'd bunk out in the stable with Albert," Rose replied cautiously, sensing a trap. "I'll be warm enough if I burrow down in some hay."

"The stable's generally crowded on nights like this," Alice said. "There'll be six, eight, maybe a dozen men out there. 'Course, maybe you'd like that." She grinned smugly. "Sharing a blanket with a couple of husky drovers'd keep you warm, all right."

Rose grabbed the back of the chair Wiley had kicked around for her, gripping it hard as the room took an unexpected dip. Her anger had deserted her, leaving only her stubbornness for defense. "I reckon not," she said, forcing the words. "I'll find some place, though."

"Well, maybe me 'n' Alice have solved ye problem," Wiley said innocently. He indicated the dark-haired whore with a tip of his head. "We figured ye could bunk with Nora. My treat, of course."

"Treat?" Rose repeated, confused.

Alice and the other whore laughed, and Alice said: "We cater to everyone, honey."

Rose took a dragging step backward, but the chair seemed welded to her hand, heavy as an anchor. She couldn't believe that Wiley could be so cruel. Hadn't she proved herself enough to men like him? What more did they want?

"What about it, Rosie?" Wiley persisted. "Sure as

hell ye didn't show much interest in men on the ride down."

"No," she said, barely getting the word out.

"No?" Wiley mimed surprise. "Are ye tellin' me ye'd rather freeze to death than sugar up with Nora?"

"Don't listen to him," Nora said angrily. "He's just hoorawing you to see what you'll do."

"You bastard," Rose said quietly to Wiley, her lower lip trembling. "You dirty bastard."

Alice laughed. "Well, hell, there ain't much you can do if they ain't bred that way, but it was fun while it lasted."

It might have been fun in the beginning for Wiley, too—a joke to see how she'd react—but it was clear his mood had changed. "How much?" he asked Nora bluntly.

Sensing the shift in Wiley's temper, Nora kept her reply neutral. "It's five dollars for the night."

"It's five dollars for the night *after* midnight," Alice corrected. "It's ten dollars for the whole night."

Wiley pushed Alice off his lap, then struggled to his feet. He extracted a $10 bill from his wallet and let it flutter to the table. "The whole night then," he said, staring at Rose as if he hated her.

Nora's hand darted like a bird in flight, snatching up the bill. She tucked it between her breasts, then got to her feet. "Come on," she said to Rose.

Rose didn't know what to do. At that point, she was half afraid even to let go of the chair for fear she'd fall on her face.

Reaching out, Nora placed her hand gently over Rose's. "It'll be all right," she promised. "You'll freeze to death, otherwise."

Rose rubbed her free hand over her face, as if wiping away cobwebs. "Oh, Lordy," she murmured, as Nora led her toward the Silver Star's back door.

The temperature outside must have stood close to freezing, but, with the wind, it felt even colder. Rose was glad of Nora's hand on her own, for the night was pitch dark, without even a glimmer of moonlight penetrating the thick clouds that had rolled in with the wind. As foggy-headed as she was, Rose was certain she would've gotten turned around and lost her way. Fortunately they didn't have to go far, and within a couple of minutes they were climbing the back steps of a two-story frame house. Nora shoved the door open and Rose followed her inside.

"Whoa," Rose breathed, backing against a wall as soon as they were inside.

"Christ, it's cold," Nora said, shivering in a thin shawl she'd draped over her shoulders when she left the saloon.

Rose remained pressed against the wall, as if afraid to let go. She'd blamed her clumsiness outside on the uneven footing of the path they'd followed from the saloon, but damn if the floor didn't seem just as tricky.

Nora crossed the room—a kitchen, Rose saw

from the light of a bronze table lamp in the front parlor—and opened a cupboard to bring down a pair of thick china mugs. Lifting a coffee pot from the warmer on the stove, she said: "Want some? It's still hot."

"I ain't generally this foolish when I get drunk," Rose said.

Nora laughed. "What's that got to do with coffee?" She poured two cups without waiting for a reply. "Besides, sometimes a good drunk is just what the doctor ordered, although I gave it up as a remedy after my first hangover."

"That's probably sound advice. I hope I remember it in the morning."

Nora sat down at the long kitchen table with her coffee. "Grab your cup," she said. "I ain't your mama."

Rose brought her coffee to the table, then lifted the mug to her face, allowing the aromatic steam to leach some of the chill from her cheeks. She took a tentative sip and, when nothing untoward happened on the way down, tried another.

"You want some cake?" Nora asked.

Rose looked up. She hadn't had cake since her wedding, and that had been burned nearly black on the bottom. "Well, maybe a smidgen," she said.

Fetching plate and fork, Nora cut a wedge that she set in front of Rose, then returned to her seat. "It pretty good," she said. "It's called Kentucky butter cake."

"Did you make it?"

"No, Callie made it. She's the colored girl who works here."

"Where's 'here'?" Rose asked, paring off a bite with her fork. As her eyes adjusted to the dimness, she was able to make out what looked like a well-put-together kitchen. Visible in the parlor was a plushly upholstered chair with doilies on the arms and an iron and glass ash-stand at its side. A gilt-framed picture of a fat tabby cat playing with a ball of yarn hung on the wall behind it. The wallpaper was a light, powdery blue, with little bouquets of flocked periwinkles running through it vertically. On the floor, a corner of a heavy Oriental rug extended under the chair, covering all but the outer rim of polished hardwood.

"Alice's," Nora said flatly. "It's a parlor house, but everyone calls it Alice's."

Rose nodded. A parlor house was basically a polite way of saying whorehouse, although it generally implied a better class of working girl.

"Alice? Is that Wiley's friend at the Silver Star?"

"Uhn-huh. She's part owner. So is Tom, but the real money comes from some well-heeled cattle-man who's already gone back to New York for the winter. They say he's got a wife back there who's scared shitless of horses and wild Indians, and has never been west of the Hudson River." Her lips curled in disgust. "I consider such a woman a bigger whore than I am."

Rose didn't know how to respond to such blunt talk. Although she used coarse language herself on occasion, it made her uncomfortable to hear it from another woman. It upset her notion of the way people—city people, in particular—lived and acted. Then she shoved the forkful of cake into her mouth and all thoughts of urban propriety vanished like a puff of smoke. The cake tasted like a sweet piece of heaven on her tongue, rich with butter and topped with a dark sauce that reminded her of crunchy molasses. "*Umm,* this is good," she mumbled.

Nora watched her curiously for several seconds, then said: "Who are you, and what are you doing riding with a saddle sore like Wiley Collins?"

Rose swallowed audibly, taken by surprise. "I'm Rose Edwards. My place got burned out and Wiley and Shorty was the first ones to come by, so I just throwed in with them for a spell. It ain't no big deal."

"Wiley told me about your place. He told me about your man, too. He sounded no-account, if you don't mind my saying so."

Rose felt a moment's vexation at Wiley for having spoken of things she might not have wanted spread around. The truth was, it embarrassed her that she'd lost her home and husband to vigilantes. She felt it reflected poorly on her character.

"He was just a man, my husband," she said finally. "I hardly knew him." Which was accurate enough to cause her a feeling of regret. She lifted another forkful of butter cake to her mouth but the taste had gone flat, thinking of Muggy.

"That says a bunch," Nora agreed. "I had a man turn out bad, too. I was young and foolish, not even fifteen years old, and that rotten piece of meat was thirty if he was a day. We never married, although I thought we were going to. Then one day he caught a train for Saint Louis and I never saw him again." She laughed. "It bothered me for the longest time that he never said good bye. Damn, I was dumb."

"I never got a chance to say good bye to Muggy, either," Rose said.

"Did you love him?"

She thought about it for a minute. "Yeah, maybe, at first." She shrugged. "I was awful wet behind the ears back then."

"Weren't we all? But you hadn't ought to sell yourself short by riding with Collins now. We all make mistakes. That's no reason to get yourself shot."

"Shot?"

"Happens to all his partners sooner or later. All except Tibbs. Those two lead charmed lives."

"Wiley and Shorty?"

"First it was Nick Janke got himself killed, then Jimmy Frakes, and both of them damn' good boys. It seems like someone else is always taking a bullet meant for Wiley Collins."

"How'd you hear about Jimmy?"

"Wiley talks too much, even when he ain't drunk." It was clear Nora didn't think much of either Wiley or Shorty.

"He must've been talkin' a blue streak tonight," Rose said irritably. Here was another topic she felt was inappropriate to discuss, at least until some one notified Jimmy's family. Then her curiosity got the better of her. "Who's Nick Janke?" she asked.

"Just a boy, not much older than Jimmy. Nick had been riding with Wiley and Shorty for a couple of months when three men tried to hold up a Deadwood stagecoach. The messenger cut loose with his shotgun. When it was over, he'd been shot in the jaw and one of the hold-up men was dead. It was Nick he'd killed."

"That don't hardly sound like Shorty," Rose said uncomfortably.

"I don't know who else was there. I just know Nick rode with Collins and Tibbs for a while, then got himself killed about the same time those two split up."

"Well, road agentin' is a dirty business, and it don't sound like something Shorty'd do, is all I'm sayin'. It's one thing to throw a long rope now and again, like they do, but I don't believe Shorty would sink so low as to rob a coach."

"Some would say throwing a long rope is pretty low," Nora replied. "There was a time when an established outfit might turn its back to a little rustling to see some hard-working drover get a start, but those days are gone. Cattle is a big business now, and businessmen . . . especially those from back East or working for some syndicate out of England or Scotland or Germany

. . . they don't see things the same way you or I might. Besides, Wiley Collins never threw a rope with any intention of starting his own outfit. It's always been fast money for him. Is that worth risking your life for? Wiley Collins's greed?"

It wasn't, and all the more so if Wiley liked to throw down on a stage from time to time. She supposed Nora was right about his rustling, too, although she had no illusions as to why she continued to ride with him. She did it because of Shorty, pure and simple. Well, maybe not so simple, she amended to herself.

"You ain't eating," Nora observed.

"I reckon I ain't," Rose replied apologetically, lowering her fork. "It's good, but it's sittin' kinda rocky on top of all that whiskey and beer I drunk today."

"There's probably some roast beef in the icebox."

"No," Rose said quickly, the thought of that much grease causing her stomach to flop like a beached fish. "Maybe I ought to sleep it off, if I ain't puttin' you out?"

"Honey, nobody puts me out unless I want to be. I've got a big bed and I've shared it before. Listen, Collins likes to shoot off his mouth, but tonight the joke's on him. I got ten dollars out of the deal and you get to sleep in a warm bed, which I'd have let you share, anyway. Hell, even Alice wouldn't turn a woman out on a night like tonight."

Rose began to feel better almost immediately. *That damn' Wiley,* she thought.

"Come on," Nora said, standing and whisking away the cake. She popped what was left in her mouth, then rinsed the utensils in a basin of cold water sitting on the counter. "Let's go," she said, after hanging up the towel. "I already invited you once. I won't do it again."

Chapter Eight

Wiley and Shorty were drinking coffee at the kitchen table when Rose came downstairs the next morning. Shorty had a cat-ate-the-canary grin on his freshly shaved face, but Wiley just looked surly, his jaw whiskered, eyes bloodshot. At the stove, a stout-framed black woman in a starched black dress and white apron and mob cap was rustling breakfast. The smell of frying meat and eggs and the buttery aroma of flapjack batter filled the air.

"Best you sit," Callie said when she saw Rose. "Breakfast'll be ready in a jiffy."

Hitching self-consciously at her gun belt, Rose took a seat opposite Wiley. Callie slid a cup of coffee in front of her, then went back to the stove.

"Ye'd best fix Rose a double helpin', Callie," Wiley said. "She probably worked up an appetite last night."

"I fix everyone that sits at my table a good breakfast," Callie replied in a no-nonsense voice.

"All I be sayin' . . ."

"You just drink your coffee," Callie interrupted. "I'll look after my guests."

Wiley snorted but lifted his mug.

"Hello, Rose," Shorty said, winking.

She couldn't help a smile. "Hey, Shorty. Why ain't you breakfastin' with that widow woman?"

"She was still asleep when I left. Besides, we've got some decisions to make, the three of us."

"Rose ain't no part of this," Wiley grumbled.

"Sure she is," Shorty replied, stirring sugar into his coffee.

Wiley's head came up. "Are ye callin' the shots now, Shorty? Ramroddin' the outfit like a regular damn' cattle baron?"

"There ain't no outfit, Wiley. There's just you and me and Rose, and we've already decided she can come. Ain't no call to cut her loose just because you're mad."

Callie set plates of steak and eggs and flapjacks on the table in front of Wiley and Shorty, then brought a third platter for Rose. "Those eggs'll get cold quick," she said, before turning back to her stove.

"This looks mighty good, Callie," Shorty said, reaching for his fork. Rose could barely eyeball her plate without her stomach roiling. Wiley, she noticed, was having similar difficulties, although he tried to mask it by glaring at Shorty. Chewing a mouthful of egg, Shorty chuckled at his partner's discomfort. "Dig in, Wiley," he said. "It won't bite."

"Awaggh," Wiley gagged, pushing his plate back. "Callie, I need some hair of the dog. Ye got any whiskey?"

"So happens I do," the black woman replied. She brought a bottle down from the cupboard and splashed an inch or so into Wiley's coffee, then gave Rose an inquiring look.

"I reckon I'll ride it out plain," Rose said gamely, taking an experimental bite of flapjack.

"Best that way," Callie opined, recorking the bottle. "Whiskey in the morning just postpones a headache into the afternoon."

"Huh," Wiley grunted. "Look who's giving advice on hangovers."

"I bet she's seen a few in her lifetime, ain't that right, Callie?" Shorty teased.

"You just mind your 'jacks, Shorty Tibbs," Callie replied starchily. "I recollect more than once I've heard you behind the house, snorting like a gaggy ol' bull to hang onto your breakfast." Although she sounded perturbed, Rose noticed she was smiling when she turned away.

They went outside after breakfast, where Wiley and Shorty lit cigarettes. The sun was just coming up, its rays sparkling off the frosty grass. The clouds had moved on during the night and the worst of the wind had settled down, but it was cold. In just her faded old shirt and canvas trousers, Rose immediately began to shiver. "What is it you boys had in mind?" she asked. "Because if it's gonna take long to tell, I ain't likely to last."

Wiley looked at Shorty. "It's your call," he said brusquely.

"She's in."

"Then by God, you can outfit her," Wiley snarled. He stalked off toward town, kicking savagely at the clumps of grass and sage that stood in his path.

"What's rilin' him?" Rose asked through chattering teeth.

"Aw, he's just hung over. Come on, let's get you a coat before you bust a tooth with all that clacking."

They took off through the sage for Main Street and the central part of town. Despite his stumpy legs, Shorty had a quick gait, and Rose had to work at it to keep up.

Although the hour was early, there were quite a few people about—shopkeepers opening up their businesses, a squad of troopers from Fort Keogh trotting past on matching bay horses made frisky by the chilly air. At the old Diamond R corral, a bull-train pulling three big blue freight wagons was just getting under way, the popping of the bullwhacker's whip cracking like pistol shots above the rattle of chains and the creak of running gears.

Overhead, the telephone lines that criss-crossed the street glistened like silver-quilled ropes. Rose kept glancing at the wires as she hurried after Shorty. She'd heard Miles City had put in a slew of them after the original line was strung from the telegraph office in town to the Fort Keogh commander's office, a good two miles away, but she'd never seen an honest-to-God telephone in her life. Although she could hardly comprehend how they might work, she suddenly had a hankering to try one.

"Shorty," she said, "you ever talk into one of them telephone machines?"

He gave her a quizzical look. "I can't say that I have. Why?"

"I want to."

"You want to what?"

"You know, dang it. Let's go find one and talk in it."

Grinning, he said: "Who do you have to talk to? Besides, they're hard on your ears."

"You said you've never talked into one."

"I ain't, but I've seen Bob Hubbell, down at Broadwater's, talking on his. He always scrunches up his face like he's in pain."

"Shoot, once wouldn't hurt. I reckon if they was all that hard on a body, Bob Hubbell would just walk across town to deliver his messages."

"Which is what a smart man should do in the first place," Shorty countered. They came to Broadwater and Hubbell's, and Shorty stopped in a patch of sunlight that was out of the wind. "We ain't got time, anyway," he added, starting a cigarette.

"Why? What's the rush all of a sudden? I thought we was gonna hang and rattle a spell."

"Not with Joe Bean poking around. Hell, I'll bet half the waddies in the Silver Star last night are having their breakfast in Dakota Territory this morning."

"Because of Joe?"

Shorty gave her a searching look. "You know what he does, don't you?"

Rose tried to piece together her conversation with Joe from the night before. "I reckon he's a range detective," she said uncertainly. "I think that's what he told me. But shoot, Joe's always been a good ol' boy, Shorty." Vaguely she recalled the anger and hurt she'd felt toward him last night, but those feelings were hard to hang onto in the bright light of a new day. When she saw him in her mind now, she saw him as he'd been years ago, fresh from the East and just learning the buffalo trade from her pap, all thumbs at times, but eager to learn.

It was clear from his expression that Shorty didn't share her opinion. "Those days are gone, as far as Bean is concerned. If you ever see him on the prairie, you'll have two choices. One is to bushwhack the bastard, the other is to crawl into a hole and hope he doesn't see you."

"Joe?"

"Joe Bean," Shorty returned flatly, lighting his cigarette. "Come on," he said. "Let's go put an outfit together."

"What for? You ain't never said."

"Well, I guess I ain't. Wolfing, Rose. I talked to Bob Hubbell about it last night, and he's willing to outfit us on credit. Said he'd take all the pelts we brought him."

Rose's spirits, heightened earlier by the prospect of talking on a telephone, suddenly collapsed. "I ain't never considered myself a wolfer, Shorty."

"Aw, a wolfer's reputation ain't no worse than a buffalo hunter's. It'll give us a job for the winter, and keep us away from Joe Bean and his boys."

Rose wasn't sure she agreed, but she felt caught as snugly as if she had her butt in a bear trap, nearly broke and without even a coat or a decent bedroll. Her options would be few if she refused Shorty's offer.

"It won't be so bad, and we can start running horses again in the spring if Bean ain't around. Come on," he said, heading for the door.

Defeated and disheartened, Rose followed.

Shorty and Bob Hubbell wasted no time getting down to business. Shorty bought the whole outfit on credit—warm clothes and grub to last the winter, traps and poison, even a case of skinning knives.

Rose got a horse-hide coat with the hair on, a seal-skin trooper's cap with flaps that folded down over her ears to tie under her chin, and two pairs of winter moccasins to wear over her boots. The moccasins were made of thick buffalo leather with the hair turned in—the last they had, according to the clerk helping her. She also got a couple of pairs of wool trousers, some socks, shirts, long underwear, and several pairs of gloves. She purchased an inexpensive toiletry set—hand mirror, brush, comb—plus a toothbrush and two pounds of baking soda for her teeth. She got a cartridge belt to hold the big .44-90 brass for her Sharps, and four more boxes of shells. She tried to get a buffalo robe for sleeping, but they were out of those. She settled for a sougan, instead—four heavy wool blankets wrapped inside a tarp to keep out the dampness.

She felt bad about putting her personal gear on Shorty's account—it came close to $75 altogether —but figured she could pay him off easy with a good season.

Shorty also bought four sawbuck pack saddles and all the rigging for the extra horses they'd brought with them from Two-Hats's. When Rose reminded him that one of those ponies belonged to Jimmy Frakes, and by rights should be returned to Jimmy's daddy, Shorty grabbed her roughly by the elbow and hauled her out of the clerk's hearing.

"You let me 'n' Wiley worry about the horses and supplies, all right?"

"I . . . I didn't mean anything," she stammered. "I just thought maybe you'd forgot."

"Nobody forgets," he said, giving her a shake. Then his grip relaxed and he let her go. "Maybe that's the trouble. Nobody forgets."

"What do you mean?"

He shook his head. "Go out back and see if Wiley's showed up. If he ain't, keep an eye peeled for him."

"Sure," Rose said, rubbing her arm.

"And keep an eye open for Joe Bean, too."

Rose went outside, taking her new coat with her. The breeze had picked up again, but she felt comfortable inside the black-haired coat. She was pulling on her gloves when she spotted Wiley across the street, waiting in the alley behind Charley Brown's saloon. He had the extra horses with him, bunched up on short leads. Sticking her hands in the pockets of her coat, she sauntered across the street as casually as possible.

"By God, it took ye long enough," Wiley grumbled as she came up. "What's Shorty doin' in there, buyin' out the whole damn' store?"

"He's just getting' an outfit together," she replied, noticing how Wiley still looked pretty green around the gills.

"He'd just better not forget the whiskey. A man doesn't mind a week or two without a drink, but I'll be damned if I'll sit out the whole winter dry."

"He bought two gallons."

Wiley looked strangely relieved at her reply. "Good," he said. "Good."

Rose swung onto Albert and accepted the lead ropes to two of the extra horses, then they jogged across the street and down another alley to the loading dock behind Broadwater's. Shorty was waiting for them there with a steel-wheeled truck piled high with supplies.

While the two wranglers sorted everything into

different panniers, Rose fit the pack saddles to the horses, adjusting cinches and cruppers and breast bands until she was satisfied they were right. Although Wiley and Shorty both seemed edgy today, she was determined that neither would find fault with her packing skills.

It took a couple of hours to line everything out. When they were finished, sweat was rolling freely down Rose's face, and Wiley's, too.

" 'Tis the damn' whiskey," Wiley had gasped at one point, "but this'll soak it outta me. I'll be good as new in no time." Then he'd walked over to lean against the cool bricks of Broadwater's back wall and heaved his morning coffee into the weeds.

Rose fared a little better, but still felt clammy and nauseated by the time they climbed into their saddles. She'd removed her coat earlier and tied it behind the cantle, but figured she'd be putting it on again soon enough.

Shorty guided his horse alongside. "Ready?" he asked.

"I am, but I ain't sure about him." She nodded toward Wiley, gulping air and clutching his saddle horn.

Shorty laughed. "He'll feel better when we get started. So will you. We'll stop early for a noon meal, and that'll help."

He reined away with one of the pack horses in tow, then hauled up abruptly about halfway down the alley, swearing. Wiley dropped the lead rope to his own pack horse and quickly rode up beside

Shorty. Rose flanked Shorty on his right, but kept a grip on the two pack horses in her string.

Joe Bean blocked their exit. He stood in the center of the alley with a double-barreled shotgun butted to his hip. Two other men stood with him. One was tall and skinny and held a sturdy Marlin lever-action gun across his chest; the other was about Joe's height, but fleshier, and, like Joe, he was toting a shotgun that he held in both hands. All three wore suits and range coats, with cartridge belts visible at their waists.

" 'Morning," Joe said pleasantly.

"What do you want?" Shorty returned.

"You're an ambitious-looking bunch this morning. Mind telling me where you're heading with all those pack horses?"

"None of ye damn' business," Wiley growled.

A smile feathered across Joe's face. "Why, bless me if that isn't Wiley Collins. I thought at first it was a sack of flour." His smile broadened. "Are you feeling all right, friend Collins? You're looking peaked."

"I'm fit enough to plow through you and yer boys if ye don't get outta me way," Wiley replied.

The tall man beside Joe guffawed, but Joe's expression turned somber as he regarded Rose. "You've chosen a dangerous path, Rose," he said. "It saddens me to see you here today."

"We're mindin' our own business, Joe. Ain't no reason you can't do the same."

"Men like Collins and Tibbs are my business.

They understand the eventual consequences of their deeds. I'm not sure you do. I'd urge you to give up these reckless habits, Rose, and settle down to gainful employment. Or a husband. Can you cook?"

"Not so good. Besides, I gave Shorty my word."

"No one would think less of you if you changed your mind. Such is a woman's prerogative, they say."

"I reckon I'd think less of me," she said.

"Maybe she don't trust ye, Bean," Wiley interjected. " 'Course, she knows ye better'n I do."

"If you were a gentleman, Collins, you wouldn't allow her to become involved in this," Joe replied. "You would force her out now, before it becomes too late."

"I ain't a gentleman, and I ain't likely to become one anytime soon. Now, are ye sniffin' for trouble, Joseph, or are ye gonna get outta our way?"

Joe looked at Shorty. "Is that your position as well, Tibbs?"

"She's a grown-up girl. She doesn't need the likes of you or me making her decisions for her."

Joe's expression relaxed, allowing that fleeting smile to cross his face once more. Glancing at Wiley, he said: "No, I'm not seeking confrontation today, Collins. I just wanted to wish you boys a safe journey . . . whichever direction you take. And you as well, Rose. Think about what I've said today. It's not too late to remove yourself from the path of destruction."

"I reckon I'll track this path for a spell yet," she said stiffly, then heeled Albert into movement. Joe and his *compadres* stepped aside as she rode past, the short one tipping his hat politely.

Wiley and Shorty followed her onto the street, where Wiley kicked his horse into a sudden lope, heading for the ferry. Shorty jogged his mount alongside Albert, saying: "You still figure Joe Bean's a good ol' boy, Rose?"

"Aw, he's all right. I don't know about them other two, though. To tell you the truth, that tall one scared me."

"That was Pine Tree Manning. The other is Amos Skinner. Pine Tree is a Hill Country Texican by birth, and they say he's handy with that Forty-Sixty Marlin. He's got such big hands, he can almost handle it like a pistol. All I know about Skinner is that he used to deputy around Bismarck, before coming out here to ride for Bean."

"Well, he seemed gentlemanly enough, him and Joe both, but that Manning character looked mean to me. I'd hate to get crosswise of him and not have a good club handy."

They reached the ferry just in time to see Wiley departing from it on the Yellowstone's northern bank. It took twenty minutes for the craft to return and carry them across, then another hour to catch up with Wiley. They didn't stop or even speak when they did, but pushed on along a faintly defined trail, each lost in their own thoughts. The wind continued to pick up as the morning progressed, and the sky looked pale and cheerless after the deep sapphires of summer.

They came to a shallow basin shortly before noon, and Wiley reined his horse to skirt it on the west. Toward the middle of the basin were some low cottonwoods and scrub willow. They'd almost ridden past them when Shorty abruptly hauled up.

"What is it?" Wiley asked.

"I reckon it's a dead man," Shorty replied.

Rose followed the direction of his gaze toward the trees. They were about a quarter of a mile away, and at first she didn't see the corpse hanging from a stout lower limb of the farthest cottonwood. When she did, it gave her a start, for she'd expected to see someone lying on the ground, not dangling from a rope.

Shorty turned his horse off the trail.

"Where are ye going?" Wiley called after him.

"I want to see who it is."

"It don't matter who it is."

"Then stay here," Shorty said.

Muttering under his breath, Wiley reined after Shorty, and, although Rose didn't really want to see who it was, either, she followed. They were still a hundred yards away when Shorty started to curse. A minute later, Wiley began swearing as well. Then Rose recognized the body of Sam Matthews, and something inside her chest seemed to lurch violently.

"Joe Bean's men must've been waiting for him outside the Silver Star last night," Wiley speculated.

He dismounted and walked around the gently swaying corpse, looking for sign. "Ground's too hard," he announced after a couple of minutes. "I can't see anything."

"Why . . . why'd they bring him all the way out here?" Rose asked. It made her feel queasy all over again to think of Sam hanging out here in last night's storm while she'd eaten Kentucky butter cake with Nora. Sam's face was swollen horribly, almost black from lack of circulation. His hands were tied behind his back but his feet were unfettered, so Rose knew he'd been strung up from the back of his horse. It was the way the vigilantes had done it with Muggy, too.

Shorty's face was livid when he looked at Rose. "There's the work of your good friend, Joe Bean," he said harshly.

"You don't know it was Joe," Rose said in a quavery tone. "It could've been someone else . . . Regulators or such."

"Jesus Christ," Shorty grated, yanking his horse around.

"Now where ye goin'?" Wiley demanded.

"I'm going on," Shorty said. "You stay and bury him. I'm tired of cleaning up other people's messes." He slapped his mount's hips with the ends of his reins, putting the horse into a lope.

"God dammit, he was ye friend!" Wiley called, but Shorty didn't even look back. "That bastard," Wiley said softly, then glanced at Rose. "I meant Bean, not Shorty."

114

"You think Joe did this, too?"

"Darlin', I *know* the son-of-a-bitch done it. He as much as told us so in the alley this morning."

"But he didn't know we'd come this way. Dang it, we ain't hardly followin' a trail."

" 'Tis trail enough, and sure he knew. Maybe not certain sure, but enough to chance this." He looked at the corpse of Sam Matthews, and his voice turned heavy. " 'Tis a warnin', Rosie, and nothin' less. One man crossed off his list and ye 'n' me 'n' Shorty told that we've moved up on it. Slick, huh?"

When Rose didn't reply, he walked over to one of the pack horses and pulled a shovel out from under the canvas. "There's a pick in there, too, if ye be of a mind to help, but if ye heart ain't in it, then ye can catch up with Shorty. I got an idea," he added quietly, "that Shorty could use a woman's ear about now, for, despite what he says, Sam Matthews was a friend to us both." He shook his head. "I reckon Joe Bean knew that, too."

Chapter Nine

It was an arduous climb out of Crooked Creek Cañon, and Rose halted on top of the divide to rest her horse. Before her lay the valley of the Pipestem, the far-off river a flat, gray sheet of ice, curving through its center in a giant oxbow. On the near side, from the divide, the land dropped sharply for perhaps a hundred yards, then sloped more gently toward the valley floor a couple of miles away. Flanking the Pipestem on the opposite bank was a line of broken cliffs ranging from five to twenty-five feet in height, the country beyond it sweeping up into the foothills of the Big Snowy Mountains far to the west.

Along the narrow strip of land between the river and the cliffs were scattered groves of cottonwood and bastard maple, with red-barked alders in the low places and the brittle, thorny branches of chokecherries growing at the breaks in the cliffs. And over it all, a mantle of snow as white as a distant swan.

They'd been out for a couple of months now, and were a long way from Miles City, or any place else for that matter. Rose figured that suited Wiley and Shorty just fine, for they'd both been thoroughly spooked by their discovery of Sam Matthews's body. Although neither admitted it, she knew the memory of Sam's corpse was like a ghost haunting the old hunter's shack where they'd taken refuge.

It was Wiley who'd brought them here, having come across the cabin the year before while running horses into Canada, just after he and Shorty split up. Rose had watched the two men closely as Wiley related the story of finding the cabin, keen for some hint as to what had brought about the rift between them, but she hadn't learned anything, and didn't want to ask.

The cabin was about fourteen feet wide and twenty deep, with a stone fireplace against the rear wall. A loose-fitting door on leather hinges faced the Pipestem about fifty feet away, and there were a couple of small windows without glass. The roof was sod, with clumps of bunch grass and cactus growing on top, furrowed by run-off and littered with old, sun-bleached bones tossed up by previous occupants. A corral was located off the south side with a lean-to built against the cabin's wall for shelter. There was grass in the curves of the oxbow for the horses, and enough downed timber nearby to keep them in firewood all winter.

It kind of surprised Rose that neither man had made any advances toward her, especially after they'd settled into the cabin, although she was grateful that they hadn't. Her life had become complicated enough since Muggy's death.

Leaning forward to rest her gloved palms against the Mother Hubbard's broad horn, Rose squinted into the distance. Several miles to the south, where the Pipestem curved out of some round-breasted hills, a lone horseman had appeared. Rose watched closely for several minutes, for the image of Sam's body was strong in her mind, too, but she relaxed when the rider started across the flat, bare land between the bends of the river. A Regulator wouldn't ride out in the open that way, nor would he come alone. When she spotted the dog, her mood brightened. It meant the horseman was probably Manuel Obreto, a sheepherder wintering his flock in the next valley to the south.

"Looks like we're gonna have company tonight,"

Rose said to Albert, heeling the gelding toward the edge of the bluff.

Although Albert snorted his displeasure at the steepness of the slope, he went over without too much fuss, and when the land leveled out with better footing, Rose kicked him into a lope. She pulled up at the cabin half an hour later, just as Manuel dismounted. The dog, a black and white shepherd with one blue eye, was rumped down in the snow out of the way, its pink tongue lolling, breath fogging the air in front of its shiny black nose.

"Hello, you gol-darn' bean-eater!" Rose called.

At that same moment the cabin door swung open and Shorty stepped out. "What the hell's all the ruckus about?" he demanded.

"*Señorita* Rose, Shorty. *Buenos días.*"

"Obreto!" Shorty exclaimed. "By God, you ought to make some noise when you ride up. I might've shot you."

Manuel was smiling broadly; even the dog wiggled with excitement. "Shorty, you were sleeping, no?"

"Aw, just a nap, though it's likely a good thing." He glanced at the sky, already fading into twilight. "I'll probably be up all night now, listening to your lies."

They'd run into Manuel soon after arriving in the valley, and for a while Rose had thought it was going to turn out badly between them. Shorty was a Texan by choice, if not birth, and the Alamo and Goliad were etched vividly in his psyche. And Wiley hated sheep with a fanaticism Rose couldn't begin to fathom. Even Manuel was stand-offish in the beginning, thinking these were ordinary cowboys and not to be trusted. But the valley's solitude had soon worn down the walls of distrust, and now they got along fine. Manuel was careful to keep his sheep away from their cabin, and Rose and Shorty made an extra effort to trap the hills surrounding Obreto's flocks. They'd taken eight wolves that first week, and Manuel had brimmed with gratitude ever since.

Lifting a slope-shouldered clay jug from his saddlebags, Manuel held it above his head. "See, Shorty, I told you. Chokecherry wine."

Shorty laughed and left the stoop in just his shirt sleeves, even though the temperature was bitterly cold. He took the jug and pulled the cork, sniffing the contents. Then he wrinkled his nose. "Smells like cough syrup."

Manuel's smile remained unchanged. "You drink a little, see if you think it is syrup." He led his shaggy bay horse over beside Albert and flopped the stirrup across the seat. "You will have a little, too, no, *señorita*?"

"Maybe," she replied. "When we get inside."

"Whew!" Shorty exclaimed, lowering the jug. He looked at Rose, his eyes twinkling. "Manny ain't lyin', this is good."

"Just see you don't swill it all," Rose said, pulling the headstall over Albert's ears and allowing him to spit out an easy-on-the-mouth snaffle bit. "It's been a long time since I drank anything besides strong coffee and crick water."

"Well, this ain't crick water, I'll guarantee you." Shorty turned toward the cabin, keeping the jug with him. "You two come on in when you're finished. I'll rustle us up some grub."

That was something else that had changed since settling on the Pipestem—Shorty taking over the cooking. It wasn't that he liked the job, he'd explained carefully one fall evening. It was just that Rose's cooking seemed to set a tad heavy on his stomach. Probably nothing more than the spices she used, he'd assured her, but if he'd been worried about hurting her feelings, he needn't have bothered. Rose welcomed the switch cheerfully, and didn't even call him a liar when they all knew the only spice she ever used was salt. Besides, there were other ways she could make herself useful—stock to look after, wood to drag up, pelts to care for.

They'd collected quite a few hides so far, and each one had to be stretched on a willow frame, then fleshed with a scraper to remove the excess fat and meat. When they were dry and stiff, Rose cut them from their frames and laced them into bundles. In the spring they would be folded and pressed into packs—forty hides to a pack, two packs to a horse—but for the time being the bundles were hung from the rafters where they would be out of reach of the mice that ruled the cabin when no one was home, or after the trappers had settled into their bunks for the night.

Rose turned Albert loose to graze, knowing he wouldn't stray far. Manuel hobbled his bay before freeing it. Then he and Rose went inside.

It was cool in the cabin, even with a fire burning. Frost clung to the interior walls around the door and windows, and the pelts swayed gently in a breeze that slipped in through the loose chinking under the eaves. Rose dropped the hides she'd taken that day on the floor beside the door, then lugged her saddle over beside her bunk, where she shucked out of her heavy coat. Manuel's dog squeezed into the cabin on its master's heels and immediately started sniffing the pelts.

"You, leave those alone," Manuel scolded. The dog slunk away, flopping down in the corner.

There was a rough-built table with benches in the center of the room. Rose poured coffee for herself and Manuel, then sat down opposite him. Manuel was a short, wiry man with thick black hair and a full mustache. He must have been fifty, but around Rose he acted as shy as a boy.

"Where's that wine?" she asked suddenly. "I think our guest could use some bug juice to warm his blood."

"Oh, I'd say Manny's warmin' up just fine," Shorty replied drolly. Still, he left his cooking to fetch the jug.

In the corner, the dog lifted its head, ears perked toward the north wall. "I reckon that's Wiley,"

Rose said, noticing how Manuel's face suddenly tightened.

Shorty was rolling a cigarette. "You'll have to give me your recipe for chokecherry wine someday, Manny."

"It takes a lot of sugar," Manuel replied. "The *patrón* always says . . . 'Manuel, what do you do with so much sugar? Do you feed it to the sheep?' . . . and I always tell him . . . 'No, just a little for my coffee.' He laughs because he thinks I use so much in my coffee. He would not laugh if he knew I made the wine."

Manuel's *patrón* had a ranch down on the Powder River in Wyoming Territory. He kept sheep on the side because they were a good investment, but hired Manuel to take care of them, and never came around himself or allowed sheep on his own range. It was an odd pact, but Manuel liked it fine. He was on his own most of the year, and never had any trouble with the *patrón*, other than his questioning Manuel about the amount of sugar he ordered each fall.

"I'd still like to try," Shorty said. "My folks used to make a heap of peach wine back in Georgia, before the war."

A horse trotted into the yard, and Rose heard the creak of saddle leather as Wiley dismounted by the corral. A few minutes later he shoved through the door, stamping the snow from his India rubber overboots. He tossed his own pelt over the two Rose had brought in, then elbowed the door shut.

Although he glanced at Manuel, all he said was: " 'Tis another damned cold day out there, and I'm gettin' mighty sick of it."

"There's stew on the fire," Shorty said. "We'll eat soon."

"Then a little drunk, eh?" Manuel nodded a wary greeting. "Hello, *Señor* Wiley."

"If ye're plannin' on gettin' drunk on my whiskey, ye can damn' well think again," Wiley replied.

"Aw, lay off a fella," Rose said. "Manuel brought his own jug."

"Whiskey?"

"Better than whiskey," Shorty said. "Manny brought some of that chokecherry wine he's been bragging about."

"I'll be damned," Wiley said, looking pleasantly surprised. He took off his coat and overboots, then came over to sit beside Rose. "Well, has the drunk commenced?"

"Not yet," Rose replied, then slid the jug toward him. "But you go ahead and get 'er started. The rest of us'll catch up after supper."

"What the hell?" Wiley said, scowling at the jug.

"It is small," Manuel admitted, "but the wine, she packs a punch. Besides, we should not get so drunk that we miss the party, eh?"

All eyes turned toward him. "What party?" Shorty asked.

"At the Lost Gulch there is to be a Christmas party, four days from now. I thought maybe we would go together? I leave my flock with the camp tender, you leave your traps?"

Interrupting their trapping wouldn't be a problem, as far as Rose was concerned. They could run them early the next morning, then either leave them sprung or bring them in until they returned. And Manuel had been fortunate to have his camp tender show up when he did. Rose had met him once, a curly-haired Scotsman with pale green eyes and a haunting skill on the bagpipes. He was an independent who contracted with several of the smaller outfits, traveling constantly between flocks to keep in touch with the shepherds and make sure everything was all right. He used a wagon rather than a saddle horse, and carried extra supplies that the herders might need between their twice-a-year resupply with the flock owners. If he hadn't shown up, Rose knew Manuel wouldn't have left his sheep even to tell them about the party, let alone contemplate riding over to enjoy it.

"Lost Gulch?" Shorty said doubtfully. "You sure there's enough people there for a party?"

Lost Gulch was a miner's camp on the eastern slopes of the Big Snowys, a day and a half ride to the west. Although it hadn't panned out the way the original inhabitants had hoped, a few die-hards remained. The last Rose had heard, the town boasted a saloon, a small general store, a livery with a blacksmith shop, and maybe thirty to forty more or less permanent residents.

"Hell," Wiley said after a pause. "It wouldn't

take many to throw a decent shindig, as long as they've got plenty of booze." He glanced at Manuel. "Their saloon still open?"

"*Sí*, and there is a whore, too, although she is old and does not have much hair left."

Laughing, Shorty said: "The hell with bald-headed whores. They'll have fresh beer and new faces, and I'll bet word will spread. Lost Gulch could be booming by the time we get there. I say let's go."

"Let's do it," Wiley agreed.

Shorty looked at Rose.

"I've been feelin' like I was buried under a snowdrift for two months now," she said. "Shoot, yeah, count me in."

Chapter Ten

They left before dawn two days later, climbing through a gap in the rimrock above the cabin and lining out, single file, to the west. Manuel led since he knew the way, although from time to time, one of the others would spell him to give his horse a break. The snow was just deep enough to be troublesome, and the cold sapped their strength. The weather had turned bitter around the first of December; some days it didn't rise to zero. It made a body cautious, for a fact, Rose thought as her roan horse struggled through yet another drift. A person wouldn't want to be caught out without the proper gear and appropriate skills, for their chances of lasting even a few hours would be slim.

It was late the next day when they came to a broad meadow surrounded by tall pines. The town of Lost Gulch sat in its center, ringed by the stumps of what had once been a thick forest. Low mountains encircled the flat, adding to its sense of exile.

The livery was across from the Gold Nugget Saloon, and the four frozen riders ducked their heads to ride inside, out of the wind, before dismounting. An old codger in a gray blanket coat limped into view, carrying a pitchfork in one hand like a scepter. Shaking his head at the sight of them, he marveled: "More strangers. By dingy, where do they come from?"

"What's it matter to ye?" Wiley asked testily.

The old man shook his head. "Hit don't matter a bit to me, long as they got money to pay for their stablin'. I won't put a horse up for free, I don't care how cold it blows outside."

Wiley flipped a silver dollar toward him, the coin blinking like a bad eye as it spun through the dim light of the stable. "What'll that buy us?" he asked.

After checking the coin's authenticity with yellow molars, the old man said: "One night's lodging for your horses. Hit's an extra two bits a person if anyone wants to spread his bedroll inside."

"Does the saloon rent rooms?" Shorty asked.

"A few, but they're full up from what I hear,

126

packed shoulder to shoulder like sardines in a tin." He dropped the coin in his pocket. "You're here for the celebration, I figure."

"I'm here for refreshment, both liquid and horizontal," Wiley replied. "Ye reckon Lost Gulch can accommodate those sins?"

"Hit can if you ain't partial to variety." The old man frowned, his gaze sharpening on Rose. "By dingy, that's a woman."

"My name's Rose Edwards," Rose said, sniffing her runny red nose. "Pleased to make your acquaintance."

"Lord God, girl, what're you doing in a hole like Lost Gulch?"

"I reckon I came to see the elephant, like everyone else."

"What's the matter, old-timer?" Wiley asked, laughing. "Ye never seen a woman in pants before?"

"No, I ain't," the old man flared. "Women wear dresses where I come from, and don't go gallivantin' around ridin' astraddle, either. And the menfolk with 'em don't talk freely of whores."

"Rosie knows what a whore is," Wiley said, just to goad the elderly man. "Ain't that right, darlin'?"

"Shut up, Wiley," Rose replied, as embarrassed by the old man's outrage as she was by Wiley's crude attempt at humor. She led Albert to an empty stall at the rear of the livery and pulled off her saddle. The old man followed, standing at the stall's entrance.

"You can store your tack yonder." He nodded toward a number of saddle racks in a dark corner.

"You won't have to worry about no drunk grabbin' your stuff by mistake, either. I don't aim to go to the party, so I'll be here to keep an eye on ever'thing."

"That's kind of you," Rose said.

"Don't know how kind it is. Could I handle a bottle better, I'd go. But I can't. I'd just end up drunk and puking blood for a week if I did."

Rose lugged the Mother Hubbard to an empty rack and slung it into place.

The old man shuffled after her. "My name's Asa Carson," he said. "Hit just struck me that mayhaps you're the Rose Edwards what used to live down on the Yellerstone."

Rose was startled by the old man's recognition. "Have we met?"

"Not personal-like, but I knew your daddy up at Fort Benton, if his name's Daniel Ames. I remember you, too, though you weren't but a sprite back then. I heard you'd married Muggy Edwards and moved onto the old Hockstetter place?"

"Well, Muggy was my husband," Rose replied warily, "but he passed away last fall."

"Uhn-huh, heard about that, too." A spark of interest had come into the old man's eyes. "Yeah, I knew ol' Muggy well, over to the Last Chance."

"He did hang around Helena some," Rose admitted, "but he died."

"Hung, they say."

She bristled. "By jealous gamblers, I reckon."

"Hit's possible. Story I heard was that it was an honest game for a change, at least as far as folks could tell. Be kind of ironic if it was, wouldn't it?"

Rose brushed past him without answering, making her way to the front of the livery to wait for the others. For a minute she worried that Asa might follow her, but he didn't. He remained close to the tack, watching like a mouse from the shadows, a shiny-eyed stare that put her instantly on guard.

It hadn't occurred to Rose that it might be a mistake coming to Lost Gulch, although when a person thought about it, the Big Snowys weren't all that far from Helena. For all she knew, Muggy could've dealt faro right across the street at the Gold Nugget, and earned himself any number of enemies, for he'd been a clumsy cheat when he drank, and was susceptible to obnoxious behavior even on his better days.

Soon the others joined her and they crossed the frozen ground to the saloon. The Nugget was larger than it appeared from the outside, at least forty feet wide and sixty deep, low-ceilinged and dark, despite the numerous lanterns hanging from the rafters. The bar was straight-grained walnut with brass hardware, and ran across the back of the room. It was jammed with men in for the celebration, the bulk of them miners, but with a few hunters, trappers, and muleskinners thrown in for good measure. A stove in the middle of the room popped and crackled, throwing off shimmering waves of heat that distorted everything behind it.

Rose could feel the warmth as soon as she walked in, a friendly, welcoming presence after the long, cold journey from their cabin on the Pipestem. Intermingled with the odors of men and leather and tobacco and booze, the rough voices and harsh laughter, the room brought back pleasant memories of her pap and brothers, who she never saw any more.

She had three siblings—John, Mark, and Luke —but had lost track of all save Luke, who was serving time in the Wyoming Territorial Penitentiary, outside of Laramie, for running whiskey to the Cheyennes over on the Rosebud. Luke had been behind bars for almost a year now, although it had been five or six since Rose had last seen him.

John and Mark had gone to Oregon even before that with the intention of buying cattle they planned to bring back to Montana to sell; the last word she'd had on them was that John had killed a man in The Dalles and was on the run. She didn't know what had become of Mark.

It didn't surprise Rose that John had turned out bad. He'd always been the mean one in the family. But it saddened her that Luke had also run afoul of the law. He'd been a gentle soul, in her opinion, though wayward by nature and prone to letting others talk him into mischief he inevitably got the blame for. From what she'd heard of the Rosebud affair, Luke had only driven the wagon that carried the whiskey, and someone else had done the actual bartering. She supposed it was splitting a fine hair to distinguish between perpetrator and moil in a game like that, but it lightened her burden a little to think Luke had been duped into another bad scheme, rather than a willing participant in such a low-down deed as selling liquor to starving reservation Indians.

Wiley and Shorty shouldered a place at the bar, and Manuel and Rose slipped in between them. It was warm enough in the press of bodies for her to remove her seal-skin cap and shake out her long blonde hair, then unbutton her coat and brush it back. A silence fell over the bar when she did, and, looking around, she saw that everyone was staring at her.

"What's the matter with you galoots?" she demanded. "Ain't you ever seen a woman before?"

"Well, yeah," said a timid voice from the far end, "but it's been a while, saving for Gabby."

Laughter rumbled across the room like a small landslide. When it died, the conversation picked up again, returning to normal.

Rose ordered a whiskey, but there was no anticipation for it now. The brief feeling of hominess that had embraced her upon entering the saloon was gone. She'd forgotten for a while, back there on the Pipestem, the full breadth of her quirkiness, and how it must look to others that she'd allowed this charade of pants and pistols to continue. At the very least, she thought morosely, Wiley and Shorty must consider her peculiar, perhaps even mentally traumatized by the horror of watching Muggy hang. Surely a normal woman would have fled to Billings after having witnessed the execution of her husband and the burning of her home. But racing to Billings hadn't even occurred to Rose until several weeks after the event.

She was starting to feel a little nervous about the whore, Gabby, too. Although Manuel had mentioned her back at the cabin, she'd been a nameless entity then. Now she had not only a name, but a presence here in the Gold Nugget that couldn't be ignored.

It was at that moment that a door opened at the far end of the room and a hard-bitten woman in a cheap red wig and a trampy red dress emerged. The woman paused in the shadows while a bearded miner came on alone. She eyed the boisterous crowd as a general might scrutinize a larger and better-equipped opposing army just before the opening salvos—subdued by the odds but resigned to the battle. Then, taking a deep breath, she set a course for the center of festivities, her jaw knotted in a frozen smile.

There were forty or fifty men in the saloon, and more likely to arrive before nightfall. The numbers twisted in Rose's gut. She couldn't help recalling Nora, from Miles City. *Was this Nora's future?* Rose wondered. *Or even my own?* Shuddering, she knocked off the rest of her whiskey, then shoved the glass across the counter where the barkeep could refill it on his next pass.

After another whiskey to deaden the chill, Rose

ordered a beer and settled in for the long haul. Soon the boys wandered off in search of fresh stories, leaving Rose to her own devices. They were barely gone when a stranger sidled up with a shy, toothy grin.

"Christ," Rose grunted, taking her drink with her as she fled the bar. She found an empty chair against the wall and slumped into it, pulling the Smith & Wesson around where everyone could see it.

Time seemed to flow more swiftly after that. Before she knew it, the evening's shadows were creeping across the town, turning the already dim interior of the saloon even gloomier. As the light faded, Rose's mood sank. She couldn't get Gabby off her mind, and kept trying to imagine the circumstances that had brought her here. Had she once dreamed of a family of her own, with a nice house and flowers in the yard and a white picket fence?

Rose sneaked a peek every time Gabby approached the bar. That she was past her prime as a dove was obvious. She might have been thirty-five or forty, but she looked at least twenty years older. Her teeth were bad, her eyes hard, yellowed around the edges like old ivory—a symptom, they said, of opium addiction. She had a whiskey-husked voice that sounded like a wood saw cutting through green lumber and a cough that bent her nearly double every time it erupted. Rose tried to keep track of the number of trips she made to the back room with some miner or trapper in tow, but lost count after fourteen, and the night barely begun.

A gnawing, nameless fear began to take root in Rose's mind, a kind of panic that made her want to bolt. It was the lack of a destination that stayed her, forcing her to sit alone, occasionally shooing off some hopeful male's approach.

It was well into the evening when the bartender ordered several tables to be set end to end along the far wall. Soon a contingent of bearded men was trooping into the room from a blazing cook fire outside, toting platters of meat and vegetables that they set out on the tables. A cheer arose from the patrons at the bar, and there was a general migration toward the food. Even Wiley gave up his seat at a poker game to join the tide.

A shadow crossed in front of Rose. She glanced up to find Shorty dragging up a chair. Plopping down at her side, he said: "Why ain't you in line for some chuck?"

"I ain't hungry."

"You ain't ate since breakfast."

"I know. I just ain't in a mood."

He smiled. "Oh, I'd say you're in a mood. You look like a hound that knows he's in for a whuppin'. What's going on?"

She couldn't stop a glance toward the far side of the saloon, where the door to Gabby's crib was closed behind yet another customer.

"Gabby?"

"She's awful used up, don't you think?"

Shorty shrugged. "I don't guess I thought about it. I knew her in Denver when I passed through there ten, twelve years ago. She was Gabriela then, the Songbird of Cherry Creek. She had a pretty voice, too."

"I heard her talkin' to a couple of boys earlier," Rose confided. "She didn't sound like no songbird to me. She sounded all fogged up, like a buffler with something caught in its windpipe."

"Well, a whore's life ain't easy," he allowed.

"Shorty," she said, fidgeting with her beer. "Shorty, I . . . I don't want to end up like that."

He looked at her in surprise. "Is that what's botherin' you? Hell, you ain't gonna end up like her, Rose. You'll find another fella someday, and better than Muggy, I'll bet. Someone who wants to settle down and raise some kids. You wait and see. Get yourself a nice little house, too."

"With flowers in the yard and a white picket fence?"

"Sure."

"Christ, Shorty," she said in consternation.

"What?"

"You're full of shit, that's what."

"Because I want to believe in a brighter future?"

"Uhn-huh."

He laughed. "Well, you go ahead and look on the hind side of life, if that's your druthers. I think I'll keep my eyes all starry and full of dreams."

She smiled in spite of her mood, and immediately felt better. "You ever meet that gal that

135

works at Alice's, in Miles City? Nora was her first name."

"Alder. Her last name's Alder."

"Alder," Rose repeated. "Then you know her?"

"Not in a professional way, but I know who she is."

"She was awfully nice to me that night. A mite salty, but I liked her."

"You miss talking to other women, Rose?"

"I reckon I do. I growed up with just my pap and brothers, and lived a rough life by most accounts, but it was all I ever knowed and I never complained. Things has sure changed lately, though. Ain't nothin' in my life seems real since they hung Muggy."

"Maybe you're getting tired of being around rough-barked men all the time. Me, I like talking to women. I like it a lot. But it'd drive me crazy if I couldn't get out with the fellas once in a while, palaver some, maybe do a little hunting or horse trading."

"You figure that's it . . . that I'm drownin' in horse talk and cow talk? Sure as heck, I ain't never give a hoot who could outdrink or outshoot anybody else."

"Likely that's the problem," he agreed. Then a twinkle came into his eyes, and he added: "But you realize there's never been any question as to who can outdrink or outshoot the whole dang' territory, don't you?"

"Outpiss 'em, too, I'll bet?"

"Coming off a ten-day drought," he avowed, laughing as he shoved up from his chair. "Come on and grab some chuck."

"Naw, you go ahead. I still ain't hungry."

"All right, but get something before the good stuff's gone. He's got vegetables over there, and we ain't likely to see the likes of those again until spring."

"Go on," she said, annoyed that he thought he had to look after her. "I ain't so pathetic I can't fend for myself."

"I didn't say you were," he replied, then winked and walked away. A few minutes later, Gabby appeared from her room, alone this time. She'd changed into a white, floor-length gown, with full sleeves and a ruffled collar. The crowd grew silent with curiosity as she made her way to a nearby table. Using a chair as a stepping stool, she climbed up awkwardly, then slid cautiously toward its center. A miner in a bear-skin coat came out of the crowd and sat down at the chair. Pulling a mouth harp from his pocket, he tapped the instrument against his dirty trousers, then placed it tentatively to his lips. Slowly he began to play, and, after the barest of pauses, Gabby started to sing.

In the unexpectedness of the performance, Rose couldn't immediately place the song. Then she recognized "Silent Night," and her throat grew tight. In her deeply melancholic mood, the beauty of the lyrics and the gentle accompaniment of the harmonica were almost too much to bear. She sat mesmerized, unable to look away. Save for the slow riffs of the harp and Gabby's gravelly yet haunting timbre, the room was as silent as a grave.

Feeling suddenly teary-eyed, Rose thought: *Maybe it ain't all over, yet. Maybe, if the Songbird of Cherry Creek can still sing, then Rose Edwards can find herself some happiness somewhere down the trail, if she just keeps looking.*

When Gabby finished "Silent Night," the crowd went wild. Somebody drew a six-shooter and fired a round into the ceiling, the concussion blowing out several nearby lamps. The report was deafening in the close confines of the saloon, but that didn't stop half a dozen others from drawing their pistols and fanning the air above their heads as well. Dust and dirt rained down from the punctured ceiling, garnishing the food with doses of sod, but nobody seemed to mind. Gabby, smiling broadly, quickly launched into another song.

Gradually the crowd abandoned the food tables and drifted toward the songbird's table, taking their drinks and sandwiches with them. A murmur of conversation rose from among them, but soft and respectful. Gabby finished a rendition on the three wise men, then began a livelier melody about Christmas on the Ohio. With the exception of "Silent Night," Rose didn't recognize any of the songs, but that didn't diminish the magic. She sat, spellbound, her beer forgotten while her mood soared higher on every note.

But it didn't last. Thinking about it later, Rose

supposed it couldn't have. Not with a bunch of drunken miners and fur trappers for an audience. After four or five Christmas songs, Gabby moved on to some of the more popular tunes of the day—"Buffalo Gals," "Blue-Tail Fly," "Lorena"— but in time the songs became more provocative, the crowd rowdier. In less than an hour, the gloriousness of the evening had deteriorated into a gutter-like crassness. Gabby started moving her hips suggestively, thrusting them toward the men in front, while they responded in kind, clutching at the hem of her dress, running their grubby hands over the white material covering her thighs. She didn't seem to mind. She hardly seemed to notice. She was perspiring heavily, sweat tracking her face, soaking through the fabric of her dress under her breasts until it became transparent.

Rose didn't know what to do. The evening was ruined, but she still had nowhere to go. She stared at an empty spot across the room until a scream from the makeshift stage made her flinch. A miner had pulled Gabby off the table and draped her over his shoulder, and her wig had fallen to the floor, exposing her real hair. It looked dark and stiff as fine wire, so thin the scalp was clearly visible. Gabby struggled on the miner's shoulder, shrieking and cursing as she reached unsuccessfully for the wig, but a lanky trapper had already picked it up. Holding it aloft, he let go a war whoop, hollering: "Lookee hyar, boys, she's done been skelped."

Laughter erupted from the crowd. Gabby screamed for the trapper to return her hair, but he shook his head. "Hell, no," he said. "I ain't never horned me a bald-headed woman afore."

"You bastard!" Gabby yelled. "Gimme my hair!"

Rose stood and drew her pistol. She intended to shoot the trapper if he didn't relent, but, before she could level the muzzle, he said: "I'll give you three dollars."

Gabby immediately shut up. Twisting her head around to look up at the fur hunter, she echoed: "Three dollars!"

"Uhn-huh, without the hair."

"Damnation, I'd give three dollars without the hair," said another.

"I'll be go-to-hell," Gabby said, allowing her arms to hang limp. "All right, three dollars without the hair." She slapped the miner who held her on his buttocks. "Lemme down, honey, I gotta get back to work."

More laughter followed Gabby's declaration, but Rose didn't hang around to hear it fade. She crossed the street in the dark and saddled Albert, turning a deaf ear to Asa Carson's inquiries. Fifteen minutes later she was riding toward the cabin on the Pipestem, alone in the frigid darkness.

Chapter Eleven

They went back to wolfing, but it wasn't the same after their holiday sojourn to Lost Gulch. At first Rose put it down to her own blue funk, for she felt as cheerless as an old mule, but it soon became apparent that Wiley and Shorty were feeling the same way. They moped through the long evenings like pallbearers, and growled more often than they talked.

January passed, then February. The bitter temperatures of midwinter moderated somewhat, but still dipped into the sub-zero range at night with an aggravating frequency. Despite the bone-numbing weather, Rose and Shorty made it a point to run their traps every day, just to get out of the cabin. They were bringing in the pelts, too. Better than two hundred so far, with most of March and some of April still to go. Even if they only got a couple of dollars apiece for them, it would be the best winter's wage Rose had ever earned.

Wiley became more lackadaisical about his trapping as the seemingly endless cold continued. He put out fewer sets, and often didn't even bait the ones he had for days on end. There were no hard feelings about it. They all understood wolfing was just a means of passing time until the grass greened up again in the spring. Still, Rose considered it odd behavior for a man of Wiley's restless nature. It wasn't until a cold, sky-blue day in early March that she discovered the cause of his discontent.

She'd returned earlier than usual from checking her traps and, after caring for Albert, went inside to warm up. To her chagrin, the cabin was cold and dark, rank with the odor of unscraped hides. Wiley was sitting in front of the fireplace with a bottle of whiskey in his lap, but he'd allowed the flame to die to a handful of dull red coals, covered by a layer of ash. Even in the murky light, Rose could see his breath puffing above the hearth.

"You're gonna freeze to death one of these days, taking your warmth from a bottle," she said irritably.

Wiley twisted in his chair, squinting into the light spilling through the door behind her. "What are ye doing back so soon?" he asked hoarsely. "Sun ain't even reached the mountains yet."

"My traps was empty."

"Now ain't that a hell of a note?"

"It is if you're tryin' to pay off a debt." She shut the door, but kept her coat and cap on, with the flaps of the hat tied under her chin to protect her ears. Kneeling in front of the fireplace, she shoved Wiley's feet to the side.

"Git them shovels outta my face," she said, then picked up a handful of kindling and began breaking it over the coals. "Dang it, Wiley, you ought to've kept this goin'."

"I like it dark. It makes it easier to think."

"Dark is one thing, cold is another."

Lurching awkwardly to his feet, he said: "Ye sure are a pretty thing, Rosie."

"Aw, hell," she breathed, sliding her fingers around a sturdy piece of firewood the size of her forearm—solid enough, she hoped, to dent even an Irishman's head.

"We've had us some good times, ain't we?" he continued.

"Some, a long time ago. We've growed up since then."

"Hell, maybe ye have, but I ain't. I'm still the horny ol' hound I always was."

"Shut up, Wiley, before you say something stupid." She pivoted on the balls of her feet, coming up fluidly while keeping the length of firewood tight along her leg where he wouldn't see it.

Wiley's expression reminded her of a small boy who'd had his feelings hurt. But instead of advancing, as she feared, he backed away until he was leaning against the table. "I know what I'm sayin'," he murmured. "I know what that hostler in Lost Gulch said, too." His voice turned suddenly harsh. "What happened to the thirty thousand in dust, Rosie?"

"Thirty thousand! Is that what you think . . . that I've got a bunch of gold stashed away somewhere?" She shook her head. "So that's why that old coot, Asa Carson, was looking at me so queersome?"

"Carson says some of the boys from Helena

made a ride past ye place last fall, after ye threw in with me 'n' Shorty. Said they found 'emselves an empty tin box that'd been buried in a corner of ye cabin. 'Tis it true?"

The box! She wanted to laugh at the absurdness of men and their obsession with riches that glittered, but then it occurred to her that maybe it wasn't all that funny. Not if half the territory thought she was toting around a sack full of gold.

"Is it?" Wiley asked.

"There was a box, but there weren't no gold. Just some change I'd saved up and some papers. Six bucks and some, is all."

"Six dollars, and Muggy known to have reached your place with the dust still on him?"

"I don't believe that. I didn't see no gold." Then she tossed the piece of firewood aside, her lips growing thin at the image of Muggy secreting the gold away somewhere, not even husband enough to let her know he was riding flush for a change. *That bastard,* she thought. She felt like bawling, but knew the tears wouldn't come. They never came any more.

She sensed Wiley slipping around behind her, saw his arms encircle her shoulders, felt his hands paw roughly at her breasts through the thickness of her horse-hide coat. "Don't," she said.

"We're pards, ain't we?" he asked, his moist breath worming through her hair to tickle the flesh along her neck.

"No!" She shrugged her shoulders, forcing his arms away. "Not like that we ain't. Not any more."

He backed off with a curse, scooping his bottle off the table and taking a long pull. Lowering it, he drew a ragged breath. "So that's the way 'tis gonna be, is it?"

"Leave me alone, Wiley. There weren't no gold, and I doubt if there ever was. I imagine they killed Muggy because of his cheatin'."

Wiley nodded resignedly. "Ye're probably right, darlin'. I came near to shootin' him meself a time or two." He corked the bottle and set it on the table, his movements wooden. "I hate this place," he said softly. " 'Tis little better'n a cell, and not near as warm." He turned and walked outside, leaving the door standing open behind him, the cold air rushing in to snuff the tiny blaze struggling in the fireplace.

Wiley was gone the next day when Rose and Shorty returned from running their traps. Rose was the first to notice the empty corral, but she wasn't alarmed. Neither was Shorty, when he cynically observed that spring must be near for Wiley to leave off his hibernation.

"He's worse than usual this year," Shorty admitted, swinging down from his saddle. "Probably because we're so far from any town where he can blow off steam once in a while."

"He has me spooked, for a fact," Rose confessed.

"It's mostly the short days, I figure. Wiley likes

his sunshine. He'd probably be rich if he lived in some southern climate."

But when they entered the cabin a few minutes later, it quickly became apparent Wiley wasn't out setting traps.

"His outfit's gone," Rose said, startled.

"So are a bunch of the skins." Shorty's face clouded over. Stalking to the middle of the room, he batted one of the remaining bundles with a mittened fist. "That coyote ran off with nearly half our catch."

"But where'd he go?" Rose had never known a man to just up and leave without even a good bye. Not even Muggy had been that inconsiderate.

"Who gives a damn?" Shorty replied. Spying a bottle of whiskey on the table, one of the dozen Wiley had brought back with him from Lost Gulch, he added grimly: "At least he left us a note."

"A note?"

Shorty nodded toward the bottle as he passed it on his way to the fireplace. "His way of saying *adiós*. He probably laughed his ass off when he thought of it."

"You're mad," Rose said, trying to sort it out.

"I ain't mad. Why should I be mad?" He leaned forward to gently blow the ash off that morning's embers, then carefully covered them with a teepee of twigs. Soon he'd coaxed a tongue of flame from the coals that curled tentatively through the brittle limbs. He added larger pieces until he was satisfied the fire had caught. Only then did he glance at Rose. "There's no point standing there wondering about it. He's gone. He won't be back."

"Is that it, then? The partnership's finished?"

"Would it matter?"

She thought it over, then shook her head. "I guess not."

A grudging smile crossed Shorty's face. "Good, although I doubt if it's over. I plan to keep trapping, then in the spring I'll mosey on down to Miles City. Likely that's where we'll find Wiley, waiting for us with some pony herd scouted out and ripe for the plucking."

"He's done this before?"

"A time or two." He rocked back on his heels, gazing at her thoughtfully. "What happened between you two yesterday? Things seemed different when I got in last night. Did Wiley try something?"

"Naw, it weren't that." She told him about the tin box that had been found inside the wreckage of her cabin, and what Asa Carson had told Wiley about it in Lost Gulch.

Shorty whistled when she finished. "That ain't good, Rose."

"It ain't so bad. It'd take a pretty ignorant lump of coal to think I've got thirty thousand dollars in gold, then want to spend the winter trappin' wolves."

"Well, there's no shortage of coal in Montana. You ought to know that. You're going to have to get the word out that you don't have it, then watch your back until the rumor dies out. It will, eventually. Sooner or later, folks'll see you ain't living the life of a nob, but you'll have to be almighty careful until they do."

"You're a worrywart, Shorty, but all right. I'll keep my eyes peeled."

Rose put the threat of assassins and gold thieves out of her mind. She considered Wiley's defection a far more critical issue. Although she didn't know how, she was sure her relationship with Shorty would change without a third party in the cabin. It was inevitable, and even a little scary, for she'd grown comfortable in her position on the Pipestem. Yet she couldn't deny a sense of fluttery expecta-tion, either, recognizing an old familiar itch, and a desire to scratch it that she hadn't felt in a long time.

After supper, they sat in front of the fire without speaking. To Rose the silence seemed deafening, the shadows in the corners of the cabin more intimidating than ever before. It was as if in all the world there was only that little ball of warmth and light directly in front of them. All else seemed cold and hostile.

In time, Shorty chunked up the fire and announced he was going to bed. The cabin had four bunks, two on the north wall, where he and Wiley slept, and two on the south, where Rose made her bed. It had been Shorty's idea to hang the bundles of pelts in a line between the two sections to give Rose a sense of privacy, although in doing so they'd also shut her off from the rest of the cabin. From the rolled-up wolf hide she used as a pillow she couldn't see anything after bedtime except the play of light along the rafters. She couldn't even see the windows. Tonight, without the murmur of conversation between Shorty and Wiley as they settled in, the sense of isolation began to overwhelm her. She endured it for as long as she could, then threw her blankets back and padded across the room in her socks and long-handles. She paused at the line of dangling hides to peek through.

"Shorty?"

"Yeah?" He was lying in bed with one arm propped under his head, smoking a last cigarette.

"I . . . I can't sleep."

"You want to talk?"

She took a deep, convulsive breath, then went over to stand above him.

"What is it?" he asked, but she could tell from his voice that he knew, that he was just making up his own mind about it. "Are you sure?" he asked finally.

"I reckon if I don't, I'm gonna go crazy."

He ground his smoke out against the wall, then scooted over, lifting a corner of his blankets. Rose slid in beside him, still in her long-handles, and Shorty dropped the blankets over her. Brushing a strand of hair away from her face, he said: "You sure are pretty, Rose. I always did think that of you."

"Shoot, we been alone so long, ol' Albert was probably startin' to look pretty to you."

Shorty smiled but didn't laugh. He continued to

stroke the side of her face, his fingers gentle as a breath of air. The sensations that poured through her body made her shudder.

"Dang," she said, quivery. "That feels good."

"I want it to feel good."

"Shorty, if I'd've known this was gonna happen, I swear I would've washed up. I'm . . ."

"Shhh," he whispered, pulling her close at last.

Chapter Twelve

They didn't have a thermometer, but Rose figured it must have been at least fifty degrees on the day they left the Pipestem. The sun was shining and the sky was deep and cloudless. Water dripped from the eaves with an upbeat, musical patter, and on the south-facing slopes, the snow was nearly gone, the short buffalo grass showing through like patches of smoked buckskin.

On the far side of the Pipestem, Shorty was driving in the extra horses. He would cross them at a shallow ford about a hundred yards above the cabin, where the ice was already breaking up. It was the creek that finally convinced them it was time to leave. As it started to rise, it quickly became obvious that whoever had chosen this site for a home hadn't done so with an eye toward spring floods. Already the ice in front of the cabin was turning rotten, buckling and popping from the pressure upstream. In another day or two the melt-off from the higher elevations would swell the creek above its banks. When that happened, it would be only a matter of hours before water started lapping at the cabin's walls.

Shorty yipped as he splashed his horse through the icy waters of the ford, bringing a smile to Rose's face. They'd gotten along all right since she went to his bunk that first time in March. For her, the past few weeks had been some of the best in her life. With Shorty, she'd been able to open up in ways she never would have attempted with Muggy or Wiley or her pap, confiding secrets that had been locked away inside her since childhood.

She told him what she could remember of her mother and their life along Grasshopper Creek in Bannock, and of the emptiness that had pervaded the family following her death; she told him of her father's fall from grace, and the craving for whiskey that plagued him still; she described her brothers and their reckless ways, and the ill fortune that had smote all three of them. She even told him about the family Bible that her pap still kept, and of the names and dates of family, written in front and going all the way back to 1780 and the Cumberland River country of Tennessee.

As for Shorty, he remained as reticent as ever. He listened and commented and smiled, but he never shared anything from his own past, nor elaborated on things he'd already revealed. One night, lying in their bunk after making love, she tried to get him to talk about his wife, but he'd clammed up like an airtight as soon as her name was mentioned, and later got up to sit beside the fire until the early hours of morning, brooding into the flames and drinking whiskey from the bottle Wiley had left them.

They didn't speak of the widow in Miles City who whored a little on the side, either, although Rose sensed she was often on Shorty's mind—the widow and Wiley, who would probably be waiting for them in Miles City with some pony herd already scouted. The prospect of returning to their thieving ways of last autumn frightened Rose; she was no longer content to ride with outlaws, fiddle-footed and daring. She wanted to go home, to rebuild the cabin the vigilantes had burned, salvage what remained of her garden, and, if Shorty was willing, maybe raise some cattle or horses.

All that would be jeopardized if Wiley talked Shorty into another raid. In Rose's opinion, wanderlust was the failing of far too many men. It had been her pap's undoing, as well as her brothers' and Muggy's, and in time she was certain it would be Shorty's undoing, if he didn't pull out now, before it was too late.

When the extra horses pounded up, Rose stepped in front of them, waving her lariat to turn them into the corral. Albert ran with them, kicking up his heels like a colt. It made Rose laugh to see him so frisky, for he was getting up in years.

She was latching the gate as Shorty swung down.

They'd spent the previous day pressing their hides into bales and sorting their gear. They had over two hundred pelts, even after Wiley had sneaked off with his divvy. Split between the three pack horses, it would make for some bulky loads, but nothing they couldn't handle if they left the heavier gear behind.

It only took a couple of hours to rig out the horses, and it was still early when Rose climbed into the Mother Hubbard's cradle. She glanced wistfully at the cabin. "I'm going to miss this place," she told Shorty.

"You wouldn't miss it tomorrow night," he predicted. "That cabin's going to be knee-deep in ice water before another day passes."

"I'll always remember it, though, even if we never come back."

"Oh, we'll be back," he replied absently, stepping into his own saddle. "Wiley has a map inside his head that's better than anything I've ever seen on paper. He won't forget this place." He booted his mount, taking the lead with two of the pack horses in tow.

Watching him ride away, Rose felt a heaviness in her chest. She supposed she'd known all along that Shorty wasn't thinking about settling down to raise cattle or horses. She should have broached the subject earlier perhaps, before the weather started to break, but she hadn't, and now she feared it was too late.

It was eight days to Miles City, what with the

snow still drifted deep on the northern slopes and the creeks running full. It would have been closer to go to Billings or Junction City, but Shorty was convinced Wiley would be waiting for them in Miles City, and Rose never spoke against it. She never mentioned rebuilding the cabin, either, and tried not even to think about white picket fences and flower gardens and the smell of a man—of leather and tobacco smoke and horses—after a hard day's work.

Her continued silence puzzled her, for every morning when she awoke in Shorty's arms, she vowed to bring it up that day, that very morning. But she never did, and the hours slipped away as Miles City crept closer.

Rose didn't know what she would feel when they topped the last rise before Miles City and saw the town sprawled below them. To her surprise, she actually found herself looking forward to reëntering civilization again. It had been a harsh winter, and even with Shorty's company, it had been kind of lonesome.

They went to Broadwater and Hubbell's first and sold their catch. Because each pelt had to be graded separately for quality, it took a couple of hours. When they finished, Bob Hubbell deducted the costs of the outfit they'd purchased on credit the previous fall, then wrote out a draft for $417. Rose nearly fell over when she heard the final tally. In her mind's eye she could envision the improvements that could be made to her place on the

Yellowstone with that kind of money. But Shorty barely glanced at the draft before shoving it into his pocket. "Is Wiley around?" he asked Hubbell.

"He was. He brought in nearly three hundred dollars' worth of pelts on his own. Said you'd be in later with the rest."

"Where's he staying?"

"The Silver Star and Alice's, is what I've heard. I couldn't say if he's still there."

Shorty thanked him, and he and Rose went out the back way to where their horses were tethered. Pausing on the loading dock, Shorty started a cigarette. He looked uncomfortable, and Rose couldn't help wondering if he was thinking of Wiley, or of the widow woman who lived over on the other side of town.

"We'll have to sit down with some paper and add everything up," he said finally, striking a match. "What Wiley brought in and what Bob just paid us, plus the extra horses, which I figure we ought to sell. We'll split what's left, then subtract your outfit from your share. It's too much to do in my head, but you ought to come out with a fair stake."

"That'd be good," Rose said, but her tone had grown cautious. "Uh, what about us?" she asked.

Shorty looked away, taking a drag off his cigarette. "What about us?"

"Dang it, Shorty."

He exhaled loudly. "I don't know," he said, keeping his gaze averted. "Let's go talk to Wiley before we make any decisions."

155

Rose felt a sudden swell of anger. "What's Wiley got to do with it?"

"We're partners, me 'n' him."

"I thought we was partners. I don't crawl into just any man's blankets."

"I know you don't, Rose. I just ain't sure how I feel about it yet."

"Meanin' now that you're back in town with your widow woman handy?"

"It ain't that."

"It'd better not be, because one of these days she's gonna be gone or married, and it might be her husband comin' to the door when you knock, totin' a shotgun."

"There ain't a time I come to Miles City that I don't wonder about that," he admitted. "Truth is, I ain't so sure I'd care if she married someone else. You're a good woman, Rose, and you deserve a hell of a lot better than a horse thief like me, but I see you done latched onto me, and, to tell you the truth, I ain't so sure I mind."

"What!" Her voice rose to a squawk. "I *latched* onto you?" She laughed derisively, but down deep she recognized the place where the pain and tears resided, where the ache twisted deep as the thrust of a saber. "You god-damn' dumb waddy. You got wool for brains and horse apples for sense if you think I *latched* onto you. If we ain't partners right down the middle . . ."

"Now, don't go flying off the handle."

"I'll by God fly off any damn' handle I take a

notion to fly off of, Shorty Tibbs, and the hell with you and what you think." She turned away, not wanting him to see the hurt in her eyes, and jumped off the loading dock. Shorty called after her, but she flung him an obscene gesture instead and got on her horse.

"Rose, don't be like that."

"Don't be like what?" she snapped, pulling Albert around.

"Like a woman," he said, red-faced.

"I am a woman, you son-of-a-bitch," she cried, then slammed her heels against Albert's ribs, riding out of the alley at a trot.

She turned west on Main, and, if the street hadn't been so sloppy with mud, she would have kicked the gelding into a run. She rode a couple of blocks at a swift jog, then slowed to a walk. "God damn him," she muttered. "God damn Shorty Tibbs."

An alley opened on her right and she reined into it. She told herself she was in search of better footing for Albert, but deep down she knew that was a lie. Pulling up a few minutes later, she eyed the rear of the Silver Star reflectively. It occurred to her that she might've been hasty in leaving Shorty without collecting at least some of her share of the wolf money, but she'd be damned if she'd go back now. She had a couple of dollars left from last year, and swore to make do with that or do with-out.

She supposed she'd expected it to be like last time, when she'd almost immediately recognized half a dozen familiar faces, but the only person she knew today was the saloon's bartender, Tom. Everyone else was a stranger, and they were all looking at her in a way that made her keenly aware of how dirty and bedraggled she must appear, how out of place she was here. She paused at the door, then hitched self-consciously at her cartridge belt and walked to the bar. Tom came down the sober side, wiping a beer mug with a damp towel. "Hello, Rose," he said without much enthusiasm.

"How, Tom."

"What'll you have?"

"A whiskey for openers, beer for sippin'."

He returned with the drinks in short order, but when she reached for her money, he waved it away. "It's on the house," he said. "For old times' sake."

"Old times' sake?" She glanced around the room, puzzled by his subdued behavior, the quiet atmosphere of the establishment. "Where's Wiley?" she asked.

"I don't know," Tom replied, lowering his voice. "I haven't seen him." His gaze slid down the bar to where a couple of somber-looking gents in dark suits were standing stiffly in front of their beers. "The clientele has changed around here the last couple of days," he added pointedly.

"Who're they?" Rose asked.

Tom shook his head. "I won't get involved in this."

"Regulators," she breathed with sudden understanding. "Is that who they are?"

"Rose, you're welcome in here any time. I mean that. But I just serve the drinks. I'm not going to get caught in the middle of anything else." He picked up the towel he'd dropped earlier and moved off.

Rose stood quietly, unsure how she should react. Then she said—"The hell with this."—and downed her whiskey in a single swallow. The amber liquid scorched a fiery path across her throat before it settled in her stomach like a cozy campfire. She sniffed and rubbed her nose, then chased away the whiskey's fumes with a sip of cold beer.

She felt better after that. It was quiet and comfortable inside the dimly lit saloon, free of the crisp, early spring breezes. After finishing her second beer, Rose noticed she was starting to feel sleepy, as she often did when coming into a warm building out of the cold. She was aware of the attention the two men Tom had pointed out were affording her, however, and knew it would pay to remain wary in such company.

She kept glancing at the front doors, half expecting Shorty to come ambling through them at any moment and half dreading that he would, but he never appeared. Meanwhile, the afternoon shadows lengthened, the light at the windows dimmed, and the crowd inside the Silver Star grew larger, although not necessarily more boisterous, as she remembered from last year.

Rose was almost through her third beer when melancholy struck. It normally did when she boozed alone. Some people drank to feel good; others, like her pap, drank to forget. But it had never worked either way for her. Liquor just made her feel drab and weepy. Caught in her own gloom, she failed to notice the two men approaching her until they stepped up to the bar at her elbow.

"Rose Edwards?" the taller of the two inquired.

She looked up with a startled expression and said, under her breath: "Dang."

"My name is John Stroudmire, and this is my associate, Theo Haus. We were hoping to ask you a few questions."

"Naw," she replied, turning her shoulder to him.

"Pardon me?"

"No, go away!" In the bar mirror she saw the look of annoyance that crossed Haus's face, but Stroudmire's demeanor remained unchanged.

"We're looking for a companion of yours . . . Wiley Collins," Stroudmire persisted. "We were hoping you could tell us where we might find him."

"Never heard of him," Rose said.

"Bull," Haus returned loudly. "You were seen coming out of the alley beside Broadwater's last year with Collins and a sawed-off runt called Shorty Tibbs. We got an eyewitness to that."

"Mister Haus," Stroudmire rebuked softly.

"God dammit, she was *seen!*"

"I'll handle this," Stroudmire said firmly.

A look of disgust puckered Haus's face, but he pulled in his horns. Stroudmire said: "We know you were traveling with Collins and Tibbs last fall, and that you likely wintered with them. You were involved in a gun battle at a rustlers' outpost on the Missouri River last October, and, for the past several years, you've run a boarding house for travelers along the Outlaw Trail."

"Boarding house, my ass," Haus interjected. "Whorehouse is more like it."

A change came over Stroudmire's face, a flicker of something so subtle Rose wasn't sure she could have even described it—but it was there, nonetheless, and a chill ran down her spine to see it.

"Mister Haus, will you wait for me outside?" Stroudmire said coolly.

"Huh?"

Stroudmire turned slightly, although he still refused to look directly at his partner. "Outside," he repeated, hard as stone.

Haus's eyes narrowed. "You want me to . . . ?"

"I want you to wait outside. That'll be all I require for the moment."

Haus paused as if to take the measure of Stroudmire's words, and then he slapped the top of the bar with an open hand, growling—"You're going to push me too far one of these days, John."—and stalked away.

Stroudmire waited until his partner had exited the saloon, although he kept his eyes on Rose. Staring back, she was struck by the similarity between Stroudmire's stark expression and the emotionless pit of a rattlesnake's gaze, and it dawned on her suddenly that she was afraid, more afraid, perhaps, than she'd been of the vigilantes who'd hanged Muggy.

"You are known to have consorted with various hardcases," Stroudmire continued mildly, "including notorious cattle and horse thieves operating within the Yellowstone Basin. You are known to have fed and sheltered these men on numerous occasions, and to have profited from your dealings with them. Recently you appear to have joined with them in their lawlessness. You are the daughter of an alcoholic named Daniel Ames and the widow of one Robert Edwards, a known cardsharp and petty thief. Now, will you tell me where Wiley Collins is holed up, or will I have to use other methods to extract that information?"

"How'd you know that?" Rose asked huskily. "How'd you know Muggy's real name, and all that other stuff?"

"I'll have my answer, Missus Edwards."

A shiver ran down her spine. "Was it Joe Bean? Was that who told you?" She shook her head. "Dang, I never would've figured he'd turn on his own. Not that far."

"My patience is wearing thin," Stroudmire warned. "I'm here under legal authority to apprehend Collins and Tibbs. If you have knowledge of their whereabouts and withhold that . . ."

"No, you ain't," Rose cut in, her voice shaky

with fright. "There ain't nothin' legal about hangin' a man in the middle of the night, like they done Sam, nor in sneakin' around in the shadows like some degenerate." She licked her lips, wondering if she'd pushed it too far, but Stroudmire's reaction surprised her.

"You have pluck, Missus Edwards. I was told that you did."

"You ought to leave me be," she said. "I got nothin' to say to you."

"Oh, I think you do. I think once we start . . ."

"Lucy!"

They both spun swiftly as the name was practically shouted at them from no more than ten feet away. Rose gasped, so intense had been the moment between her and this steely-eyed killer operating under the guise of a lawman. It took her a moment to recognize Nora Alder, swooping forward like a hawk on a mouse; when she did, there was such a rush of relief she had to tighten her grip on the bar to keep her knees from buckling.

"Lucy, I've been looking all over for you," Nora said, still in that too-loud voice. She grabbed Rose's arm. "You're late."

"Late? For what?"

"Don't be thick, *Lucy,*" Nora said, leaning heavily on the unfamiliar alias. She dug her fingers into the muscled flesh of Rose's upper arm. "Come on, we've got to get you gussied up."

"Hold on," Stroudmire said, scowling. "What is this business?"

"This business is getting Lucy dressed for work," Nora replied, constructing a slap-dash smile. "This is Lucy . . . Alder. She's our newest gal, but we've got to get her dolled up first. If you're interested, you can come by later."

Stroudmire's color deepened at the suggestion. "So this is how you want to play it?" he said to Rose. "We can do that, but remember that I'll be watching. Sooner or later, we'll finish this conversation. Just the two of us." With the promise made, he turned and strolled toward the door.

They watched until he exited the saloon, then Nora looked at Rose. "Are you all right?"

"Yeah, a little rattled is all."

"Stroudmire and Haus have been hanging around the Star for several days, making a bunch of noise over Collins and others."

"Shorty!" Rose exclaimed, pushing away from the bar.

Nora pulled her back. "Alice has already sent someone after Shorty."

"Are you sure?"

She nodded. "Tom sent word to the house as soon he saw Stroudmire approach you. He figured something was up, and Alice said that, if you were around, Shorty would be, too. She sent Eben after him. Eben's the house bouncer at Alice's. He'll find Shorty quick enough, if he ain't already. Alice thought he might be over at Nellie's. That's where she sent Eben to look first."

"Nellie?" Rose's repeated softly. "So that's her name."

"Didn't you know about her?"

"Not her name."

"Are you sure you're all right?"

"Yeah, I'm fine." She forced a lop-sided grin. "I'm glad you showed up, though. I ain't sure anyone else would've helped."

"Everyone's afraid of Stroudmire, including me. You looked into his eyes. What did you see?"

"Weren't no soul in there, that's sure."

"You're safe for now, but you ought to come back to the house before Stroudmire puts someone to watching the rear door."

"I can't, Nora. I got a horse out back, plus I need to locate Shorty. He's still got my money."

"Don't worry about Shorty. Eben'll bring him around when it's safe, and Callie's already taken care of your horse."

"Callie? The cook?"

"Come on," Nora said. "But keep that pistol handy. Stroudmire ain't a man who likes to be made a fool of, and I suspect that's what he'll be feeling like real soon, once he starts thinking about it." She paused, glancing over her shoulder at Rose. "When he thinks about it a while, I figure he's going to want to kill somebody. You shouldn't be around when that happens."

Chapter Thirteen

Standing at an upstairs window in Alice's parlor house, Rose stared across the town. The view was interesting, although not especially attractive. She thought the lights from all the windows looked like a diffused reflection of the stars, and shadows that were buckboards and pedestrians moved in a steady flow along the streets. But for all that, it was a lonely scene, and exclusive. All those homes, all those families, yet how many among them would welcome Rose Edwards if she were to show up on their doorstep?

There was a sound behind her and she turned, letting the curtain fall. Nora came into the room, looking harried and relieved at the same time. "Callie and Eben are back," she announced. "They've got your stuff."

Callie came in first, lugging Rose's saddle in one hand, the Sharps in the other. "My goodness, girl," Callie said, puffing. "How'd you ever throw all this stuff onto that horse of yours? I had enough struggle just pulling it off." She dropped the saddle next to a chest of drawers, then leaned the rifle in the corner.

Eben came next, carrying the weathered canvas pannier that Rose and Shorty had used for their personal gear on the trip back from the Pipestem. He set the pannier on the floor beside the saddle and straightened slowly, his black face sheened with perspiration. "This here's all of it," he said, arching his back. "Mister Tibbs said this is all your gear, plus some extras, some blankets and skillets and such. He said you was to keep it." Plucking a fist-size buckskin pouch from inside his shirt, he held it toward her. "He said to give you this, too. Said he hadn't had time to figure it all out on paper yet, but thought this would cover your share of the pelts."

Reluctantly Rose extended her hand; Eben set the pouch in her open palm. She recognized it as Shorty's money poke, the once golden buckskin now stained nearly black, the cotton drawstring raveled. "Did he . . . ah . . . did he say anything else?" she asked.

"He said he was sorry," Eben replied gently. "Said he was going to light out for Junction City to look for Collins."

Rose's fingers closed over the pouch, crushing the soft leather in her fist. "Well, I reckon that's that then," she said, feeling suddenly light-headed.

"That bastard," Nora said vehemently.

"Yeah, ain't he though," Rose replied, unable to mask her disappointment.

"I'd like to whack that Shorty Tibbs upside his head," Callie declared. "Men don't know half the heartache they cause."

Looking uncomfortable, Eben began an unobtrusive retreat. "I'll just let Alice know I'm back," he said genially.

He'd almost reached the door when Rose said: "Eben."

"Yes'm?"

"Thank you."

"Why, you're welcome, Miss Rose," he answered, then left the room.

"Humpf," Callie said, regarding the empty doorway. Then she turned to Rose. "If it helps, Shorty told Eben he wouldn't have left if he hadn't been sure you were safe." She made another snorty sound of disgust. "Just proves there ain't no critter thicker skulled than a man, except maybe a Missouri mule, and even that ain't a sure-fire guarantee. I've met many a mule I'd consider downright intelligent compared to some of the men I've seen traipse through parlor houses over the years."

"They're all bastards," Nora said, "but crying about it won't change anything." To Rose, she added: "You're welcome to stay here as long as you like."

"I don't hardly know what to do. I'd been thinkin' about goin' home and rebuilding the cabin, but I guess I'd counted on Shorty to help with that. I ain't sure I got the wherewithal to go it alone any more."

"Maybe you ought to just go to burrow for a while," Callie suggested. "Ain't nothing you can do tonight that you can't do next week."

"That makes sense," Nora said. "Take some time and think about what you want to do."

"I can pay," Rose said.

"If you can pay, Alice will charge you a dollar a night," Nora said. "You'll have to share a bed with someone, though. There ain't no empty rooms."

"We got us a full house," Callie agreed. "Pearl and Jessie are already sharing a room. Miss Alice is gonna have to build herself a larger place if this keeps up."

"It'll just be for the convention and roundup," Nora explained. "We're expecting a lot of men through here in the next few weeks. The ranch owners and ramrods will come for the cattlemen's convention. After that, they'll start one of the district roundups from nearby."

"Be a barrel full of drovers in for that," Callie predicted.

"Won't I be in the way?" Rose asked.

"No," Nora assured her. "You can bunk in here with me. I don't allow men in here, so you won't be bothered. Besides, I doubt if you could even find a room in a hotel. They've reserved all their beds for the ranchers, and a lot of them will be double-bunking, too."

"Well, then," Callie said briskly, as if everything was settled. "I'll go heat some water. You'll want a bath, I expect."

"I . . . ah . . . naw." Rose blushed at the thought of taking a bath indoors, where people would know what she was doing, or could even walk in on her accidentally. Although the prospect of hot water was appealing, she considered it more modest to bathe in a river or creek, where she could see someone approaching from a long way off. But Callie wouldn't hear of it.

"Don't start fretting over foolishness," she chastised. "You ain't the first gal to show up here needing a bath and a change of clothes. You dig out what you've got, I'll freshen it up while you're scrubbing. If you need anything else, we'll find it around here somewhere. How's that sound?"

It was what an educated person might call a rhetorical question, Rose decided, for sure as shooting the stern look on Callie's face precluded any further argument. Shrugging submissively she said: "Why, now that I think on it, that sounds like a fine idea."

The next few weeks turned out to be perplexing ones for Rose, who'd never in her life been in the presence of so many women. She was certain they must consider her as backward as a woods waif, if not outright ignorant, yet as time went on she began to strike up tentative friendships with several of them, and to lower her guard around the rest.

Callie was a big help. It was she who encouraged Rose to reach out first, rather than always hang back. In many ways, Rose's relationship with the heavy-set black woman reminded her of a small child's dependency on its mother. It irked her that she should crave such bonds now, in her twenty-fifth year, yet she couldn't deny something immensely gratifying about it, too.

It was to Rose's deep regret that she was unable to forge the same level of intimacy with Nora. If Callie had become a kind of surrogate mother to her, then Nora remained very much a distant, salty cousin. Not that they didn't get along. Nora was as conversant in the harsher realities of a fallen woman's lot as any whore, and she and Rose shared a mutual respect based on the experiences each knew the other had suffered and survived. But in the end, neither women possessed the skills necessary to bridge the barriers those circumstances had created. They became good friends; they just never became close ones.

One day near the end of her first week in Miles City, Rose was sitting on the top step of Alice's front porch with her face tipped to the warming rays of the sun. The snow was gone and the land was drying out. A fresh blush of green shaded the hills, and songbirds warbled in the budding trees. Her head was bobbing, and she might have drifted off to sleep in another minute or two if the door hadn't swung open on its squeaky hinge. Glancing over her shoulder, she saw Nora coming out of the house in a demure blue dress. A matching pill-box hat was perched atop her dark curls, and she carried a cloth purse in one hand, decorated with embroidery and small beads. She might have looked downright pretty if not for the stub of a cheroot jutting from a corner of her mouth.

"Dang," Rose exclaimed, twisting around for a better view. "You clean up right pert."

"Smart ass," Nora replied, squinting into the sunlight.

"Well, flattery ain't my strong suit," Rose admitted, "but I do like that dress. It's eye-catchin'."

"Christ, that sun is bright." Nora moved into the shade near the front wall. "You could go blind in this much light."

"Feels good to me," Rose said.

Nora gave her a calculating look. "You ought to get yourself a better dress. That thing you're wearing looks like a wrung-out rag." She took the smoked-down cigar from her mouth and flipped it into the yard. "I'm going into town. You want to come along?"

Caught off guard, Rose quickly shook her head. "Naw, I'll stay here."

"You ain't been into town since you got here. Scared?"

"No, I ain't scared." She stood and hesitantly ran her hands down over her hips, eyeing her get-up. It was a fact she'd been feeling rather homely of late. The old gray dress she'd salvaged after the fire at her cabin last year had acquired a large, reddish stain along one thigh, absorbed from the leather of her saddlebags. Plus the fabric was worn thin over her shoulders and under her arms, the color faded so badly a person could hardly make out the thin pink stripes that ran vertically through the material. "I reckon I could use a new one," she concluded.

"Sure, get yourself a new dress, maybe some new knickers."

Rose's cheeks grew warm. She'd been wearing her old long-handles under her dress, although with the sleeves and ankles rolled up so that they wouldn't show. Still, she didn't suppose a new pair of bloomers would bankrupt her.

She hurried upstairs to get her money while Nora waited on the porch. She felt an odd mixture of excitement and apprehension as she shoved Shorty's buckskin poke down beside the Smith & Wesson in the bulky cloth purse Callie had loaned her. She knew from Nora that Stroudmire and Haus were still buzzarding around town, although they were keeping a low profile, and lately had avoided the Silver Star.

The rumor floating around Miles City was that the two shootists were waiting for someone connected with the upcoming cattlemen's convention to give them the go-ahead. No one seemed quite sure what that go-ahead might pertain to, but such limitations of fact did little to check the flood of speculation. All the girls at Alice's were convinced the mysterious *they* were about to unleash the Stranglers once more, to finish hanging the thieves and rustlers they'd missed on their first sweep.

Rose held a different notion. Having been something of a participant herself during the Stranglers' raid in 1884, she remembered all too well one of their most intimidating tactics—their secretive-ness. No one had known what to expect or who to trust, and that uncertainty alone had convinced many of the territory's worst scallywags to seek out more tolerant ranges.

In Rose's opinion, there was nothing covert about Stroudmire and Haus; they were about as inconspicuous as a couple of dead horses lying in the middle of the street. Because of that, Rose was convinced there was no connection between them and the Stranglers, other than the monied interests that probably financed both parties.

Although the two gunmen were prominent in Rose's thoughts, she didn't bring them up. In fact, she and Nora didn't speak at all as they entered the business district, when her nervousness began to increase for entirely different reasons.

Traffic along the streets and boardwalks was forcing Rose to take more notice of her attire. Her stained dress and wind-roughened face and hands, her long, loose hair with neither bonnet nor hat or even a simple ribbon to control it hadn't caused her much concern at Alice's, where everyone knew her story and accepted her. But it was different here, and she could well imagine what the people they passed must think—a big, oafish girl tagging along like a simpleton beside a properly costumed woman such as Nora.

The irony of her embarrassment, that she felt more awkward in a dress than she had earlier that week trotting Albert down Main Street in male garb, didn't escape her, but it was also a fact that she'd always felt like a charlatan whenever she tried to make herself look more appealing. She could still hear the voices of her pap and brothers, ridiculing her efforts at femininity.

What's an ox need a ribbon for? her pap had once queried, the last time she'd pleaded for such foofaraw. Even though she knew he had a mean streak, and that others considered her attractive, the question still haunted her.

Rose figured Nora was taking her to Broadwater and Hubbell's, but they passed the big brick mercantile without so much as a glance in the window. Instead they turned into a narrow log structure a block east of the larger store, where a small bell on a leaf spring above the door announced their entrance. A woman looked up from a table in a corner of the front room where she was pinning a hem on a dress. She was petite and blonde and had hard eyes, but she smiled when she recognized Nora. Rose pegged her as another survivor, although she had no idea from what. Nora introduced her as Doris Bochner, an old friend from Kansas City.

"Doris has a dressing room in back, where horny old men can't hang around trying to catch a peek," Nora explained.

While Nora browsed through bolts of cloth out front, Rose followed Doris down a hall to a small cubicle at the rear of the building. Rose hadn't known what to expect from a dressing room, being unacquainted with the term, but she decided, once she'd seen one, that her ignorance had probably stood her in good stead. Had she anticipated much at all, she likely would have been disappointed. There was a short bench, nails in the walls for hangers, and a full-length mirror on a cherry wood stand. A window admitted light, although its panes were covered with brown butcher's paper for modesty's sake. Pink wallpaper, peeling and water-stained, hung on the walls.

"It isn't fancy," Doris admitted, "but at least a woman doesn't have to order her unmentionables in public, or from a male clerk. You can try on a dress, too, to make sure it fits properly."

"It's . . . nice," Rose said lamely, eliciting a strained smile from Doris.

"Honey, it's a scant step up from a dirt-floored tent, which is what I started in, but it'll have to do until we're all rich and can afford mansions. Now, what did you have in mind?"

Rose hadn't a clue, and Doris quickly took charge. By the time they left the back room a couple of hours later, Rose had bought two new dresses—one of dark blue serge with pearl buttons down a pleated bodice, and the other linen in a soft shade of green, with white piping and a green bow that tied in back. She'd also purchased stockings with garters, petticoats, bloomers, camisoles, a pair of pointed-toe black shoes that laced to above the ankle, and a flat-crowned straw hat with a narrow, straight brim and a piece of black ribbon for a hatband. Some small white handkerchiefs and a woolen shawl for evenings completed her ensembles. In addition,

Doris helped her with her hair, showing her how to fasten it above her head with long pins in the current, casual fashion.

Nora was slumped in a chair in the front room when Rose emerged from the rear of the shop. She looked tired and irritated, but came over to lend a hand when she saw the boxes in Rose's arms. Rose paid the bill with money she'd earned from trapping, and the two women left the store.

"Do you like ice cream?" Nora asked when they were outside.

"Ice cream? Shoot, everybody likes ice cream."

"There's a place down the street that sells it. It's an apothecary shop, and I promised Pearl I'd pick up a tin of cocaine powder for her."

Rose frowned. "Pearl ought to stay away from that stuff. I think it's making her brain jittery."

"It ain't your business or mine," Nora replied. "I promised her I'd pick some up. You want to come along or not?"

"Sure."

The apothecary shop was located in a small, wood-framed building overshadowed by a two-storied brick bank with lawyers' offices overhead. Rose and Nora found seats by the window, and when a heavy-set older woman came to take their order, Nora asked for two bowls of ice cream with chocolate sauce and a sprinkling of crushed pecans over the top.

"Lordy," Rose murmured when the woman returned with their orders. She rubbed a hand self-consciously across the back of her neck, made bare by her new hairstyle.

"It's been a long time since I've had any, too," Nora said. "The first time I tried it was last summer, right before they ran out of ice. I've been starving for another bowl ever since. It was Jessie told me they were serving it again."

Rose tried a spoonful, closing her eyes, and shaking her head in wonder as the concoction melted on her tongue. "I reckon this is near about as good as Callie's Kentucky butter cake," she declared.

"It'll taste even better this summer. It ain't hardly hot enough yet. This summer, when you eat it fast, it'll give you a headache."

Rose looked out the window at the traffic on the street, the flow of people along the boardwalks. It amazed her how rapidly Miles City was growing. It seemed like every time she came to town there was something new or different to be seen, and she said as much to Nora.

"Were you here in the early days?" Nora asked.

"Not the early, early days, but I remember when they still called it Milestown, and shipped buffalo hides downriver on steamboats. That was before the railroad came in 'Eighty-One and ruined everything. Shoot, they used to be ricks of buffler skins a quarter mile long down by the wharf, and mountains of bones for the china factories and fertilizer plants back East. Wasn't a drover in sight in them days, either. Now they're buildin' all them cow pens over by the tracks . . . all that fresh lumber . . . it looks like a whole new city goin' up."

"I hear they plan to ship five thousand head out of Miles City this year, and most folks think it'll just keep growing."

"That's a lot of beef. I reckon was a person smart, they'd take up ranching."

"They'd have to be rich as well as smart. Even on the range, cattle are expensive."

Rose looked at Nora. "How'd you get to know so much about cows?"

"I've learned more about cows than I ever wanted to from peckerwoods who are too bashful to shuck their pants until they've talked my ears off first."

Rose smiled. "Just the same, I can't get over the way things has changed. Only a few years ago there weren't no telephone lines or ice cream parlors or ladies' stores or anything. Just regular businesses and saloons."

"It'll keep on changing, too. I remember how Kansas City turned so fast . . . telephone and electric lines criss-crossing the streets, trolleys to take you anywhere you wanted to go, brick streets downtown instead of mud and dust, gaslights on every corner. After a time it got to be like a foreign city, like London or Paris. Not that I've ever been to either of those places, but it was strange to watch. The same thing'll happen here someday."

"I ain't so sure I'd want to live in a place like

that," Rose confessed. "Just thinkin' about it makes me miss the old days."

"At least you've got that land up the Yellowstone. If I had a place like that, I'd kick the dust of Miles City off my heels in about a minute."

"Homesteadin' ain't all it's cracked up to be," Rose said vaguely.

Nora looked almost surprised. "You sure don't sound very enthused about it. I was under the impression from Collins that you loved that place."

"I do. It just ain't what folks that's never done it before thinks it is, is all. The loneliness can near about kill you sometimes. Especially in the winter. It weren't like that in the beginning, but it gets worse after a few years."

"Get yourself a partner."

Rose's voice took on an edge. "Someone like Shorty?"

"Uhn-uh, someone you can count on. Someone who'd love the place as much as you."

"You?"

"No, not me. I'm just a whore and a dreamer, but . . . I don't know. Doris was a dreamer." Her eyes became unexpectedly moist. "She was one of us, you know, back in Kansas City?"

"Doris?"

"Uhn-huh. A hook shop girl, but she was smart and took care of her money. After a few years she was able to buy a partnership in a dress shop. Not long after that, she got married and turned respectable. That was when she and her husband moved out here. Her husband fell in the river and froze to death that first winter, but Doris stayed."

Nora looked out the window, her ice cream momentarily forgotten. "I kind of have that same dream, I suppose. I've been cautious with my money, saved what I could. I haven't decided what I want to do with it, though. I ain't got the skills for a dress shop, or much else for that matter, but after I met you last year, then some of the boys told me about your place and what you'd done with it . . . well, I thought that was pretty impressive." She smiled. "I think I'd actually enjoy some isolation for a change. I sure as hell don't get much around here."

"Homesteadin' ain't an easy life," Rose pointed out.

"Neither is whoring," Nora returned bluntly.

"I didn't mean it that way."

Nora shrugged dismissingly, but it was clear she was perturbed. "The hell with it," she said. "It wouldn't have worked out anyway."

"We could try," Rose ventured half-heartedly.

"No, you were right. It was just wishful thinking."

Rose nodded, feeling suddenly sad again, not so much for herself as for Nora. She knew what it was like to feel trapped and hopeless. She'd felt that way most of her life. But the thought of a friend experiencing that same level of despair troubled her. Nora deserved better than a life wasted in frontier whorehouses.

Glancing at the boxes of new clothes stacked on

a nearby table, Rose felt a twinge of guilt for having squandered so much of her hard-earned money on foolishness. Then she smiled and shook her head.

"What are you grinning about?" Nora asked suspiciously.

"I was just thinkin' how I wasted my money buyin' dresses, when what I should've bought was some britches and new work gloves."

Chapter Fourteen

The days passed swiftly into weeks and the balmy weather held. The green on the hillsides deepened into a rich emerald hue, and in the flower beds the tulips and crocuses poked their tiny heads above the soil like chicks emerging from eggs. Among the citizens of Miles City an air of indolence prevailed. People went about their chores, but stopped often to gaze at the distant hills or breathe deeply of the fresh spring air. No one neglected their jobs or lost sight of the essentials, but everyone seemed willing to slow down a bit, to enjoy a moment of quiet celebration at having survived another harsh winter.

For Rose, that April of 1886 was a time of rare leisure, an opportunity to recuperate from the strenuous days of wolfing without the usual responsibilities of planting and repair. She would sit on Alice's porch for hours on end while her imagination roamed, or stroll alone along the Tongue or Yellowstone Rivers, listening to the roar of mountain run-off.

She hadn't forgotten the more somber images of her recent past, and would occasionally wonder if anyone had informed Jimmy Frakes's family of the young man's death. Or she would recall the Indian she'd shot on the Musselshell, and cringe when she remembered the way the Sharps' slug had flung him backward like a paper doll in the wind. The wolf carcasses she and Shorty and Wiley had left scattered for miles around their Pipestem cabin bothered her, too, as did thoughts of Muggy's death and the fire-gutted cabin on the Yellowstone. But for the most part she tried to keep those memories at bay, her sights elevated toward happier targets. She napped and walked and daydreamed, and spent at least a couple of hours each day with Albert, currying his coat and brushing his mane and tail, or just holding him out on fresh grass with a long rope and talking.

When the cattlemen's convention got under way, Nora and the other girls became rare sights. They were almost constantly engaged at either the Silver Star or entertaining guests in Alice's parlor or in one of the cribs at the rear of the house. It wasn't until the convention ended and most of the ranchers and their hands returned to the range that Nora and Rose were able to spend some time together again.

Mostly they talked. Neither would approach

anything too personal, preferring instead to focus on the more benign experiences of their past— things they'd seen or done, stories they'd heard. Rose told Nora of the wild times she'd shared with her pap and brothers, knocking around Montana Territory, while Nora described growing up poor in Chicago, where her father had worked sixteen hours a day in the meat-packing industry and her mother had taken in laundry.

Nora's description of city life from an indigenous point of view was sobering. The dilapidated wooden buildings constructed side by side and as tall as five stories; the alleys where death was as cheap as a Virginia cigar and the air was rife with the throat-burning, acidic grit of coal smoke spewed from a hundred thousand homes and factories; the stench of garden refuse, excrement, dead cats, dogs, rats, and even an occasional horse or ox, left to rot along the sidewalks. Her memories made Rose realize how unrealistic her notions about the world outside Montana had been, and how unprepared she was for any kind of life other than the one she lived now.

One afternoon they went down to the bottoms along the Yellowstone, where Rose taught Nora some of the finer points of shooting a pistol. They used both Rose's Smith & Wesson and Nora's little .32 Colt Rainmaker. Afterward Rose demonstrated some of the tricks Sam Matthews had taught her. Nora was most impressed by the road agent spin, and was soon able to hold her little pearl-handled self-cocker around the cylinder in a grip-first position, as if to give it up, then smoothly tip it sideways and twirl it around on her trigger finger until it was cocked and pointed at an imaginary foe. Although slower than Rose, Nora displayed a natural ability that convinced Rose it wouldn't take much practice for her to become as good as any gun handler currently roaming the Yellowstone Basin. She was already better than most.

Although the subject of partnering with Nora hadn't resurfaced, the idea continued to rattle around inside Rose's skull. It wasn't until the evening of the day they practiced their pistol shooting that she was able to steer the subject back in that direction.

They were dining in a tiny Chinese restaurant close to the Northern Pacific tracks when Rose started talking about the spring-fed creek and the rich grass on her land. She described the trees along the creek, and the tract of forest to the west where timber was free for the cutting. When Nora wondered aloud how many head of cattle such a place would support, Rose's reply was: "As many as a person could brand."

"It's the water that makes it so valuable," she continued. "Shoot, you could graze a thousand head over unclaimed land, but you have to have reliable water, and along that bluffy stretch of the Yellowstone, there ain't a lot of places where a cow can get down to the river. That spring of mine ain't run dry once in the four years I lived there.

Not even during the hottest part of the summer."

"So it's just a matter of how many cows you could afford?"

"Plus an outfit. I've got just about enough right now to rebuild the cabin and supply it for the winter, but Albert's too old to pull a plow, and I couldn't afford a mule to work a big garden, let alone buy a bunch of cattle."

"What if someone bought the cows for you?"

"It'd be costly. Last I heard, cows was runnin' eight to ten dollars a head."

"I know men who'd sell them cheaper, especially a small bunch."

"Who?"

Nora's expression hardened. "Arrogant little bastards who'd think it was cute if I asked. But I bet they'd let me buy forty head or so."

"Forty head!" Rose whistled under her breath. "That'd be a good start, for sure. Not like most of the spreads poppin' up hereabouts, but enough to keep a place goin'."

"All you'd need is enough to make a simple living."

"What about you?"

"Me? Hell, I'm fine where I'm at." Bitterness coated her next words. "A whore's gotta stay where the men are."

Scowling, Rose said: "That ain't fair. I wouldn't take advantage of a friend like that."

"There're no strings attached, if you're interested."

"I know, but I wouldn't feel right investin' your life's savings in something as risky as livestock. Why, a disease could wipe out a whole herd in a week, or one good lightning strike could kill a dozen head in the snap of a finger."

"There are risks involved in everything," Nora reminded her.

"That's true, but I still won't take your money. Not that way."

A rail-thin waiter in a white jacket brought their orders—steaming plates of ham-fried rice and chow mein, plus hot tea served from a small porcelain pot, the handle formed in the shape of a dragon. Rose eyed the food skeptically, unsure how to attack it with only a pair of slim wooden skewers, and neither spoon nor fork in sight. Picking up one of the tiny lances, she turned it inquisitively in her fingers. "I reckon I could stab the meat and most of the vegetables with this, but I'm danged if I know how I'm gonna get much rice."

"They're chopsticks," Nora said. "Use them like this." She maneuvered the two sticks in her right hand, showing Rose how to grip them between her fingers. "It ain't hard, once you get the hang of it."

"I reckon," Rose replied doubtfully. She tried it, but was immediately showered in a spray of rice when one of the sticks flipped loose in her fingers. "Lively little things, ain't they?" she said, embarrassed.

Nora started to laugh, so hard that tears soon

came to her eyes. The waiter returned with a fork, which he placed next to Rose's plate with a look of exasperation, then quickly backed away.

Red-faced, Rose picked up the fork.

"I wouldn't worry about it," Nora said. "I imagine you could easily outshoot him."

Rose allowed a crooked grin. "It's no wonder he's so danged ribby. I'd probably be skinny myself, was I to take up eatin' with sticks."

"What about the money, Rose? Will you take it?"

"Nope."

"Will you consider it?"

"Uhn-uh, although I appreciate the offer. Maybe someday, but . . ." She burped, looking at her plate in surprise. The rice and chow mein swam before her eyes, and she had to put out a hand to catch the edge of the table.

"Something wrong?" Nora asked.

"I don't feel so good all of a sudden," Rose admitted. Then a sharp pain lanced through her lower abdomen, driving toward her groin, and she cried out.

Nora pushed her chair back in alarm, then paused uncertainly. "Rose?"

Sweat beaded Rose's upper lip as she struggled to her feet. The waiter, who had been watching from a distance, hurried over. His gaze darted between the two women. "What wrong?" he asked. "Food good?"

"I need some air," Rose said, feeling panicky. She gripped the backs of chairs as she made her way around the table. Then Nora was at her side, slipping a shoulder under her arm. Together they headed for the door, but Rose had to stop when another cramp struck. She jerked convulsively, her body almost doubling over in pain. *"Jesus,"* she hissed, after the worst of it had passed.

"Must pay," the waiter said, moving quickly to intercept them. "You pay first!" A second man appeared from the kitchen holding a bloodied cleaver, the sight of it causing Rose's stomach to heave violently.

"Here!" Nora shouted, flinging a handful of coins against the waiter's chest. "Keep the damn' change!"

They stumbled outside, then paused while Rose gulped deeply of the fresh spring air. She felt a little better after that, but continued to support herself against the restaurant's front wall.

"Are you all right?" Nora asked.

"Yeah, I'm fine. I don't know what it was, but it sure kicked like a dang' mule." She tried to smile, then another spasm twisted her guts and she cried out and nearly collapsed.

"I'm getting you to a doctor," Nora said firmly.

"No!" Rose gasped. "Privy, I . . ." She bit down on her lower lip as another wave of agony exploded downward from her abdomen.

"Rose!"

"Privy," Rose grunted desperately. With Nora's aid, she rounded the restaurant's corner and lurched as rapidly as possible down a trash-filled alley. At its far end sat a weathered two-seater, its doors incised with quarter moons to allow ventilation.

Grasping a frayed rope strap, Rose yanked open the right-hand door and stumbled inside. Fighting waves of dizziness, she quickly hiked up her skirt and petticoat and pushed down her bloomers. Another surge of pain rammed through her as she sank gratefully to the time-polished oak seat. She rested her forehead on white-knuckled fists while her elbows drilled into her knees and the pain slid down and out in a warm, soupy coagulation. Then it was over, the razor-sharp spasms passing from her body, her limbs turning weak and trembly.

Nora pounded on the door. "Rose! Are you all right?"

Too weak to reply, Rose sagged against the wall at her side. As the sweat began to cool on her brow, a chill passed over her. Then Nora opened the door, her hand flying to her mouth, stifling a scream.

Rose kept her eyes closed, even after she awoke. She was lying in a bed, distantly aware of strange voices floating through thin walls. There was a male's husky growl, a woman's laughter, and, far off, the scratchy squeal of a violin. When her eyelids finally fluttered open, she recognized the cracked ceiling above her as belonging to the room she shared with Nora. Lamplight from the bedside table emphasized the shadows in the corners, telling her night had fallen while she slumbered. Then Callie's ebony face loomed above her, her chubby cheeks taut with concern.

"Sugar?" Callie said gently. "Can you hear me?"

Rose ran her tongue over parched lips. "Water," she managed.

"Sure, honey, I got a pitcher right here." Callie filled a beer stein, then held it to Rose lips, keeping one strong hand cupped under her head.

Rose drank tentatively at first, just enough to wet her throat and wash away the sour scum that had collected there, but as her thirst grew, so did her greed, until Callie finally pulled the mug away.

"You can have some more in a bit," she promised. "It's best you go slow for now."

"I'm drier'n corral dust," Rose admitted.

" 'Course you are. Your body's craving water after what you've been through. It's only natural."

"Been through?"

"Oh, sugar, why didn't you tell someone?" Callie sat on the edge of the bed, brushing the blonde hair back from Rose's forehead.

"Wha- . . . what? Tell someone what?"

Callie's fingers slowed. "Don't you know?"

"I got sick as a dog, I know that. I remember Nora helping me here." Her voice dropped when she recalled the blood, its warmth soaking through the dark blue fabric of her skirt. Looking away, she said: "I was kind of . . . messy, I suppose."

"Oh, sugar, you don't know, do you? You miscarried, Rose. You lost your little baby."

"Baby?" Rose whispered, struggling to bring the loose ends together, to make sense of it all.

"I figured you knew," Callie said. "Didn't you miss your monthlies?"

Rose started to reply, then abruptly shut up. Squeezing her eyes shut, she thought: *Lord God, how could I have been so stupid?* Tears welled in the corners of her eyes but she angrily fought them back. Putting the joint of her index finger between her teeth, she clamped down hard in an effort to diminish the larger ache that was piercing her heart.

"Here," Callie said, pulling Rose's hand away. "You don't need to be causing yourself any more pain, sugar. I expect you're hurting enough without chewing on yourself."

"Shorty's . . . ," Rose said in a cracked voice, but was unable to complete the sentence.

"I expect," Callie agreed. "But it wasn't far along. You got that to be thankful for."

The bed shifted, and Rose heard Callie fumbling at the nightstand.

"I want you to drink this," Callie said. "It'll help you sleep."

"I don't want to sleep."

"You need to rest. Sleep's the best thing for you."

"I'm a failure," Rose whispered almost frantically. "I'm the worst kind of human being, to have killed my own . . ." There was a loud, fleshy smack in Rose's ear, and her head rocked to one

192

side. It was a moment more before she realized Callie had slapped her, hard.

"I don't want to hear that kind of talk," Callie said fiercely. "It was the Lord who took your baby, and the Lord who's holding it in His loving arms right now." Her voice softened as she held out a deep-bellied tablespoon filled with a thick liquid. "Here, take this."

"What is it?"

"Laudanum. Miss Alice keeps it on hand for when one of the girls needs it. It'll help you sleep."

Rose opened her mouth and Callie tipped the spoon between her lips. It had a tart flavor, and Rose made a face.

"It ain't butter cake, is it?" Callie asked gently.

Rose licked her lips in an effort to get rid of the taste, but she felt too limp to wipe it away. Within minutes her body started to relax, her eyelids to grow heavy.

She was alone when she awoke next, and for a while she was content to lay unmoving, collecting her thoughts. The lamp had been extinguished and the bright blue of a new day poured through the window. A deep, comfortable silence had replaced the music and laughter of the night before, and a feeling of well-being came over her that lasted only until the memory of her lost child returned. She closed her eyes with a small, anguished moan.

Nora was there when she opened her eyes the next time, sitting in a chair beside the window where she could keep an eye on the door. Her Colt Rainmaker and Rose's Smith & Wesson lay on the sill within easy reach. She still wore her low-cut working dress, and her eyes were puffy with fatigue.

"Nora?"

Nora didn't immediately respond. Then her gaze swung to the bed and a smile tilted the corners of her mouth. "So, are you awake?"

"More or less."

"How do you feel?" She came over to stand at the foot of the bed, one hand on a post.

"Middlin', I reckon." Rose sat up cautiously, but there was neither pain nor light-headedness.

"Callie says you'll be fine in a few days. The bleeding stopped almost immediately. That's the important thing." She patted Rose's foot through the quilt. "Callie's seen this before, Rose. Lots of times. If she was worried, she'd have sent for a doctor."

Rose nodded. "I know."

"We have to talk," Nora said.

"I figured we did." Her gaze went to the pistols lying on the window sill.

"Last night," Nora said, "Stroudmire gave me a message to deliver to you. He said it was time."

"Time? For what?"

Nora shook her head. "He said you'd know. I'm sorry. You don't need this after what you've just been through, but Stroudmire scares me. Miles City ain't big enough for you to hide in forever."

Rose kept her gaze on the window. "Are you sayin' I have to leave?"

"What else can you do?"

Fight, she wanted to say, but she knew, if she did, she'd risk pulling Nora and Callie and the others into it with her. "Hell, it was time to move on, anyway," she said with resignation.

"Do you have somewhere to go . . . friends or family?"

Rose was careful to keep her voice neutral, her expression calm. "I reckon I can stay with my pap in Billings."

"You ought to leave Montana. I've got friends in Kansas City who'd help, if you wanted to go there."

"Kansas City? With all them trolley cars roamin' the streets like grizzly bears?" She gave Nora a crooked grin. "Now what would an ol' cob-rough gal like me do in a place like that?"

Tears welled in Nora's eyes. "It ain't fair, god dammit. Women like us can't even turn to the law for help."

"The law weren't set up for the likes of you 'n' me, and that's a fact," Rose agreed, "but nobody ever said it was fair. It's just the way things is." She looked around the room, remembering the first time she'd come here. "You've been a good friend, Nora. Everyone here has. I'm gonna miss this place somethin' terrible."

"We're going to miss you, too." Tears tracked Nora's cheeks; she wiped them away with her palm. "Can you stand?" she asked, as if needing to change the subject.

"Sure." Rose slid her legs out of bed and sat up. "See, fit as a fiddle."

"It'll be dark in a few hours. Eben'll bring your horse around and Callie will fix some things for you to take on the trail. Or we'll help you catch the train, if you'd rather travel that way."

"No, I want to keep my horse."

"We thought you would. Come downstairs as soon as you're dressed. Callie has a warm meal waiting."

Rose nodded but didn't try to speak. Nora set the Smith & Wesson on the nightstand, within easy reach, then walked to the door. Pausing, she glanced over her shoulder. "Good bye, Rose."

"I ain't gonna see you again?"

"I have to go back to work. Besides, that way I can keep an eye on Stroudmire and Haus. I'll send word if I think they're up to something."

Rose didn't know how to respond. She felt over-whelmed by the changes that were occurring even as she sat on the edge of the bed in a borrowed nightgown. But she did know that, if she truly cared about Nora and Callie, or any of them, the only sensible alternative she had was to ride away as swiftly as possible. Bucking up to her grief, she said: "Thank you, Nora. I don't know how I'm ever gonna repay you for all you've done."

"Hell," Nora replied, her lips trembling. "You already have. You're my friend."

Chapter Fifteen

"That'll be Eben," Callie said several hours later. She moved to the window, although Rose doubted if she could see much beyond her own reflection in the glass, for the night was dark, the moon not yet risen.

The clopping of a horse's hoofs came faintly from the back yard. Standing, Rose pushed her chair under the table. She felt suddenly awkward and uncertain, standing in Callie's kitchen in her old wolfing clothes. Although Callie had scrubbed them as best she could, they were still stained and ratty-looking, her hat as shapeless as any tramp's. Silently she strapped the Smith &Wesson around her waist, then pulled on her canvas jacket.

Watching, Callie said: "God bless you, sugar. I'll pray for you."

Rose hesitated beside the table, then walked over and wrapped her arms around Callie's broad shoulders. "I won't forget you, Callie," she whispered. "Not ever."

"Hush, now. Don't talk like that. I expect you'll be back soon as this Stroudmire foolishness dies down."

The door opened and Eben came in. He looked nervous, and was carrying a shotgun in addition to his revolver. Rose pulled away from Callie. "Sure," she said. "More'n likely I'll be back in a couple of weeks." Then she hurried outside before her throat closed completely.

It was a rare warm night for spring in Montana. The air was fresh, the wind behaving itself for a change. Rose took Albert's reins and swung him around to the light, running her hands over the pannier Eben had strapped behind the cantle, checking the saddle strings. She and Callie had gone through the pack that afternoon, sorting out the heavier stuff, keeping only what she'd need for the immediate future.

"Well, ol' pard," she said, adjusting her reins above the gelding's withers. "I reckon it's just you and me again." Albert swung his head around to push his velvety muzzle against her elbow. Rose grabbed the saddle's broad, flat horn and swung carefully aboard. It was a stretch getting her leg over the bulky pannier, for she was still sore, and the top of the pack came above the small of her back when she was seated. She didn't attempt a final farewell. They'd said their good byes earlier, and Rose was afraid that if she tried to speak now, her voice would betray her.

She rode west until she was sure darkness had engulfed her, then turned Albert to face Main Street. For a minute the lights of Miles City blurred like smudged thumb prints on glass, and a harsh choking sound raked at the back of her throat. She lifted her face to the starry sky, her jaw clenching until the tendons in her neck stood taut.

Then the moment passed, the pain sliding back

and down until it was locked securely behind a cold, hard shell of resolve. She forced herself to relax, and for a while she just sat there as the memories of the past few weeks flowed through her mind. Then she put those away, too, storing them with the grief, deep enough that they wouldn't become bothersome. Gathering her reins, she said: "Come on, hoss. I reckon it's time we paid Stroudmire a call."

Rose hadn't been to the Silver Star since her first night back in Miles City, and was surprised to find so many horses hitched out front. She had to dismount across the street and loop her reins through the spokes of an empty Diamond R freight wagon, the rails were so full.

In the shadow of the tall wagon she removed her jacket and hung it over the saddle horn, then pulled the Smith & Wesson around where it would be easier to reach. Finally, taking a long breath, she crossed the street and climbed the steps to the saloon, ignoring the curious stares of the beer drinkers clustered along the verandah.

Even expecting it, the size of the crowd was startling. Rose recognized Tom behind the bar and several of the girls from Alice's, but everyone else was a stranger. A lot of them, she figured, were drovers who'd followed the season north to work the roundup, only to lose out to older, more experienced hands. Not a few were muleskinners and bullwhackers, with the usual sprinkling of Fort

Keogh swaddies in their dark blue soldier uniforms.

Rose spotted Nora at the bar with a cowboy pressed to her side like a brand. He had one arm draped over her shoulders, his fingers absently stroking the soft flesh at the tops of her breasts. Nora saw Rose at the same instant, and an expression of alarm crossed her face even as she glanced toward the rear of the room. Following the direction of her gaze, Rose saw John Stroudmire sitting alone at a table with his back to the wall. A bottle of whiskey and a half-filled glass sat at his elbow, with ranks of cards spread across the green felt in front of him in a game of solitaire.

Making an oblique turn, Rose headed for Stroudmire's table. Silence accompanied her. Groups of men parted before her, then came together again in her wake. Stopping before the gunman, she hitched self-consciously at her cartridge belt, then let her hand rest lightly against the double-looped holster. The Smith &Wesson's hard rubber grips pressed against the inside of her wrist. Stroudmire didn't look up, but Rose knew he was aware of her presence. Planting her feet solidly, she said: "John Stroudmire."

"What might I do for you, Missus Edwards?" he replied, tapping thoughtfully at a nine of clubs with a long, tapered index finger. Then he raised his eyes, and Rose stiffened as they came to rest on her like hot coals. "Or is it still Lucy Alder?"

"You know who I am. I came to let you know I'm leavin' town."

"In other words, I am to leave your friends alone?"

"Your business is with me, not them."

"Go away, Missus Edwards," he said mildly. "I have other fish to fry, and little patience for making war on women. Leave now, and relieve me of this distasteful dilemma." He slid the black nine off the end stack and placed it over a ten of diamonds, revealing a three of clubs with no harbor for it.

Rose hesitated. "Nora said you had a message for me."

"Did she deliver it?"

"Yeah."

"Then that objective was accomplished." He dealt three more cards off the deck, turning up a jack of clubs. Rose shifted uncertainly, and Stroudmire paused, his gaze as cold and hard as a rattler's. "Do you intend to draw on me, Missus Edwards?"

"I will if you ever bother me or my friends again. I ain't afraid to do it, if forced."

His cheeks seemed to darken, and his voice grew rough. "Then I'd suggest you either pull your piece now, or leave."

"I'll leave, but I won't be far away or hard to find."

"I shall keep that forever in mind," he replied, his voice laced with sarcasm.

Rose paused indecisively. It seemed the encounter was at an end, although it had taken her in a direction she hadn't expected. Nodding stiffly, she walked away, the noise of the crowd rising abruptly at her back. She heard one man say—"I'll be damned."—and another—"Stood right up to the bastard. . . ."—and still a third—"Backed him down like the cur he is. . . ."

She shoved through the doors and down the steps, her pace quickening as she crossed the street. She could feel the eyes of the men at the Silver Star's doors following her, no doubt wondering who she was and where she'd come from. While she wondered, was she really that tough that she could challenge a man of Stroudmire's mettle and walk away unscathed?

Rose had no answer for any of them. At Albert's side she stopped long enough to grip the Mother Hubbard's skirt with both hands, her fingernails scalloping the soft leather of the *mochila* with tiny half moons. Then, knowing the cowboys at the Silver Star were waiting to see what she'd do, she yanked the reins free and stepped into the saddle. Wheeling smartly, she rode out of town at a gallop.

It was after midnight when Rose finally stopped. She picketed Albert in a grassy draw, then wrapped up in her blankets to catch a few hours' sleep. By dawn she was in the saddle again, riding west toward Billings. She kept the Yellowstone a couple of miles to her left to avoid the toll road that ran along the river's north bank, and stayed to higher ground where she had an unobstructed view of the surrounding country. She was feeling better today, stronger and not nearly as sore, although she didn't push it as hard as she could have.

At noon she halted to lunch beneath a rocky ledge, pulling off Albert's bridle and loosening the cinch so he could graze unencumbered. With the Sharps and the cotton sack of food Callie had prepared, she climbed higher among the crumbling yellow rocks until she found a place where she could rest and eat and still keep an eye on her back trail.

Stroudmire's affected disinterest last night hadn't impressed Rose one whit. If anything, it convinced her that she'd been moved up on the cattlemen's target list, the one Joe Bean had warned her about last fall. No doubt her recent association with Wiley and Shorty had a lot to do with that, even as her wolfing had directly benefited the ranchers.

The irony of her situation was not lost on Rose— that she was an outcast in the eyes of men who probably wouldn't even be here if not for her pap and others like him. But the tables had turned in the last few years, and those very trailblazers— the hunters and trappers and scouts—who had opened up eastern Montana to the cattle barons were now, as a class, vilified by them.

In a life spent on the woollier side of the frontier, Rose couldn't recall ever having witnessed the degree of viciousness she'd seen perpetrated by the wealthier stockmen since taking control of the range with the Stranglers' raid in '84. Not even during the Indian Wars, including that period immediately following the Custer debacle, had she observed such a desire for one class to eradicate another. At least between the United States military and the various Indian tribes there had existed a mutual respect, based on an acknowledgement of the other side's skills as warriors.

Nothing like that seemed to exist between the monied interests currently controlling local politics and the smaller, earlier outfits, which included, in Rose's opinion, the hard-scrabble settler families even now moving into the territory. Regardless of whether or not these people had ever stolen a cow in their lives, they were being conveniently lumped together in catch-all categories such as "stock thieves" or "undesirables"—guilt-by-association titles that granted the larger ranchers a conscience-balming license to rid the ranges of nuisances.

To Rose, these land-hungry cattlemen were every bit as parasitical as the worst rustler, and far more so than the average hunter or settler. Everywhere she looked, it seemed that the big ranchers were willing to destroy what they couldn't control, to plunder for their own benefit that which others had built before them, and, in her mind, their methods made them as much a class of thieves as the men and women they sought to displace.

What she found even sadder was the idea that, in all this empty land, there still wasn't going to be enough room for everyone.

Finishing her meal, Rose stood and brushed the crumbs from her trousers. Down below, Albert was grazing hungrily on the new grass. The sight of it brought a rare smile to Rose's face. They'd been together a long time, her and that rangy roan gelding with the graying whiskers. She'd bought the horse off a Fort Benton dealer back in her pap's hunting and trading days, and could still recall his outrage when she returned to camp with the roan in tow. Daniel Ames had made it clear he considered the purchase a waste of hard cash, the whimsy of a starry-eyed girl who'd forgotten that her only job was to drive a team of mules and keep caught up on the camp chores. He'd ordered her to return the animal, and threatened her with a switching if she didn't, but Rose's affection for the strawberry-colored horse had already taken root, and she'd clung stubbornly to her right of ownership, even when her pap came after her with a quirt. Although he'd eventually given in, he'd grumbled about it for months afterward.

It felt odd to remember those days now, the way she'd been all gangly and overgrown. Her pap had been a terror even then, but still holding his own against the bottle, and her brothers had helped with the hunting and skinning, although they'd lacked the diplomacy for trading. So much had happened since then—her family scattered to the winds and all of them in trouble, one way or another—that it hardly seemed real any more. Only Albert had remained constant.

At first Rose didn't notice the trio of horsemen who appeared out of the timber along the Yellowstone. It was only when Albert lifted his head, nostrils distended to test the wind, that she turned her gaze toward the river. She immediately hunkered down among the rocks, pulling the Sharps across her knees.

Two of the horsemen rode in advance, stirrup-to-stirrup; the third brought up the rear, leading a pack horse. Judging from their line of travel, Rose figured they must have spotted Albert and were coming to investigate.

Grimly she scampered down off the ledge and hurried to the roan's side. Although it was likely the three intruders were only drifters, she didn't intend to take any chances, especially after last night's conversation with Stroudmire.

Keeping a wary eye on the approaching horsemen, Rose tightened the cinch, then slipped the bridle over Albert's head. Although she considered it encouraging that the horsemen weren't picking up their pace when they spotted her, she also noticed that they weren't turning away, either. Keeping the Sharps in her right hand, Rose stepped into the saddle, then reined toward the top of the ridge. She would ride in the opposite direction as if to snub them, and know their intent by their reaction.

Turning west on the far side of the ridge, she kicked Albert into a canter. She kept looking over her shoulder, expecting to see them pounding after her, but she was almost a mile away before they finally hove into view. Slowing, she watched as they came together on top of the ridge as if to confer, but when they came on, it was obvious they were following her.

Cursing both Stroudmire and the cattlemen who'd hired him, Rose kept Albert at a jog. She held to the north of the ridge, far enough out to avoid the coulées that fingered down on her left. For the first half hour or so she was content to try and put as much distance as possible between herself and the three horsemen, but she eventually realized that, although they hadn't yet made any effort to close the gap, they also had no intention of being left behind. Deciding that a confrontation was inevitable, Rose began to study on how best to make it work to her advantage.

In time she came to a broad, deep coulée— almost a shallow cañon—that headed in a tangle of rocks near the summit. At the top was a V-shaped pass leading to the other side. Instinctively she reined toward it. She slowed to a walk as she entered the coulée, but didn't find what she was looking for until she was almost three-quarters of the way up—a sharp bend in the trail with a cutbank high enough to hide behind, providing she kept low in the Mother Hubbard's seat.

Pulling Albert alongside the crumbling dirt wall, Rose took off her hat to peer cautiously downhill. Her breath thinned when she spotted the horsemen, still a mile away but on a line with the mouth of the coulée. Although she figured they'd pause when they reached it and discovered she was no longer in sight, they didn't. They entered the coulée, single file, without hesitation, and she wondered irritably if they would've been so lax had they been trailing a man.

She'd been carrying the Sharps unloaded across her saddlebow. Now she lowered the trigger guard to open the breech in much the same manner a Winchester's lever is opened. Fingering a shell from her cartridge belt, she slid it into the chamber, then slapped the breechblock closed with the flat of her hand. She stayed down, but kept her eyes on Albert's ears, knowing the roan would warn her when the horsemen were close.

That moment came all too soon. Albert suddenly lifted his head, ears pricked forward, and Rose hauled back on the reins to cut off any questioning nicker. Seconds later she heard a low cough, then a man's voice speaking a question, another answering. Her pulse accelerated, but it was too late to back out now. Muttering a nervous—"Lordy."—she heeled Albert into the bend, in plain view of the men coming up from below. She held the Sharps butted to her thigh and kept her chin thrust forward in what she hoped was an authoritative pose.

The horsemen were about fifty feet away, their eyes glued to Albert's prints in the soft soil. The man in the lead looked more stocky than fat. He wore a narrow-brimmed bowler over curly red hair, his unshaven cheeks giving his face an appearance of rust. The man behind him was slim and poorly dressed, not yet out of his teens; with his hunched shoulders and scowling mien, he reminded her all too much of Jimmy Frakes.

The third man was tall and middle-aged and black, with a full curly beard and shotgun chaps striped with rope burns. It was the black man who spotted Rose first. He pulled up with a low warning to the others, the pack horse bumping up beside him. The red-headed man looked up next, then jerked his horse to a stop. The skinny teen-ager hauled up last.

"By hell, girl, you led us a merry chase," the red-haired man called.

"Why are you followin' me?"

"We just want to talk. We mean you no harm."

Rose felt a moment's apprehension. She'd braced herself for Stroudmire's men, no matter how inept, but it was plain these three didn't work for any stockmen's association. They looked more like saddle bums than Regulators, and were poorly armed to boot. Then the red-headed man spoke again, and Rose knew she hadn't been a victim of chance, after all.

"You're that Rose Edwards gal, ain't 'cha? The one whose husband stole all that gold in Helena? Nearly fifty thousand dollars is what we heard."

It was the absurdity of the question that wiped away her fear. She let the Sharps tip deliberately forward until its muzzle was pointed down the coulée. "Do I look rich to you?" she asked.

"Christ, girl, don't get careless with that thing!"

the red-headed man cried. "That's a buffalo gun."

"I know what it is. I'm glad you do, too."

"We ain't here to hurt you," the black cowboy hurried to interject. "We just want to talk."

Rose cocked the Sharps, the sound loud in the narrow confines of the coulée. "I reckon that's a lie. You gonna tell me it ain't?"

When no one denied her accusation, she continued: "What I want you boys to do is what I tell you to do, and no arguin' about it, understand?"

"Axel," the skinny kid said in a ragged voice, "we ain't gonna let this woman hooraw us, are we?"

"Hush now," Axel replied. "I'm thinking we made a mistake."

"Maybe you did," the kid snarled, reaching for his pistol, "but I'll be damned if I'll . . ."

Rose fired, the Sharps like a clap of thunder going off in her hands. The 450-grain lead bullet smacked the ground in front of the kid's horse like a small cannonball, kicking up a geyser of dirt that struck the animal squarely on its nose. The horse jumped straight up with a squeal, its hoofs churning the air a good three feet above the ground. Then it returned to earth like a streaking meteor. The kid grunted loudly as his crotch slammed into the saddle. His face turned pale and the pistol tumbled from his fingers.

"Son-of-a-bitch!" Rose exclaimed, then hurriedly ejected the spent cartridge and chambered a fresh round. Axel and the cowboy were so caught up in watching the kid that Rose had the Sharps reloaded and cocked by the time they turned back to her.

"God *damn*," the kid wailed, sitting folded over his saddle horn, hands pressed to his crotch.

"Listen up," Rose said loudly, her eyes wide. "Axel, pull that hogleg and let it drop."

After Axel did as instructed, Rose had the black cowboy drop his revolver. Then she ordered all three men to back their horses away from their guns. Riding down, she dismounted and gathered up the revolvers, wedging them under the pannier behind her saddle. Then she clambered back into the Mother Hubbard's seat, not once taking her rifle off the three men.

"Now get off your horses," she commanded.

"Go to hell," the kid grated, but Axel and the cowboy complied without hesitation.

"Loop your reins under their headstalls." Rose pointed her rifle at the kid. "You, too, friend."

"Get down, Bud," Axel said resignedly. "There ain't no point in getting shot."

"God damn it, she ain't gonna shoot nobody," Bud argued. "She ain't got the craw for it."

Axel glanced at Rose. "Oh, I'd say she's got plenty of craw."

"You boys start walkin'," Rose ordered.

"You're taking our horses, too?" the cowboy asked, looking truly frightened for the first time.

"I ain't stealin' 'em. You can catch 'em after I'm gone. I'll drop your pistols off up top, too. But you boys listen now, don't you ever follow me like this again. I won't be so easy to get along with next time."

"You ain't been all that easy to get along with this time," Axel pointed out.

"You damn' yellow dog," Bud said to Axel, then carefully dismounted, mindful of his injured crotch. He tied his reins above his mount's neck. "You satisfied now?" he asked Rose, looking like he was just about to burst into tears.

"I'm gettin' there," she said, then made a motion with the Sharps. "Go on now, before I start thinkin' too much about what you boys tried to do. Start walkin'."

Silently Axel and the cowboy turned down the coulée. Bud stared at her a moment longer, then spun and followed his partners. When they were far enough away, Rose circled their horses and drove them toward the top of the ridge. She stayed behind them until she was sure they wouldn't immediately stop or go back, then pulled up. Glancing over her shoulder, she saw that the three would-be thieves had stopped about a hundred yards downhill and were waiting for her to leave.

Returning the Sharps to its scabbard, Rose continued on toward the pass. She'd entered the coulée aimlessly, not knowing where she wanted to go or what she wanted to do, but as she climbed toward the notch above her, a new goal came to mind. She would go to Sheridan and talk to Jimmy Frakes's daddy, let him know what had happened to his son. It was something that had been nagging at her ever since they'd left Miles City last fall to trap wolves, and it was time, she decided, to tie up that loose end from her past. Time to close one door firmly, before opening the next.

Chapter Sixteen

Rose crossed the Yellowstone that same afternoon. The rickety ferry that served the tiny community of Rosebud creaked and groaned as it bucked the river's swollen current, but made the trip without mishap. Albert stood with his legs braced wide, his nose nearly brushing the weathered oak decking, then scampered up the opposite shore like a frightened colt as soon as the ferryman lowered the gangplank. Rose paid two bits for the ride, then walked up the bank to catch her horse.

A twelve-mule jerk-line rig with merchandise bound for Sheridan was just pulling out as Rose passed through town, but she declined the teamster's invitation to accompany the wagon southward. It would be a wearisome two-day ride to the isolated little cattle community as it was, and she had no hankering to prolong the undertaking.

The days were growing warmer as spring turned into summer. On the hills south of town, the roundup was in full swing. Rose saw cowboys nearly every hour, hazing small bunches of cattle toward distant holding grounds. In all her years in eastern Montana, Rose had seldom ventured into this country below the Yellowstone, once the heartland of the stalwart Sioux and a sort of no-man's land for whites. She was struck now, as she had been on those rare southern excursions in her past, by the contrast between the timbered, well-watered valleys here and the more arid region to the north that some called the Big Lonesome.

In that vaguely flat-iron-shaped wedge of country bordered roughly by the Musselshell on the west and pinching down between the Yellowstone and Missouri to the east, there were as yet no large ranches, and precious few cattle. That would change in a very short time, Rose knew. In their quest for more land, the cattlemen would invade that last stronghold of the buffalo as they had already invaded the better-grassed country along the Rosebud, Tongue, and Powder Rivers, changing forever the face of the country and the spirit of its people.

Rose took pains to avoid the cowboys and their working grounds, knowing that even a distant sighting of a woman on horseback would raise speculation. She wasn't necessarily hiding, but she didn't want to furnish the Regulators with an itinerary, either.

She stayed as close to the Rosebud as she could until it began its curve toward the Cheyenne Reservation to the southwest, then crossed the divide to the Tongue River, skirting the reserve on the east. She kept a wary eye on the hills for Indians as well as drovers. The Cheyennes were deemed friendly nowadays, but *friendly* could be a subjective term in that land.

The town of Sheridan lay at the confluence of Big and Little Goose Creeks, south of the Tongue, a crude square of humanity cradled in a broad, beautiful valley, the majestic Bighorn Mountains towering above it in the west.

It was dusk when Rose entered town, feeling tired, hungry, and out of sorts. She'd eaten the last of Callie's provisions for breakfast the day before, and had subsisted on river water and old jerky from her wolfing days since then. After paying a hostler 50¢ to stable Albert overnight, she walked toward the business district with her saddlebags over her shoulder, the Sharps rocking easily in her left hand, tolerating the snooty stares of the townspeople in silence. It had been her intention to find a place to eat first, then locate lodging for the night, before seeking out old man Frakes in the morning, but the reaction of the town's citizens convinced her it was time to retire her old, blood-stained wolfing apparel.

Turning into the first dry goods store she came to, she purchased a new suit of clothes—sturdy wool pants, vest, and a light sack coat, all in brown, plus a white shirt with a detachable collar, second-hand boots in good repair, and a flat-crowned dove-gray Stetson with a kettle-curled brim. On impulse, she added a pair of polished spurs with a bronze heart brazed to the outside of each shank and jinglebobs on the rowel pins for

215

extra ching. While she was in the mood, she also bought a red silk bandanna to wear around her neck and a $1 pocket watch with a twelve-inch chain and an elk-tooth fob.

It grew dark while she suppered in a tiny hotel café. She went upstairs afterward and stretched out on a squeaky, iron-framed bed. Light from a waning moon slanted through the window, illuminating the cubicle's sparseness. There wasn't even a carpet to dampen the sound of footfalls.

Staring at the ceiling, Rose contemplated her loneliness. It hadn't affected her so deeply on the long ride south, when she'd been able to occupy her mind with details like caring for her horse and worrying about cowboys and wandering Indians, but it was bad tonight. Lying in bed, listening to the heavy snores that bled through the walls on either side, or the murmur of conversation between a husband and wife across the hall, made her realize how much she missed Nora and Callie and the others. She even missed Shorty, and it occurred to her that she felt more alone tonight than she ever had in her cabin above the Yellowstone.

She fell asleep in her clothes and awoke the next morning feeling grumpy as a bear. At the livery where she'd stabled Albert, she learned that Maxwell Frakes had a spread south of town, although the hostler doubted if he was there.

"Old man Frakes is probably with the roundup somewhere along Big Goose Creek," he told her. "Assumin' he ain't at the bank countin' his money."

Saddling Albert, Rose rode out to find him.

She located the holding grounds shortly before noon, guided the last few miles by clouds of dust kicked up by the milling herds. Roundups generally consisted of several area ranches combining their efforts to cover a larger section of land. Reps from the more distant spreads would be on hand to help with the branding and cutting, and to claim any far-wandering cow that might turn up. The spring roundup was sometimes called the calf roundup. It was when the ranchers brought in the spring crop of new calves to brand. Bull calves were also castrated, the severed testicles tossed into a nearby bucket for roasting at the campfire in the evening. Mountain oysters, they were called, and about the only good thing to come out of the cattlemen's invasion of the northern plains, to Rose's thinking.

She halted beside the chuck wagon, but the cook didn't even look up until she called a greeting. Grudgingly he ventured out from beneath the shade of a canvas fly stretched over the long tailgate that served as his table. Rose asked for Frakes and the cook allowed he was probably at the branding fire, keeping tally on his stock. Rose thanked him and was about to rein away when he made a statement that brought her up short.

"I'm Miser," he said, then paused expectantly. When she didn't immediately reply, he got an angry look on his face and retreated into the shade of the fly.

Although puzzled by the exchange, Rose was too nervous about her impending conversation with Frakes to worry it. She guided Albert to where the dust looked thickest. There she found a cowboy on a chunky bay dragging a calf to the fire. The calf's mother, a lanky black and white animal with traces of Texas in her widespread horns, was nervously trotting back and forth nearby. A couple of calf-throwers grabbed the young one and tossed it on its side. One of them pinned the calf's head to the ground, the other stretched its upper rear leg all the way back. The mounted cowboy called—"Three-Bar-Clover!"—and a grizzled man with an air of authority walked over with the appropriate branding iron. Back at the fire, a dozen irons from three or four different outfits were heating in the coals.

An elderly man in a nearly new hat spied Rose and came over. He had a white handlebar mustache and a long white goatee, and carried a dirt-smudged tally book in one gloved hand. The muscles across the back of Rose's neck tightened when she recognized Maxwell Frakes.

"Yes, ma'am?" Frakes said in an unexpectedly congenial tone.

"Mister Frakes, my name is Rose Edwards. It used to be Rose Ames. I knew you when you lived up on the Gallatin."

Frakes didn't even bat an eye. "Yes, how may I help you?"

"I . . . ah . . . it's about your son Jimmy."

"What about James?"

"Look, can we get away from all this dust and noise? I got some news I ain't lookin' forward to sharin'."

"Would that message be that James was murdered on the Musselshell by one of Frank Caldwell's accomplices?" the old man asked.

"You've heard!"

"I suspect most people have by now. Was that your message?"

Rose nodded. "Uhn-huh."

"Then if you won't consider it rude, I should get back to my duties. Feel free to stop by the chuck wagon for a meal. Tell the cook I said it was all right."

But Rose couldn't let it go that easily. "Don't you care?"

With the kindly countenance of an indulging grandparent, Frakes said: "There's plenty of food, Missus Edwards. We won't run short. Help yourself to all you want."

"I meant Jimmy. He was your son."

"Of course. Yes, Missus Edwards, I do care. Very much. Not about his death, but about how he died, and in whose company. But James was his own man, and responsibility for his actions, beginning on the day he left home, fell exactly where it should. Yes, I regret his death, but I regret the circumstances surrounding it even more. He brought shame to the good name of Frakes. The Lord might forgive him for that. I won't."

"Do you know he blamed me for your leavin' the Gallatin?"

For the first time there was a noticeable change in Maxwell Frakes's expression. The pasted-on smile faded and his brows drew down like gun sights. "I'll not allow you back into my life, Missus Edwards. What passed between us on the Gallatin is behind us. I would suggest you forget those days."

"Wha- . . . what passed between us?" Rose echoed incredulously. "What in blue blazes are you talkin' about?"

"Let sleeping dogs lie, Rose."

"You god-damn' old goat," she said in sudden comprehension. "You're the one who started that rumor, ain't you?"

"Are you finished?"

She straightened, gathering her reins. "I ought to shoot you, not for what you said about me, but for what you did to Jimmy."

"I've warned you for the last time," Frakes replied stiffly. "I'll not suffer this abuse any longer."

"You killed him, Mister Frakes. Just as sure as you squeezed them triggers yourself."

Frakes seemed to pull himself up even straighter. "You are hardly in a position to lecture anyone, Missus Edwards. Now, I'll ask you to leave a final time. I suggest you do it, with haste."

"You go to hell, you sorry old goat bastard," Rose said thickly, pulling her horse around. She slapped Albert's hips with the ends of her reins, racing for the tree-lined creek and the trail that would take her north again. Her eyes blurred from the dust and the wind, tearing up so she could hardly see. It was a long time before they cleared up completely.

She picked up the Rosebud road above Sheridan and stopped that night at a freighter's campground along the Tongue, where she shared a cup of coffee with the muleskinner she'd met on the Yellowstone several days before. It was the muleskinner who told her about the resumption of hangings throughout the Yellowstone Basin, and of the deaths of some of Montana's more notorious horse thieves, including Wiley Collins and Shorty Tibbs.

It was funny how a person's priorities could change so abruptly, Rose thought two days later, guiding Albert down the rutted Fort Custer trail to the Yellowstone River. Below her, the lights of Junction City beckoned. That evening back on the Tongue, when the muleskinner told her about the renewed activities of the Stranglers, Rose hadn't even paused for details. She'd dumped her coffee on the ground, shoved the cup into her saddlebags, and ten minutes later was riding north toward the heart of the Crow Indian Reservation, that sprawling, grass-rich reserve that bordered the Cheyenne Reservation on the west. Only a few days earlier she'd fretted over just being close to Indian country—that concern didn't even enter her thoughts now.

She hadn't experienced any trouble, and ran into only one Indian, that on the day after leaving the freighter's camp. She'd stopped to water Albert at a spring running into the Little Bighorn, then bellied down to slake her own thirst. When she looked up, there he was, not forty yards away and proud as a peacock aboard a handsome black and white pinto rigged with a McClellan saddle and a jaw-line bridle of woven horse hair. He wore moccasins, baggy wool trousers, and an Army vest decorated over each shoulder with quilled epaulets. His hair was long, braided with red trade cloth, and included the familiar high pompadour of a Crow warrior. He carried a bow and a quiver of arrows across his back, and an ivory-handled revolver in a holster at his waist.

Such a blending of cultures was no surprise to Rose, who'd cut her teeth on Montana's quirky frontier. Standing, she wiped her lips with the back of her wrist. The Indian watched stoically for a moment, then deliberately lifted his gaze to the empty miles surrounding them. A slow, haughty smile touched the corners of the brave's mouth, at which point Rose said the hell with this and drew her Smith & Wesson, informing the Indian that she was in no mood to tolerate male foolishness, be that male red, white, or some shade in between. Then she cocked the revolver for punctuation.

Although it was unclear to her whether or not the Crow understood English, the Smith & Wesson effectively transcended any barrier of the tongue.

He yanked his pony around and rode out of there at a fine gallop, the pinto's hoofs kicking up little spurts of dust from the green grass.

She passed the Custer Battlefield site early the next morning, but didn't ride up to inspect the gray stone obelisk towering impressively against the sky, shielded from vandals and name-carving, souvenir-chipping curiosity seekers by a tall iron fence. The tenth anniversary of the Seventh's inglorious defeat was only a few weeks away now, and she'd heard there were plans for a memorial service, complete with visiting dignitaries and returning veterans, although there were no signs of prepara-tion for it as yet.

Rose tried not to look at the weathered bones still visible in the grass. That there were a few left was something of a shock. She would have expected them to be gone by now, either buried or dragged off to some distant coulée by the military. She knew they were just the skeletal remains of horses—the graves of fallen troopers were clearly marked by wooden stakes dotting the slopes above her—but it was still disconcerting. It gave her an odd, spooky feeling to ride that winding trail below Custer Hill, a sense of unresolved *presence* that made her scalp crawl and the hairs along her arms stand up. Even Albert seemed disturbed, and Rose was glad to leave the place behind. She thought she under-stood now why the Crows never camped there.

Mindful of her status as a trespasser on the reservation, Rose rode in a wide arc around the

Crow Agency headquarters and Fort Custer, near the forks of the Bighorn and Little Bighorn Rivers. Shortly after dusk she guided her weary mount down the long slope of the Fort Custer Road to the Junction City ferry.

Junction City was a dying town, and everyone knew it. Built near the sites of old Fort Pease and, later, the supply dump known as Terry's Landing, it sat at the head of steamboat navigation on the Yellowstone, a jumping-off point for settlements both military and civilian to the west, south, and north. But when the Northern Pacific Railroad laid its tracks across the less broken country south of the river, on the Crow Reservation that was off limits to white settlement, it had sealed the town's fate as effectively as a cholera outbreak.

Nowadays Junction City was slowly strangling between the more prosperous communities of Miles City to the east and Billings on the west, while the Yellowstone itself carved huge chunks of land from the banks below the town each spring. Soon, the local wags claimed every time a few more feet of the town peeled off into the river, the city's limits would stretch all the way from the Bighorn River to the mouth of the Yellowstone, some two hundred miles away.

Junction City had a reputation as a tough town. It was a favored watering hole along the Outlaw Trail, which wasn't rightly a trail at all, but a general route with numerous branches—including the one that ran past Rose's cabin to the west—

chosen for characteristics favorable to the rapid advancement of stolen livestock and men on the dodge. As a result, the town attracted a rougher element than most, and it was a rare individual who walked its streets unarmed. Perhaps it was for that reason that Junction City was considered a relatively safe haven on the frontier. As far as Rose knew, no one had ever been robbed or murdered in Junction City, which was a lot more than could be said for Miles City and Billings.

Reining up in front of Hannahman's Saloon, Rose dismounted awkwardly, hanging onto the saddle horn until she could put her full weight on her legs. She was sore all over and so tired her eyes burned. She'd lost track of the number of days she'd spent in the saddle since leaving Miles City. Less than a week, she supposed, but it seemed longer, having covered so much territory. Walking up beside Albert's head, she ran a hand over his clipped roach, scratching the dusty hair beneath his headstall.

"I reckon you've earned some time off," she told the gelding affectionately. "Just let me check out how things is standing hereabouts, and, if it looks all right, we'll bunk in for a few days."

Albert twisted his head sideways, allowing her better access to his itchy hide.

"You're a dang' ol' con pony is what you are," she accused, scratching harder. Then she patted the roan's neck and climbed the steps to the saloon.

Hannahman's was similar to most of the drinking

establishments Rose was familiar with. The lighting was poor, the furnishings few but sturdy, the odor strong yet not unpleasant. There was a bar with a brass foot rail, spittoons scattered around the room like metallic stumps, and a backbar that glittered with an assortment of whiskey bottles. Kegs of beer under the counter constituted the bulk of the saloon's business, but there was bottled beer, too—Coors from Colorado; Falk's & Schlitz's out of Milwaukee; and Bullards, freighted in from Miles City. There was a faro table up front and chuck-a-luck in the rear, but no women. Some saloons, like the Silver Star, employed either dance hostesses or hookers, but most didn't. Mostly, or so Rose had been told by those who knew, a Western saloon bore more resemblance to a quiet East Coast tavern than it did the orgy-infested houses of Kansas cow town fame, although there were exceptions to that rule, even in Montana. Rose considered it an indisputable fact that wherever there were men and money, there were bound to be hookers.

She studied the crowd carefully for anyone who might be a Regulator, but it appeared a fairly common lot. There were a few cowboys who hadn't been hired for the roundups, some mule-skinners who probably freighted for the Fort Custer sutler or the agency, plus the usual array of drifters. She didn't see anyone who looked like a bona-fide range detective, although she knew that could be a dangerous assumption.

She was about to push inside when her gaze was arrested by a slim figure in striped pants and a red leather vest, standing at the bar. Her fingers tightened on the top of the swinging door, and for a moment she thought she might faint, so great was her relief. Then she slipped inside and moved up next to him, saying: "Howdy, Dave?"

Dirty-Nosed Dave Merritt turned a pair of bloodshot, green eyes on her. "Huh?" he said.

"Dang!" Rose swayed back from the stench of his breath. "What have you been eatin', skunk cabbage with alkaline sauce?"

"He's drunk," the bartender said, coming over.

"Lew!" Rose exclaimed.

"Hello, Rose." There was a welcoming smile on the bartender's face. "How have you been?"

"Fit enough, I reckon. Keepin' my hinder outta trouble as much as possible." She felt a sudden giddy happiness that not everyone she knew had been strung up or shot by the Stranglers. Dirty-Nosed Dave Merritt and Lew Parker were both old hands on the frontier, men Rose had known for years. "It looks like you're doing the same," she added.

"Sometimes a fella needs to just set a spell," Lew confided. "Figures I'd pick a town like Junction. The Yellowstone must've washed away another thirty feet of bank this spring."

"At least you're alive." Rose lowered her voice confidentially. "I heard about Wiley and Shorty and them." She gave Dirty-Nosed Dave a quick glance. "I reckon ol' Davey here must've hid out. I'd heard they got him, too."

"What are you talking about?" Lew asked, puzzled.

"The Stranglers. Ain't you heard?"

"I guess not, though I know for a fact Wiley and Shorty ain't been hung. Not unless it was within the last hour. I saw both of them this afternoon, shooting tin cans down by the river."

Rose licked her lips. "Shorty Tibbs?" she repeated hesitantly. "You saw Shorty, just today?"

"Sure. Him and Wiley have been hanging out at Levi Wilson's digs for a couple of weeks now, playing poker. You know Levi, don't you?"

"Levi! He ain't been hung, either?" She felt thoroughly confused now.

Frowning, Lew said: "Who have you been talking to?"

"Ben Bradley, that freighter who runs an independent line outta Miles City."

"That old liar!" Lew laughed, but then quickly sobered. "You had me going, Rose. I'd heard there'd been some more hangings recently, but nobody seems to know any of the particulars. But Bradley . . . hell, that ol' boy couldn't get a story straight if it was written down for him on a piece of paper."

Rose hooked her elbows on the bar. "That dang' windbag. I been worried half sick the last couple days. About wore Albert to a frazzle gettin' up here from Sheridan. I don't know why. I reckon I had some fool notion of havin' to bury you-all." She looked at Lew, expecting a chuckle. Instead she saw an unexpected warmth. "Now, don't go gettin' doe-eyed on me," she warned. "I wasn't gonna plant you deep, just enough to keep the smell down."

"But you still would've done it. I can see you now, riding up and down the Yellowstone Valley with a shovel and a bunch of crosses strapped to the back of that old roan horse of yours. You're a good woman, Rose, and if I wasn't so fiddle-footed . . ." Looking suddenly embarrassed, he pushed away from the bar. "What'll you have?" he asked gruffly. "It's on the house, so pick something expensive."

"Lew, I'm too danged bushed to want a drink, even a free one. Where at's Levi got his digs? Maybe I'll mosey over and say howdy to the boys before I find a place to throw my bedroll."

"Levi's got a tent down by the river, just up the bank from where his cabin used to sit, before it got washed away, but if they don't have room, come back here. I'll find you a bed, with a mattress and pillow if you want one."

"Thanks, Lew, I'll keep that in mind." She looked at Dirty-Nosed Dave, standing as he had when she first walked in, oblivious to the world. "Good bye, Dave," she said.

"Yeah, g'bye, Dave," Dirty-Nosed replied, jerking his head around in a startled fashion.

"Dang," Rose murmured. "That boy is *drunk!*"

Chapter Seventeen

Levi Wilson's big wall tent was set up between a narrow coulée on one side and a cluster of small wagons and a blacksmith shop on the other. There was a corral behind the tent, the rushing sound of the river just beyond it. Lanterns from within silhouetted the shapes of several men sitting at a table in the middle of the tent, and at least two more standing toward its rear.

Rose paused on the street to listen to the rumble of conversation. She recognized Wiley's snappy Irish brogue first, followed by Shorty's even-toned reply. Had she been capable of real tears, she likely would have sat down in the middle of the street and bawled her eyes out. Instead she had to content herself with a sniff and a determined tug at her cartridge belt. Dropping Albert's reins over the footboard of a wheelless buggy, she walked up to the tent. She searched for something solid to knock on, but Levi heard the jingle of her new spurs, and yelled: "Come on in, god dammit! There ain't no doorman."

Rose ducked through the flaps and stopped. Wiley and Shorty were playing cards at a table with two other men; Levi stood at a makeshift bar at the back of the tent with another. Looking up, Levi's face turned red as a brick. "Oh, hell,

Rose, I'm sorry. I wouldn't've used such rough language if I'd've known it was you."

"It ain't no matter, Levi," she replied, "though I appreciate the sentiment." She was staring at Wiley, who was facing the door with a deck of cards frozen in his hands.

"Well I'll be go to hell," Wiley said.

"Likely you will," Rose agreed. She let her gaze drift across the table. "How, Shorty?"

Shorty didn't reply. Slapping his cards to the table, he got up from the empty keg he'd been using as a chair and walked over to the bar. "Gimme a whiskey, Levi."

Wiley chuckled. "Hurry up with that drink, Levi. Ol' Shorty looks like he's about to apoplexy."

"He does for a fact," Levi said, fetching a bottle from beneath the bar. He arched a brow questioningly to Rose. "A little hair of the dog?"

"No thanks," she said. "I ain't been bit." She came into the tent, casting a furtive glance toward the other three men; although they had the look of hunters, she didn't recognize them. To Wilson, she said: "I didn't know you was runnin' a saloon, Levi."

"I ain't. If I was, I'd have to buy a license, and I can't abide that kind of government meddling." He recorked the bottle and put it away. "That'll be two bits," he told Shorty.

"What are ye doin' in these parts, darlin'?" Wiley asked, resuming his deal. "Did Alice kick ye out? I heard ye'd turned hound dog on her, sleepin' on the front porch and scratching fleas all day."

"Shut up, Wiley," Rose and Shorty said at the same time.

Laughing delightedly, Wiley turned up a card for the man on his left. "Seven and a king showin'. Nothing there that worries me. Shorty, are ye in?"

"I'm folded," Shorty replied. He looked at Rose. "I didn't expect to see you here. Can I buy you a drink?"

The offer caught her unprepared, but she shrugged and walked over to the bar. "I reckon I'll have a beer, after all, Levi." She started to dig for the buckskin poke that had once belonged to Shorty, but he tossed a 50¢ piece on the bar before she could find it.

"My treat," he said.

"I can pay," she said stiffly.

"Watch ye fingers, Shorty," Wiley said. "She's liable to bite off a couple, ye ain't careful."

"Come on, Collins," one of the hunters grumbled. He was heavy-set and weathered, and had a knobby briarwood pipe canted sideways from the black tangle of his beard. "Either play cards or go palaver with your friends."

"Have a care there, friend Simons," Wiley replied recklessly. "I be a happy-go-lucky sort, but I'll take no guff from a lousy wolfer."

Simons's face darkened above his beard. "Either play cards or quit the game, else I'll pop that damn' mick head of yours like it was a boil."

Silence fell over the makeshift saloon. Wiley carefully set the deck of cards aside, then slid his hands back until just the fingers rested on the edge of the table. "All right, Simons, come pop my mick head."

A change came over the hunter's face. Taking the pipe from his mouth, he slowly leaned back. "I came here to play poker, not fight."

"Are ye backin' off?"

Simons's lips thinned inside the shaggy mat of his beard. For a full minute he sat rigidly, glaring across the table at Wiley. Then he cursed and pushed to his feet, kicking away his stool. "Come on, Jake," he said to the man at the bar. "Let's go find a place that caters to a better class of customer." He stalked from the tent, and, after a moment's hesitation, Jake shrugged and followed.

"Well, 'twas nice of the man to leave his share of the pot," Wiley observed, though keeping his voice low, and his head cocked to listen to the sounds from outside.

"Simons won't try anything underhanded," Levi said. "I've known him a spell. He's a good enough sort."

"A coward, though, eh?" Wiley said.

"Look at it how you'd like, but I'd ride the river with him." A go-to-hell smile crossed the bartender's face. "I'd rather partner with a man with brains enough to walk away from a fight than some dumb Irishman always on the prod to start one."

"The hell with him," Wiley said, "and you, too, Levi." He glanced at the man on his right. "And ye, Mace?"

"I reckon I'll call it a night," the lanky hunter replied. He gathered his money, then exited the tent.

"You're hard on business, Collins," Levi said darkly.

"Aw, to hell with all them soreheads." He came over to the bar. "Give me a whiskey and quit complainin'."

While Levi poured, Wiley turned to Rose. "By damn, ye're lookin' good, Rosie. Pretty as a newborn colt."

"My heart's all a-flutter," she replied acidly.

"Sassy as ever, too! Damn if it doesn't do me heart good to see ye again."

"I wasn't sure you'd care. I noticed neither one of you are big on good byes."

Wiley laughed, and sheepishly, Shorty said: "Didn't Eben tell you why I cut my pin?"

"Yeah, he told me. I reckon one excuse is as good as another when you're in a hurry."

"By damn, what happened up there on the Pipestem after I left last winter?" Wiley asked. "You two're railin' at one another like an old married couple."

Rose and Shorty ignored him, and for a couple of minutes the four of them drank in silence, even though Wiley continued to grin into his glass as if enjoying a private joke. When a pistol shot cracked flatly across the town from somewhere down the street, all four flinched and reached for a weapon.

"God damn' nobs," Levi muttered, meaning the Eastern ranchers and their hired guns. He leaned a double-barreled shotgun back under the bar. "They've got us all jumpy as hens in a thunderstorm."

"I wonder where Davey is?" Shorty said thoughtfully.

"Dirty-Nosed Dave?" Rose asked.

"You saw him?"

"At Hannahman's."

"What were ye doing in a dive like that?" Wiley asked.

"I was lookin' for you. Figured it'd be quicker to start low and work up, rather than the other way around."

Levi guffawed, but Wiley cold-shouldered him. "Was he still on his hind feet? Dirty-Nosed Dave, I mean."

"He was right well-lubricated, but still standin'."

"You boys ought to get him out of town before he drinks himself into a grave," Levi opined.

"The hell with him," Wiley said, although a trifle uncertainly, Rose thought.

"It wouldn't be to our advantage if he started talking to the wrong people," Shorty pointed out.

"Maybe," Wiley replied, "but I'll be damned if I'll run after 'im like he was some kid in a soiled diaper. A man can't hold his liquor's got no business drinkin'." He glanced at Rose and his cat-ate-the-canary grin returned, full-blown. "Are ye figurin' to ride with us again, darlin'?"

She hesitated, glancing at Shorty.

"We've got enough hands," Shorty said brusquely. "We don't need another."

"We didn't need another last fall, either, but she worked out."

"Things were different then," Shorty countered. "She needed a stake."

"I'm needin' a stake now, too," Rose said to Wiley.

"Not this kind of stake," Shorty replied. He looked at his old trail pard. "She ain't coming, Wiley."

That was the wrong position to take with Wiley Collins. Even Rose knew that. "What was it ye told Joe Bean last year, Shorty? That our Rosie here be a growed-up gal, capable of makin' her own decisions?" His smile faded. "I say if she wants to come, she comes. How about it, hon? Ye want to ride with ye old partners ag'in?"

"What'd you have in mind?"

Wiley glanced at Levi.

"Aw, hell," the bartender said in disgust. "Go ahead and talk to her. I gotta see a man about a horse, anyway." He came out from behind the bar. "Keep an eye on things for me, will you? And stay out of the liquor unless you pay for it."

"If she comes, you'll pay her wages out of your share," Shorty said to Wiley, when Levi had left.

"Naw, if she comes, she'll get an equal share,

same as the rest of us. 'Tis only fair. What do ye say, Rose? Ye want to help us drive some horses up to Canada?"

"They'd be horses lacking a bill of sale, I reckon?"

"Well, they might have one somewheres, but we won't be carryin' any."

"Who else is in on this?"

"Me 'n' Shorty and Dirty-Nosed Dave, if he can sober up long enough to saddle his horse. A couple others waitin' down south. There'll be six of us altogether, if ye throw in."

Meeting Shorty's hard stare, Rose said: "All right, but only under one condition."

"What's that?" Wiley asked warily.

"I don't cook."

Wiley paused with his mouth slightly agape, then he laughed and said: "Why, darlin', I knew that the first time I ate a meal at ye house."

They left Junction City five days later, calculating that by now most of the roundups would be completed, the ranges less crowded as crews moved back to headquarters to regroup. They crossed the Yellowstone under cover of darkness and made their way south in easy stages. Rose took charge of a pack horse carrying supplies to make their trip more comfortable—tinware, a coffee pot, extra blankets, and enough food to last them to Mexico, if they got turned around.

Bringing up the rear was Dirty-Nosed Dave

Merritt, riding a scrawny buckskin that would have looked better proportioned under a ten-year-old boy. Not that Rose would have advocated such a swap, for the runty mustang had a heart as black as a pirate's. The first time she approached it, the buckskin tried to take a bite out of her arm; the second time, its rear hoofs had punched the air next to her left hip like an iron-shod battering ram. After that, she steered clear of the horse unless she was equipped with a club of adequate heft.

What made the relationship between Dave and his mount so irksome to Rose was that, in the five days since her arrival in Junction City, she hadn't seen him fully sober once. That he could even find the horse in a crowd of three amazed her; that he could saddle it, then climb onto its back without being mauled to death left her nearly sputtering with indignation.

Dave remained drunk all that first night of travel, even falling off his horse a couple of times. By dawn, Wiley was so incensed by the delays that he busted all of Dave's bottles on rocks. Sitting cross-legged under the buckskin's fight-scarred muzzle, Dirty-Nosed Dave stared owlishly at the broken shards of glass. "That ain't good," he said foolishly.

"What ain't good is wastin' such sweet nectar because some saddle tramp can't control his urges," Wiley snarled.

They didn't move out again until after sunset,

when Shorty guided them south along the foothills of the Bighorn Mountains. Two nights later, just before daybreak, they spotted the lights of Sheridan twinkling in the valley below. This time Wiley didn't call a halt at dawn. He had a destination in mind, and Rose figured it had to be close for him to risk traveling after sunup.

Several hours later they came to a ranch about twenty miles south of Goose Creek, a ramshackle collection of sod-roofed log buildings and crooked-pole corrals, located within a grove of towering cottonwood trees. Several dogs set up a clamorous barking as they jogged into the yard. At the cabin's door a naked child with hair the color of old straw watched indifferently as they dismounted at the corral. The skinned carcass of a beef hung from a limb beside the house, its meat glazed by the wind. Trash—the busted-out seat of a cane-bottomed chair, rusting tin cans, rotting vegetables scraps—was heaped in a pile beneath the window on the near side of the cabin; a gnawed leg bone, probably from the same cow whose carcass hung in the shade of the cottonwood, lay in the front yard where one of the dogs had dragged it. Behind the cabin, beyond the garden patch, and nearly hidden by tall spring weeds, sat a weathered privy, its sole link to the rest of the ranch a narrow path tramped to hardpan.

Rose had seen some fancy spreads since the influx of the big cattle outfits to the Yellowstone Basin—two-story frame houses with slate-shingled roofs, covered verandahs, and tiny round cupolas; sprawling complexes of corrals, runways, and breaking pens; gaily painted barns and stables capped with fancy weathervanes. There were even a few well-maintained polo fields—that sport of European royalty having caught on locally, chiefly through the influence of foreign investors. But for the most part what she saw before her now was the norm, and in many ways the true backbone of a cattle kingdom that stretched all the way from south Texas to the Milk River country of northern Montana.

On the whole they were a dirt-poor and seedy lot—under-educated, narrow-minded, suspicious of strangers even as they were hospitable to a fault, zealously cautious of every hard-earned nickel. They were a hang-and-rattle kind of people, tough as tom turkeys. They had to be, because without their bull-headedness, their prejudices, their abrasive arrogance, they never would've lasted, never would have secured that first perilous foothold in an uncompromising wilderness. They were the ones who forged the way for the softer elements that always followed. *Foundation people,* Rose thought, loosening Albert's cinch. As she herself had been, before taking up the aimless ways of a vagabond.

A woman appeared at the cabin's door, young and pretty in a shy, work-gaunt sort of way. Her long, blonde hair was pulled back in a loose ponytail, and bare toes peeked out from under the hem of her faded cotton dress. A taut round belly disclosed the early stages of pregnancy.

"Della, me darlin'!" Wiley bellowed while still some distance away. "Ye be as lovely as ever."

A faint look of pleasure crossed the woman's face, but she lowered her eyes anyway, as if embarrassed. Her gaze fell on the naked child, and she said: "You, Chad, get in the house."

"Is Fred about?" Wiley called.

"He's acrost the crick yonder," Della replied, "but likely he heard the dogs barkin'. I expect he'll be along directly."

"And Jeremy?" Wiley asked—cautiously, Rose thought.

"He's with Fred." Della's eyes were on her child. "Chad, come here!"

The boy looked up but made no effort to comply. From the scrub across the creek a covey of sage grouse exploded skyward. Minutes later a husky young man on a gray horse emerged from the brush, followed by a second man on a flaxen-maned sorrel. Something about the second man caught Rose's attention, but it wasn't until he was splashing his horse across the shallow creek that she grunted as if sucker-punched. Hearing her, Shorty edged over with an apologetic look.

"Hell, Rose," he said, "I wish I'd have said something, given you some warning."

"That's all right," she replied. "I should've remembered. Sure . . . Jeremy, Della, Jimmy. But that was so long ago. Shoot, Della was just a kid when her folks left the Gallatin." She watched as Jeremy Frakes drew up in the yard, the resemblance between him and his brother Jimmy unmistakable. Della, too, bore a similar visage—heavy brows, a small straight mouth, sharp cheek bones.

"I expected you here a week ago," Jeremy said to Wiley. "Where the hell have you been?"

Laughing at the younger man's brashness, Wiley said: "Whoa, young buck, afore ye find yeself eatin' dirt." Jeremy's face reddened, but Wiley had already turned to the stocky young man on the gray. He walked over, holding out his hand. "Howdy, Baylor."

"How do, Wiley."

"Tolerable, by damn, tolerable." He stepped back. "I brung ye some stuff I was hopin' ye'd accept without arguin'."

"I ain't looking for charity. I told you that last time."

"No one said anything about charity. It's just some vittles and such I thought ye woman and kid might enjoy while ye was gone. Hell, we'll dig into some of it tonight, if it'll make ye feel any better."

"Well," Fred said uncertainly, "maybe we could leave a little behind, as long as it won't be needed on the trail, and as long as you let me pay for it out of my share of the horses."

Jeremy suddenly forced his mount between Wiley and Fred. He was looking at Rose, struggling with his memory. "Who are these people?" he demanded.

"Why, that there's Dirty-Nosed Dave Merritt," Wiley said by way of introduction. "And the lady is none other than Rose Edwards. *The* Rose Edwards, who stood up to John Stroudmire in a Miles City saloon not a month ago." Wiley smiled cockily. "Ye've heard of Stroudmire, ain't ye, boy?"

"I've heard of Rose Edwards," Jeremy returned flatly.

Rose saw Della standing in the cabin's door with her hand over her mouth. It was a gesture she'd seen Indian women use when startled, covering their mouths to prevent their spirit from escaping. It made her feel ill at ease to know what Jeremy and Della must be thinking, what lies of their father they must have overheard. She supposed they also blamed her for their mother's death, as Jimmy had.

It didn't surprise Rose that Wiley had heard of her encounter with Stroudmire, even though neither he nor Shorty had mentioned it. Both Lew Parker and Levi Wilson had questioned her about it at length, however, and it was Lew who'd filled her in about Stroudmire.

It turned out the gunman was fairly well-known in the mining camps of Idaho, where he was considered a deadly pistol shot and no man to trifle with. Stroudmire favored a pair of .45-caliber Merwin Hulbert revolvers, which they'd both agreed spoke highly of his taste in firearms. Rose considered the Merwin Hulbert to be one of the finest pistols on the frontier, easily the equal of Smith & Wesson or Colonel Colt's popular six-shooters.

It was Lew's contention that the ranchers had upped the ante considerably by hiring Stroudmire and Theo Haus—Haus having created something of a shooter's reputation down in the Pecos River country of New Mexico a few years earlier. Although the consensus was that Joe Bean was still officially in command of the loosely con-federated body of Regulators—and no one outside of a select few seemed to know exactly how large a body of men that was—Lew reckoned it was only a matter of time before he was dethroned.

"Joe's bit off more than he can chew," Lew had confided to Rose on her second day in Junction City. "Or maybe someone *fed* him more than he can chew. Joe ain't fool enough to hire men like Stroudmire and Haus without someone forcing them on him."

Rose was inclined to agree, in part because she trusted Lew's opinion.

Rose had been impressed with Lew the first time she allowed him and his on-again, off-again hunting partner, Gene Sidwell, to bunk in her small barn one rainy night several years ago. Although Lew wasn't a horse thief, and was, as far as Rose knew, as honest a man as any the territory had ever produced, he understood the idio-syncrasies that made the Yellowstone Basin tick—including its shadier aspects. That he'd ridden the

Outlaw Trail a time or two meant little to Rose, for it was common knowledge that not everyone who rode the Trail was a bona-fide desperado.

"You got a problem riding with a woman?" Shorty asked, bringing Rose back to Wyoming.

"I got a problem riding with her," Jeremy Frakes replied. He was glaring hard at Shorty, an expression Rose remembered well from his brother Jimmy.

"Rose rides with us," Wiley said flatly. "I don't give a damn what you do. I've ridden me butt into the ground settin' up this deal. The money's waitin' for us in Canada. All we have to do is run the horses up there and collect it."

"We don't need any of you," Jeremy flared. "Me and Fred'll do it alone, and Miser'll help."

Miser. The name jogged Rose's memory, but it took Wiley's reply to put a face to it.

"Miser ain't givin' up no cushy job slingin' beans to go run the Owlhoot with a pup like you," Wiley said.

That was when Rose remembered old man Frakes's cook, and his words as she'd started to rein away from the chuck wagon. *I'm Miser,* he'd said, as if the name might mean something to her. Suddenly it did. As one of the roundup cooks, Miser was in a position to know the latest plans for the spring gather—what valleys would soon be populated with working cowboys, what ranges they wouldn't get to until later. He would know about such things as the winter cavvy, too—those

245

horses that had recently been turned loose for the summer while the cowboys used their summer string to work the calf roundup. And of course Jeremy would know Miser, and how to approach him without the old man catching on. It was even possible Miser had known who she was; it would explain his boldness in introducing himself that day.

But Rose knew there was more here than met the eye. It took deep feelings to turn a man against his own kin, to dredge up the kind of anger young Jeremy was demonstrating. Recalling the elder Frakes and his new hat, string tie, and sturdy range clothes—all marks of a successful rancher— Rose was struck by the sharp contrast with the scene before her now, his own children and grandchildren living such a hard-scrabble life.

It was the stocky man on the gray who salvaged the deal. Dismounting, he stepped between Wiley and Jeremy. Turning to his brother-in-law, he said: "I vote we go with Wiley's plan, Jer. He's done this before and we haven't. I'd like to have his help."

"He don't know everything," Jeremy replied, giving Wiley a withering look.

"No, but he knows more about it than I do. All I want is to get those horses to Canada and get back home without being seen. With a little luck, nobody'll even know we're gone."

"Son-of-a-bitch," Jeremy grated. "All right, but I don't like it."

Fred smiled. "Things'll be fine," he promised. "You'll see."

Wiley and Shorty exchanged wary glances. Then Wiley walked over to Rose. "Ye and Davey take that pack horse over to the house and unload what we won't need. We'll leave most of it here with Della."

"I'd been wonderin' what all them extry supplies was for," Rose said. "You ain't goin' soft-hearted on us, are you, Wiley?"

He shook his head. "I just don't like seein' kids go hungry, but I'll tell ye, Rosie, I'm about ready to skin that Frakes boy out and peg his hide to a wall."

"Aw, Jeremy's just young and ornery," Rose replied as she turned away. "Kind of like you'd be, if you was still young."

"It ain't funny, dammit. I've been puttin' up with that boy's temper all spring, and I've about reached the end of me rope."

Rose's expression abruptly changed. "I expect you'd best hang onto it a while yet," she said soberly. "It's a long way to Canada, and there's liable to be a lot of Regulators betwixt and between."

Chapter Eighteen

They found the horses where Jeremy said they would. Or rather where the cook, Miser, had told Jeremy they would be—about halfway between old man Frakes's spread and the Three-Bar-Clover headquarters to the east. It was the winter cavvy they were lifting, as Rose had suspected. The herd was grazing in a sheltered valley, and in another few weeks would have been too scattered to locate, but, having just been turned loose for the summer, the horses were easy to find, and easier still to gather.

They didn't take the whole herd, but by the time they abandoned the valley at dusk, they'd collected forty-two of old man Frakes's best saddle stock, already toughened to the long trail ahead by the winter of hard work just behind them.

The horse thieves crossed the Tongue River before midnight and were well into the Crow Reservation by dawn. They shadowed the old Bozeman Trail as much as possible, staying out of sight among the piney ridges to the west. The rough country slowed their travel, but Rose appreciated the proximity of the Bighorns. The rugged mountain range was like a haven towering over her left shoulder, a place of easy retreat, should the need arise.

Shorty rode point and gave the orders. Rose hadn't seen Wiley all day, but she knew he was out there somewhere, ranging either ahead or behind among the rolling hills. It was a comfort to know it was Wiley doing the scouting. As much as he often infuriated her, she knew there was no one better at this kind of work.

They broke for a meal and a couple of hours' rest late that afternoon, but were on the move again before the light drained out of the sky. A chill crept over the land as twilight deepened, and Rose slipped into the sack coat she'd purchased in Sheridan. Dawn found them within a mile of the Yellowstone, where Shorty called another halt, then sent Dirty-Nosed Dave ahead to locate Wiley. Those who remained behind gathered below the herd to share a cold breakfast of jerky and raw potatoes, peeled and eaten like apples. Jeremy opted for sleep, curling up nearby with his coat pulled over him like a blanket. Within minutes he was lost to the world.

Listening to the younger man's snores, Shorty shook his head in disgust. "Just like his brother. Jimmy was a hog for shut-eye, too."

"Jimmy wasn't as testy as this one, though," Rose said around a mouthful of spongy potato. Although she felt a certain sympathy for the Frakes boys, knowing their daddy as she did, she wasn't going to let that blind her to their short-comings.

Dirty-Nosed Dave returned within the hour with the news that Wiley was waiting for them a couple of miles above Pompy's Tower, the stubby butte named after the mixed-blood son of Sacajawea, who had accompanied the Lewis and Clark expedition to the Pacific eighty-odd years before. Wiley's plan, according to Dave, was to use the trail past Rose's cabin to cross the Bull Mountains, then follow the Musselshell to the Missouri.

"Wiley figures we'll make the foot of the Bulls

by sundown, if nothing goes wrong," Dirty-Nosed Dave added.

It was midmorning when they climbed through the notch in the bluffs above the Yellowstone and topped out on the rim. As he'd done so many times in the past, Wiley guided the herd off the trail and let it spread out to graze.

Purposefully Rose reined her mount—she was riding a line-back dun today, while Albert ran with the rest of the horses—away from the cavvy and pulled up, facing the cabin. The place looked pretty much as she remembered it. The cabin walls weren't quite as black as they'd been on the day she left, and a top pole on the corral had somehow been knocked down and busted, but the wagon was still in the barn, the harness still hanging from pegs in the wall beside it. Across the creek, too far away to read the brand, were a couple of hundred head of cattle, ranging across the rich buffalo grass. Then her gaze touched the old, lightning-struck pine at the lip of the bluff, and for a moment a blackness fluttered at the edges of her vision, as if she were going to faint. Then Wiley and Shorty reined over beside her, having also spotted the disinterred grave.

"God dammit . . . ," Wiley started, but Rose cut him off.

"No!" she said, her voice sharp but fragile. Gripping the saddle horn with her free hand, she gigged the dun forward. She didn't want to deal with Wiley's outrage or Shorty's sympathy today.

She just wanted to do whatever needed to be done and put it behind her.

But the boys wouldn't be dismissed that easily. Spurring alongside, Shorty said—"Don't, Rose."—and reached for her reins.

Batting his arm away, she said: "I already buried him once. I reckon I can do it again."

"You shouldn't have had to do it the first time. It ain't right that a woman has to lay her own man to rest that way."

"I ain't the first wife to dig a grave for her husband. I doubt I'll be the last."

Having no reply to that, Shorty meekly gave up his objections, although he remained quietly at her side as they rode toward the grave. Wiley also stayed close, following a couple of horse lengths behind.

From a distance, Rose had assumed the site had been dug up by wolves or badgers. It wasn't until she got close that she noticed the shovel and grubbing hoe lying next to the despoiled grave. She dismounted stiffly, her legs like oak as she approached the torn earth. Behind her, Wiley was swearing softly but viciously.

"Who the hell would've done this?" he finished.

Staring at the rusting implements she'd once used in her gardening, Rose suddenly knew the answer. "They was lookin' for the gold."

"What gold?" Shorty asked.

"The gold they thought Muggy stole off them Helena miners."

Her comment created a moment of silence. Then Shorty said: "I'll be damned."

Rose's steps dragged as she approached the grave. It wasn't until she was nearly at its edge that her breathing returned to normal. "Lazy misfits," she said with relief. "Didn't even have enough gumption to go all the way down."

"Likely they got spooked," Wiley said. "It chills my heart just thinkin' about it."

Rose stared into the shallow pit until her vision started to blur, then looked away. Whoever had done this had given up after digging down only a couple of feet, so perhaps Wiley was right. Maybe they had turned yellow-livered at the thought of disturbing a corpse, when all they'd wanted was its gold.

"Get out of here, Rose," Shorty said gently, picking up the shovel. "Me 'n' Wiley'll fill this in."

"You boys don't have to do that. Shoot, there ain't much to throw back, anyway. I could dang' near scrape it in with the side of my boot."

"No, there's more than that," Wiley said, reaching for the grubbing hoe as if grateful for the diversion. "Go on, we'll take care of this."

Rose didn't argue. Turning, she walked down to the cabin. Across the creek, one of the cows lowed plaintively. It galled her that folks could be so careless in letting their stock wander. Although she was tempted to catch her horse and chase them off, she knew it would be a waste of time. It would take most of a day just to round up the cattle she could see from here, and Wiley would never stand for that kind of delay. Besides, left unattended, the cattle would soon drift back. It was the water that attracted them. From a cow's point of view, Rose supposed there wasn't much logic in making the difficult descent down through the bluffs to the Yellowstone when there was such a clear-running creek so close.

Approaching the cabin, Rose saw that the inept grave robbers had been busy here, too. They'd deepened the hole she'd dug last fall to retrieve her cash and legal documents, then burrowed several inches into the other corners. In the barn, the dirt floor was pockmarked in half a dozen places. Judging from the amount of débris in the bottoms of the holes, she estimated they'd been here sometime last autumn, before the ground froze.

The sound of approaching hoofs drew Rose from the barn. She found Shorty sitting his cayuse nearby, the reins to the line-back dun in one hand, the shovel and hoe balanced across his saddle like a pair of skinny rifles.

"We can't tarry, Rose," he said apologetically, "but if you want to stay a while, then catch up, nobody'll mind."

"No, I've seen all I need to see." She put the tools away, then came back to accept the dun's reins. Out on the prairie, Wiley was starting the cavvy northward. Hooking a toe in the stirrup, Rose swung into the Mother Hubbard's cradle.

Shorty's mustache twitched above a smile.

"You'll come back one day," he said. "You've got the makin's of a fine spread here."

"I ain't sure I want to come back," she confessed.

"Aw, you don't mean that. You're just upset about Muggy's grave."

It not being a point she wanted to belabor, Rose let the subject drop. Staring at the grazing cattle, she said: "Who's got hisself an outfit nearby, Shorty? I can't think of a soul who'd own that many cows."

"I can't either, unless it's one of the Musselshell outfits pushing south. You knew it was only a matter of time before someone started grazing the Bull Mountains."

"Maybe," she said thoughtfully, but the question continued to nag at her as she reined away.

They made good time after that, and still had a couple of hours of daylight left when they reached the trail that would take them to the fenced-off box cañon where they'd cooked supper last fall, on Rose's first day riding the Owlhoot. Wiley was all for pushing on while there was still some sunshine left, but the others talked him out of it. It was Dirty-Nosed Dave who made the most persuasive argument, pointing out that they'd covered a lot of territory already, and left a poor trail for anyone to follow in the process.

"We're doin' good, Wiley," Dave said earnestly, "but these bronc's are pure frazzled. We need to hole up, rest 'em a spell, and it ain't likely we're gonna find a better place than this until we reach the Mo'."

"Davey's right," Shorty said. "We've pushed awfully hard so far. It's time we started saving something for the long haul."

"All right," Wiley grumbled, "but we hit the trail again at first light. By God, this ain't no picnic we're on." He rode off along the path that led to the box cañon a couple of hundred yards away, his spine rigid with nervous energy.

Rose and Shorty took the point positions, guiding the weary herd off the main trail toward the cañon. Rose could just make out the top of its rim from here, etched as sharply as a serrated blade against the blue Montana sky. It took only a few minutes to reach the little flat below the jack-leg fence where she'd gathered wood last year; the coulée where they'd eaten supper away off to the east, out of sight.

Rose was still among the junipers, though, when she spied Wiley sitting hunched in his saddle just ahead, as if frozen in place. Muttering— "Here's trouble."—she put her hand on the Smith & Wesson. Coming around the last bushy tree, she drew up suddenly, unable to comprehend what she saw even as she stared at it straight on.

"Sweet Jesus," Shorty rasped, jerking his horse to a stop.

The cavvy, without guidance and still being driven from the rear by Dave, Fred, and Jeremy, started to fan out across the flat, unaware of the dead men that hung before them like grotesque *piñatas*.

Chapter Nineteen

It took a few minutes for Rose to make sense of it all, to understand how someone had rigged a gallows from poles dragged off the fence, binding them with pigging string to create a pair of tripods tied off about ten feet above the ground, then running a crossbar between them.

It seemed like a lackadaisical affair to her, something that would probably blow down in the first strong wind, but it had served its purpose, and not just as a means of execution. Here was notice served to those who would use this trail for nefarious purposes, as plain as any road sign. The Stranglers were back, and they hadn't forgotten how to tie a noose.

The man on the right and the one in the center had died slowly, their faces still showing signs of asphyxiation, but the neck of the man on the left had snapped cleanly and his features were barely disfigured, save for the neck which, with the spinal column severed and the weight of the body pulling at it, had stretched out like a giraffe's, until it was at least two feet long and thin as a man's wrist. His head was cocked at an almost one hundred and twenty-degree angle from the rest of his body and his feet, bent at the ankles, rested loosely on the ground.

For a long, painful moment, no one moved or

spoke. Then Dirty-Nosed Dave said: "Hey, I know that jasper on the right. That's Roy Green . . . used to run horses outta the Little Mo' country."

"Lordy," Rose gasped, averting her gaze just as Fred Baylor tumbled from his saddle and staggered away with the dry heaves.

"Look at the neck on that fella," Jeremy blurted. Of them all, only he seemed unaffected by the ugliness of the setting. "How long do you figure he's been hanging there?"

"You're a dumb little shit," Shorty said tautly.

Dismounting, Rose turned her back on the dead men and breathed deeply. Fred Baylor had finally quit trying to bring up his breakfast. He stood with his hands on his knees, sucking in great gulps of air. His pale, hollow-eyed look made Rose remember Della's expression on the day she'd watched him ride out, the toddler, Chad, perched on her hip, the worn-thin material of her dress drawn tight over the mound of her pregnant stomach. With a cry of outrage, Rose jumped at Fred, whipping off her hat and slashing it across his face.

Fred hollered in surprise and stumbled backward, but Rose followed, beating him about the head and shoulders, crushing the stiff brim of her Stetson against his upraised arms. She slapped at him until her shoulders ached and her arms trembled, driving him back and forth among the junipers while the others watched in slack-jawed astonishment. Then the hat slipped from her fingers and she drew her pistol and fired a single round. With a howl, Fred pitched into the cushioning branches of a juniper.

"Rose!" Wiley roared, leaping from his horse. He grabbed her around the shoulders, but before he could wrench the Smith & Wesson from her grasp, she twisted free and leveled the revolver on him. Wiley jerked to a stop, staring into the muzzle. "Ye'd best start usin' ye noggin, girl, afore I take that shooter away from ye and blister ye butt with it."

"Shut up, Wiley! Just shut up!"

"Tighten ye reins, darlin'."

"Shut up!" she screamed.

"Are ye believin' them tales they be tellin' on ye, Rosie? Is that what's got ye hackles so ruffled?" He backed off a step, straightening and relaxing. "I know ye stood up to Stroudmire there in the Silver Star, and the boys all admire ye for it. But ye got off lucky that night, gal, and shouldn't be countin' on it happenin' again. John Stroudmire's a heller with them pistols, and not given to patience with folks like ye 'n' me."

"What are you talkin' about?" Her gaze darted to Shorty, then came back to Wiley. "What's that got to do with anythin'?" Then her shoulders sagged and the Smith & Wesson's muzzle dipped toward the ground. "Damn you, Wiley Collins," she said without heat.

"Put the pistol up, darlin'," he said gently, and she holstered the Smith &Wesson.

"I'm shot," Fred yelled from beneath the juniper where he'd fallen. Shoving aside several low boughs, he struggled to sit up. One hand was clamped tightly to his thigh, where Rose's bullet had ripped the flesh along the outside of his leg. His face was welted and red where the brim of her hat had battered him, his nose bleeding. Looking at Rose in bewilderment, he said: "What'd you do that for?"

"Because you need to go home," she said wearily. "It don't matter so much about the rest of us, but you need to go home."

"You shot me!"

"You wouldn't've listened, otherwise. This way you ain't got no choice. Besides, you ain't hurt bad, are you?" She started toward him, but Fred scuttled deeper into the protective branches of the juniper.

"Keep her away from me!" he hollered. "She's crazy."

Laughing, Wiley said: "She's makin' damn' fine sense for a crazy woman, if ye ask me. Be quiet now, let her look at ye wound." Turning to the others, he barked: "Davey, Jeremy, go find some soft dirt and scoop out a grave. I reckon the least we can do is give these fellas a decent burial."

Rose kneeled at Fred's side, drawing a clasp knife from her vest pocket. "I'm sorry, Fred," she said.

"Dammit, Rose, we needed that money."

"Think of your kids, dang it. Think of Della."

"I was!"

Steeling herself to the task, Rose carefully sliced the bloody material away from the wound. Despite her efforts to be gentle, sweat was soon rolling down Fred's face, and his leg was extended as rigid as a jockey stick, though twitchy with nerves.

"Hold still," she scolded. "You're jumpin' around like I'm holdin' a brandin' iron to your butt."

"There's a hole in my leg you could lay your finger in," he reminded her through gritted teeth.

"Better a hole in your leg than your wife a widow. Listen, Fred, when I get done here, I want you to make a beeline to Junction City. You know where that is?"

"I've been there."

"Good. Look up a man named Lew Parker who tends the bar at Hannahman's Saloon. Tell him I sent you. He'll see that things is taken care of until you're fit enough to go home. You do that, and I'll make sure you get your share of the money."

He looked at her in puzzlement. "Why are you doing this? I hardly know you."

"I don't know why I'm doin' it," she admitted. "Just do what I say, and don't argue."

He lay back in resignation. "Well, whatever your reason, I owe you. I figure Della will feel the same."

"You just hush about that. Hush and go home, where you belong."

They buried the three men in a common grave, scraped out of the hard earth with a cast-iron skillet. Rose didn't know how they arranged the corpse with the stretched neck, nor did she inquire. She stayed in the junipers with Fred until the bodies were covered, then went over to stand above the grave for a moment of respectful silence. Afterward they started the cavvy north. Nobody wanted to tarry at the box cañon now. Not with the ghosts of hanged men hovering about its entrance.

Mounted awkwardly on his gray, Fred waited until the herd was under way before reining in the opposite direction. Rose and Shorty rode with him for a ways, mostly to see how he'd fare with his wounded limb, but he seemed to manage, his pain numbed by a flat pint bottle of whiskey Shorty had given him from his saddlebags. Dirty-Nosed Dave had eyed the bottle hungrily as it changed hands, but made no claim for a snort.

"I got a bad feeling about this, Shorty," Rose said, after Fred had left them.

"So do I, but there's nothing either one of us can do about it. Come on, it's a long ride over the top, and I doubt if we'll stop again until we reach the Musselshell."

It was just after dawn the next day when Rose spotted the familiar bend of the Musselshell in the distance. An exhausted smile came to her face. She'd lost track of the time they'd spent in the saddle, the days and nights having merged into a solid sheet of sight and sound and smell. They could all use a rest. Even the horses looked nearly dead on their feet.

It was while coming down that last stretch before

the river that Shorty pulled his horse aside and waited for Rose to catch up. "Got a minute?" he asked.

She reined Albert—she'd returned the line-back dun to the cavvy that morning—away from the herd. "Sure, what do you want?"

"I've been thinking about that Indian you shot last fall."

Rose's gaze went to the ridge top where the Indian had stood, taking aim on Jimmy Frakes with a Springfield rifle. "What about him?"

"It's always bothered me that we didn't take a look."

"He was dead," she replied brusquely. "I hit him square."

"I know, I just want a look. Care to come with me?"

After a pause, she shrugged. "All right."

While Wiley and the others took the cavvy on to the river, Shorty and Rose rode to the top of the ridge. Near its crest, Rose urged Albert into the lead, reining up a couple of minutes later above the remains of the only human being she'd ever killed. Staring at the weathered cadaver created a fluttery feeling in the pit of her stomach, but nothing else.

"Looks like you plugged him center," Shorty said, after dismounting. At some point on the ride up he'd shucked his rifle from its scabbard; he carried it with him now as he approached the corpse.

"You ain't likely to need that Winchester," Rose said hollowly. "I doubt he's been playin' 'possum this long."

Shorty gave her a funny look but didn't reply. He used the rifle's barrel to sweep back a gray-green sage bough, exposing more of the corpse to view. It had decomposed considerably over the winter. Tufts of stiff black hair were lodged in the grass nearby, framing the white skull, and rotting leather leggings clung to the thigh and shin bones. A coiled rawhide lariat was draped over the body's shoulder, forming a sort of crossed bandoleer look with a cartridge belt that hung from the opposite shoulder. The Springfield lay nearby, rusted beyond salvation.

"He was looking for horses, all right," Shorty said, pointing out the rawhide rope.

"A lariat Indian," Rose said reverently; it was an old-timers' expression, used to describe an aboriginal horse thief. It had been a sort of rite of passage in the old days for young men to venture out on foot in search of horses to steal.

Stooping, Shorty started to reach for a knife in a beaded sheath propped against the Indian's pelvic bone.

"Uhn-uh," Rose said sharply. "Leave it."

He looked up, scowling.

"Just leave it be, Shorty Tibbs. We ain't lowered ourselves to robbin' the dead yet." He straightened with a piqued look, but, before he could argue his point, Rose added: "Folks has got a sour outlook on redskins, but they weren't bad neighbors, all things considered."

"Folks with sour outlooks toward Indians might be remembering some dead and scalped relative they had to bury," he reminded her.

"I ain't defendin' 'em. I just admired their straightforward way of tryin' to kill all us White Eyes. It was a lot simpler to understand than what I saw yesterday."

"Oh, I thought what we saw yesterday was pretty straightforward," Shorty replied, yet when he turned away, it was without the knife. He went to his horse, then paused with his gaze on the distant bend. "Did you hear something?"

Rose twisted in her saddle for a better look. The cavvy had reached the river and was spreading out to drink, the men drifting upstream to find a clean place to satisfy their own thirsts. Yet even as she watched, Wiley jerked his horse around and started spurring down the front of the herd, trying to turn it back. A puff of gray smoke appeared on the far bank like a giant, frayed cotton boll. Shorty cursed and vaulted onto his horse as the report of the shot echoed up the ridge.

It seemed like everything happened at once then, and too much of it for Rose to keep track of. A ragged volley of gunfire erupted from the far shore, and, in the horseshoe bend, horses screamed and men cursed. Powder smoke seemed to blossom from every direction, until a haze floated over the water like morning mist. Shorty was racing recklessly down the steep slope, riding pell-mell to the aid of his comrades, but Rose held back. Jumping from her saddle, she yanked the Sharps from its scabbard and slid it across the Mother Hubbard's seat. Then she lowered the breech and thumbed a hefty brass cartridge into the chamber. The Sharps was a long-range weapon, and Rose knew she could provide more support from her ridge-top position than she could down below, where the rifle's single-shot capacity and excessive weight would become a liability.

The cavvy was bolting back up the coulée to the south, while the echo of gunfire rattled off the hills. Rose saw Dirty-Nosed Dave's mount bolting with the rest of the herd, its head high and to one side to avoid the trailing reins, its empty stirrups flapping. She saw Jeremy slammed from his saddle to sprawl, unmoving, on the sandy river-bank. In the Musselshell, Wiley's horse had reared, its hoofs churning the river's surface. Still in the saddle, Wiley jerked convulsively under the impact of a slug, then jerked again when a second bullet struck him. His horse, nearly crazed by the thunder of guns, remained on its rear legs, but Wiley lost his grip and tumbled into the current. A second later, another bullet caught his horse in the head and it went over backward, crashing down on top of Wiley's drifting body, pinning it to the bottom of the Musselshell.

All in less time than it took to work up a good spit. Desperately Rose eared back the Sharp's big side-hammer. Sighting on the figure of a man half hidden in a tangle of sun-bleached logs on the far bank, she squeezed the trigger and the rifle bellowed. Powder smoke blew back in her face, and Albert whickered and shuffled. Something small and hard whizzed past Rose's left shoulder as she reloaded. She fired again, but from this distance she couldn't tell what effect her shots were having. Most of the stolen cavvy was already gone; only a couple of animals remained, crippled by stray bullets. In the river, Wiley's horse was floating downstream, but there was no sign of Wiley or of Dirty-Nosed Dave. Jeremy lay on the beach where he'd fallen, and even through the pall of gunsmoke, Rose could see the deep red stain on the white sand around his head. On the far bank, the bushwhackers—there must have been half a dozen of them—were keeping up a steady fusillade, peppering the sky around Rose's hat, tearing up the soft earth at her feet, and making Albert dance nervously.

Rose wasn't sure what she would have done next if not for Shorty. From the corner of her eye she saw him clinging to his saddle at the bottom of the ridge, his horse fighting the bit, wanting to run. Shorty had lost his hat in the struggle, and in the bright sunshine his bald head seemed to gleam like polished marble. With a cry of alarm, Rose swung into her saddle, resheathing her rifle on the fly so that by the time she reached Shorty's side, her hand was free.

"Hang on!" she shouted, pulling the reins from Shorty's unresponsive fingers. A bullet whined past her cheek and she swore and flinched at the quick burn under her right ear. Across the river, several of the ambushers had emerged from cover, concentrating their fire on the two surviving horse thieves.

"Come on, dang it!" she yelled, hammering at Albert's ribs with the sides of her stirrups. They made a mad dash back down the coulée toward the Bulls, the sound of bullets whisking past becoming almost like the sound of the wind itself. It took less than two minutes to round the first deep curve in the coulée, putting them safely, if temporarily, out of the line of fire from the bush-whackers' rifles.

Rose hauled up a few miles into the Bulls, dismounting and scrambling onto a nearby rock, where the winding course of the coulée could be scanned for pursuit. Although she saw nothing to indicate they were being followed, she knew that meant little. Returning to the horses, she quickly mounted and led off into the hills, tugging Shorty's horse along by its reins.

She took them into a maze of broken ridges and winding cañons, and when she judged they'd gone far enough, she stopped and helped Shorty out of the saddle, laying him in the shade of a cutbank. The left side of his shirt was soaked with blood, and a pink froth had collected at the corners of his mouth. Moving aside the torn material of his shirt, she caught her breath. "Dang it, Shorty," she said.

He gave her that old, familiar smile. "I ain't dead yet."

"You need a doctor. I reckon they nicked a lung, at least."

"Busted a rib, too, the way it feels." He put a hand on his side and pressed gently, wincing at the sudden pain. "I've seen worse," he said. "They only shot me once. I recollect a time a Mountie north of the line put four slugs into Sam Matthews, and he wasn't down but a week."

"Shorty, I ain't never knowed nobody to tell so many lies as you." She wiped her eyes with the back of her hand. "I always said that about you, Shorty Tibbs, that you was . . ." Her voice broke and she looked away.

"Rose, we can't stay here. We've got to find a place to hole up. I've been thinking about that cabin on the Pipestem. It ought to be dry by now."

"That's three days from here," she protested. "Maybe four, the shape you're in."

"Naw, we can make it in three. Hell, we could make it in two if we rode all night. Help me on my horse."

"Just settle down," she said, pushing him back. "At least let me wrap that wound, before you bleed out right here."

"You need to keep an eye behind us, too," he said, his voice wheezy.

Pulling her knife, Rose deftly sliced the fabric

away from the wound, taking confidence from the experience she'd gained yesterday with Fred. "I been keepin' my eyes behind us," she said.

"Those boys were good," Shorty murmured, letting his muscles go slack. "They slickered us clean, and Wiley ain't a . . ."—he paused, then went on doggedly—"Wiley wasn't a man to be slickered easily."

Rose ripped the shirt away from the wound and didn't reply. The bullet had entered close to the center of Shorty's chest, breaking one of his ribs and probably striking a lung, although she was relieved that there wasn't any sign of the lung starting to collapse. Still, it frightened her that the bullet hadn't exited anywhere. It meant the slug had hit the rib and probably ricocheted Lord knew where inside his body.

"Bad?" he asked, keeping his eyes closed.

"I reckon you'll live," she replied, although she wasn't sure he believed her.

Smiling, he said: "Well, there's no point looking too far ahead, even on a good day. I've got a spare shirt in my saddlebags. Why don't you wrap it around this, then we'll get on down the trail. If whoever jumped us decides to follow, we'd be in a poor position here." Then his eyes snapped open and he grabbed her forearm, squeezing hard. "If they come, Rose, promise me you'll hightail it outta here without me. I can't . . ."

"You might as well forget that notion. I ain't going nowhere without you."

He gave her arm a shake. "Listen, dammit, if they come, don't you play brave. Just get, and take both horses, too. Sure as hell, I won't need one where I'll be going."

Rose pulled away, then put her hand on his shoulder. "Shorty," she said quietly. "Would you leave me?"

"Rose, I'm a sentimental ol' saddle tramp, and that's a fact, but just because I ain't got the brains God gave a honking goose doesn't mean you have to be stupid, too."

"No, it don't have to mean that, but it does." She went to his horse and found a checked shirt that had only been worn a few times. Returning to his side, she began pulling it apart at the seams. Shorty's eyes were closed again, his slim chest rising and falling shallowly. Brushing impatiently at the tears gathering in the corners of her eyes, Rose set about bandaging his wound.

Chapter Twenty

It was nearly noon on the third day after the ambush when Rose and Shorty exited a break in the hills and spotted the distant, tree-lined course of the Pipestem.

Although it hadn't been a particularly taxing journey—Rose had kept the pace to a walk the entire time—she was feeling as wrung out as a December weed. She figured it was Shorty's dying that was taking such a heavy toll, for she'd discovered, as others had and still others would, that living with an impending death wore on a body more than hard labor.

Halting Albert, she pulled Shorty's horse up beside her. Although Shorty had either been dozing in the saddle or flirting with unconsciousness, he roused himself when Rose remarked that they'd made it. He was wearing her Stetson, with a leather thong knotted under his chin to hold it in place, it being a size too small for his head. She'd loaned him the hat the same day as the ambush, after noticing how quickly his bald pate was starting to burn.

"Where are we?" he asked, narrowing his eyes against the glare of sunlight.

"Somewhere above the cabin, I expect."

Even in the shade of her hat, Rose thought Shorty's complexion looked jaundiced, as if maybe there'd been some liver damage, too. His cheeks were sunken, the flesh under his chin as loose as a turkey's wattle. He looked as if he'd aged twenty years in the last three days, the changes so striking that Rose wondered if she would've recognized him if she hadn't witnessed the transformation herself.

"Not too far above it, though," he said approvingly, judging their location by the mountains to the west. "You did good, Rose."

"If you can hang on a while longer, we'll stop at the creek and rest."

"Naw, let's keep going. I'm looking forward to seeing the cabin again."

It was a theme he'd come back to often since the ambush, as if reaching the cabin had become a goal of sorts. She didn't ask him what it meant. She was afraid she already knew the answer.

She led off gentle and they reached the river half an hour later. There was immediate relief from the sun when they rode in among the trees, causing her to take notice of how hot the days were becoming. Summer was upon them now, spring but a memory; soon the green grasses would turn to brown, and the creeks and water holes would begin to shrink.

Rose led them downstream at a walk, glancing back often. She wouldn't have been surprised at any point to see Shorty sitting there dead, but he clung as stubbornly to life as he did his saddle horn, and was still hanging on several hours later when they came to the valley above the cabin where Manuel Obreto had wintered his sheep.

The valley was empty, as Rose had expected. The lambing and shearing had probably been completed a month ago, the sacked wool carted off to market in Miles City or Billings. By now Manuel would be making his slow journey into the high, verdant meadows of the Big Snowy Mountains, where he would graze his flock among the pines. He wouldn't be back on the plains until October, barring early snows.

Even forecasting a deserted field, Rose couldn't help feeling disappointed. It would have been comforting to have a second opinion on Shorty's condition, not to mention the solace of a friend to see them through the rough days ahead.

It was Shorty who spotted the carcass of a sheep on the prairie side of the trail and pointed it out to Rose. She reined up, scowling. The sheep lay in a shallow gully some yards away and had been dead for at least a month. By itself, a dead sheep didn't warrant much notice, but once her attention had been drawn to the first one, she suddenly found herself looking at thirty or more carcasses scattered over several acres a couple of hundred yards away.

"Let's take a look," Shorty said. "I want to know what killed them."

"It don't matter what killed them," Rose replied. "We gotta get you to that cabin before you fall off your horse."

"I've hung on this long. I can manage another fifteen minutes."

She sighed. "To tell you the truth, I ain't keen on the idea, Shorty. I'm afraid if we go pokin' around out there, we might find Manuel, and I ain't sure I could stand that right now."

"If Manny was out there, we'd see his body. If he's dead, he's probably ahead of us somewhere, hanging from a tree limb like those fellas back at the box cañon."

Although Rose hadn't considered it quite that graphically, she knew Shorty was probably right. Still, she was confident that whatever had killed these sheep hadn't been an element of Nature—

lightning or wolves or a sudden change in weather. No, this was the work of a two-legged predator, the kind that wore pants.

They rode into the sunlight and stopped above the first carcass. A glance told her she'd been right.

"Sons-of-bitches," Shorty said.

Rose kept her own opinion to herself, although it complemented Shorty's nicely. Her gaze was locked on the bullet hole that had shattered the top of the sheep's skull, staining the curly mop of wool with blood.

Shorty was squinting toward the trees they'd just vacated. "Take a gander, Rose. My eyes are so blurry I can't make out a thing."

Her heart gave a twitch at the helplessness in Shorty's words, but she kept her expression neutral as she pulled Albert around. She looked hard but didn't see anything out of the ordinary. With considerable relief, she said: "He ain't there, Shorty."

"Maybe they cut him down after they hung him. Or maybe they just shot him. Let's poke around a little."

"No!" Her voice was raspy with fatigue and anger. "Dammit, Shorty, we're going on to the cabin. I can come back later and look for Manuel."

But Shorty was already shaking his head. "There's no need. Hell, I'm sorry, Rose. This ain't very fair to you, is it?"

"Just don't go frettin' over fair, not with a bullet burnin' a hole in your gut. Come on, we're almost there."

They angled back to the trail, and were soon winding through a stretch of small round hills. Coming out the other side, Rose drew up with a curse. Shorty looked but was unable to make out the smoke rising from the chimney of the cabin, a mile or so away, or the cattle grazing on the land to the east, toward Crooked Creek Cañon.

"What is it?" he asked.

"Company, I reckon."

They crossed the Pipestem at the ford above the cabin, although it was hardly necessary. Even the deepest pools wouldn't have reached their horses' knees. It brought a smile to Rose's face to remember the last time they'd crossed here. Lordy, but the water had been cold—high and wild and flecked with ice. Today it looked as tame as a house cat, comfortable enough to just flop down in butt-naked and close your eyes.

She halted on the left bank, about fifty yards away to study the cabin. The place hadn't changed much. Upon first spying the smoke, she'd feared a settler had moved in, bringing along a wagon-load of kids and chickens and hogs and such. Nesters hadn't entered Shorty's thoughts, however. He was still thinking like a wrangler. Or a horse thief. "Can you see a brand?" he asked.

She eyed a pair of horses in the corral. "Looks like an oblong O with a wing on each side," she said.

"An O with wings? That doesn't ring a bell."

"It don't with me, neither." Lifting her voice, she hailed the cabin. "Hello, anybody to home?"

The door opened and a slim young man carrying a rifle stepped into the yard. He seemed to relax when he saw there were just the two of them, but Rose wished now that she'd taken the precaution of loosening the Smith & Wesson in its holster.

A second man appeared on the stoop. He was hatless and toting a piece of red meat in one hand, a large butcher knife in the other. "Who is it?" he called.

"I got an injured man here. He's needin' a bed."

"Dang it, Rose, tell 'em it's our cabin and to get the hell out," Shorty said.

She looked at him tenderly, knowing she'd miss his feistiness almost as much as his humor and gentle spirit. "I don't reckon it's ours any more than it's theirs," she replied. "Besides, we ain't in a position to be tellin' folks to git."

After a moment's palaver with the man holding the rifle, the man with the knife called: "Come on in! We've got a spare bunk where you can lay your man."

"They think you're my woman," Shorty said out of the side of his mouth. "That's good. Let 'em keep thinking that."

"I lived out here a good many years on my own, Shorty. I don't reckon it matters what they think."

He chuckled, although the effort cost him dearly for pain. "You are the contrariest woman I've ever met, and I lived in Texas before I came up here."

"Yeah, you told me. Come on now, and mind your manners. We're goin' visitin'."

They rode up to the cabin and the man with the rifle quickly set it aside and came over to help when he saw the blood on Shorty's shirt. The one with the knife remained on the stoop, watching. Up close, Rose saw that he was bootless as well as hatless.

"What happened?" the booted man asked.

"He accidently shot himself whilst cleanin' his pistol," Rose replied innocently.

"Looks like he accidentally shot you, too," the man remarked, staring at her neck.

She touched the wound under her right ear self-consciously. The bullet's passage, back above the horseshoe bend of the Musselshell, had burned the flesh deeply enough that it would likely scar, but it hadn't torn the flesh or drawn more than a mild seepage of blood. It was sore, though, the flesh tight and hot, and she'd learned not to twist her neck too far or too fast.

The booted man was watching her, waiting for a reply.

"He'll be needin' to get off his horse today," Rose said in sudden annoyance. She slipped from Albert's back and moved around to help Shorty dismount.

The booted man took the reins of both horses, and when Shorty was clear, he said—"I'll tie 'em to the corral yonder."—and led them away.

Rose looked at the man with the knife, who finally moved aside. She helped Shorty inside, to her old bunk against the south wall. The man with the knife followed, though keeping his distance. "How bad is it?" he asked.

"Bad enough, I reckon." She eased him down on the hard pine slats. "You wouldn't have an extra mattress, would you?" she asked.

"Uhn-uh, just what the ramrod brung us."

Although she gave him a hard look, it was clear he had no intention of giving up his own comfort for a stranger. Not even one with a bullet hole in him.

The booted man returned, keeping his rifle in hand. "You're that woman they call Rose of Yellowstone, ain't you?"

Rose looked up, frowning. "What's that?"

"We heard about you in Billings, before we came up here," the man with the knife said. "They say you faced down John Stroudmire, made him crawl like a baby."

"They say you shot a Mexican named Garcia," added the other, "and threatened to hang Frank Caldwell's scalp from your saddle horn the next time you saw him."

"That's foolish talk," Shorty said from his bunk. Looking at Rose, he added: "Get me a blanket, will you?"

"You cold, Shorty?"

"Yeah, I'm real cold."

Rose looked at the two waddies, but neither man moved; they stood in the middle of the room like a pair of village idiots, while her anger swelled. Then Shorty touched her hand and nodded toward the door. "Go on," he said, smiling. "I gotta ask these gents a couple of questions."

"You ought to save your strength," she replied, although she knew he wouldn't listen.

She went outside and around the cabin to where Albert was tethered to one of the corral posts, his nose poking over the top rail to make acquaintance with the horses inside. Loosening the saddle strings that held her bedroll in place, she slid it over her shoulder, then paused to eye the stock of her Sharps, jutting from its scabbard. She wondered if she ought to take it with her. It wouldn't do her much good out here if a bunch of Regulators showed up, but she was also leery of alarming the two cowpokes inside; they were already acting wall-eyed by the tales they'd heard of her in Billings. Then the sound of gunfire erupted from the cabin and she dropped the bedroll and raced around th corner with the Smith & Wesson drawn. Before she could reach the door, however, the bootless man lurched into view. Rose skidded to a halt, but the man died before she could call for him to stop, crumbling across the stoop without even seeing her.

Light-headed with anxiety, she leaped across the dead man and ducked through the door. The first thing she saw was the booted man lying on the floor next to the table, his rifle on top of his ankles, where it had fallen. There was a small, neat hole in the middle of his forehead, but no blood. His eyes were open, the pupils rolled back until only the whites were visible.

Shorty lay curled on his bunk with his eyes closed, his right arm draped over the edge. His Colt lay on the floor beneath his fingers, its muzzle dribbling smoke. Holstering the Smith & Wesson, Rose hurried to his side.

"Shorty?" she whispered urgently. "Shorty, are you all right?" She stroked his forehead, then leaned forward to plant a kiss just above his brow. His eyelids fluttered but didn't open.

"That was nice," he said, the words barely audible.

She lay her head on his shoulder. "What am I gonna do with you?" she murmured into his ear. "People are gonna quit invitin' us over if you keep behavin' like this."

He chuckled, then choked and coughed up a bloody froth. Biting her lip, Rose gently wiped it away. She was glad he kept his eyes shut; she wouldn't want him to see the anguish on her face. "You hurt yourself, didn't you?"

"He shot me."

"What?" She drew back, startled. "Who shot you?"

"The cook. He had a little belly gun I didn't see. Couldn't have been bigger than a Twenty-Five, but I didn't see it until it was too late."

"Where are you hit?" She kept her hand on his shoulder, afraid to move him until she knew where the wound was.

"It's all right. Hell, it might even . . . even be for the best. I was dying, anyway, and we both know it." Then he changed the subject so abruptly it took her a second to catch up. "I'm sorry, Rose. I'm sorry as hell. Manuel's dead."

"What are you talking about?"

He opened his eyes then, but they had a filmy, faraway look in the murky light. "On the wall there, beside the fireplace."

She glanced over her shoulder, then caught her breath. Tears came to her eyes, but she didn't say anything.

"They killed the dog, too," he explained. "As soon as I saw the hide, I knew they had, but I wanted to . . . to find out what happened to Manuel first."

"Is that why you sent me outside?"

"I didn't want 'em blurting it out in front of you."

"Shorty, Shorty, when are you gonna learn I ain't some fragile porcelain doll that's always needin' protectin'?"

"They shot a bunch of sheep, trying to run him out. When Manny tried to stop them, he . . . caught a bullet. They buried him in the hills, then scattered his sheep for the wolves."

"Are you sure?"

"They said it." He slid his hand along the bunk until it rested on top of her wrist. "There's something else."

"No." She jerked her hand away. "That's all I want to hear right now. I can't . . ."

"It's time," he said, his voice growing weaker. "I wish it wasn't. I feel like I'm running out on you again."

"God dammit, Shorty."

"I told her about us, that widow woman I used to see . . . in Miles. I told her."

Rose swallowed hard, lifting her eyes to the rafters. "What'd you tell her?"

"That I wouldn't . . . be seeing her any more. That I'd met someone else. Then I . . . ran like a frightened colt." There was a rattling in his chest now, growing louder with every breath. He made an effort to clear it, but when he couldn't, he pushed on doggedly. "I guess I ain't . . . ain't much of a romantic . . . but I won't lie about it. I knew I didn't want to see her again, not that way."

"Nellie?"

"Yeah, Nell. She's a good woman. You would've liked her. But it just . . . didn't feel right after . . . last winter. You 'n' me, that felt right. Comfortable, you know? Like an old pair of boots. But instead of telling you that, like I should've, I ran. I wish . . . wish to God . . . I hadn't. I don't know, maybe I had to sort it out . . . in my mind, and Stroudmire and Haus was my excuse. But I was wrong . . . to leave. I know that. Knew it as soon as I heard about you standing up to Stroudmire . . . there in the Silver Star." He smiled. "The funny thing is, it wasn't Stroudmire or Haus I was . . . was running from. It was you who scared hell outta me."

Rose laughed and wiped her eyes. "I've been known to have that effect on men."

"Naw, that ain't true. Everybody likes you. Everybody. Shoot, you think that trail past your cabin . . . is the closest route to anywhere? Or the easiest? It ain't, I can tell you that. But it was always good . . . to swing past your place and see the look on your face when we rode up. It was worth a couple of extra days in the saddle . . . just to see that smile."

He fell silent then, closing his eyes. It took Rose a moment to realize he'd never open them again.

Five days later she rode across the Tongue River bridge into Miles City. Avoiding the main part of town, she followed a riverside path to Third Street to approach Alice's parlor house from the rear. She was still a couple of blocks away when she spotted several women behind the building. As she approached, she recognized Callie and Nora among them. They were hanging bed sheets on a clothesline, the squares of dingy cotton rippling gently in the breeze. It was auburn-haired Jessie who spied Rose first, but they all stopped to look.

Rose reined up a few yards away, and for a while no one spoke or moved. Rose figured she must have looked a sight—dirty, disheveled, probably smelling more like a horse than a human being. Her clothes, which had been new only a few weeks before, had taken a beating on the trail, and the once-flat brim of her hat hadn't been the same since the thrashing she'd given Fred Baylor. She wore her pistol pulled around where it would be easy to grab, and had kept the Sharps loaded and balanced across her saddlebows ever since leaving the Pipestem. She was loaded for bear, for a fact, but hadn't seen so much as a jack rabbit all the way in.

Nora was the first to move. She came forward in jerky strides, as if the bottoms of her shoes were sticking to the dry grass and bare earth of the back yard. Rose squared her shoulders uncertainly.

"We heard about Wiley, what happened up on the Musselshell," Nora said, stopping beside Albert's shoulder. "The papers are calling it the 'Mussel-shell Massacre,' and rumors have been flying all over about it. They're saying the whole Collins gang was wiped out, including you." Tears came to her eyes, and she looked away. "Dammit, Rose, we thought you were dead."

"Naw, I ain't dead, but I'm god-awful tired, and I've seen so many dead things since I left here I can't hardly stand it no more."

"What do you need?"

"Is that offer of a partnership still open?"

Cautiously Nora asked: "To rebuild your cabin and raise some cattle?"

"Uhn-huh."

Taking a deep breath, she nodded. "Yeah. I've been thinking about that a lot since you left. I believe I'd like to try it, after all."

"So would I," Rose said, booting the Sharps. "So would I."

HOMESTEADER

Chapter Twenty-One

It was the birth of the little bald-faced bull calf in early November that convinced Rose it was time to make the trip into Billings. Nora had been urging her to go for the last six weeks. They needed basics to see them through the winter—flour, salt, sugar, tea, coffee, canned goods, ammunition—plus warm clothing and overboots for both of them. But mostly, with the arrival of the wobbly legged whiteface, they needed a branding iron to mark this new addition as A-Bar-E owned.

They'd settled on the design for the iron only a few weeks before, when it became obvious the birth was nigh. The A stood for Alder, the E for Edwards. It wasn't a complicated brand, and Rose knew it was possible someone else had already registered it, or one similar, with either the Montana Stockgrowers Association or the Yellowstone Basin Cattlemen's Association. To be on the safe side, they'd worked up several variations on the A and E theme, and Rose was confident they'd be able to record one of them.

It was a big step, though, registering their own brand, and a little scary, too, the way things had been changing recently. In all her years on the frontier, Rose had never felt particularly threatened, but she reckoned that would change when word of a new ranch spread across the range. The big outfits would view such a fledgling upstart as the A-Bar-E as an affront to their own way of life, their own concept of world order. That the operation was run by a couple of women would only add to the insult.

Nor would Rose's own reputation help matters. Although she was already on Joe Bean's infamous list of suspected stock thieves, it would be her association with Wiley Collins and Shorty Tibbs that sealed her image among the larger outfits.

Nora thought her worries were exaggerated, and even Rose had to admit they rang with shades of paranoia when spoken aloud. But she also understood that there was more involved here than just who owned a piece of property or controlled a source of water. For the more affluent cattlemen, especially those who still sported foreign citizenship, it was a matter of station and lineage. Those feelings were no doubt being intensified by the massive influx of European immigrants deluging the Eastern seaboard of the United States, then flowing westward by rail, water, and wagon.

That fear of outsiders, or perhaps more correctly, that fear of the lower classes, was something Rose had trouble comprehending, having spent the better part of her pigtail days in the rough-and-tumble mining camps of western Montana, before coming to the buffalo ranges with her pap. In Bannock or Virginia City it hadn't been uncommon at all to hear the ebb and flow of conversation in a dozen different languages, and she'd learned early in life to recognize Shoshone, Portuguese, French, German, Spanish, Norwegian, Salish, Italian, Flathead, Finnish, and Mandarin—men and women working side-by-side for a chance at a better life, free of the thumb of oppression.

But if provincialism was a recent addition to the plains—carted in alongside baby grand pianos and crystal chandeliers—it was hardly difficult to spot, even to an uneducated frontier gal of Rose's caliber.

Halting at the edge of the timber west of the cabin, Rose pushed those darker thoughts aside as she studied the A-Bar-E. A smile tugged gently at her lips. They'd rebuilt the cabin first, using logs snaked out of the forest behind it. It hadn't been easy, but by the time they'd cleared off the ruins of the old cabin and cut down the trees they'd need for the new one, they'd toughened to the task. From time to time travelers along the Outlaw Trail had stopped for a few days to help, but mainly the accomplishments were their own.

The cattle had arrived in August, and were grazing off to the east where the grass was better. Nora had contracted for the herd before leaving Miles City last June, purchasing forty head of shorthorn cows and a good range bull from a Little Missouri outfit that was planning a drive to the mining camps of central Montana later that summer. Nora had met the rep during the Stock-growers Convention in April and broached the idea to him then, but it wasn't until Rose's return after the Musselshell fiasco that she'd concluded the deal via telegraph. They hadn't expected any of the cows to freshen before spring, but the newborn bull calf proved them wrong. Judging from the looks of several other cows, there would soon be more.

Nora had been ecstatic when she saw the little bull for the first time. "That's pure profit," she'd exclaimed. "A one hundred percent return on that cow. By next summer our herd will be twice this size, and by the following year we'll be marketing some of the two-year-olds."

Watching the calf nose its mama's udder, Rose couldn't deny a tentative hopefulness. Still, she'd been around livestock all her life, and knew it could be a risky venture. She recalled the time her pap had bought two new spans of young mules to pull a second hide wagon, only to have all four animals sicken and die within a month. But Nora refused to be brought down by such morbid cautions, and Rose soon quit bringing them up.

In Rose's opinion, Nora's transformation since leaving Alice's was a wonder in itself. As the summer progressed she'd become a different woman. The hard edges had softened and her language had mellowed out until it was nearly salt free. Sometimes Rose would hear her humming or singing quietly to herself, and it seemed she could find delight in the damnedest things—a butterfly, or the trilling of a meadowlark. Not even the morning frost the last few weeks, clinging to the corral poles and the iron rims of the wagon wheels like bristles, had dampened her mood.

She seemed to thrive on the challenge of rebuilding the A-Bar-E, too. Her once seemingly frail physique had turned as sinewy as a catamount's after months of hard labor, and her milk-white skin had darkened to a rich walnut; calluses marked her palms and the first small wrinkles crinkled the flesh around her eyes. These changes might have demoralized another woman, but they seemed only to strengthen Nora, widening the gap between who she was now, and who she'd been six months before. Last June Rose might have fretted about leaving her new partner behind while she went to Billings for supplies, but Nora had been quick to assure her that some time alone would suit her just fine.

"I'm looking forward to it," she'd confided to Rose. "Besides, I'll have the shotgun and my pistol, and I know how to use them."

Rose didn't point out that a shotgun—the more deadly of Nora's two weapons—would be a poor defense against a sore-tempered grizzly bear or marauding Indians. Besides, she had other things on her mind now that the Billings trip was imminent—largest among them being her pap, who she hadn't seen in more than a year.

Daniel Ames lived in Billings, or had the last time Rose was there. He was getting on in years, and wasn't as spry as he used to be. Nor was he as keen-witted, although she attributed that more to drink than age. Still, as an only daughter, she considered it her duty to look in on him from time to time, to make sure the bottle hadn't claimed him completely.

Sighing, she heeled the buckskin toward home, half a mile away.

Dirty-Nosed Dave's scrawny horse had been another little surprise. Rose had discovered the buckskin grazing along the creek one morning in July and recognized it immediately. Almost frantically she'd searched the barn, then the trees along the creek, but Dave was nowhere to be found. Nor was there any indication the buckskin had been ridden recently. Thinking back, Rose recalled that Dave hadn't used the horse at all once they'd started north with old man Frakes's winter cavvy. The buckskin had likely been drifting south ever since the ambush, and, given time, probably would have returned to whatever pasture Dave had stolen it out of. But the tawny gelding had taken a shine to Albert, and showed no inclination to move on.

At first Rose ignored the horse in the hope that it would go away on its own. She didn't relish the prospect of some previous owner showing up to level charges of theft against her or Nora, but, when the gelding was still around a few days later, she decided to let it stay. Had the buckskin been marked in any way, she would have taken it into the trees and shot it, rather than risk being found with stolen property, but since the horse was unbranded, and a runt to boot, she figured it wouldn't pose much of a threat. And she was glad she didn't have to kill it. Death was a part of life that anyone who lived with Nature understood, but Rose had seen enough of it in recent months to last her a good long time.

If the buckskin got along well with Albert and the mules, its attitude toward humans hadn't improved at all. Within the first week Rose had been bitten at and kicked—the latter a glancing blow that had sent her sprawling in the dirt. It was the unprovoked kick that angered her into challenging the buckskin for control. The next morning, before breakfast, she roped the gelding and snubbed it to the strongest corral post she could find. Then she slapped the Mother Hubbard onto the horse's back and tightened the cinch. She handled the struggling bronco quickly and efficiently, taking no guff and showing no fear, and when she threw her leg over the saddle a couple of minutes later, the horse was thoroughly enraged.

It was a hell of a battle, with lots of dust and noise but very little strategy on the buckskin's part. Rose rode him out easily, then swung down and tied him to the post before he could catch his wind. She went inside for a cup of coffee, peering through a crack in the shutters while she drank. The horse continued to fight the rope, the make-shift snubbing post, and its own frenzied wrath, but when she went outside thirty minutes later, it was standing quietly, lathered with sweat, its flanks heaving.

The rest was mostly anticlimactic. The buckskin had already been broken to the saddle; it had just required proof that Rose had the pluck to handle it. Still, she knew she'd never be able to trust the buckskin the way she did Albert.

So they had an extra horse that would take some of the load off of Albert, a pair of mules they'd purchased in Miles City to pull the wagon, and forty head of cattle—forty-one, counting the little bull calf. The cabin was rebuilt better than the original, the corral repaired, and they'd added a lean-to to the side of the barn where they stored their tools and harness.

Logs had been hauled down from the forest for a smokehouse, and firewood was cut and stacked against the north and west walls of the cabin, where it would serve as a windbreak until it was needed for the fireplace or cook stove. They'd hauled in several wagonloads of coal for the stove from an outcropping some miles to the east, then cut a couple of acres of hay that they stacked close to the corral.

They hadn't gotten to everything. They still needed a fence around the haystack to keep the deer and elk at bay, once the deep snows of winter drove them down from the high country, and Rose wanted a door on the barn. Eventually they hoped to add a couple of rooms off the back of the house for separate bedrooms, but that would have to wait, too. Now the season had ended. Four inches of snow had fallen before dawn that morning, and, even though it had melted off before noon, Rose knew it was time to start thinking of the smaller tasks that needed to be done before winter clamped its icy hand over the range.

Riding into the yard, she stripped the saddle and hackamore—the buckskin still refused to take a bit—from the horse and stowed them in the lean-to. Nora had already forked hay into the corral for the stock and topped off the water trough that the cabin's previous owner had carved out of a cotton-wood trunk.

Wafer-thin strips of lamplight were glowing from around the window frame in the cabin, illuminating cracks that would have to be caulked before the temperatures turned bitter, but Rose found the sight comforting at this time of day. Recalling the hundreds of times she'd returned alone to a cold, dark cabin reminded her of the gratitude she felt to have a friend like Nora.

Nora was standing in front of the stove when Rose entered, sliding a cast-iron pan of biscuits from the overhead warmer. The aroma of baking sourdough and simmering meat was like a breath of succulent air.

"Lordy, that smells good," Rose said, sniffing loudly. "I hope you don't ever get tired of cookin'. I reckon we'd starve if we had to go back to eatin' my grub."

"Oh, I doubt if we'd starve," Nora replied blandly.

"We might shoot ourselves after a couple of weeks, though." Setting the biscuits on the table, she added: "I was beginning to think you'd chopped off your foot."

"I lost track of time," Rose admitted. With the snowy weather that morning, she'd opted to hold over a day and girdle trees rather than begin the long trek into Billings under such soggy conditions.

"How many'd you strip?" Nora asked, setting out bowls and spoons.

"Twenty-six." Using a scythe-like tool with a hook on the tip of the blade, Rose had peeled away two-foot-wide strips of bark all the way around the trunks. Without that flesh-like connection to the soil, the tree would soon die, allowing it to be cut down next summer for the cabin's addition. Although deadfall for firewood was plentiful, good straight logs of a suitable diameter for building required more effort.

Rose hung her coat and hat on a peg beside the door, then washed her hands in a pan setting on top of the water barrel. She had to resort to the harsh lye soap they normally reserved for laundry to remove the pine sap. While she was doing that, Nora poured coffee, then set the kettle from the stove in the middle of the table. Taking her seat, Rose pulled the pot close to peek inside. "Stew?"

"Slow elk," Nora replied matter-of-factly.

Rose bent closer, allowing the food's warmth to caress her face. Slow elk was a local term for some-one else's beef, in this case a Flying Egg yearling

Nora had shot and butchered the week before. Although technically rustling, it was another of those largely bygone practices Rose had grown up with, and which the old-timers—the foundation people—mostly understood. Like stealing horses from Indians, always with the full expectation that they could have their own stolen in return at any time.

Reaching for her wooden spoon, Rose said—"I saw a bunch of Egg cows at the edge of the timber, north of where I was workin'."—then almost immediately regretted opening her mouth.

Plopping down opposite her, Nora said: "I've about come to the end of my patience with that outfit. They ought to show more respect for their neighbors."

The Flying Egg was actually registered as the Crooked Bar-O-Bar, the outfit having established itself along the upper Musselshell the preceding summer, even though the first of its cattle had come onto the range two years ago, in '84. Its brand was a short, wavy line on either side of the letter O, but the blacksmith who'd fashioned the branding irons for the spread had failed to create a perfect circle. The result was more of an oval, with the wider side on the bottom, creating the effect on a cow or horse of an egg flanked by a pair of wings.

"Likely they do, if their neighbors is flashy enough," Rose said. There were several large outfits north of the Egg, Granville Stewart's D-S and the N-Double-Bar being two of the better-known spreads. But the A-Bar-E was the only ranch to the Flying Egg's immediate south, and Rose figured a company like the Crooked Bar-O-Bar would hardly credit such a rawhide outfit as theirs as worthy of respect.

The Egg was owned by an Englishman toting the unlikely handle of Howard Archibald Ostermann, who laid claim to being the third son of the Fifth Earl of Brackenridge. His Montana friends called him Howie, and generally over-looked his some-what boorish manners in light of the fine polo ponies he'd brought with him from the East. Polo's popularity was growing by leaps and bounds among Montana's aristocratic set, and it was widely held that the fresh bloodlines Ostermann was introducing to the region could only enhance the sport.

Although Howard Archibald wasn't your typical Montana homesteader, he wasn't all that unusual, either. In the parlance of the times, Howie was a remittance man, a victim of the Old World custom of birthright, where only the eldest son inherited any real title, along with the lion's share of what-ever family fortune might exist. Howard was forced to survive on a meager—by blueblood standards at any rate—stipend that barely covered his purchase of a Montana cattle ranch, plus an occasional vacation to one of the world's more celebrated resorts. He'd wintered in Cannes last year, which gossip had somewhere in France, although Rose had never personally seen a map confirming the location of either Cannes or France.

There were those who pitied the Howard Ostermanns of the world, who saw them as lost youths—albeit sometimes pushing forty or better —forced to wander the continents in search of the respect their older siblings obtained through simple inheritance. Neither Rose nor Nora fell into that company, however.

"We'd be within our rights to start shooting some of his cows," Nora said, prying apart a biscuit.

Rose looked up uneasily. "Well, that'd only aggravate matters, I'm feared."

"This is your land, Rose!"

"It's our land," she corrected. It was a thing they'd agreed to last summer, splitting not only title to the property, but to the cattle and other commodities as well—an equal partnership right down the middle. All that remained was to find an attorney in Billings to make it legal.

"All right . . . our land. They still don't have any right to crowd it with their cattle."

The Flying Egg and the arrogance in which its managers ran the spread was a constant source of irritation to Nora. There wasn't much that could darken her mood quicker than mention of the Egg or Howard Ostermann's name.

Rose tried to avoid both topics when she could, in part because she'd learned it was Egg cowboys Shorty had killed up on the Pipestem last spring, but also because she'd come to depend upon Nora's stalwart good nature to get her through her own rough days following the Musselshell Massacre and Shorty's death. Although Nora's anger toward the Flying Egg paralleled her own in many ways, it was a handful to bear when they both fell into the same sour disposition on the same day.

"I reckon if we started shootin' cattle, they'd just sic the law on us," Rose said finally. "We got to hang and rattle a while, see what happens."

Nora snorted. "You know what's going to happen. It's going to get worse."

"Well, I guess I feel like our hands is tied, is all. If the Egg wants this range, it'll be a tough fight for us. They won't just bull onto it like in the old days. They'll bedevil us until we do something stupid, like shoot a bunch of their cows, then haul out some hundred-dollar lawyer with all his loopholes and twisty words. Next thing you know, we'll be throwed in jail for breathin' Egg air. They won't fight fair, Nora, if it comes to a fight. I'll tell you that for dang' sure."

"But you have the deed."

"Yeah, I got a deed, but I ain't got any money. That's what'll hurt us." She ran her spoon absently around the rim of her bowl. "It's a complicated thing, and all the more so because of that butchered Flyin' Egg beef we got hangin' in back of the barn."

"Rose, there isn't a small outfit in the territory that doesn't lose calves every year to big ranchers who aren't particular about where they slap their brand, especially during the spring roundup. Not to mention being crowded off the better ranges, like Ostermann is trying to do to us. Or stealing our grass the way his cows do every day. Butchering a Flying Egg beef for meat once in a while doesn't complicate anything as far as I'm concerned."

"I been makin' that same argument in my head for a couple years now, but it seems to get muddier the more I study on it."

"Sometimes you have to consider justice over legality. Do that and you'll have a harder time condemning the smaller outfits for what they do take. Especially considering how many of those smaller outfits go belly-up every year, fighting fat wallets and shady lawyers."

Rose sighed. "I ain't ag'in' you on this, Nora. I just figure we need to sit quiet a spell, not draw too much attention to ourselves. If nothin' else, it might give us time to think up some better way we can fight 'em."

"Don't kick up a dust?" Nora asked, her sarcasm impossible to miss.

"More or less, dang it."

"And when Flying Egg cows come onto our land?"

"We chase 'em off, like I did today. I ran 'em back into the Bulls."

"Sooner or later Ostermann will send his men down here to push them back. They'll come armed, too, to make sure they stay. What do we do then?"

Rose looked up, a peculiar hardness coming into her eyes. "Then we'll fight. By God, win, lose, or jail, we'll fight."

Chapter Twenty-Two

Although it was an easy day's ride from the A-Bar-E to Billings by horseback, the trip took considerably longer by wagon. Because the trail that ran up through the gap in the bluffs behind the cabin was too narrow to accommodate a wheeled vehicle, Rose had to drive east almost ten miles before she came to a break in the wall where she could get down to the Yellowstone. There, she picked up the road that followed the river's north bank, making camp about fifteen miles east of town and getting a leisurely start the next morning to arrive about 9:00 a.m.

Billings was about as pretty a little burg as any to dot the Northern Pacific railroad. It sat under the same line of bluffs that ran past Rose's cabin to the east, and was surrounded by good grass and plenty of trees. In its own way the town was a tribute to the same type of shenanigans that had marked the cattlemen's advance onto the plains, and proof, Rose figured, that avarice existed just about every-where.

Billings had been laid out in 1882, a couple of miles above an existing community called Coulson. The citizens of Coulson had naturally assumed the NP would build its depot there, and had marked off plots of land to sell for the expected boom. But the big money they'd set their sights on had gone into the pockets of more enterprising men when the railroad, for purely political reasons, built its depot west of the city. Nowadays there wasn't much left of Coulson—a couple of faltering businesses, a handful of homes, an overgrown cemetery. It seemed to Rose the town shrank a little more each time she passed through.

Wheeling into a Billings alley beside the Jepson & Lane Livery, Rose halted beside the complex of small corrals and holding pens out back and stepped to the ground. She was wearing a warm wool skirt and blouse in concession to the morals of the day, but had retained her sack coat, Stetson, and boots, recognizing a long time ago that while propriety might have its place in society, a sharp wind demanded its own code.

After snapping the tether-weight to the bit ring of the near mule, she stared across the animal's dusty roach at a squalid shack about fifty feet beyond the farthest corral. She wasn't looking forward to this, but she knew that delay wouldn't change the inevitable. Gathering her skirts in one hand and pulling determinedly at the brim of her Stetson with the other, she headed for the shack.

"He ain't there."

Rose jerked to a stop, her hand dropping instinctively to her hip for the reassuring touch of the Smith & Wesson, but it wasn't there, either; it was tucked safely under the wagon's seat next to the Sharps, where she'd placed it that morning before entering town.

A tall black man in a heavy, plaid coat stood at the livery's rear door, chewing on a stem of straw. "Danny Ames ain't there, if that's who you're looking for," he said. "You his daughter?"

Rose nodded, returning to the wagon. "Is he all right?"

"I expect he is, though he'd likely disagree. He's in jail."

Resignation settled over her. "I ain't all that familiar with Billings. Can you direct me there?"

"Why, surely." He stepped into the alleyway and nodded toward the center of town. "Couple of blocks down, is all. You're welcome to leave your rig here, if you'd like."

"I'd be obliged," Rose said. "Do you know my pap?"

"Sure, I know him. Folks call me Skinny Jim. I been friends with Danny a couple years now."

Rose reached under the seat to extract the Smith & Wesson, and Skinny Jim's eyes grew wide.

"Oh, my," he said with a hint of veneration. "Is that the pistol you used to run John Stroudmire out of Miles City?"

"Skinny," Rose said, "you'd do well to discount most of what you've heard about that incident. It weren't that impressive."

"I heard you run Stroudmire out of town like a dirty dog. I'd call that impressive."

"I would, too, if there was a lick of truth to it. Stroudmire didn't run anywhere, and I was the one who left town." She buckled the belt around her waist, then settled the holster on her hip, under her coat. She considered taking the Sharps but decided too much armament might be misconstrued. Jails made her nervous, though—jails and forts and other hubs of civil authority. She'd always gotten the impression they were built for the convenience of others, and not the likes of her.

"What's my pap doin' behind bars?" she asked.

"Poaching."

Rose had been so certain Skinny's reply would include some reference to booze that it took a moment for what he'd said to sink in. "Poachin'! Are you sure?"

"Uhn-huh. They got laws against shooting buffalo nowadays."

"Buffalo!" For a minute she thought surely he'd gone daft. Then, with a sinking sensation in the pit of her stomach, she knew he hadn't. "That old fool!" she exclaimed angrily, starting back up the alley. "Keep an eye on my wagon for me, will you, Skinny?"

"Sure, miss," Skinny Jim promised. "Won't nobody bother it here."

But Rose wasn't fretting about the wagon as she turned toward the center of town. She was thinking of her pap and all the damned fool things he'd done in his life—and those being just the ones she knew about.

With her mind thus occupied, Rose barely noticed the handsome stranger in a sharply-tailored herringbone suit and cream-colored derby until he

305

pushed away from the telephone pole he'd been leaning against to intercept her. Doffing his hat to reveal a thatch of yellow hair as fine as corn silk, the young man said: "Good morning to you, ma'am. I'm Deputy Phillip Allen, of the Billings Police Department. Might you by chance be Martha Jane Cannary, otherwise known as Calamity Jane?"

Rose came to a wary halt. "No, I ain't."

"Then you'd be Rose Edwards, alias Rose of Yellowstone?"

There it was again, that same sobriquet the cowboys up on the Pipestem had tossed at her last summer, just before they killed Shorty. It disturbed her that the appellation kept popping up. Coupled with the outlandish tales she'd already heard about her encounters with Stroudmire and Caldwell, it was adding up to quite a character, and considerably larger than the actual person. Worse, it was putting her on a pedestal she knew she was doomed to topple from.

"I don't like that name," she said curtly. She didn't care much for Deputy Allen, either, having long ago developed a distrust of men who used too much bay rum or dressed too nattily.

"Then I must apologize," the deputy said. "I didn't mean to offend such a lovely lady, nor did I mean to presume you were . . ."

"I'm her," Rose interjected irritably. "I didn't say I wasn't Rose Edwards. I said I don't like that other name . . . Rose of Yellowstone. It sounds dumb."

"Why, I disagree," he replied, flashing a smile. "It's a colorful title. You should wear it with pride."

"You got a reason for whoain' me here in the middle of the street, Deputy? Other than makin' a fuss over my name?"

"I do, if you are indeed Rose Edwards."

"I thought we'd already established that."

"Then Missus Edwards, it's my misfortune to inform you that your father has been incarcerated in the city jail."

Rose's fingers twitched impatiently at the deputy's overblown style.

"Please." He gripped her elbow and attempted to steer her toward a nearby bench. "Won't you sit down?"

Planting her feet, she said: "Deputy, this conversation is wearin' me out, so just for the record . . . and I'm sorry as heck if I'm wrong . . . but I ain't likely to be wooed by someone with enough toilet water in his hair to choke a skunk." She pulled her arm free. "I ain't partial to bein' grabbed uninvited, either. Now, what's the charge against my pap?"

Deputy Allen seemed to lose all his puff in a single heartbeat. In a voice several degrees less amiable than before, he said: "Daniel Ames was arrested for poaching bison in Yellowstone National Park, in violation of federal law. I should add that this isn't his first offense for the crime, in case you're unaware of his recent history."

"Well, he was a buffalo hunter in the old days,"

Rose acknowledged. "I reckon it's in his blood."

"Times have changed, Missus Edwards. The days of wanton slaughter are over. Save for a few head kept on preserves, the buffalo are all but extinct."

"What do you intend to do with him?"

"Your father was apprehended attempting to sell the meat, hides, and heads of three bison to a local butcher. He was arraigned on Thursday last and will stand trial this coming Monday, day after tomorrow. It is to my utmost chagrin that he'll probably be released with little more than a slap on the wrist, since the local courts seem averse to upholding federal jurisprudence. Be that as it may, I'll not lessen my efforts to uphold the law. In co-operation with the United States Marshal's Office, of course. You may wish to inform your father of my will in this matter, Missus Edwards. I fear for his safety if he continues this course."

"Just for my own curiosity, what's your definition of a slap on the wrist?"

"In the last incident, Daniel Ames was found guilty of destruction of federal property, to wit, killing a bison for profit. He was fined fifty dollars and the evidence . . . the robe, a head suitable for mounting, and meat . . . was confiscated by federal authorities and turned over to the local community. If I had my way in the matter, he would have served time in the Deer Lodge penitentiary. I don't consider these trivial infractions."

"If he had his way, he'd probably kick your butt up between your shoulder blades and tie your ankles together above your ears, so it's probably a good thing neither one of you got your own way. Now, how do I go about gettin' my old man outta jail?"

Although he remained stiffly at attention, Deputy Allen kept his temper in check, his reply coolly professional—a feat Rose admired in spite of herself. "Your father's bail has been set at seventy-five dollars," he informed her. "You can pay it at the jail. Is that your intention?"

Rose's intent was suddenly sliding into turmoil. That amount represented almost everything she'd brought with her for supplies, and she knew she could lose it all if her pap jumped bail to avoid his court date, which he was just ornery enough to do. But the thought of letting him languish in a tiny, iron-strapped cell, even for a few days, gnawed at her more. Sighing, she said: "I reckon it is. Let's go bail him out."

Rose waited in the outer office while a jailer in a smart-looking blue uniform disappeared into the bowels of the two-story brick building to fetch her pap. A feeling of dread hammered at her as she fidgeted on a polished hardwood bench. She figured it was the jail that was making her feel so flustered. The last time she'd rescued her father from a cell had been in Bozeman, where he'd staggered out of the back room lashing the air with his raspy curses. His shirt had been half torn from his shoulders from fighting, and a dried urine stain had darkened the front of his trousers. The thought of seeing him again in such wretched condition made her want to bolt, but she forced herself to remain seated, allowing only an occasional twitch of her leg or jerk of a shoulder.

Fearing the worst, she was more than a little dubious when the jailer returned with an elderly, well-behaved male in tow. She had to look twice to be sure it was her pap. His hair, which had once been a stringy salt and pepper, had gone almost completely white in the past year and a half, and he'd grown it long again, in the fashion of an old-time plainsman, combing it back over the collar of a red, double-breasted shirt. His mustache was equally canescent—a great, drooping monster that hid his mouth like a dead trout balanced precariously atop his upper lip.

His face was thin and deeply lined, the cheeks hollowed from missing teeth along either side of his jaw, but he was clean-shaven save for the stubble he'd sprouted behind bars. He wore buckskin trousers and worn but cared-for boots, and carried a broad-brimmed black hat in his left hand; a light-weight buckskin jacket was draped over the same arm, its fringe nearly sweeping the floor. He didn't sparkle. There were grease and blood stains on his clothes from handling the carcasses of dead bison, and the cuffs on his sleeves were fraying, but he looked no worse for wear than any self-respecting buffalo hunter in town for a spree, and nothing at all like the whiskey-soaked bum she'd feared.

Their eyes met across the room and he winked broadly. "Be with you in a bit, Kitten," he said in a voice gone scratchy from too much booze, too many cigarettes. "Gotta get my rifle."

"Sure," Rose said, standing uncertainly. She didn't know what else to say. She felt as if she were meeting an old friend of the family, someone she didn't remember at all, but who could recall even the tiniest details of her own early years— such as that her pap had always called her Kitten when he was in a good mood.

Daniel Ames waited in front of a large oak desk while the jailer went to fetch his rifle. Deputy Allen stood nearby, disapproval stamped across his brow like an official seal. The jailer soon returned with a long gun encased in fringed elk-hide and a cartridge belt that gleamed with heavy brass shells.

"I hope they ain't no damage to this here rifle, sonny," Daniel remarked to Deputy Allen. "They don't make 'em no better'n this."

"If you value that firearm so highly, I'd suggest you quit using it for unlawful activities," Deputy Allen advised.

Daniel snorted, glancing at Rose. "Onlawful, he calls it. 'Course, when a lawdog takes what ain't his'n, they call it confiscation. But for the rest of us, it's on*laaaw*ful."

"It's stealing, Mister Ames," Deputy Allen replied. "And to clarify . . . proceeds from confiscated items go toward the purchase of new equipment for the city."

But Daniel was unswayed. "You expect a hard-workin' citizen to buy a bucket of crap like that? What's the matter with you, boy? Your mama drop you on your head when you was a baby?"

Deputy Allen drew himself up rigidly, his jaw thrust forward like a chunk of granite smothered in bay rum. "These loopholes that release men such as yourself back into society will eventually be closed, Mister Ames. Take my advice and find gainful employment while there's still time." He spun sharply toward Rose. "I'd encourage you to aid your father in that, Missus Edwards, before he ends up in Deer Lodge. As a further word of caution, the open carrying of sidearms is prohibited within city limits. I'd advise you to remove your pistol as soon as practical and either store it somewhere safe or keep it pocketed. I shan't overlook a second infraction." With both opinion and position made clear, Deputy Allen exited the room.

Daniel whistled, clearly impressed. "That was pure for fancy," he said to the jailer. "That boy'll go far with a line like that."

"Deputy Allen was trained in Philadelphia," the jailer replied with a trace of civic pride. "He ain't like the old-time lawmen we used to have."

"Screw Deputy Allen," Daniel retorted cheerfully. He crossed the room to his daughter's side. "Hello, Kitten. You finally come to see your old pappy, did you?"

"Hello, Pap," Rose said hesitantly, reaching out

to give him a light tap on the shoulder. "You're lookin' fit."

"Feel it, too, by damn. I'm huntin' again, did they tell you?"

"Yeah, the deputy told me."

Daniel laughed. "I can imagine what that little pissant said. Thinks they can outlaw huntin', for Christ sake." He shook his head at the audacity of such sentiment. "Come on, girl. All I've had to eat for a week is jailhouse slop. I'll let you fix me a decent meal. You've learned to cook, ain't you?"

"Sure, I can fix somethin'."

Handing her his jacket and cartridge belt, he said—"Here, make yourself useful."—then headed for the door with the rifle canted proudly across his left arm. Lowering her head from habit, Rose hurried after him.

Rose knew the shack behind Jepson & Lane's Livery was a reflection of more hard-pressed times in her father's life, days when booze had dominated his every waking moment. Empty whiskey bottles scattered around what passed for a yard were testimony that he still drank.

Home was nothing more than a squat, flat-roofed hut constructed from cross-ties pilfered from the Northern Pacific reject pile. The sharp smell of creosote assaulted Rose's sinuses as soon as she walked in, and she knew from past experience that if she stayed more than a day or two her skin would break out in hives.

Old newspapers and pages torn from back issues of the *Police Gazette* were tacked to the walls for insulation. The floor was lumpy and thick with dust, not having been swept or sprinkled in months, for even a dirt floor required attention. There was a small coal stove in one corner, a narrow rope-sprung bunk in another, a table and two mismatched chairs. A low cowhide trunk with the hair still on sat at the foot of the bunk. Had she looked inside, she would have found her pap's reloading gear for his rifle—he'd never trusted factory ammunition for hunting purposes—the family Bible, and some personal items of her mother's that he never unwrapped any more. An opening in the back wall that could hardly be called a door allowed access to a small storage area where he kept his saddle and what odds and ends of gear he hadn't hocked to buy liquor.

Nor had his manners improved, Rose was quick to learn. He was still the same old Daniel Ames, more likely to break wind or blow his nose with his fingers than offer a lady assistance with her chair. Yet for all that, she sensed less hopelessness in his outlook, more enthusiasm in his voice. It was the hunting, she thought; it had brought purpose back into his life, given him a renewed strength that, if it couldn't conquer his alcoholism, could at least provide some balance for it.

"Leave the door open," Daniel instructed as he laid his rifle on the table and sank into a chair. He fished a sack of Lone Jack and a little bible of smoking papers from his pocket and began a cigarette. "Get a meal burnin'," he said, without looking up. "I traded breakfast this mornin' for this tobacco. I ain't had shit to eat since supper last night."

Rose laid his jacket and cartridge belt on the bunk, then went to the stove. It hadn't been emptied in a long time. The top was layered with dust, and ash and jagged, rock-like clinkers were piled up in the middle of the firebox. She knew she should haul the old ashes outside before kindling a fresh blaze, otherwise it might be days before the cast-iron stove cooled enough to be cleaned, but she also knew her pap would poorly tolerate such a delay. He wanted his breakfast.

She kindled a fire with wood, then added a few fist-sized chunks of coal she found on the floor beside the stove. When she was satisfied the flame would catch, she brushed her dust-blackened fingers off on a rag. Her pap looked up as she did, and Rose knew he'd been watching from the corner of his eye all along.

"There's some beef in the back room," he said.

She nodded and went to the small opening in the rear wall. Wrinkling her nose, she said: "It smells pretty ripe in there, Pap. Don't you have any beans or rice?"

Daniel looked up, his eyes narrowing. "Yeah, there should be some rice in there. Fix it with the meat."

Rose licked her lips. "I'm thinkin' that meat's gone bad."

"Cut the bad off. What the hell, girl? You gone soft?"

"Naw, I ain't gone soft."

"Then get your ass in there and get me some meat, god dammit."

Resolutely Rose took a deep breath and ducked through the opening. Although it was dark, she had no trouble locating the meat. It hung from an iron hook fastened to a rafter. Taking it down, hook and all, she scuttled backward into the main room, then took what looked like part of a shoulder outside.

The outer rim of meat was flyblown and rotting, soft as mush and stinking to high heaven, but she found enough red stuff closer to the bone to make a meal. She hauled what was bad around back and tossed it onto a pile of manure carted down from the livery; the good stuff she took inside and set on the table.

She fetched water from the livery's well and rice and coffee from the back room, and soon had a hearty meal sizzling. While she cooked supper, her pap stripped the elk-hide cover from his long gun and brought it into the light. It was a nearly new Remington-Hepburn, with an engraved action and checkering on the wrist and forearm—a single-shot, breech-loading hunting rifle, built on the same principle as her Sharps. It had a long, telescopic sight to replace the more familiar iron sights his fading vision had forced him to give up.

Whistling appreciatively, Rose said: "That's a mighty fine-lookin' shooter, Pap."

"Best damn' rifle ever made."

Save for a couple of small dings in the stock, the gun looked spotless, as clean and sharp as a bull elk's bugle during rut, and she said as much. Her father beamed at the compliment, but his expression clouded over when she asked permission to look through the scope.

"I ain't never had a peep through one," she added hastily. "I was just wonderin' what things would look like, is all."

"Is that meat burnin'?" he asked.

"It shouldn't be. I just turned it."

"Turn it again. It's burnin'."

Rose retreated to the stove, properly chastised. Although the meal didn't require it, she turned the meat anyway, then stirred the rice. Meanwhile her pap examined the Remington carefully for any sign of damage incurred while in possession of the Billings police department. Evidently satisfied that it had survived the encounter unharmed, he laid it on top of the elk-hide case, then leaned back to roll another cigarette. His gaze went out through the open door, but Rose knew his thoughts were turning inward, his expression darkening by the minute. Her own mood sank at an equal pace, as if father and daughter were emotionally linked.

Daniel Ames's chameleon-like humor wasn't entirely unexpected. Rose had seen it happen before, brought back after some form of excitement—a binge or a fight or a good hunt—to the realities of his hard-scrabble existence. Although she needed to take care of the mules, she was afraid that if left alone for even a few minutes, her pap's spirits would sink beyond recovery. So while the meal cooked she sat in the chair opposite him and tried to distract him with conversation.

"How'd you get started poachin' buffalo?" she asked.

He gave her a lingering glance, then took the cigarette from his mouth and jetted a stream of smoke toward his lap. "It ain't poachin'," he said finally. "That's what the law calls it, but it ain't." He stirred, warming to the subject. "That there's a national park, right?"

"Yeah, I reckon."

"Reckon, my ass. It's a national park, owned by the people of the United States. Right?"

"All right," she agreed warily.

"So ain't I a citizen of this here country?"

She hesitated, knowing where he was taking this even as she recognized the futility of arguing the principles of public ownership. Her brother Luke had tried to differ with him once, and suffered a broken nose for the effort.

"Yeah," she said in defeat. "I reckon you got as much right to shoot buffalo up there as anyone."

"Damn' right I do." He leaned back in his chair. "There's good money in it, too. I went up there the first time last summer, camp doggin' for a

Bozeman outfitter haulin' a bunch of Eastern dudes up to see the geysers. It was an eye-opener, girl. God, they've got some buff' up there. Saw one bunch that must've numbered sixty head. Biggest herd I've seen since 'Eighty-Two. 'Course, the damn' park ranger won't let you shoot 'em, but he's just one man and that's a big country. I ain't worried about him. The problem is they've got the Army stationed at Mammoth Hot Springs now to keep the hunters out. But I figure if I can dodge them and kill just two or three a year, I'll be sittin' pretty." He laughed, shaking his head. "What'd we used to get for a hide . . . four, five bucks apiece for a good one? Today I can get fifty dollars for every one I haul out, plus another two hundred for mountable heads. All to fancy up some dude's house back in Boston."

Rose's jaw nearly dropped in astonishment.

"It's because it's the *West*," her pap continued. "Ten years ago, most of the peckerwoods east of Saint Louis thought we ought to give this country back to the redskins, but now that it's disappearin', they all want a piece of what it used to be. God damn, if I'd've known this, I'd have saved every damn' robe and head I could lay my hands on. I'd have fifty thousand dollars, easy, and never have to work another day in my life."

"Lordy," Rose said softly. "Think of all them heads we just throwed away."

"That's what I'm sayin'. I could've been rich."

"What about skulls?" Rose asked, recalling the

trip she, Wiley, and Shorty had made last year between Two-Hats's trading post on the Mussel-shell and Miles City. In places, she remembered, the ground had been almost white with the bones of dead buffalo, their black-horned skulls scattered everywhere. But her pap was already shaking his head.

"Done thought of that, but nobody wants 'em. They ain't scarce enough. Hell, they've got 'em piled up along the N.P. tracks higher'n the smokestacks on their locomotives, waitin' to get hauled to some fertilizer plant in Pennsylvania. Naw, skulls are worthless except to the bone pickers, and I ain't a god-damn' bone picker. I'm a hunter."

"But if robes and mounted heads is worth so much today, maybe skulls will be, too, down the road."

"Daughter, you're just plain dumb when it comes to finances. It's the girl in you, I figure. Skulls ain't worth the sweat a man'd break pickin' 'em off the ground. Not to a real hunter."

Rose let the subject drop, but vowed she'd talk to Nora about it when she got home. There were plenty of skulls out east of their place, and it wouldn't take much to gather a wagonload or two to store in their barn, just in case.

"I heard about Muggy's gold," Daniel said out of the blue. "Been hearin' about you, too. They say you're raisin' hell out on the plains."

"Been dodgin' it as much as possible. Don't go believin' them tales they're tellin' about me. Folks are just havin' fun at my expense, is what I think."

"What about Muggy's gold?"

"There weren't no gold that I saw, though there's knuckleheads about that believe there was."

"Maybe folks aren't as easily fooled as you'd like to think," her pap said shrewdly.

Rose bit her lip but held her tongue. She turned to the stove to check on the meat, aware of her father's gaze lingering on her.

"What do you mean, there wasn't any gold?" he asked after a pause.

"Just what I said. Maybe someone else took it and blamed it on Muggy. Or maybe the vigilantes found it and split it amongst themselves. I ain't even sure any more there was any gold. But everybody thinks Muggy had it, and now they think I've got it, which is pretty dang' funny, considerin' I just spent nearly every nickel I had to bail you outta jail."

Her pap's brows wiggled suddenly, like worms touched with hot steel, and Rose immediately grew cautious; her pap's brows were like a barometer that could register a change in mood seconds before it touched any other feature on his face. Over the years, she'd grown adept at reading them.

"Girl, I'd watch that mouth of yours," Daniel said coolly. "I'll slap you silly if you get smart with me."

"I ain't gettin' smart, Pap," Rose said quickly. She kept her back to him, but also kept one eye cast warily over her shoulder. "I didn't mean nothin', other than I ain't got the money folks think I've got."

"I figure you're lyin' about that. I won't put up with lyin' from my own kid."

"I ain't lyin'."

"You do and I'll slap you silly."

She flinched when he surged to his feet, but he only laughed. Sweeping his chair aside with a foot, he headed for the door. Rose dropped her stirring fork and followed him outside. "Where you goin'?"

He tossed what was left of his cigarette to the ground. "I'm gonna find something to drink, if it's any of your damned business. You stay with that meal, make sure it doesn't burn. And clean the place up a little. It looks like a pigsty."

"Don't go. We ain't seen one another in more'n a year."

"Whose fault is that?"

"Pap, please."

A look of fury crossed his face. "You just do what you're told for a change. If you wasn't so bull-headed, I wouldn't have to drink."

Tears sprang to Rose's eyes as her father turned away. "Don't," she called, though keeping her voice low so that Skinny Jim wouldn't hear her beg. "Pap."

But Daniel Ames might as well have been deaf.

Chapter Twenty-Three

Her pap didn't return home that night, nor did Rose expect him to. Still, she kept the meat and rice and coffee warm for as long as she could; if he did show up, he'd expect to be fed.

At dusk she went outside to care for the mules. It angered her that they'd been forced to stand in harness all day just because of her pap's temper, but she'd come to realize a long time ago that Daniel Ames didn't feel the same way toward animals as she did. Horses, mules, oxen, dogs— they were all just tools to him, soulless brutes to be used until worn out, then discarded and replaced. Any regard he'd ever shown had been based on economic factors, since it was usually cheaper to provide superficial care for a beast than purchase a new one.

Rose stabled the mules with Jepson & Lane at four bits a night, letting Skinny Jim take them to a corral where there was fresh water and shelled corn for feed. She left the wagon where it was and piled the harness in back, then returned to the cabin to supper on overcooked meat and rice.

The following morning, with frost clinging to the weeds and the ringing of church bells echoing off the bluffs, Rose began her search. It didn't take long. She was an old hand at this, and knew all the likely places to look, even in a strange city.

She found him, lying drunk in a vacant lot behind the Blue Heifer Saloon, clutching a bottle of sour mash to his stomach that still held an inch or so in the bottom. The smell of booze emanated from his body like the stench of last night's rotting meat.

"God damn you," Rose said gently, staring down at the curled form with a mixture of anger and pity. Kneeling at his side, she jostled his shoulder, wallowing him around until he started to resist. "Pap!" she said sharply. "Come on, dang it, wake up. You're gonna freeze to death, lyin' here."

His lids slid back vacantly and his breath came in quick, shallow puffs on the chilly air, like the chuffing of a locomotive.

"Come on," she said crossly. "Let's get some coffee down your gullet." She gave him another shake. "Get up, dang it."

He tried to speak, but the words were too slurry to follow. Impatiently Rose hauled him half off the ground by his arm, then let him flop back. It would make him mad, she knew, but it would take anger to get him on his feet now.

Soon she had him standing—swaying and cursing—but on his feet. She tried to guide him toward a path that would take them home via the alleys, but he balked and pointed to the gap between the Blue Heifer and the building next to it.

"Naw, let's go this way," Rose said. "It'll be quicker."

"Street," he squawked like a petulant parrot.

Rose didn't fight it. She knew the simplest way

home at this point would be the route he wanted. "But listen," she warned. "It's Sunday out there, and they's church folks about. You mind your manners, hear?"

"Street, damn," he snapped, trying to yank his arm away.

Tightening her grip, Rose said: "All right, but hang onto me so you don't fall down." She pulled his arm across her shoulders, sliding her own around his gaunt waist. Side-by-side, they made their way through the litter-filled lot.

There wasn't as much traffic out front as Rose had feared. A couple of buggies were wheeling toward a frame church at the far end of town, and a cowboy leading a second saddle horse was riding east into the rising sun. There were a few people along the boardwalk, but they were all saloon-keepers and swampers—no one who hadn't seen a drunk stagger home on a Sunday morning before. She was beginning to think they might make it without incident when a man stepped out of a hotel doorway not twenty yards ahead and paused to light a cigar.

Rose jerked to a halt, her breath catching in her throat. She'd left her Smith & Wesson at the shack because of Deputy Allen's admonitions, and knew her pap was unarmed, too. She tried to steer him into the recessed entrance of a closed grocery, but he wouldn't have it. It was their almost comic struggle there on the boardwalk that drew the man's attention. Rose hoped he wouldn't recognize her, that without her pistol and dusty male attire, he wouldn't make the connection, but it was a futile wish.

"Well, well, if it isn't Wiley Collin's little blonde whore." He spared her pap a glance. "Find yourself another customer?"

"Go to hell, Caldwell."

A thin, cold smile twitched at the corners of Frank Caldwell's mouth. "So what brings you to the big city, besides rolling drunks?"

Rose felt her blood rise. Pulling on her pap's arm, she said: "Come on."

But her pap had planted his feet wide on the plank walk and refused to budge. Glaring at the blond gunman, he said, bold as brass: "Who's this stack o' shit?"

"Aw, hell," Rose said under her breath. She knew Caldwell was a dangerous man, and the twin bulges under his long black coat showed plainly what he thought of the city's ordinance on firearms. Tugging desperately, she said: "He ain't no one. Come on, quit fightin' me all the time."

But Daniel had his footing now, and neatly jerked away from her shoulder. He continued to scowl at Caldwell in a way that would have been funny if it hadn't been so provoking.

Caldwell looked unimpressed. To Rose, he said: "Don't tell me you've given up squatting on that place above the Yellowstone and moved to town?"

Rose frowned. "I ain't squattin' there. That land's mine."

Caldwell sauntered over, his smile fading around the cigar jutting from between his lips. "I've been intending to pay you and your little whore friend a visit. You still owe me for those three horses you and Collins stole last year."

"You'd best take that up with Wiley," Rose said.

The smile returned to Caldwell's face. Or a smirk. It was difficult to tell with him. "I doubt I could hold my breath that long," he replied, and Rose knew he was referring to the Musselshell Massacre. But how had he known that Wiley had gone to the bottom of the river, trapped beneath his own horse . . . ?

"Son-of-a-bitch," she breathed. "It was you, wasn't it? Up there on the Musselshell?"

"It could have been anybody, from what I heard," he returned blithely.

But Rose knew she was right. "Why, Caldwell? Because of three lousy horses?"

Taking the cigar from his mouth, he said: "Did you know I've been working for Howard Ostermann since March?"

The chill that had invaded Rose's veins when she first spied him turned suddenly to ice.

"I've been wanting to explain the new property lines to you all summer," he added, "but Mister Ostermann decided he'd do that himself. I suspect he has some further business to discuss with you concerning that land."

"You bastard," she said softly.

"Mister Ostermann is visiting friends in New York City right now, but he's expected back before Christmas. Maybe we can pay you and your little Miles City tramp a call when he returns. Spread around some holiday cheer, as it were." His smirk grew as he returned the cigar to his mouth. "Oh, by the way, I ran into an old *amigo* of yours a few months back. You remember Billy Garcia, don't you?"

"I remember him," she said cautiously.

"Ol' Billy's feeling mighty put-out with you. Seems you shot the top of his ear off that night up at Two-Hats's. He hasn't forgotten."

"He ought to consider himself lucky," Rose replied pointedly. "There were other appendages I could've aimed for."

Caldwell laughed. "Now, that's true, and I'll be sure to tell him the next time I see him. I'm certain he's looking forward to seeing you, too."

"I'll be around."

"Don't be too hasty. Listen to Ostermann's offer. You might decide it's the wiser course. Especially when you consider the alternatives."

"Get outta my way, Caldwell," she said. "I want to go home."

But Caldwell was looking at her pap now. "Hello, Dan'l."

"You leave my little girl alone, Frank," Daniel warned.

Stepping close, Caldwell blew a cloud of cigar smoke into the older man's face, causing him to sway back, blinking. Laughing, Caldwell stepped around him and continued on his way.

Moving to a bench in front of the grocery, Daniel lowered himself to the seat, then eased his legs out straight. He was breathing heavily, as if he'd just run around the block. "So it's true," he said, looking at his daughter. "About you running with Collins and that trash, stealing horses and shooting up the territory like wild Indians?"

"Wiley Collins wasn't trash," Rose replied dully, "and you ought to know better than to listen to saloon gossip."

If she was worried that her words might upset him, she needn't have been. Her pap had a one-track mind at this stage of sobriety, and right now it wasn't on saloon gossip. "I reckon that gold's real, too, ain't it? You're just lyin' about it so you won't have to share it with your old pap."

But Rose wasn't listening to him now. She was watching Caldwell make his way along the boardwalk. It had shaken her to her boot soles to learn that he was working for Ostermann at the Flying Egg, although when she thought about it, it made sense. Caldwell might be a killer, and he'd certainly been a major operator along that upper segment of the Outlaw Trail, where horses and cattle were spirited back and forth across the border with Canada, but she doubted if there were many men who understood the business better— and not just the routes and contacts, but all the little tricks of the trade. It made her nod her head in admiration for Ostermann's foresight. She'd never met the man, but she knew now that he'd be a formidable opponent, putting to the test all the theories she'd developed about the big ranchers over the past couple of years.

Her pap's scratchy voice interrupted her thoughts. "Where at did you rub Frank Caldwell the wrong way?" he asked.

"It don't matter," she replied absently.

"Kitten," her pap replied seriously, "you'd better get that notion out of your head right now, because when a man like Caldwell marks you for a target, it damn' well matters a lot."

On Monday, the court fined Daniel Ames $75 for shooting bison in a federally protected area. As anticipated, the evidence from all three buffalo became the property of the city of Billings, signed for by none other than Deputy Phillip Allen himself. Add that little tidbit to the fact that his fine was the exact same amount as his bail, and there wasn't a soul in all Montana Territory who could have convinced Daniel that the whole shitaree was anything other than a dirty, rotten scam.

It was a fact Rose wouldn't have argued the subject with him, although as morning slid into early afternoon, she was discovering more pressing matters that needed her attention. Such as that after registering the A-Bar-E brand with the Montana Stockgrowers Association, then ordering a $5 branding iron from the Jepson & Lane smithy, she had less than $30 remaining in Shorty's old buckskin poke. No more—and $150 worth of supplies waiting for her at Sutherland's Mercantile, goods she and Nora would need desperately if they were to survive the winter.

Seeing no other alternative, Rose swallowed her pride and went to see Herman Sutherland about getting the merchandise on tick. Having been carried before and knowing she was considered a good risk, Rose wasn't surprised when Herman agreed to her proposal, but there was no pleasure in it for her. Although Sutherland probably carried half his clientele on credit from time to time, and made a small but fair profit by charging three-quarters of a percent interest, it always chafed her to buy her provisions that way. She never went on tick that it didn't seem like she was slipping backward a little.

It was late when they finished loading the wagon, tying everything down beneath a sheet of canvas for protection against the weather. Even though the sky was overcast and threatening, Rose was determined to make her start back to the ranch as quickly as possible. By pushing, she hoped to reach her old campsite east of town by nightfall, then make it home before sunset the following day. But she had to swing past Jepson & Lane first and pick up the new branding iron. And if her pap was around, she wanted to say good bye. She wasn't optimistic about finding him, though. He'd stormed out of the courtroom that morning in a fit, flinging curses like they were handfuls of candy in a Founder's Day parade. But she had to try. It would eat at her all winter if she didn't.

Skinny Jim met her at the livery with the branding iron in hand, his heavy coat buttoned to his throat against the deepening cold. A smile creased his ebony face as he held the iron up admiringly. "Sure is a pretty thing," he remarked.

Rose didn't try to suppress her grin. "Dang, who'd've ever thought it."

"A Bar E. Someday that mark'll be on a million head, I expect, and I'll get to say . . . 'I held the original iron.' "

Laughing, Rose accepted the branding iron, her blue eyes sparkling as she turned it over in her hands. "Lordy," she said reverently. "Ain't that handsome?"

"It sure is," Skinny agreed. "It surely is."

Then the moment passed and Rose gave Skinny an embarrassed look. "Well, shoot, where's that blacksmith? I want to thank him personal."

"He ain't here," Skinny replied. "He had business up Livingston way, but he gave me this here iron this morning and asked me to pass it along."

"Well, you pass my thanks right back then. He done a good job."

"I sure will," Skinny Jim promised, but something had changed in his tone. "You figuring to go see your pa, are you?"

"I thought I would. Is he home?"

"Yeah, but he's in a foul mood. Mean, like he gets sometimes."

Rose's muscles drew taut, recognizing the intent of Skinny's words. "Drunk?" she asked.

"Ought to be by now."

"Gol-dang it, where's he get money for booze?" She didn't expect an answer. She knew men like her pap had their ways, and figured she was probably better off not knowing what they were. Hefting the iron, she said: "Take care of yourself, Skinny."

"Thank you, miss. I will."

She shoved the branding iron under the tarp, wedging it between a couple of one-hundred-pound sacks of flour, then started down the alley at a deliberate stride. She was anxious to get this over with, knowing from past experience that the sooner she left Billings, the sooner she'd lose that smothery feeling she always got around her father.

She was dressed as she'd been on her arrival—skirt, blouse, coat, hat, boots—but in the wake of her encounter with Caldwell, she was toting the Smith & Wesson at her waist, Deputy Allen be damned.

The door to the shack stood open despite the cold, but there was no smoke from the tin stove-pipe, no glow of lamplight in the window. In the sepia-toned twilight, the place looked deserted and forlorn. A gusting wind sweeping down the Yellowstone batted the weeds in the yard and sent a chill down Rose's spine. She knocked tentatively at the door.

"Go away," Daniel snarled.

"Pap, it's me. I come to say good bye."

"Then say it and get. I ain't got no rich husband left me a sack of gold when he died."

Rose's lips narrowed. For a moment she considered just walking away. Then she ducked through the entrance, stepping quickly to one side so that she wouldn't be silhouetted in the door. It didn't take long for her eyes to adjust to the dimness.

"You never did listen worth a shit," Daniel growled. He was sitting on his bunk with a clay jug of whiskey balanced on the frame within easy reach. His eyes were bloodshot, his expression murderous.

"I come to say good bye," Rose repeated doggedly.

"Going back to your whoring?"

"Don't do that, Pap. Only idjits say things like that."

His eyes glazed over in rage and he tried to rise, but the effort proved too taxing and he fell back. "Little trollop," he puffed. "How'd a girl of mine turn out like you?"

"I got my own land, some cattle. I didn't turn out bad."

"Everything you've got was leeched off some man. Poor ol' Muggy, givin' up his life so you could squander it all on crazy dreams. I don't know what a gal wants to own land for, anyway.

You ought to be findin' yourself a husband, havin' me some grandkids. It ain't right, the way you've been livin'."

Rose licked her lips. "That ain't true. You know Muggy never gave me nothin' but heartache."

"You're lyin' now," he said. "I know for a fact he gave you that land. Gave it to you by gettin' his neck stretched by vigilantes. Gave you that gold dust, too, so you can just forget any seventy-five dollars I owe you . . . that I *don't* owe you. God damn good-for-nothin' cow. How long did I feed you while you was growin' up? Huh? How long?" He struggled to his feet, then stumbled over to grasp the back of a chair. "How many pounds of beans have you ate at my table?"

Rose's breath was coming quick and thin, her hands shaking. She remembered Shorty dying in her arms, and Wiley shot up and drowning in the Musselshell; she remembered the Indian she'd killed, the baby she'd miscarried, and the wolves she'd skinned. And, by damn, she remembered the buffalo she'd skinned, too, helping out when her pap and brothers had shot too many to peel themselves—that on top of the hides she was responsible for back at camp, keeping them turned and free of bugs, and having supper on when the men got in and the mules cared for, and then there was a flash that was like a mist of red paint sprayed in her eyes and a harsh jerk of muscles across the back of her head. She blinked and looked at her father and laughed, laughed *at* him—in his face—

and said, shouting: "You god-damn' old drunk. You god-damn' worthless *bum!* How many beans have I ate at your table? You ain't even *owned* a table except this one since I was little, and this you stole off someone's junk pile." She smacked the rickety piece of furniture with her fist, hard enough to make it jump. "God damn you, I tried! I *tried,* but nothin' I ever did was good enough!"

Daniel's face turned pale as whey. From somewhere upcañon, thunder rumbled like an old-time buffalo stampede. For perhaps a full minute, neither spoke, the silence between them almost electric. Then her pap started around the table, using it as a crutch. His face was mottled red now, his breath like a rasp drawn across wood. "You ungrateful bitch," he hissed. "You worthless little tramp of a daughter. I should've smacked you silly years ago."

She sidled toward the door, having to will herself not to bolt, as she would have done when she was ten. "How dare you act as if I owe you anything?" she whispered fiercely. "How dare you treat me like a clod of dirt? Who do you think you are? Who do you think *I* am, that you can talk to me that way?"

"Come here!"

She refused, standing white-knuckled just inside the door, her pulse pounding. "I worked my butt off for you. I did a man's work and never got nothin' for it *except* beans. Nothin'!"

Daniel lunged across the short space separating

336

them. Expecting it, Rose darted for the door, but she'd misjudged her father's swiftness, the anger that propelled him. His fist struck her cheek like a mallet and she slammed into the doorjamb with a sharp, indrawn cry. Her toe caught the threshold and she stumbled outside, sprawling in the dirt. Dazed, she rolled onto her back. A keening wind stung the hot, throbbing flesh under her eye, and the sky was dappled with tiny flakes of snow that danced so lively in the gray light she wasn't at first sure if they were even real. She tried to stand up but her pap loomed above her. She felt his fist strike her again but the pain seemed less severe now, the blow muffled, distant. She didn't remember drawing the Smith & Wesson, and was as startled as he was by its solid roar.

Daniel staggered backward as the sound of the report echoed over the town. Coming up hard against the side of the shack, he leaned there breathing heavily.

"You bastard," Rose grated, climbing to her feet, the Smith &Wesson trembling in her right hand. "If you ever raise a fist to me again, I swear I'll put a bullet between your eyes."

"You spoiled little brat. I never thought I'd see the day my own little girl . . ."

"Shut up!" she screamed, and, for perhaps the first time in all her years, her pap complied. Stooping, she picked up her hat and clamped it on her head. Her cheek was already starting to swell, promising to close off the vision in her left eye;

it burned as if someone had shoved a live coal under the flesh, but it was the heat of the growing bruise that kept her anger alive, that prevented her from caving in to the guilt that rippled just below the surface, demanding that she apologize, beg forgiveness. She backed away until she was sure there was enough distance between them that she was safe, then holstered her revolver. Lifting a finger, she said—"Never again."—then turned and walked to the wagon.

The wind lashed at her back as she drove out of Billings and the snow thickened as an early darkness fell, but she never looked back.

Chapter Twenty-Four

It was still snowing when Rose sighted the lit window of the cabin the next day. Although it couldn't have been much past 4:00 p.m., the sky was layered with dingy clouds that made it seem a lot later.

Nora must have heard the rattle of the wagon, because she stepped out of the cabin in her coat, cap, and mittens as Rose wheeled the small wagon into the yard. They wasted only scant seconds on greetings, then hurried to get the supplies inside before they froze any more than they already had.

It was dark when they finished. Wrapping herself in a blanket, Rose sank to a stool in front of the fireplace. With Nora settled on the edge of the hearth, Rose related her adventures in Billings, leaving out only the details of her final parting with her father. No mention was made by either of them about her swollen eye and discolored cheek.

Nora immediately recognized the gravity of Frank Caldwell's employment with the Flying Egg. Although she'd never met the man, she'd heard about him through her associates at the Silver Star.

Of the money Rose had spent on her pap's fine, and the title change on the property she'd been unable to secure because of it, Nora seemed unaffected.

"I'd have done the same," she assured Rose. "Don't worry about it."

Her response brought instant relief to Rose. Had it been others she'd known—her pap or Muggy or Wiley—she wouldn't have heard the end of it. But Nora understood that sometimes a person needed to roll with the punches, else be destroyed by them.

Nora's time alone at the A-Bar-E had been uneventful. Riding Albert, she'd driven some Egg cattle north into the Bulls one day, but hadn't Seen another human being at all. She'd spent her days chopping firewood, her evenings puttering inside. This would be her first winter away from the security of a town, where there were others to turn to for help in an emergency, and she admitted she was nervous about it.

Her confession made it easier for Rose to acknowledge—as much to herself as to Nora—

that she'd always been kind of skittish about wintering alone out in the middle of nowhere, but she reassured Nora that she'd survived more than one season on her own, and that the two of them together could come through this one.

It was still snowing lightly when they awoke the next day. They spent the morning sorting out the supplies Rose had brought back from Billings, then putting everything away. By the time they finished, the snow had stopped and patches of blue sky were showing through the clouds. It was Rose, peering out the frost-webbed window, who spotted the two horsemen approaching from the east.

"We got company," she announced tersely, then went to fetch her rifle.

Nora moved to the window. "Who are they?"

"Could be some of Caldwell's men."

"Would Caldwell's men be leading pack horses?"

Rose returned to the window. Although the two men were only a couple of hundred yards away, the brightness of the afternoon sun reflecting off the freshly fallen snow prevented identification. Even so, she had to admit they didn't look very menacing. Each man led a pair of horses laden with bulky packs, and were bundled in heavy fur coats.

"Hunters," Nora said with sudden conviction, then went to the corner to retrieve her shotgun. "Just in case," she added.

"Well, we don't want to shoot 'em if they don't mean us no trouble."

"Men are always trouble," Nora replied, breaking open the double-barreled Remington to chamber a pair of brass, twelve-gauge shells. Then she looked up with a sly smile, snapping the weapon closed. "Although if they ain't too dumb, I can sometimes put up with a little trouble."

Keeping the Sharps handy, Rose went to the door and pulled it open. A wave of cold air swept into the cabin, causing the flames in the fireplace to crackle loudly. Nora came to stand at her side.

"What do you aim to do if they ain't overly smart?" Rose asked. "I'm only curious because I think I recognize one of 'em now, and it'd be a chore to dig a grave in this weather."

"We won't worry about a grave. We'll just haul 'em into the woods and let the buzzards have them."

Feigning surprise, Rose said: "My, my, when'd you turn so bloodthirsty?"

"When I recognized the other one," Nora replied. "That's Gene Sidwell if I ain't mistaken, which means that other yahoo is probably Lew Parker, who must've given up his bartending job in Junction City."

"Yeah, that's Lew," Rose said, allowing the Sharps' curved steel butt plate to gently strike the floor. "Dang' fool. It'd be just like him to give up a good indoors job with the first snowfall."

They had venison for lunch, compliments of a young muley Gene had kicked up in a draw earlier that morning. The women supplied brown rice, beans, and a couple of cans of Blue Hen tomatoes, with a dried apple pie for dessert.

They idled the afternoon away in front of the fireplace, drinking coffee laced with bourbon and catching up on old news. It soon become apparent to Rose that Nora and Gene were more than casual acquaintances. Lew must have seen it, too, or else he'd known about it all along. It was he who suggested, after a light supper, that Rose accompany him to the barn to check on the stock.

Rose pulled on the heavy horse-hide coat and seal-skin troopers' cap she'd worn last winter while trapping wolves with Wiley and Shorty. Slipping into a pair of four-buckle India rubber overboots, she followed Lew through the ankle-deep snow to the barn. It was early evening and the sky, dark but clear, with a sliver of moon riding low in the east. Glancing skyward, past the transparent clouds of her breath to the twinkling canopy of stars, Rose was struck by the artistry of the night, the immensity of the blue-black dome. She felt small beneath it, insignificant.

They stopped in front of the barn, and Lew said: "You knew about Gene and Nora, didn't you, Rose?"

"No, Nora never mentioned him."

"I guess I ain't surprised. Gene asked Nora to marry him last winter, but she wouldn't on account of him being so fiddle-footed. He's got his heart set on winning her over, though. That's why we're heading into the mountains. Gene wants

342

to use the money he makes trapping to start a business. He wants to see if Nora'll reconsider."

Rose kept her expression neutral, her eyes locked on the pitch-dark interior of the barn. "I didn't even know they was acquainted. Are you sure Nora feels the same? Seems like she would've men-tioned it if she did."

"Whoever knows what a woman thinks? No offense, Rose, but a man generally gets better odds bucking the tiger at faro than he does courting a female. It's only a sad phenomenon of nature that some men are attracted to it. Courting, I mean."

"But not you, huh?"

"I might regret my wandering ways someday, but I ain't even thirty yet, and that's young to think about settling down like Gene wants to do."

"Well, Nora has an obligation here," Rose said bluntly. "She's part owner of the A-Bar-E, and can't go gaddin' off after some wayward hunter who don't know his butt from a bull-hide ledger."

Lew gave her a searching look. "They're fine people, Rose . . . Gene and Nora. Most folks would think it was a good thing if they hitched."

Rose glanced at the cabin, feeling a panic growing in her breast. It rattled her mightily, and made her feel so light-headed she thought she was going to pass out.

"Rose?"

"I'm fine," she said, forcing a smile. "I just got to feelin' a mite . . . discombobulated, thinkin' about runnin' this place by myself again."

Alone, again.

"Hell, you ain't got nothing to worry about until spring, at the earliest. Gene ain't even set his first trap yet."

They went into the barn where it was marginally warmer, although there wasn't anything to do in there; they'd fed and watered the stock before supper. Rose didn't even light a lantern, and after a while she and Lew settled down against the rear wall, sharing a thick wool blanket out of one of Lew's packs. At one point he placed a hand on her knee, then let it slide a few inches up her thigh—a question she responded to by pushing his hand away. She did it without rancor, though, and Lew, always a gentleman, didn't pursue it. Under different circumstances she might have obliged him, but she was still feeling unbalanced over Shorty's death, as well as her miscarriage last spring.

They sat in silence, snuggled together against the cold, each pursuing their own thoughts. Finally Rose remembered Fred Baylor, who she'd shot in the leg last summer, and asked Lew if he'd made it to Hannahman's Saloon in one piece.

"Well, he did for a fact. That hole in his leg had festered up pretty bad, but the town barber has some experience in those matters. He lanced it, then put leeches on the flesh around the wound, and it healed nicely."

"Did he say anything about how he got shot?"

Lew chuckled. "He told folks he was on his way to Fort Benton when bandits jumped him. Said there was four or five of them, and that he fought 'em off until one of them put a bullet in his leg, then he had to make a run for it." Lew's voice turned sober. "Of course that was before we heard about the ambush on the Musselshell. That took the starch out of him real quick. He told me everything, including how it was you who'd shot him to make him give up the Owlhoot. He was pretty shaken. Nobody knew what'd happened. There was some that said you was there, and that you'd been killed, too. Fred and I kept our yappers shut, and when he could ride again, he went home to Wyoming. They say his woman had a little girl not too long ago."

Rose smiled. "I knowed Della when she was playin' with dolls. Dang if it ain't funny to think of her having young 'uns of her own."

"I'd wager Fred has given up the outlaw life for good. I imagine he and Della are mighty thankful for what you done."

"He seemed like a nice enough fella," she admitted. "He just got caught up with the wrong crowd. Not that I'm in any position to be talkin'."

"They took young Frakes's body back to his daddy, along with the stolen horses. They say the old man didn't even come in to attend the funeral. That he sent word to the undertaker to bury the boy at Sheridan, and that he'd stop by later to pay the tab."

"That old man is a rocky son-of-a-bitch," Rose allowed. "Them boys of his might've turned out different, was he a better pap."

Lew was silent a moment, then said: "There's talk they might elect the old man president of the Bighorn Valley Land and Cattle Association, and that he's promising to clean out the undesirable elements for good. That's a pretty popular sentiment right now. Was a bunch of boys hung in the Little Missouri country this past summer, then a family burned out and run off over by Powderville."

"I heard about that," Rose replied quietly. "Little girl got killed, right?"

"Trampled by a horse, though they say it was an accident."

"Still dead, though."

"Yeah, still dead, and not a soul brought to justice for it, either. The word is her daddy wasn't doing anything illegal. Not that it matters any more." He cleared his throat. "I guess you've heard about their list?"

"I reckon that'd be the same one Joe Bean mentioned to me last year."

"Probably. They're saying John Stroudmire is growing impatient with the way Joe's handling things for the Montana outfits, and that the local cattlemen are starting to feel the same way. They want the Outlaw Trail shut down from Utah to Canada. I'd say that'll include the A-Bar-E."

"They've got some right to their opinion of me, but they're tootin' on the wrong horn if they think I'm any kind of threat. I learned my lesson on the Musselshell."

"It's not just the rustlers they want out, Rose. It's the competition."

"Competition?" She laughed. "I got forty cows and a little white-faced bull calf against the thousands of head a fella like Frakes or Ostermann will run. I ain't no more competition to them than a whistle is to a windstorm."

"Maybe not outright, but you've got that little crick yonder, and you know a reliable source of water is more important than grass to a stockman. Especially after the dry summer we just had."

"The Yellowstone's less than an hour's ride from here, Lew, even on a poky horse. They ain't got enough cattle in Montana to drink that dry."

"The Yellowstone is the northern border of the Crow Reservation, and that's trouble enough right there. Plus there's the railroad and the toll road, and people going back and forth winter and summer. It's getting congested along the Yellowstone, and it'll only get worse. It stands to reason a cowman would want another source of water. Then you've got those bluffs out there, a natural barrier between the high plains and the Yellowstone Valley. Using those, it wouldn't take much fencing to keep an outfit's cattle up high and out of the way. More important, it'd help keep sodbusters down below. Nesters ain't a big problem in Montana yet, but they will be, just like in Kansas and Nebraska."

Sighing, Rose said: "You ain't told me nothin' tonight I ain't already thought of myself, but, dang it, why can't they leave a body alone?"

"They can, if you ain't got something they want."

A silence grew between them after that. Finally she said: "Now that's scary, hearin' you say it out loud like that. It makes it seem more real, somehow."

"It is real," Lew said gently. "It's scary, too. That's why I'm telling you. Times are going to get rough, Rose, and it's looking like you're going to be right in the middle of it."

Chapter Twenty-Five

Lew and Gene saddled up early the next morning. Coming out to see them off, Nora exhibited a flush to her cheeks that Rose never would have expected. Standing beside the corral, she studied Gene's face, wondering what it was that Nora saw in him. Certainly it wasn't his looks. Gene was long and lanky and as graceless as a newborn colt. His hair was close-cropped and red as a brick, and his ears stuck out on either side of his head like tiny skillets. Even his grin was lop-sided.

Yet there was no denying an attraction, so obvious it was almost funny. Even Lew seemed amused. Looking at Rose, he declared: "If we'd have stayed out in the barn another hour last night, they might've been engaged by now."

"I dang' near froze my hinder off as it was," Rose reminded him, her breath coming in quick, vaporous clouds. "We'd've had to've had a funeral and the wedding on the same day."

"You two just hush," Nora said, laughing.

Gene's face reddened to a point that he almost lost his freckles. Mounting and taking up the lead rope to his pack horses, he said: "I'll be back in the spring, Nora honey."

"Don't get your toes caught in a bear trap," she advised.

Gene's blush deepened. "We ain't got a bear trap, Nora."

Lew snorted loudly, then swung onto his horse, and the two rode off. They skirted the corral to pick up the Helena trail, which ran a little south of northwest from Rose's cabin, rather than the more northern route that would have taken them over the Bulls to the Musselshell. Rose and Nora watched for a while, but it was too cold to linger and they soon retreated to the cabin. Rose poured a cup of coffee, then went to stand in front of the fireplace, but Nora confined herself to the area immediately surrounding the stove. "I like him," she said at last.

"Who?"

Nora gave her a strained look but let it slide. "It wasn't fair that I didn't tell you about him earlier."

"Lew says he asked you to marry him."

"Last year. I said no, but he's been tenacious."

"You gonna do it?"

"I don't know." She glanced almost sheepishly at Rose, a new look for someone who, until recently, had seemed iron-skinned and nearly indestructible. "Do you think I should?"

Rose's answer surprised them both. "Yeah, I

reckon I do." Setting her coffee aside, she went to get her coat and hat. "I'm gonna take a ride up along the north line, see if any Egg cows has drifted down with the storm."

"Rose . . ."

"Naw, I'm goin'." She paused, one hand on the latch. "But listen, I'm happy for you, Nora. For you and Gene both. All right?"

For the next several weeks the weather remained dry but bitterly cold, like a blue Arctic cap pulled over the land. Although Rose and Nora continued to work outside every day, cutting firewood and nursing calves—two more newborns had joined the ranks of the A-Bar-E herd—the unforgiving temperatures were starting to worry Rose.

They'd fared well during the summer, having only a small herd that had been brought in late, but Rose knew most of the cattle ranges were suffering badly after last summer's drought. For several years now, the best ranges had been increasingly overgrazed by the big ranchers, their vision of the whole blinded by a high market value on beef sold by the head, rather than the pound. Heaping insult upon injury were the prairie fires that had ravaged the vast grasslands, while many of the water holes and small creeks had dried up by August. For the majority of cattlemen, Rose knew, it had been a brutal summer; she doubted if many of them could afford an equally harsh winter.

Still, not even their concern over the long freeze

could distract them from the memory of Frank Caldwell's words. The gunman's intimation that he and Ostermann would visit the A-Bar-E sometime before Christmas had been taken seriously by the women, and, as the holiday neared, they found their gazes turning more and more to the north, the direction from which they expected the Flying Egg owner and his hired shootist to appear.

It snowed again in December, then, after another brief cold spell, a blizzard swept down out of the Arctic regions with winds that howled like demons. When the storm blew itself out three days later, Rose and Nora rode out to check on the cattle. They found one of the calves dead—a little black and white heifer, already partially devoured by wolves—but the rest of the herd had come through unscathed. To their chagrin, they found an inordinate number of Egg cattle mixed in with their own stock.

Nora, on Albert, eased over as close to Rose's ornery-tempered buckskin as she dared. Her eyes, between the muffler wrapped around the lower portion of her face and the bill of a red-plaid hunter's cap, looked like twin coals of rage. "They aren't even trying to keep their cows off our land any more!"

"So I noticed," Rose said.

"How long do we put up with this?"

"I don't know." Rose could sense Nora's deepening frustration, and, to an extent, she shared it. But she'd done an awful lot of tossing

351

and turning in her bunk the past few weeks, and still hadn't come up with a reasonable response, something that wouldn't give Ostermann the excuse he needed to sic his attorneys on them. Or worse, Caldwell.

"The law belongs to them that pays for it, I reckon," Rose said, after a pause.

"And justice takes a hind teat?"

"Generally speakin', yeah."

With a curse, Nora hauled Albert around roughly, kicking him into a gallop for the cabin. Rose watched until horse and rider had grown small in the distance, then guided the buckskin into the mass of cattle to begin weeding out the Flying Egg stock. Nearly an hour passed before Nora returned. Rose was crowding a brindled Egg cow off to one side when she heard the pounding of Albert's hoofs. Glancing around, Rose saw Nora approaching with her shotgun balanced across the saddle in front of her. Pulling up, she shook the double-barreled Remington toward Rose. "It's time we fought back," she declared.

"What you got in mind is likely gonna start a range war."

"What other way is there when the law chooses sides? This is our home, Rose, and Ostermann has more cows grazing on it than we do. I don't want a war, but I won't let him take this place without a fight, and that's just what he'll do if we don't stand up to him. He'll nibble away at our land and our patience until we don't have anything left."

Taking a deep breath, Rose lifted her gaze to the distant ridge line of the Bull Mountains. Then she lowered her eyes and straightened in the saddle, reaching back to touch the Smith & Wesson. "It's them," she said flatly.

Nora turned to look. A long carriage pulled by four matching sorrels was moving swiftly toward them. The car was flanked by several outriders, and Rose had little doubt that one of them would be Frank Caldwell, eager to throw his weight behind whatever offer Ostermann made.

The carriage and riders were a quarter of a mile away and closing rapidly. Casually loosening the Smith & Wesson in its holster, Rose said: "I hope that shotgun's loaded."

"It isn't," Nora replied guiltily. She started to reach for the pommel bag where she carried her shells, but Rose stopped her.

"They're too close. It might make 'em churlish if they saw you poppin' shells into your scattergun. Best we can do is see can we bluff 'em. They ain't likely to start anything today."

Men like Caldwell, Rose knew, didn't function well in daylight, when others might unexpectedly happen upon their skullduggery. She figured Ostermann's presence would also subdue the gunman's conduct, if it were indeed the Fifth Earl of Brackenridge's third son riding in that carriage. Men like Howard Ostermann might be cruel and ruthless, but they generally liked to be far away when the work got bloody.

Within minutes the carriage was braking to a halt in front of them, its bright yellow wheels crunching loudly through the wind-sculpted snow. The carriage was a closed-bodied, goose-neck affair with etched glass in its windows and polished brass running lamps mounted on either side of the driver's box for night driving. Camping gear, including a small stove and a tent with collapsible metal poles, was strapped to the car's roof in concession to the long, empty miles separating the Flying Egg headquarters from the A-Bar-E range. The driver sat in the middle of a button-tucked, patent-leather seat on the outside, bundled in a buffalo-hide coat.

Frank Caldwell was riding a well-put-together chestnut. Four other men rode with him, all of them strangers. The five lined up with almost military-like precision between the women and the coach, with Caldwell in the center. It was Caldwell who spoke first. Smirking, he said to Rose: "I didn't figure you'd last long in a skirt."

"I wouldn't let that concern you overmuch."

Glancing at Nora, he allowed a lazy smile to tilt one corner of his mouth. "You must be the little whore."

"Wait a minute," Nora said. "I've heard of you. You're Frank Caldwell, the one the girls call Little Stub-Horn."

One of Caldwell's men snickered and Rose tensed up to reach for her pistol, but then the nearside car door sprang open and a giant gray hat poked out into the sunlight.

Although Rose had never met Ostermann in the flesh, she'd observed enough English fops around southeastern Montana to have a fair idea of what to expect. Howard Ostermann was hardly a disappointment. He stood about five-foot-six and was lean as a longhorn, save for a little pot gut that even a full-length camel-hair coat couldn't hide. He had dark, curly hair, a thin mustache, bushy eyebrows, and wore wire-rimmed glasses over eyes the color of Yellowstone mud. His gauntleted gloves were brain-tanned doeskin, soft as chamois and decorated with Crow beadwork, and his wide-brimmed hat could have shaded a small family, had a small family been handy and in need of shading.

Ostermann paused dramatically on the snowy ground beside the carriage's open door, one booted foot propped on the brass step, his head tipped back to allow him a view of the women without interference from his hat. Then, tugging proudly on his ornamented gloves, he strode briskly forward. The two men on Caldwell's right obediently side-stepped their horses out of the way, offering Ostermann a straight shot. The efficiency of the move caught Rose's attention, and she whistled.

"That," she said emphatically to Caldwell, "was some for fancy. Do them boys of yours know any other tricks, or is scootin' out of the boss' way their only talent?"

Although Caldwell declined a reply, Ostermann seemed amused. "Superlative," the Egg owner gushed, "simply superlative. I was told you had a sharp wit. To be quite honest, I find a cutting intellect refreshing in this Boeotian country." He came forward, holding out his hand. "I am Howard Ostermann, of the Crooked Bar-O-Bar. You must be Rose Edwards."

Rose stared at Ostermann's outstretched hand for a long time before reluctantly accepting it. Inclining her head to the side, she said: "This here's Nora Alder. She's half owner of the A-Bar-E."

"Miss Alder," Ostermann said, taking Nora's hand graciously. Stepping back, he broadened his smile. "It is indeed a pleasure to meet you both. I've heard so much about you, and you especially, Miss Rose of Yellowstone. You're something of a frontier luminary, I'm told."

"It's Missus," Rose corrected. "I'm a widow, and I don't hold much with that Yellowstone stuff."

Ostermann laughed heartily. "Ah, but sometimes our reputations do precede us, do they not? Based on half-truths and groundless fears, as unflattering as they are inaccurate. Take my own situation, for example. The local populace seems to have created an image of me as a monster who breathes fire and eats children. They are convinced my intentions are dishonorable, that I wish to re-create the feudal lifestyle of my ancestral homeland. Yet nothing could be further from the truth. If I am guilty of anything, it is of being a competent businessman, in possession of skills I've cultivated every bit as diligently as Mister Caldwell does his as a shootist. The fact that my father funded my education, or has the good sense to offer monetary assistance from time to time on my own sound recommendations, lessens my accomplishments not one whit.

"Yet above that, and I do recognize the immodesty this must imply, I truly believe I have been blessed by the Lord's own hand with an uncanny ability to see into the future. Not as a soothsayer, but as a visionary. I see a future as it *might* be, and the emphasis on *might* is notable here, Missus Edwards, because if left in the hands of the insipid, that vision quickly becomes lost. I see possibilities the common man, with his limited economic opportunities and a mind stunted by labor and a lack of formal education, is incapable of seeing."

He shifted position, taking a stance that might have better suited an actor or politician, but which Rose feared would be lost on his present audience, most of it half frozen and clearly bored, having in all probability heard this recital many times before.

"I see a Montana dotted with cities, Missus Edwards. Can you see that?" Here, Ostermann flung an arm toward the distant horizon, causing everyone to look in that direction. "I see a skyline defined not by emptiness, but by the smokestacks of factories supplying goods to a worldwide market. I see a state where a territory now exists, hills populated with the homes of honest employees rather than degenerate natives riddled with lice and disease. The world, Missus Edwards, not Montana, but the *world* is in the midst of an industrial revolution that will redirect the evolution of mankind, and not a dozen people in this entire territory can understand that. Cattle? Posh! Cattle are not the future of this land, merely its genesis. Cattle to feed the worker, of course. Wool from the backs of sheep to clothe them, certainly. But at its center, at its very heart, the clanging gears and spinning belts of industry. That, Missus Edwards, is the true future of this grand but currently desolate territory. Mechanical industry."

He looked at Rose and smiled, and for a moment she was afraid he was going to bow, or that someone might applaud. But only silence—deep and disturbingly charged—greeted the conclusion of Howard Ostermann's monologue.

"Does that surprise you, Missus Edwards?" he asked after a moment. "A future so unlike the one you must have envisioned? Or have you ever considered the future, and by that I mean the forward development of society?"

But it wasn't Rose who answered him. It was Nora. "I lived in Chicago, Mister Ostermann. I saw the future you're talking about. The air there was black with smoke from the factories. It left a gritty taste in my mouth day and night. People died of it. Not the rich. They lived outside the slums. But the poor, the men, women, and children whose backs your factories were built on."

Ostermann's smile remained undamaged. "Small-mindedness, Miss Alder, though hardly a surprise from a prostitute. Please, take no offense at my dismissal. I do appreciate the necessity of the oldest profession, I just don't consider a whore's opinion pertinent." He clapped his hands as if to call them to attention. "Now then, shall we proceed? Missus Edwards, you have approximately six hundred and forty acres under a somewhat dubious title filed in Bozeman in Eighteen Eighty-One. While I'm confident a skilled attorney could render such a document invalid, I would prefer an outright purchase. Since I'm equally certain you are both aware that even twice that acreage would be insufficient to maintain a profitable cattle station in such a semi-arid region as southeastern Montana, I can only assume your recent acquisition of shorthorns is a ploy to escalate your asking price."

Ostermann's smile widened, so smugly self-righteous, Rose wanted to laugh.

"Does that surprise you, Missus Edwards, that I would see through your little charade so easily? I can assure you, the minds of most men . . . and dare I include women? . . . are as easily read to me as the *London Times*. But I digress. I do recognize the value of your property, and especially its water, and I'm willing to pay handsomely. Does, say, a thousand dollars pique your interest? I should think that it would."

Rose glanced at Caldwell but the gunman refused to meet her eyes. He did smile, though, acknowledging Ostermann's presumptuousness, as well as her own dangerous predicament.

Tugging impatiently on his gloves, Ostermann awaited her reply. Apparently he was expecting it immediately.

Looking at Nora and noting the stubborn set of her jaw, Rose suddenly grinned. "I reckon we'll hang and rattle a while," she told the Egg owner.

"We'll hang until hell freezes over," Nora added defiantly.

The cocksure smile left Ostermann's face. "I see. I was told you were independent. Apparently you fancy yourself something of a business-woman, as well. Let me assure you, such tactics could cost you more than you wish to lose. You know as well as I that men of Mister Caldwell's abilities are a necessary tool in this environment, but I suspect you also realize that the real power lies with those of us who have the means to . . . shall we say, *coax* the law into a proper direction. I daresay I could have title to your property inside of three months if I so choose, and for much less than what I've offered here today."

"You can't just take our land," Nora said angrily. "What right do you have to come here and threaten us like this?"

Ostermann looked genuinely puzzled. "I need your land," he began vaguely, then shrugged and added: "I want it."

Rose waited for him to elaborate, but it appeared that Ostermann had said all he was going to say. At his side, Caldwell guffawed. "It's a hell of a note, ain't it?" he said to Rose.

Ostermann half turned to hold up a gloved hand. His gaze remained on Nora and Rose, shifting rhythmically between the two. After nearly a full minute, he said: "Surely you realize the futility of refusal. You, Missus Edwards, of all people. While I know nothing personally of the efforts some men have made to eradicate the territory's lawless element, haven't you at least heard . . . *rumors* . . . of your own position within that effort?"

"I ain't a part of that crowd no more. All I want is to go about my business without no trouble."

"I'm afraid that won't be possible."

Rose sighed. "Do you love this land, Mister Ostermann?"

"Love it?" He looked around as if he'd heard a strange noise. "You cannot love an inanimate object, Missus Edwards, no more than you can love your horse."

"Oh, but I do." She gestured toward Nora's mount. "That there's Albert. I consider him one of the finest friends I've ever had, and there ain't much I wouldn't do for him. I feel the same about this land. This is my home, Mister Ostermann, and you're tryin' to take it away from me. I don't cotton to that."

"Don't be preposterous," Ostermann said. "Such theatrics won't work on me, Missus Edwards."

"Then I reckon this here palaver is finished," Rose said, gathering her reins. "Mister Ostermann, we've been more'n lenient with your cattle comin' onto our range, but we don't intend to ignore the problem forever. If you want to run cows south of the Bull Mountains, you're gonna have to establish some kind of line camp where your boys can keep an eye on 'em, keep 'em off our grass."

A tic jumped in Ostermann's cheek. "That will not be a continuing problem, Missus Edwards." He walked stiffly to the carriage, there to pause with one foot on the brass step that would take him inside. "We will not meet again. Any further negotiation will be through my agents."

"Good bye, Mister Ostermann," Rose said calmly.

With a curt nod, Howard Ostermann disappeared inside his coach. Five minutes later the rig was little more than a black smudge against the white landscape, rolling swiftly away with Caldwell and his men loping in its wake.

Chapter Twenty-Six

Christmas dawned clear but frigid. Even in the wan light before sunup, Rose could see the gray fog of her breath with every sleepy exhalation. She remained in bed until the first bright rays of the new day tinted the ice on the window glass, then threw her blankets back and quickly dressed.

Nora was still asleep in her own bunk across the room when Rose slipped outside to care for the stock. She turned the mules and Albert loose for the day, then fetched hay and broke ice in the water trough for the buckskin, which she kept penned. Tomorrow she'd switch the rotation so that the buckskin could graze loose while Albert or one of the mules remained in the corral.

Rose scanned the country to the east, but the cattle were nowhere in sight. That wasn't particularly alarming. The A-Bar-E might be small compared to outfits that encompassed thousands of acres, but it was still large enough to hide a herd of forty shorthorns.

What did worry her was Howard Ostermann. She and Nora had rehashed their conversation with the Flying Egg owner daily since the encounter, and were in agreement that he'd follow through. Ostermann had been challenged by someone he considered inferior to himself, and that was an affront a man of his station couldn't ignore. Especially if it stood in the way of something he coveted.

I need your land. I want it, he had told them. The simplicity of his reply, the logic behind it, sent a chill down Rose's spine even today. That men like Ostermann expected preferential treatment, and were usually granted it, had been made abundantly clear to her during the Stranglers' raid three summers before, but she hadn't grown up in the company of such men. It had taken Howard Ostermann to personalize it, to give elitism countenance and voice and quirky mannerisms. No longer were "they" a nameless entity somewhere "out there." She understood now that *they* were *here,* and had been all along, living on fine country estates or in secluded enclaves, growing fat and opulent on the sweat of the others.

To men like Howard Ostermann, raised in sheltered environments, skating through adulthood secure in the knowledge that, no matter how difficult times became, someone—father, uncle, brother—would always be there to bail them out, life could be that simple.

I want it, Howard Ostermann had declared. And so he would come for it, Rose knew.

Entering the cabin with thoughts of Ostermann still on her mind, Rose didn't immediately pick up on the changes that had been wrought since she had gone outside. It was only as she was slipping free of her outer garments that a splash of color on the mantle caught her eye.

"Nora?" she said uncertainly.

"Just don't make a big deal out of it," Nora replied.

Turning, Rose took in the cabin's interior. A new red candle sat in the middle of the table, its base wreathed with tiny juniper limbs, their dusty blue berries still attached. Evergreen boughs were draped over the mantle, held in place with red ribbons, and on Rose's bunk lay a package wrapped in brown butcher's paper. Nora stood at the spice cabinet beside the stove, her hands powdered with flour, the smell of yeast and cinnamon and percolating coffee suddenly strong in the warm air.

"What's goin' on?" Rose asked.

"It's Christmas, ain't it?"

"Yeah, but . . ." She nodded toward the package on her bunk. "What's that?" She shrugged out of her coat and hung it on a peg beside her cap.

"Something to celebrate all the hard work we've done around here. I figured we could use some holiday cheer." She made a face. "Just open it. It ain't that much, anyway. I bought it last summer in Miles City because I thought you could use it, but I swear if you make a fuss out of it, I'll throw it in the fire."

"Naw, I ain't gonna make a fuss about it. It just caught me by surprise. My kin weren't never much for exchangin' gifts, but since I figured you might . . ." She went to the roughed-together chest at the foot of her bunk and lifted the lid. Nora followed, peering over her shoulder. Rose dug down under her extra clothes until she found what she was looking for, then brought it into the light. "I wish I'd thought to wrap it," she said.

"Why, that's pretty," Nora exclaimed. She took the cup and saucer in her hands, turning it slowly. They were tiny things compared to the dented tin mugs they normally used, the cup shaped like an inverted bell with a delicately sculptured handle; both pieces were made of bone china, the color of fresh-churned cream save for a row of little blue flowers on a green border around their rims.

"It's a tea cup," Rose explained. "I considered the whole set, but it was pricey."

"I'm not sure I'd want a whole set," Nora said, taking the gift to the table and setting it next to the red candle. "Having only one makes it more personal." She gave Rose a quick look. "Not that you can't use it once in a while."

"Naw, I been frettin' over that thing ever since I brought it back from Billings. I wasn't sure it'd make it to Christmas without gettin' broke. Now that I'm shet of it, I got no need to handle it any more, although, if you wanted to, you could set it on the mantle when you ain't usin' it. Them flowers remind me of summer."

"I will," Nora promised. "But now it's your turn." She retrieved the package from Rose's bunk and handed it to her. "Open it."

Carefully Rose slid the string from the package, then unfolded the paper. Her eyes widened as the gift was revealed—a dark green riding skirt with a double row of brass buttons down the front. Nora smiled hesitantly at the look of pleasure that crossed Rose's face. Holding the skirt to her waist, Rose said: "It looks like a perfect fit."

"Doris kept your measurements after you bought those dresses from her last spring."

"Is that where you got this?"

Nora nodded.

"Shoot, I don't know what to say."

"Don't say anything, just take it."

"All right, but . . . thanks." Rose's thoughts flashed back to Christmas a year ago, and the bald whore named Gabby. That day seemed years gone now.

"Well, thank you for the cup and saucer, too," Nora said. "And Merry Christmas. Come on, let's have breakfast."

The brindled cow with the crooked horn was the last to drop its calf that winter, a bull born in early January. It brought the total number of newborns on the A-Bar-E to seven, not counting the little heifer they'd lost in December's blizzard. Although calves were the purpose of the cows, Rose was glad to see an end to the birthing. She considered it poor luck to have so many little ones born in the middle of winter, rather than in the spring when their chances of survival would have been better. With the worst of the season yet to come, she figured they were bound to lose a few more calves before warmer weather.

Rose discovered the spindly legged calf late one afternoon on her way back from the hills south of the Bull Mountains. She knew something was up as soon as she spotted the wolves. There were six of them, led by a cream-colored doyen with a dark-tipped tail. The other five members of the pack were various shades of gray, all noticeably smaller than the alpha. Rose slid the Sharps from its scabbard while still several hundred yards away and chambered a cartridge. Although never particularly afraid of wolves, she'd developed a healthy respect for them. She knew the wild canines were becoming desperate, hunted and trapped at every quarter, their food sources dwindling as overgrazing by cattle drove the deer and elk—the wolf's natural diet—to increasingly higher elevations.

The cow and calf were alone, the cow having instinctively sought out a sheltering grove of wild plums as her time of calving neared. It was there the wolves had cornered her. Never very far away, the pack must have scented the warm, musky odor of the birth. Although the cow had kept its predators at bay so far, Rose knew it was only a matter of time before one of them slipped past her and got at the calf. Likely the cow would have been doomed as well, had Rose not come along when she did.

She rode to within two hundred yards of the pack and dismounted. Keeping Albert's reins in her left hand, she dropped to one knee and took careful aim at the lead wolf, squeezing the trigger. The big rifle slammed into her shoulder, and the cream-colored wolf was knocked spinning across the snow. Rose quickly reloaded, but the rest of the pack was already scattering toward the Yellowstone. At the edge of the thicket, the cow continued to pace nervously, the calf wobbling at her heels. Keeping the rifle in her right hand, Rose stepped into the saddle and jogged over. The cow lowered its head threateningly as she approached, but moved off when Rose yelled. The little one stumbled after it, emitting a series of short, plaintive bleats.

Dropping her reins over a handy plum branch, Rose cautiously approached the wolf. It lay on its side in the trampled snow, its jaws parted to reveal a curved, yellowed incisor; although its eyes were open, they were already glazed in death, the liquid film freezing around the lids. Exhaling loudly, Rose lowered the Sharps' hammer to half cock. The tangling of emotions that had accompanied the death of every animal she'd taken since she started hunting as a girl thrummed through her.

"It weren't nothin' personal," she assured the limp form. "Kill or be killed, eat or be eaten." She could have said more, but figured the spirit of the wolf would understand. Besides, she'd never set much store by people who prayed too long or too loud.

Setting her rifle aside, Rose knelt next to the carcass and ran her gloved fingers through the thick, luxurious hide. Then she pulled a clasp knife from the pocket of her coat and leaned forward to skin the wolf of its $5 pelt. She was rolling the hide into a bundle to tie behind her saddle when she noticed the sky to the northwest. "Oh, Lordy," she breathed, unable to look away.

A storm approached. Low-ceilinged, massive, its belly as black as midnight, its dark, angry front towering thousands of feet above her. Even as she watched, a gust of wind swept across the plain, flinging up sheets of grainy snow that tossed and writhed and fell back to earth. She stared in awe as the clouds began to swallow the sun, plunging the afternoon into an eerie, early twilight.

Hurrying to Albert's side, Rose sheathed her rifle

and flung the pelt across the pommel, then vaulted into the saddle. Albert needed no urging. He could sense the danger speeding toward them as readily as she could, and ran like a two-year-old, as if the wind itself were a quirt.

The cabin was less than a mile away, but the blowing snow obscured it until Rose was within fifty yards of the buildings. She reined into the barn and dropped from the saddle. Nora was already there, a lantern lit at the entrance to guide her home. The buckskin and mules were already secured inside, and Nora hurried forward to help Rose strip the rigging from Albert's back. Rose tossed everything, including the hide, into the lean-to while Nora led Albert to an iron ring stapled to the wall and tied him firmly in place.

With the stock sheltered, the two women plunged headlong into the maw of the storm. The wind immediately snuffed the lantern's flame, while battering gusts tried to knock them off their feet. They reached the cabin and followed its walls with their hands until they came to the door, then almost fell inside.

"Thank God," Nora gasped, after they'd pushed the door shut. "I was afraid you wouldn't make it."

"I'd have hated to've been much farther away," Rose agreed. "Folks is gonna die in this one."

"Don't say that," Nora said. Shivering, she went to stand at the fireplace, crossing her arms under her breasts.

"Shoot, we won't have any trouble," Rose said.

"We got plenty of wood and enough feed to last till spring."

"It scares me," Nora confessed. "Back in Miles City I thought I'd enjoy the solitude, and I did last summer. But it gets to be too big sometimes."

"It's a big land, all right, but the only part we got to worry about is right here in this cabin and out at the barn. We can string ropes between here and the barn and here and the privy if we have to. This storm'll wear itself out soon enough."

"Of course it will," Nora replied. "Besides, it's only snow."

"Sure, it's only snow."

But before it was all over, it turned out to be quite a bit more. Rose's prediction that the storm would blow itself out didn't come to pass for another couple of days, and then not before it had dumped almost two fresh feet of snow on top of what was already on the ground. There was no way she could have foreseen what would follow, though. No one could have known that, when the snow quit falling, the temperature would plummet, bringing the north-central tier of an entire nation to a jarring halt.

For weeks the thermometer ranged well below zero, sometimes as much as forty-five degrees below. Although those bitterest temperatures lasted less than two weeks, it was almost March before a warm, South Pacific wind—a Chinook—arced up over the Rockies to melt the tortoise shell-like cap of ice and snow, releasing the grass underneath.

The winter of 1886 and 1887 was a time unlike any in Rose's memory. Unable to turn the horses and mules loose to forage for themselves, they quickly depleted their meager supply of hay and grain. The creek froze solid and they had to melt snow over the stove for water not only for themselves, but for the livestock. They kept the fires in the fireplace and cook stove burning constantly, and began working in shifts so that one of them would always be awake to monitor the twin blazes. Even that failed to keep the frost from creeping inside, whiskering the interior walls along the chinking and completely obliterating the view through the tiny front window. The cold was so intense that in the early hours of dawn, the sound of trees popping and splitting in the forest to the west reminded Rose of the tales Wiley'd told her of the battles he'd fought in during the Civil War.

They stacked all their canned goods in front of the fireplace and around the stove to keep them from freezing and bursting, and piled a small mountain of sacked potatoes, turnips, apples, and dried fruits in the middle of the room for the same reason. On the worst nights, they slept on the floor beside the stove, their feet shoved so close to the firebox that whoever was awake would also keep an eye on the blankets, in case they caught fire.

Near the end of the first month, with the hay gone and the water coming less frequently as the women's pace slowed, the horses and mules started to grow unruly. As if they also sensed the gravity of the situation. With nothing else available, the women began feeding them potatoes and apples, and when that ran low, they gave them flour.

It was nearly six weeks into the freeze that Rose discovered the buckskin had broken its halter and disappeared. She trailed it for nearly half a mile, far enough to determine that it was headed for the gap that would take it down through the bluffs to the Yellowstone, then she returned to the cabin. By the time she stumbled inside, her eyelashes were frozen, her hands and feet painful to touch.

"You could've died," Nora scolded, rubbing Rose's pallid toes by the fire. Then she abruptly shut up, a haunted look coming into her eyes.

Rose regretted the loss of the buckskin. It had been a connection to a past she could never retrieve, friends she still missed. She hoped it was for the best, that things weren't quite so harsh down below. She couldn't help thinking the horse would stand as much of a chance on its own as it did trying to subsist on a dwindling supply of paste and dehydrated fruits.

After a while the unrelenting cold and the exertion it took just to get through another day began to take its toll on the women. Their steps became draggy, their speech slurred with fatigue. Their cheeks shrank to craters and the flesh under their eyes turned dark and puffy. And as their strength waned, their pessimism grew. Dreams as dark and ugly as a grave robber's soul began to plague Rose's sleep, so that she often awoke trembling, her heart pounding.

At first she kept the disturbing images of her nightmares to herself, burying them under her work as she had so many other unpleasant memories, but as the freeze continued and her hopes flagged, that effort became more and more difficult.

It was noon on a hazy day well into the seventh week of the freeze that Rose finally caved. The temperature had warmed to around five degrees below zero. Tiny ice crystals danced and twinkled in the still air, and the snow crunched like crushed glass underfoot. Rose and Nora had paused on their way back from the barn, although Rose couldn't have said why. Perhaps it was to search the plains to the east for some sign of their cattle. Or maybe it was to stare wistfully at the indistinct sphere of the sun, remembering when it had been more kindly, more forgiving. For whatever reason, they stopped and turned together to face the brittle, gray-white world, a hushed and featureless landscape that was without perspective or even horizon, so perfectly did the shades of earth and sky blend together. Neither spoke, and in the silence, Rose began to shake. A chill wracked her shoulders and her limbs weakened until it seemed her knees would surely buckle and throw her to the ground.

"Rose?"

It passed then, with that single query from Nora, but she was badly shaken and it showed. They went inside, but even there Rose was unable to slow her chills. She was so cold she kept her cap and coats on, and stood shivering in front of the fireplace.

Finally Nora said: "What's wrong?"

"I can't seem to warm up."

Coming over, Nora touched the inside of her wrist to Rose's forehead. "You don't seem warm."

"I sure as heck don't feel it, either."

"Would you like some tea?"

"Yeah, tea sounds good." She sat down on a stool, and after a few minutes sweat began to bead up above her brow. She removed her coats—the horse-hide outer coat and the sack coat and vest she'd purchased in Sheridan—and tossed them on her bunk. Even then she couldn't stop the tremors. By the time Nora returned with a cup of Earl Grey, Rose was certain she was going to explode.

"Rose," Nora said, kneeling at her side. "What is it? Are you sick?"

"I don't feel so good." Her teeth chattered and her legs and arms tingled with an unfamiliar numbness. After a couple of minutes the feelings began to subside, replaced by an incredible sadness. She wanted to cry, but couldn't. The tears wouldn't come. The tears never came, not the way she needed them—fast and furious, washing away a torment she didn't fully understand.

"You look like you've seen a ghost," Nora said gently.

Rose almost laughed. "Maybe that's it. Maybe I'm seein' ghosts." She stared into the fire, watching the flames blur into shimmying waves of yellow and gold.

"What ghosts?" Nora asked.

"That Indian. The one I killed up on the Mussel-shell."

"When you were running with Wiley and Shorty?"

"Uhn-huh. I been thinkin' about him again lately, wonderin' did he have a family that maybe looked but couldn't find him. I been thinkin' about Wiley and Shorty, too." She wiped her lips with the back of her hand. "And the Frakes boys. I get these dreams, Nora." The panic was returning, digging its claws inside as if reaching for her soul. "They won't leave me be, and I don't know why."

"What kind of dreams?"

"The baby . . . ," Rose began in a tiny voice.

"Oh, Rose, that couldn't be helped. There wasn't a thing you could've done."

"I could've buried it. I could've gotten the body outta there. That ain't right, the way that happened."

"No!" Nora said sharply. "Don't even think that." She gripped Rose's shoulders, giving her a shake. "Listen to me, don't you dare think such thoughts! Nothing good can ever come from them."

"It was my baby," Rose said in a choked voice. "Mine 'n' Shorty's." She trembled, tears pooling in the corners of her eyes.

"There wasn't any way to recover the body, or likely even a body to recover. It was too early, Rose. It was a miscarriage."

"I dream of it cryin' for me, Nora. Sometimes I dream about Muggy, too . . . that I'm in the grave with him and people is throwin' dirt on top of us and I'm tryin' to get out but Muggy keeps holdin' me down. Sometimes I dream it's Wiley up there, throwin' the dirt in, and sometimes I dream Shorty's tryin' to get outta his grave while I'm standin' on top of it, whackin' it with a shovel. They keep comin' back, Nora, all these dreams, all these people. They're tearin' me apart."

"Oh, Rose," Nora breathed, stroking her hair. "Why didn't you say something?"

"What was I supposed to say? Don't be scared, Nora, but you're trapped in a mountain cabin with a loony?" She shuddered. "Lordy, that's it, ain't it? I'm losin' my mind?"

"No, you're not losing your mind, but you have to start talking about these things. You can't bottle them up and not expect them to haunt you." She shook her head. "I should've realized that growing up the way you did, you'd think it was wrong to speak of something so personal."

Rose lowered her head, the chills subsiding. "There ain't nothin' to talk about," she said softly. "They's just dreams."

"Then talk about the dreams. Your past is eating you up inside. Talking is the only way I know to get through it. That's something I learned in half a dozen hook shops between here and Chicago. If you don't, then you probably will go crazy."

"I . . . I don't know what to say."

"Why, hell," Nora said, taking a seat on the hearth and handing Rose her tea. "You just open your mouth and see what comes out."

Chapter Twenty-Seven

Of all the weather phenomena a person was likely to encounter in Montana over the course of a year, Rose considered none more pleasant than a Chinook. Not even a summer thunderstorm could compare favorably, since those events were far less singular and normally preceded by gusting winds and cracking bolts of lightning.

A Chinook would generally start as a subtle shift in sound, almost always too imperceptible to grasp on a conscious level. Nine times out of ten, Rose would be working on something around the cabin and intent on the task at hand, or else asleep in the middle of the night, when she would become aware of a disturbance in the pattern of her existence that frightened the bejesus out of her until she figured out what it was.

Usually what the sound was—and thinking about it, she'd realize it had been there for quite some time, like the ticking of a clock in the next room—was the patter of melting snow. Only then would she become aware of the rising temperature, or note the blessed moisture permeating the normally dry air. And always she would stop whatever she was doing and turn to the warming winds, or if the Chinook arrived during the night, she'd pull on her overboots and go outside to stand on the stoop and absorb it, while hope for a future beyond drifting snowbanks and numbing cold blossomed once more.

That was the way it was in the spring of 1887, if a person in that northern latitude could rightly call February a child of spring. The Chinook swept over the A-Bar-E sometime before dawn, so that a steady dripping from the cabin's eaves was the first thing Rose heard when she awoke that morning. She threw her blankets back with a hoarse shout and padded to the window in her wool socks.

In her own bunk across the room, Nora elbowed her blankets back to squint quizzically at Rose. "Whazzit?" she mumbled.

"Summer's come," Rose announced, running a fingernail across one of the windowpanes and scraping away a slushy layer of ice to reveal the glass underneath. With a disinterested groan, Nora flopped back to her pillow, pulling the blankets over her head.

Because the temperatures had moderated some-what since the worst of the freeze in January, they no longer slept in shifts to watch the fires at night. Some days now, the thermometer on the outside wall of the cabin would climb to twenty above, although Rose knew such temperatures were misleading. She had to resist the urge to throw off her coat and mittens and bask in the newly arrived warmth, reminding herself that it was a false warmth, and that a person could die almighty quick in twenty-degree weather.

But this was different. This was a bona-fide

Chinook, and by afternoon the red mercury in their thermometer had climbed well above freezing. Although there would be more cold and snow, Rose knew the worst was over. It was only a matter of time now, a few more weeks would put the season behind them for good.

Hanging on had become easier for Rose since Nora had encouraged her to start talking about the things that bothered her. It had been a struggle at first, what with her pap's voice constantly harping that a woman was to be seen and not heard, and that her problems were small when compared with others.

It helped, Rose figured, that Nora was a woman. It enabled her to talk not just about her past and family, as she'd done last winter with Shorty, but about her feelings and hopes, the things she still wanted in life—a good man who loved her, a home, kids. And dammit, what was wrong with a white picket fence and a flower box under the window?

She wasn't blind to the fact that she was still shying away from the darker subjects of her dreams, but that was all right. Now that the nightmares had retreated, she was content to let the whole affair slide. Besides, with winter breaking, they were finding more pressing matters to contend with.

Rose had been out on Albert several times in the weeks preceding the Chinook, and what she'd seen worried her. The range was a mess, their own land rife not only with Flying Egg cattle, but with other northern brands as well. And their own A-Bar-E stock had vanished altogether.

Nor were the cattle she did find faring all that well. With a hard cap of ice under the snow, the range had yielded little to keep an animal going. The body fat had melted off the stock at alarming rates, creating washboards out of rib cages, bony, protruding knobs out of hip joints. Long before the thaw began to release the life-saving pastures, Rose was looking at cattle so thin she could have wrapped her arms around their stomachs and clasped her hands on the opposite side.

At first the sudden melt created about as much trouble as it alleviated. Lowlands flooded, and the footing on even the higher slopes was made uncertain by the deep slush. It was more than a week into the thaw before Rose felt confident enough to venture onto the range.

She rode east first, but the land that only a few weeks before had seemed crowded with stray cattle was now empty. Except for scattered carcasses, she didn't even see a Flying Egg cow.

Knowing that the open-range herds would have drifted south ahead of the bitter, lashing winds, she shifted her search to the bluffs above the Yellowstone. It was there she began finding the cattle she sought, in far larger numbers than she'd anticipated. It was there, too, that Rose began to discover the true scope of the winter's legacy.

Dead cattle were stacked like cordwood in the draws and coulées above the bluffs. Caught by drifting snows and too weak from hunger to fight their way out, they'd simply given up and died. The piles of bodies emerging from the melting snows reminded Rose of tangled, broken driftwood left in the wake of a flood. Wolves and coyotes feasting on the half-frozen remains trotted lazily out of her path, their bellies obscenely distended. On the ride back to the cabin, Rose counted fourteen wolves and over a hundred dead cattle—the beeves all carrying the Crooked Bar-O-Bar brand of the Flying Egg.

There was very little conversation in the cabin that night, following Rose's description of what she'd seen on the range. The next day she left before Nora awoke, riding Albert down through the gap in the bluffs to the valley below.

If what she'd discovered yesterday had frightened her, what she saw today nearly broke her. At least five hundred head had tumbled to their deaths from the bluffs above, and those just along the short stretch of cliffs where she explored. She had little doubt that the number of perished livestock would climb into the thousands, if not hundreds of thousands.

Among the dead she counted thirty-nine of the forty-five head of A-Bar-E stock they'd started the new year with. All of the calves were there, even the little bull she'd saved from wolves the day the blizzard struck.

Reining away from the bluffs, Rose entered the timber along the Yellowstone. It was here she began inding a few live ones. Although none of them carried the A-Bar-E brand, she couldn't help but feel some hope. Yet as she rode among them, even that tiny ray was extinguished. The cattle she found had hardly escaped unscathed. Many were crippled beyond recovery. She saw scores of hoofs that had frozen and split, so that the animal was left with only bloody stumps to stand on; others had knees swollen to three times their normal size, their agony apparent in their runny, infected eyes. None appeared capable of moving. Most didn't even swing their heads to watch her pass. Their time now would be short, Rose knew. Soon these pitiful survivors would succumb to infection, shock, or scavengers; those that didn't would die an even more horrible death, consumed from the legs up by maggots and rot.

Nora had supper waiting by the time Rose got back, but neither of them were very hungry. They drank tea laced with whiskey kept on hand for medicinal purposes, then fell into their bunks as if drugged. The next morning, they sat on the stoop in their coats and talked.

"It ain't lookin' too good right now," Rose said tentatively.

"You warned me last spring that livestock was a risky investment, but who could've imagined a winter like this?"

"It wasn't just the winter. The range was in poor shape to begin with. Cows was thinny even last fall, when they should've been fat."

Nora's features drew taut. "Well, no one will have to worry about overgrazing this year, will they?"

Taking a deep breath, Rose said: "Nora, we got bills to pay. We owe Sutherland over a hundred dollars, and I figure they'll tax this place this year, too. We got a registered brand now, and you can bet ol' Ostermann is gonna make sure the tax inspector knows how to find us. We might scrape together enough money to get by one year, but we'll sure as Hades go belly up next, assumin' we could scrounge up enough supplies to see us through. Herman Sutherland'll outfit a body on credit if he thinks the odds is good, but ours ain't so shiny no more."

In a ragged voice, Nora said: "I won't go back to whoring. I'd rather rob stagecoaches."

"Nobody said anything about whorin' or robbin' coaches, but we're gonna have to come up with something."

"Maybe I could get a job in a restaurant," Nora said after a pause.

"That'd help, and I reckon I could skin mules. Ol' Calamity Jane's done it aplenty."

"We could get by," Nora said.

But Rose was already shaking her head. "I reckon that'd be all we'd do. We'd never get enough money ahead that way to restock the place."

They were quiet for a long time then, until finally Nora stood, brushed off the seat of her skirt, and went inside. A couple of minutes later, Rose heard the clang of a skillet as she started breakfast.

In the weeks that followed, Rose spent as much time as possible scouring the plains to the east and the Yellowstone Valley to the south in search of the six remaining head of A-Bar-E stock, but she never found them.

By April, life had returned more or less to normal. Still haunting the timber along the Yellowstone, Rose began to encounter travelers using the Miles City to Billings toll road. Through them she learned the extent of the winter's devastation. People had died by the hundreds, livestock by the millions; tragedy had been wrought as far east as Minnesota and as far south as Colorado. Some newspapers estimated that as much as eighty percent of the cattle that had roamed the northern ranges in the autumn of 1886 had perished by the spring of '87.

"Buzzards are so heavy they can't get off the ground, and coyotes'll just lay up along the road and watch you pass," one old bullwhacker told her on a sunny afternoon toward the middle of the month. "Damnation, but it stinks. Everywhere you go."

Rose nodded morosely. It stank up above, too, and the wolves and crows and magpies were fat and indolent.

As spring advanced she saw several Flying Egg cowboys roaming the land, but they never came near. Still, they made her wonder what Ostermann was planning now that his herd was gone. Would he still be intent on taking control of the A-Bar-E, or would he return to his home across the Atlantic to mourn his losses among the gambling dens and whorehouses of London?

Word along the trail revealed that some ranchers were settling the question of their future with a bullet in the brain, but Ostermann hadn't struck Rose as possessing that kind of fortitude. He'd invested some time and effort, and potentially a great deal of someone else's money, into the Flying Egg, but she doubted if he'd put any of his own heart or soul into the venture. In her opinion it generally took that kind of commitment to induce a man to take his own life when an undertaking failed.

Rose and Nora still hadn't come up with any kind of solution to their own dilemma. The lost cattle and the debt they owed Sutherland continued to hang over them, tinting their every decision—even the trivial ones.

The grass was turning green on the day they spotted an approaching horse. Although it was late evening and the light was poor, they both noticed the meandering animal as soon as it exited the trail that had brought it up through the bluffs. Coming to a stop, Rose let her hand swing back to touch the Smith & Wesson's butt. She continued to carry the pistol even around home—Ostermann had made that kind of an impression.

"Why, it's a horse," Nora said in surprise.

"Looks more like an overgrown jack rabbit," was Rose's droll reply.

Nora took a couple of steps forward. "Isn't that . . . ?"

"I reckon so."

Twenty minutes later, Dirty-Nosed Dave Merritt's stunted buckskin wandered into the yard. Rose moved to intercept it, but the horse snorted and trotted off.

"Contrary ol' hammerhead," Rose commented.

But Nora was laughing so hard that tears were streaming down her cheeks. "It ain't dead, Rose. It survived. Do you know what that means?"

"That if only the good die young, this nag is gonna live to be a hundred and twenty-nine?"

"I'm serious."

"Nora, if you're thinkin' any of our cows survived just because this jughead did . . . well, I wouldn't get my hopes up."

"Why not?" She was clearly in an optimistic mood. "If eighty percent of the herds were destroyed, doesn't that mean twenty percent lived? And doesn't it stand to reason that some of them might be ours? They were in better condition than most of the stock on the range."

"That last part's true, but I been up and down the Yellowstone a dozen times. There ain't no A-Bar-E cows out there."

"Then where are they? If they aren't along the Yellowstone or under the bluffs, where'd they go? And where's this horse been?"

"I don't know where that buckskin's been, but them cows is dead. Maybe they're buried under a pile of other dead critters and lost to sight, but they've gotta be dead."

"What if they aren't?" Nora insisted. "What if they crossed the river onto the reservation?"

Rose hesitated. "It wouldn't be like cows to leave good shelter along a river to cross the open plains in the middle of a blizzard," she said finally. "They'd want to stay in amongst the trees where the wind wasn't so sharp."

"What if they were starving or freezing or chased out by wolves?"

"Then I'd say if they crossed onto the reservation, they've already been in and out of some hungry Crow family's bellies."

"Oh."

"Aw, hell," Rose said, seeing the crestfallen look that came over her friend's face. "Maybe they did cross over on the ice. It wouldn't hurt to ride down that way and take a look."

But Nora's mood had already crashed. "Whites aren't allowed on the reservation, are they?"

"Not unless you've got special permission from the agent, but I been over there a hundred times without no one knowin' it, just like them Crows come north of the river all the time. I reckon Indian agents need to know only what they need to know, and that sure as shootin' ain't everything."

Fetching her lariat, Rose went after the buckskin, grazing beside the barn. She wanted to put it in the corral with Albert and the mules, but the undersize gelding wouldn't be caught. It wouldn't even allow her within roping distance. After several failed attempts, Rose gave up and returned to Nora's side. "That's a cantankerous little bronc'," she said.

"It wants to be left alone," Nora replied. Heading for the cabin, she added: "That doesn't seem like a lot to ask for any more."

Chapter Twenty-Eight

Rose spent three days combing the northern reaches of the Crow reservation but didn't find anything sporting an A-Bar-E brand. She returned home late on the third day to discover several extra horses in the corral, packs and piles of gear stacked outside the fence. Although she loosened the Smith & Wesson in its holster as a precaution, she'd already recognized Gene Sidwell's bay and the seal brown mare belonging to Lew Parker.

Lew wandered out of the barn as she rode up, looking as ragged as any derelict after his winter trapping. His hair was long and unkempt, his beard like a shaggy bib covering the front of his shirt. He wore a poorly cured wolf-hide vest over a threadbare shirt, and knee-high buckskin leggings over his trousers.

"Dang," Rose said, eyeing his attire. "You look like you been rode hard and put up wet."

Taking her in a bear hug, Lew lifted her clear

of the ground. "Hello, Rose. Gimme a squeeze."

"Here now," she said, cuffing the side of his head. "Put me down! What's got into you?"

"I been six months in those hills and ain't seen a woman since we left here last fall."

"Well, don't go gettin' no randy notions around me." She pushed him away. "What you've seen or ain't seen since you passed through here ain't my bailiwick."

"Why, I never said it was," Lew replied solemnly. "It was a friend I greeted, that's all."

"Well . . . shoot." She thrust out her hand. "All right, ya dang' horse thief. How'd you fare over the winter?"

"We done all right," he said, shaking her hand formally. "We found a sheltered valley with plenty of grass for the horses and enough meat to feed an army. It was cold, though. Froze the ears off a couple of the pack horses."

Rose told him about the cattle she'd found below the bluffs, and of the huge losses suffered by ranchers across the northern tier of the nation.

"Nora told us you lost your herd, too," Lew said. "I'm sorry to hear about that."

"It was a rough winter," she agreed, "but we come through with our ears intact."

Lew laughed. "I've got some meat and coffee in my packs. Let's find a place along the crick and fix ourselves something to eat?"

"You got to be joshin'!" She turned to the cabin, noticing for the first time that its chimney and stovepipe were smokeless, the single window dark as the eye socket in a skull. "When'd you get in?"

"Last night, but I didn't get booted out until this afternoon. I consider myself fortunate to have spent one night under a roof, although I'll admit I didn't get much sleep."

"I'll be damned," Rose said. She'd been looking forward to sleeping inside tonight herself, with a fire to warm her toes and a rope-sprung bunk to cushion her slumber.

"If it's any consolation, we didn't take many hides," Lew told her. "The furs were prime, but once the big freeze hit, it took all our efforts just to keep us and the horses alive. I doubt we'll clear more than a few hundred dollars, and that won't be near enough for Gene to buy a freight outfit."

"Is that what that fool has in mind, a freight outfit? As if there's a teamster in this territory that ain't scramblin' for whatever business the rail-roads has left like crumbs on the floor?"

Chuckling, Lew said: "Come on, let's camp out under the stars like a couple of kids in the back yard. It'll be fun."

"You been out 'way too long, Lew Parker, if that's your notion of fun!" Rose called after him, then turned to strip the saddle from Albert's back.

But Lew was right, and even Rose had to admit she had a good time. She'd always enjoyed Lew's company, and she found it especially refreshing tonight, after her long winter's confinement with only another woman's voice, another woman's point of view. They didn't see Nora at all, but Rose heard her sharp, happy squeal a couple of times right before sunset. Later Gene came out in just his long-handles to rummage through his panniers for something or the other, but he took no notice of the campers along the creek. He looked quite a bit less woolly than Lew, which surprised Lew more than it did Rose.

"Nora must've cut his hair and made him shave," Lew said in wonderment. "I swear I've never seen a woman have a spell over a fella like she has over Gene."

"Casting a spell over a man ain't hard work if you can stomach the consequences," Rose replied. "It always made me feel a mite queasy, though."

Lew had kindled his fire about a hundred yards from the cabin to increase the lovebirds' sense of privacy, then whipped up a meal that came largely from his own packs. They had meat from a black bear he'd shot in the hills and spotted pup—a concoction of rice and raisins—along with biscuits, coffee, and some early greens.

They bedded down with the sun and let the fire die out. It was a mild spring night, the stars twinkling and the creek running fast and furious. Overhead the budding cottonwood limbs swayed in the breeze.

They slept late the next day, burrowing deeper into their blankets as the sky grew light. Although Rose considered the weather agreeable, she knew there were some who'd be put off by the frost that clung to the rocks along the creek when they awoke. Eating another meal over a smoky campfire was more than she was willing to endure, however.

"Enough's enough, dang it," she declared, pulling on her boots. "I don't know about you, but I aim to eat breakfast at a table this mornin', even if I got to throw a bucket of water on them two rabbits to do it."

"I ain't arguing with you," Lew replied, skinning into his clothes.

Gathering their gear, they headed for the cabin. The buckskin had showed up again during the night and was standing hipshot in front of the barn, its head drooped sleepily.

"You want me to lasso that critter for you?" Lew asked manfully. Rose had mentioned last night how she'd been unable to catch Davey's little gelding since its return.

"You're welcome to try," she said, thinking it might be fun to watch. "They's a lariat in the lean-to." She set her bedroll and rifle aside, then headed for the corral to turn the stock loose for the day.

"That horse is too small to be so hard to catch," Lew said, lifting his voice so she could hear. "Likely a man could run it down afoot if he . . ."

Rose paused with one hand on the gate, the abrupt silence pulsing with intimidation. Cautiously she looked over her shoulder. Lew lay on the ground in front of the lean-to, his long hair splayed out in the dirt. The buckskin hadn't moved, but it was standing straighter, its head up, ears laid malevolently backward. Taking a deep breath, Rose slowly pivoted, though careful to keep her hands away from the Smith & Wesson.

"Did you think I'd forgotten you?" John Stroudmire asked. He stood above Lew like a vulture, wearing a tall-crowned black hat and a tan, ankle-length range coat, brushed back to reveal the ivory grips of his Merwin Hulbert revolvers. He held a length of firewood in his left hand, but tossed it casually aside.

"If you killed him, I'm gonna take it personal," Rose said thickly.

"We've some unfinished business, you and I. My regret is that I've waited this long to see it through."

"We don't have no business together. Why don't you just ride on outta here?"

"An armed woman presents a delicate situation," Stroudmire went on in an eerily conversational tone. "I could've killed you easily that night in the Silver Star, yet had I done so, I would have hanged, for no other reason than your gender."

"I imagine if they'd've hung you it would've been for other reasons, like that little girl that got trampled over to Powderville last summer."

"A hangman's noose won't be a concern today. What happens here will remain in this yard forever."

"Dang, Stroudmire, are you hearin' anything I'm sayin'?"

"After today," he assured her, "petty little

cowboys won't snicker into their drinks when I sit down at a table, or speak of roses with thorns when I pass them on the street. After today, I shall be vindicated."

"Jesus," Rose breathed.

"I'll offer you a rare opportunity, Missus Edwards," he said calmly. "I'll allow you to draw your pistol first. Can anything be more fair?"

"I can think of a few things."

"Shall we proceed?"

"Dammit!" She glanced at the cabin. It seemed they were talking loud enough to wake the dead, yet there was no sign of Nora or Gene. Then she sucked her breath in sharply, her eyes suddenly ablaze. "What'd you do to 'em, Stroudmire?"

"What's your preference?" he inquired. "We could count backward from ten, draw our pistols on one?"

Rose's pulse roared in her ears. "You son-of-a-bitch!" she yelled, her hand diving for the Smith & Wesson.

Stroudmire moved at the same time, although neither of them was very fast. Despite her best attempt, Rose quickly found herself locked in a three-way struggle between the Smith & Wesson, the gripping leather of the holster, and her own gut-wrenching panic. Even Stroudmire, who made his living with six-shooters, had to separate leather from steel with the ball of his thumb against the top of his holster. In a land of rugged terrain and hostile weather, speed was seldom as important as a good, tight-fitting sheath to hold a revolver snugly in place.

But Stroudmire was still the more practiced of the two, still the swifter. He was leveling his pistol before Rose could even loosen hers. He fired casually and without aim, and the heavy .45 slug smashed into the gatepost at her side. Rose jumped at the Merwin Hulbert's bark, loosening her grip on the pistol. The buckskin started and swung its hips toward Stroudmire, its ears flattened. Stroudmire took a step forward, then another. He was smiling, a taut little upward curl at each corner of his mouth. His eyes sparkled with triumph. The buckskin hunched its croup as if in anticipation of another shot.

Rose wrapped her fingers around the Smith &Wesson's grips but dared not draw it. "Shoot, you bastard," she hissed. "Get it over with."

Lifting his arm, Stroudmire thumbed the hammer back to full cock. "Who did you really think was the quickest, Missus Edwards?"

She would have said he was and made it unanimous, but, as it turned out, they were both wrong. Stroudmire settled the Merwin Hulbert's sights on her breast. Rose wanted to close her eyes, but couldn't; it was as if a morbid curiosity compelled her to watch to the bitter end. And then the stunted gelding that had once belonged to Dirty-Nosed Dave struck so fast that Rose barely saw the flash of its hoofs. She did, however, hear the crisp snap of Stroudmire's right arm, saw his face go pale as the Merwin Hulbert spun out of his hand as if spring-loaded, landing a good thirty feet away. The gunman staggered, then caught his balance.

"Damn horse," he muttered with no more emotion than if he'd nicked himself shaving. Using his left hand, he reached for his second pistol, carried butt forward on his left hip.

"Wait!" Rose shouted, yanking the Smith & Wesson free. "Don't be a fool, Stroudmire! I'll shoot!"

But Stroudmire didn't even hear her. At this moment in time, he was like a machine—precise, methodical, without conscience. He'd forgotten the buckskin as he had the arm that hung crookedly at his side. He was unaware of Rose as a human being, immune to any threat she might pose, incapable of being approached or recalled. He had come here to kill. Nothing else mattered.

A chill gripped Rose's heart. Her mouth went dry and the Smith & Wesson's muzzle began to waver. As if through a haze she saw Stroudmire's weak-side Merwin Hulbert clear leather, watched the barrel begin its long ascent to level. A whimper escaped her. Then the Smith & Wesson clapped like thunder, and, twenty feet away, Stroudmire stumbled backward from the bullet's impact. Blinking swiftly, he glanced down not at the finger-size hole that had appeared in his vest, but at his own ivory-handled .45 that refused to come to taw. Rose watched in disbelief as he struggled to tighten his fingers around the smooth grips, to bring up the muzzle.

"God damn you," Rose quavered, cocking the Smith & Wesson a second time. She held the pistol in both hands to steady her trembling aim; her finger tightened on the trigger. "God damn you for making me do this."

Chapter Twenty-Nine

Nora and Gene were alive. Rose could have fallen to her knees and shouted hallelujah, so great was her relief when she discovered the pair tied together on Nora's bunk, naked as jaybirds. Pushing open the cabin door to peek inside had been the hardest thing she'd done since the morning she cut Muggy down from the lightning-scarred pine to bury him.

There was a bruise on Nora's cheek, an ugly gash across Gene's forehead that had stained the mattress with blood. Their fingers were swollen like fat sausages from being bound too tight, but there was nothing wrong with them that time wouldn't heal.

Lew remained unconscious for nearly an hour after Rose and Gene brought him inside and laid him out on Rose's bunk, but, once he came around, he refused to stay in bed. Lew was mad clean through for having allowed Stroudmire to get the drop on him.

"The son-of-a-bitch should've gone ahead and shot me for being so stupid," he grumbled from his seat on the stoop.

"Stroudmire won't be shooting anyone any more," Gene said. He looked at Nora, and the two of them quietly slipped away.

"Stay with me," Lew said, grabbing Rose's wrist when she started after them. "I'm feeling kind of woozy yet."

She jerked her arm away, growling: "I ain't no dummy, Lew Parker. I know what they're doin'." But after a pause she sat down again. Rose waited until she figured Gene and Nora had had enough time to load Stroudmire's body onto a pack horse and take it away, then abruptly stood. "I'm gonna bust if I sit here much longer. I think I'll turn the horses loose."

"You'd best hold off until we talk this through," Lew said. "We may not want to take time to catch those horses if we decide to cut our pins."

"I ain't runnin'," Rose replied curtly. "That slick bastard ain't chasin' me off my property, alive or dead."

"Killing a man creates complications, Rose, even if it was self-defense. A lot of people heard you threaten Stroudmire in Miles City last year."

"We ain't takin' him to Miles City or any other place. If Gene and Nora ain't buryin' him, I'll get a shovel and do it myself."

"I'm not suggesting we take him in. I'm just

wondering if maybe we ought to leave Montana for a spell. They say California's nice."

"I reckon not," she replied coolly.

"You're as bull-headed as a stump, Rose."

"Maybe, but I ain't runnin'." There was movement at the barn and Rose touched her pistol, but it was only the buckskin. Letting her hand fall away, she said: "I must've come close to shootin' that jughead a dozen times since he came back. Now I reckon I'll have to feed him until one or the other of us dies of old age."

"It's a small price to pay," Lew remarked somberly. He looked away, but not before Rose noticed the scrunched look of pain that flashed across his face.

"You got a headache, Lew? I could hot up some tea if you'd like."

"I've got a dent in my head you could lay your finger in. Hell, yes, I've got a headache."

Rose went inside to kick up a fire in the stove. Nora and Gene returned by the time the tea was ready, and Nora passed out crackers and huckleberry preserves for breakfast. They stood in the yard and ate, talking about what they should do. It was Nora who made the final decision.

"Rose and I will stay here. Stroudmire and his gear is buried, and you boys can turn his horse loose along the river for someone else to find. Gene and Lew will go on to Junction City like they planned and sell their furs. If we all act like nothing's happened, no one should suspect anything."

"Oh, they'll suspect plenty," Lew said. "Rumors will float up and down this valley for another twenty years."

"Let 'em talk," Rose said stubbornly. She noticed Gene watching Nora closely, but Nora gave him a quick shake of her head. As soon as they finished eating, Gene and Lew went to the corral to saddle their horses and rig their packs. Rose and Nora remained behind.

"Are you sure?" Rose asked, seeing the mist of tears in her friend's eyes.

Nora shrugged angrily. "Who the hell is ever sure?" she snapped, then went inside.

By the end of the month the killing of John Stroudmire seemed as far away to Rose as last January's blizzard. At first she'd worried that the incident might trouble her sleep, as the Indian she'd killed up on the Musselshell had, but her nights passed uneventfully.

Unfortunately Nora didn't fare as well. It wasn't Stroudmire's death that bothered her. If anything, she seemed to approve of that.

"There's no telling how many innocent lives you've saved by what you did today," she'd told Rose on the evening of the shooting.

Yet as the season progressed it became evident Nora was slipping into a blue funk that not even the warming temperatures of spring could cure. Rose suspected the problem was twofold—Gene Sidwell and the loss of their cattle—but she couldn't think of anything that might help.

"Maybe we should go on a picnic," she suggested one day in late May. "We can shoot at empty tin cans and practice our road agent spin."

Nora stopped what she was doing at the stove to look at Rose. "What for?"

"To get you outta the house before you lose all your color, is what for."

Nora's gaze hardened. "Men prefer pale women. It makes them think we're fragile."

"Dang it, you got to quit lookin' on the mossy side of things. The sun's shinin', in case you ain't noticed."

Nora walked to the window to stare across the empty plains. "Maybe I was too hasty, saying I wouldn't go back," she remarked softly.

Although she didn't elaborate, Rose knew what she meant. "Whorin's no life for you. We got a place here. We'll make it work."

"There's no future here. Not for me."

"Don't talk that way. You've worked too hard to get away from parlor houses to go back now."

Nora smiled bleakly. "You're a good friend, Rose. I'll bet with a little luck we could've made something of this place." She turned away from the window. "But that didn't happen, did it?"

"The winners is them that hang on."

"Sometimes the winner is the one who knows when to let go."

"Not if it's a brick wall they're fixin' to walk into."

Nora went to the door and slipped outside. Rose followed only as far as the jamb, standing there with one hand on the frame, an ache in her heart that was like a length of steel post embedded there.

They were standing at the corral one morning in early June, having just turned the stock loose for the day, when Rose heard the buckskin whinny. Looking up, she saw the runty gelding standing about a hundred yards out, his ears pricked toward the gulch that led down through the bluffs.

"Son-of-a-bitch," Rose grunted, scurrying over the corral poles. She raced into the cabin, and was back outside with the Sharps by the time a couple of horsemen hove into sight. Although her heart was pounding, she could tell at a glance that neither man was Frank Caldwell, and some of her worst fears subsided.

Nora appeared at her side, shotgun in hand; her face was flushed, eyes wide. "I wish you wouldn't do that," she said. "You scared me half to death."

"Riders comin'."

"I see them, but you shot out of that corral like a cannonball. It wouldn't have taken ten extra seconds to go through the gate."

Rose let that one pass. Propping the Sharps against her hip, she quickly buckled on her gun belt. "You'd think after what happened with Stroudmire I'd have better sense than to wander around outside without my pistol," she murmured, mostly to herself.

"I don't recognize them," Nora said. "Who do you think they are?"

"Horse thieves, I reckon."

"They look more like hunters. They're wearing buckskins."

"Take a gander at that second horse, the black with the star that fella in front is leadin'. Ain't no wolfer owns an animal like that."

Nora nodded but remained silent. As the riders drew near, Rose felt a chilling pessimism. Something about the lead rider nagged at her, but it wasn't until he rode into the yard that she realized what it was.

"No," she breathed, the Sharps hanging slackly in her hand. "No, god dammit . . . no." She started forward in a stiff walk, but quickly picked up speed. By the time she reached the lead horseman, she was almost running, the Sharps raised above her head like a club.

"Nooo!" she screamed. *"God dammit, no, no, no, noooo!"*

Before she could bring the rifle crashing down against the horseman's head, the second rider spilled from his saddle and grabbed her, forcing the rifle down, pinning her arms at her side. "Rose!" he shouted. "It's all right, Rose! It's all right!"

Rose kept her gaze on the first horseman, tears pooling in the corners of her eyes. "You was supposed to be dead," she whispered fiercely. "God dammit, you was supposed to be *dead!*"

"I know," Wiley Collins replied. "I'm sorry."

Chapter Thirty

Rose jerked away from the arms holding her. They belonged to Dirty-Nosed Dave Merritt, and under different circumstances that would have elicited a major jolt in itself, but, at that moment, she hardly noticed. Dirty-Nosed Dave stepped back cautiously. Then Nora appeared, her shotgun leveled at Dirty-Nosed Dave's belly. Both hammers were cocked, and Nora's expression was furious.

"Get away from her!" Nora screamed.

Dirty-Nosed Dave back-pedaled quickly, throwing his hands up. "It's me, Nora, Dave Merritt."

"I don't give a damn who it is. Grab her like that again and I'll blow your head off."

"Christ," Dirty-Nosed Dave squawked, his Adam's apple bobbing. "Has everyone gone crazy?"

The Sharps hung loosely in Rose's right hand, its muzzle nearly brushing the ground. She was looking at Wiley as if in a trance. "I saw you drown," she said distantly. "I saw it."

"Mind if I get down, darlin'?" Wiley asked with uncharacteristic humility. "Me knee be sore as blazes, and it'd help to walk it some."

Rose hesitated, then nodded. "For a while, but you can't come inside. I don't ever want you in my house again."

Wiley smiled. "I'm not dead, though I appreciate

ye concern. I've developed a healthy respect for ha'nts meself of late."

He was different, Wiley was, and not just in his dress—the fringed buckskin trousers and a thigh-length leather jacket embellished with floral patterns of beadwork. His hair was long and he had a beard and mustache, although combed and recently trimmed. When he dismounted, she saw that his right leg was missing below the knee, replaced by a peg carved from a juniper tree, held in place by a criss-crossing of leather straps.

Firming her grip on the Sharps, Rose backed away. She wasn't afraid of him, but she didn't want him standing too close, either. In her mind, Wiley had been dead for so long that some of the taint still remained. "What do you want?" she demanded.

"I'm wantin' nothin' from ye," he assured her. "We're on our way to Canada, Davey 'n' me, and I stopped to tell ye we was still alive, and to say good bye. 'Tis a bit selfish, perhaps, but I wanted to apologize for the hardships I put ye through."

"You never put me through no hardships."

A gentle look crossed his face. "Could we water our horses, Rosie? I didn't want to linger on the Yellowstone, as I was a-feared men might be watchin' the crossin's."

"Just like old times, huh?"

He shrugged self-consciously.

After a pause, Rose nodded toward the water trough in the corral. "You know where it's at."

Taking the reins from Dirty-Nosed Dave, Wiley led all three horses toward water. His limp was pronounced under the peg, as if the stump were still tender. They watched until he was out of earshot, then Rose turned to Dirty-Nosed Dave. "Put your hands down," she said curtly.

"I would've thought you'd be glad to see us," Dirty-Nosed Dave muttered indignantly as he lowered his arms.

"Well, you thought wrong," Rose replied. Her gaze returned to Wiley. "I saw him get shot," she said. "What happened?"

"He was shot. Once in the leg, a second time in the back. I was knocked off my cayuse, too, and both of us was in the river. I'd lost my pistol and was tryin' to burrow under a crawdad when I saw Wiley's nag floatin' past. You and Shorty was still shootin', so I figured that was my chance. I kicked out to Wiley's horse and grabbed hold. That was when I saw Wiley, tangled up in the downside stirrup. He was near drowned but still strugglin', so I got my shoulder under his head and kept his face above water as best I could. I figured soon as things slowed down, them cusses would come after us, so when we got around the bend, I cut Wiley loose and we swum for shore. Wiley was unconscious by then, but I floated him into some alders to lie low. It was as poor a hidey-hole as you're likely to find, but it turned out them buggers wasn't all that interested, after all. A couple of 'em rode up and down the bank a few times, but they never looked close. They'd 'a' spotted us easy if they had.

"We holed up till dark, then floated downriver some more. The next day, when I pulled Wiley outta the water, he was in bad shape. I reckon he'd've died . . . hell, I reckon *both* of us would've died, had not some Red River 'breeds come along. Bone-pickers, they was, waterin' their horses. Turned out there was a whole caravan of 'em back in the hills, thirty or forty of them squallin' carts they favor, plus a passel of squaws and kids and dogs and cats. A regular damn' village on wheels. It was a 'breed squaw what took off Wiley's leg with a handsaw. He carved his own peg."

Dirty-Nosed Dave followed Rose's gaze to where Wiley was watering the horses, smoking a cigarette and staring absently at the skyline.

"He ain't the same, is he?" Dirty-Nosed Dave said softly. "I picked up on it last summer. He ain't dumb or nothin', but he's lost his fire."

"I barely recognized him," Rose admitted.

"He's different, and better in some ways because of it, but he ain't cut out for this kind of work no more."

"Where'd you get that horse?" Rose didn't specify the well-groomed black; Dirty-Nosed Dave knew which animal she meant.

"Wyoming. It's what they call a polo pony. After we left the bone-pickers last fall, we went north to Alberta. I got a job snappin' bronc's on a spread outside of Medicine Hat, while Wiley played cards for money in town. He did all right for a while, but he ain't got the patience for that kind of work full time. Around Christmas he ran onto some fancy dude outta British Columbia who offered him top dollar for that horse. It's called Midnight Blue and I reckon all hell's breakin' loose for its return right about now."

"If he ain't cut out for stealin' horses, why'd you let him take such a famous one?" Rose asked testily. "Dang it, even I've heard of the Lazy-Sixteen's Midnight Blue."

"Well, it ain't that we haven't seen the error of our ways," Dirty-Nosed Dave assured her. "It's just that this is the only thing we know how to do."

"The lad's tellin' ye true, Rosie," Wiley said, returning from the corral. "Times have changed too much for old sods like me 'n' Davey. We don't fit in any more." He looked at Dirty-Nosed Dave and Nora. "Would ye mind giving me 'n' Rose a couple minutes privacy?" he asked politely.

Nora glanced at Rose, but she nodded that it was all right, and the two of them wandered off toward the barn.

"How are ye farin'?" Wiley asked when they were alone.

"I miss Shorty. I miss him a lot."

A look of anguish crossed Wiley's face. "So do I, darlin', so do I."

"Why didn't you come back, or at least send word?"

"Ye know the answer to that. I was shot up bad

and couldn't run. I couldn't risk word that I was still alive gettin' back to Caldwell or Joe Bean."

"What are you goin' to do now?"

"I'm bound for British Columbia. Maybe with the money I make from this"—he indicated Midnight Blue, standing, high-headed and nervous, at the corral—"I can buy some land and raise horses legal."

"You figure they'll let you stay in British Columbia after showing up with a stolen polo pony? That ain't gonna impress the neighbors much."

He grinned. "Ye could be right. California, then."

Rose bit her lower lip. "You ain't comin' back, are you?"

"No, darlin', I ain't. I be too well-known in these parts. Sure as shootin', I'll hang if I stay."

"Then you ought not tarry. There's been enough killin' around here of late."

He nodded, then limped forward to kiss her gently on the forehead. Stroking her cheek with his fingers, he said: "Ye be a beautiful woman, Rose, me love. Have ye realized that yet?"

"Get outta here, Wiley," she said, shoving him back. Shoving him so hard he almost fell over on his wooden leg. "I got no time for blarney."

Wiley squared his shoulders, then motioned for Dirty-Nosed Dave to bring their mounts. Glancing at Rose, he said: "Watch out who ye buy a horse from, darlin', for there be scoundrels lurkin' in every corner of this territory."

She smiled in spite of the tears stinging her eyes.

"If ever I wonder, I'll just compare 'em to you, for I'm danged if I've ever met a bigger scoundrel than Wiley Collins."

Laughing delightedly, he accepted the reins Dave handed him. Mounting awkwardly because of his leg, he took a hitch around his saddle horn with the lead rope from the big stallion called Midnight Blue. "So long, Rosie!" he called. Then, nodding a farewell to Nora, he reined toward the Helena trail, the one Muggy had come down the night they'd hung him.

Dirty-Nosed Dave held up a moment, eyeing the buckskin. "He found his way back, did he?"

"He saved my life," Rose said simply.

Another man would have asked how, but not Dirty-Nosed Dave. He smiled and lifted his reins. "Watch them hoofs," he warned, meaning the buckskin's. "He's wicked with 'em."

"Take care of yourself, Dave. Take care of Wiley, too."

With a quick wave, Dirty-Nosed Dave spurred out of the yard. Watching him go, Rose touched the scar below her right ear where she'd been creased by a bullet during the Musselshell fight—a finger-wide stretch of ruffled flesh, less than an inch in length, yet a lifelong reminder of the smoke and thunder of that bloody day that changed her life forever.

Rose was working in the garden a couple of hours later when she heard the pounding of hoofs in the gulch through the bluffs. Her pulse quickened as she moved to the edge of the pumpkin patch to retrieve her rifle and pistol. The horsemen came out of the coulée at the head of the trail like wine spilling from a jug. Rose didn't recognize the rider in the lead with the nickel-plated star pinned to his vest, but she could tell at a glance he wasn't a man to abide foolishness. He jogged his big chestnut horse toward her, pulling up only at the last minute to avoid trampling the fist-size green-and-black striped squash hidden among the vines.

"I'm looking for Collins. How long ago was he here?"

"Collins who?" Rose asked, feeling a quick anger at the lawdog's abrupt manner.

"I'll not banter with you, Missus Edwards. How far ahead is he?"

Rose let the Sharps' muzzle dip a couple of inches, then come back up, a move not lost on the lawman. "You're talkin' mighty big for a tres-passer," she pointed out.

He scowled, and Rose thought surely the fat was in the fire then, but the scowl faded, replaced by a wry grin. "You're feisty. If I hadn't been married to the same good woman the past twenty-three years, I'd consider calling on you."

"You're too old for me," Rose said. "You'd probably break something."

"Well now, I've ridden some mighty rough horses in my day."

"It's the long haul I'm thinkin' of. Collins passed

through here four or five hours ago, heading northeast."

"Little lady, you might be surprised at my endurance. What was his destination, did he say?"

"Up the Musselshell to the Mo, then east into Dakota."

"I don't hold your lies against you. I was told you were tight with the Collins gang."

"Collins never had no gang, and I ain't tight with him. I trapped wolves with him one winter, but that don't make us married."

A second horseman came up, also wearing a star, although he was clearly a subordinate. "Jed," he said to the elder lawman, "the lady back there insists it isn't Collins we're chasing. She says she's never seen them before."

Jed continued to stare at Rose. "Nobody wants to believe it was Collins on account of the Musselshell Massacre, but I know the truth of it well enough, and can guess the rest." Turning to his deputy, he said: "Gather the posse, Leroy. We'll ride north toward the Bulls and see what we see."

When the deputy was gone, the lawman said: "My name's Jed Plover. By rights my authority ended at the territorial line in Wyoming, but I'm not a man to give up easily, no matter what you might think of my endurance. I know your reputation, Rose Edwards, so understand this. I'll tolerate no lawlessness in my jurisdiction. You keep your shenanigans out of Wyoming and we'll do fine, you and me. Try something crooked in it and I'll hound you to the Yukon."

"I'll remember that," Rose said neutrally. She remained where she was while Plover returned to his posse, heading it north at a brisk trot. When they were gone, Nora came over with her shotgun.

"There were some hardcases in that bunch," she observed, her gaze following the dust of the retreating posse.

"That lawman didn't seem too bad," Rose replied. "I'd say he was a determined feller, though not much of a tracker." The posse was angling slightly west of north, toward the trail that would take them over the Bull Mountains to the Mussel-shell. Wiley and Dave had taken the Helena route, swinging slightly south of northwest and skirting the Bulls.

"He might be fooled, but I doubt if the others are."

"What others?"

"A couple of Caldwell's old bunch, Larson Web and Billy Garcia."

A chill slid down Rose's spine. Web was the old man she'd met at Two-Hats's, and she still remembered what Frank Caldwell had told her in Billings about Garcia and his vow of revenge for shooting off part of his ear. For a moment she considered it odd that neither man had come forward to confront her, but then she realized such a straightforward approach wouldn't be their style. She also thought Nora was right when she said those two wouldn't remain duped for long. They were old hands at this game, and would soon discover that the trail they were following had no fresh tracks on it. They'd know about the other trail, too. The one that led to Helena.

"I have to go after them," Rose said suddenly. "I have to let Wiley and Dirty-Nosed Dave know who's trailing them."

"What does it matter who's trailing them? They knew when they stole that horse that somebody would."

"The law's one thing, Nora. Garcia and Web is something else."

"Let them go, Rose. Don't get dragged into something that's none of your concern."

"They was my friends. I won't turn my back on 'em."

"Shorty Tibbs might've been your friend. Wiley Collins was never anyone's friend, and Dave Merritt's a drunk and a fool."

"They took me in, Nora. They accepted me when I hit rock bottom, when the fancy, God-fearin' kind wouldn't've given me the time of day. I can't no more turn my back on them than I could you or Callie. I just can't."

She saddled Albert and gathered some grub, then took off at a gallop, following the Helena trail. The prints of Wiley's horse, the black stud called Midnight Blue, and Dirty-Nosed Dave's mount were as plain as newsprint in the dust, which vexed

Rose no end. Wiley, of all people, should have known better than to be so careless, especially after leaving her cabin, which was sure to be a focal point in the minds of any pursuing posse.

The trail led her over a gently undulating plain for most of the day, skirting to the north of the small pine forest that lay west of her cabin and southwest of the Bulls. It wasn't until late in the afternoon that the land began to change, the hills becoming more rugged, marred with rocky outcroppings. Although a warm day, it wasn't especially hot; early grasshoppers leaped buzzing out of her path, and meadowlarks trilled sweet tunes in the grasses. Rose kept Albert at a steady pace, alternating between a jog and a slow lope, and his ears remained perked forward, as if he were enjoying himself.

By nightfall Rose estimated they'd covered thirty miles, and Albert was starting to show the strain. Sweat darkened the gray-peppered red hair around the gelding's cinch, and his head hung low as Rose picketed him next to a creek. Her heart ached for the aging gelding. She knew his spirit was willing; it was his muscles and joints that had seen too many hard miles, endured too many frigid winters.

The land began to climb in earnest the next day, the snow-streaked peaks of the Crazy Mountains looming dead ahead. The trail to Helena would swing north of the Crazies, but Rose was hoping that Wiley and Dave would leave it at its bend and disappear into the mountains. It continued to aggravate her that they weren't making any effort to hide their tracks.

By noon the country was becoming increasingly broken. Sparse groves of lodgepole pine shaded the hills, and aspens as green as lime shimmied in the gulches. Despite a cooling breeze, there was a trace of perspiration across Rose's upper lip when she topped a small rise and saw a scene below her that made her throat constrict and her scalp crawl.

"Lordy," she croaked in a dust-dry voice, then grimly heeled Albert forward.

Chapter Thirty-One

She rode slowly into a clearing surrounded by piney hills. Two men sat on a sloping boulder near a large oak growing alongside a creek. One of them was smoking a cigar; the other held a rifle across his lap. Both stood as she approached, expressing neither alarm nor embarrassment. Behind them, hanging from nooses tied off over a high limb, were Wiley Collins and Dirty-Nosed Dave Merritt. Both were dead, and Rose knew this time they wouldn't be coming back.

"I'll be damned," the man with the cigar said. "If it ain't the wild woman of the Yellowstone."

Rose recognized them as members of Ostermann's entourage from the previous winter. Although she hadn't known their names then, Lew Parker had identified them based on her descriptions. The one with the cigar was Ted Keyes. The man holding the rifle was Dutch Weinhart. Both were reputed veterans of past range wars, most notably those in central Texas, although rumor also implicated Weinhart in the Lincoln County conflict in New Mexico, the one that had made Billy Bonney so famous.

Fighting to control the jerky pattern of her breathing, Rose halted some ten yards away. Her right hand was clenched tightly on the top of her thigh, close enough to the Smith & Wesson that she could grab it quickly if she needed to.

"Come to rescue your friends?" Keyes asked, then cackled loudly. He'd been drinking, Rose realized; she could see it in his eyes and in the darting unsteadiness of his hands. "You're a little late if that's what you had in mind," he added.

For a long moment Rose didn't say anything. Staring at Wiley, it was all she could do to keep from screaming. She wanted to pull her pistol and empty it into Keyes's face, to smash Weinhart's skull with the butt of her rifle until it resembled a flattened gourd, but reason prevailed. "I guess I came to take 'em home," she said eventually.

"Ve vill be taking keer of dem, miss," Weinhart replied.

"We aim to let 'em rot," Keyes added.

"They're my friends," Rose persisted, forcing herself to look at Keyes and Weinhart, to keep her gaze away from Wiley's limp form, the wooden leg cocked at an unnatural angle. "They deserve a proper burial."

"No, to leave dem hang is vhat Mister Caldwell told us to do, and dhat is vhat ve do."

The fingers of Rose's right hand stretched flat along her thigh, then came back into a loose fist. Albert shifted nervously, sensing her tension. "Naw, I'm gonna take 'em home."

"No," Weinhart stated obstinately.

Rose blinked and glanced around the clearing. It was empty save for the three of them and Wiley and Dave. She saw a pair of Flying Egg horses that belonged to Keyes and Weinhart, but the black stud and Wiley and Dave's mounts were gone. "Where's Caldwell?" she asked.

"He is not here," Weinhart replied. "It is us you today 'ave to deal vith."

"But he was here," Rose said with sudden comprehension. She looked at Weinhart. "Where's the horse, Dutch? The one they call Midnight Blue."

Keyes laughed brashly. "It got away."

"Shut up, you," snarled Weinhart. "Too much talk."

"He stole it, didn't he?" Rose charged.

"Dhat is foolish talk," Weinhart replied, his accent thickening. "Is best you don't say dhat tings no more."

"Maybe we ought to hang her, too," Keyes suggested. "I'll bet ol' prissy-britches Howie would appreciate our initiative."

"Vhen to take keer of dis von is to be done,

Mister Caldwell vill tell us," Weinhart answered. "You!" he said to Rose, then pointed to the trail behind her. "Go now. Go home."

"I ain't some dog that's gonna be shooed off."

"Yah, you go."

"They're my friends," she repeated. "I won't leave without them."

"Dead men are not so much vorth dying for, are dey?"

Rose stared hard, but she knew there would be no back-down in a man like Dutch Weinhart. "How far," she asked, her voice drawn thin, "how far do you let others push you before you fight back?"

Weinhart shook his head sympathetically. "Maybe I tink only you can answer dhat question, eh?"

"Yeah," Rose said through clenched teeth. "Maybe you're right." Wheeling, she rode back the way she'd come. Half an hour later she pulled up in the middle of the trail. After a couple of minutes she turned Albert to face the way they'd come. Yanking the Sharps from its scabbard, she shoved a cartridge into its chamber, then rested the rifle across her saddlebows. For a long time she just sat there, staring in the direction of the clearing. As she did, a peculiar calm began to replace the anger. Finally, resolutely she squeezed Albert's ribs with her calves and rode back toward the clearing. She kept the Sharps across her thighs and loosened the Smith & Wesson in its holster, but there was no fight. By the time she came in sight of the oak and its grisly crop, Keyes and Weinhart had already departed. Crude Ts had been scrawled across Wiley's and Dirty-Nosed Dave's shirts in blue chalk, marking them as thieves.

Rose cut down the bodies, then tossed the severed nooses into some nearby bushes where she wouldn't have to look at them. Although she would've preferred burying the two men on the A-Bar-E, she had no way of getting them there. Besides, she knew it wouldn't have mattered to Wiley or Dave. They'd both loved the wide-open places.

Using her knife and fingers, Rose scraped a shallow trough out of the flinty soil, ruining the blade and making her nails bleed, but managing an adequate grave. After positioning the bodies side-by-side in the hole and scrubbing the chalk off their shirts as best she could, she covered the corpses with loose soil, then finished the job with stones hauled up from the creek. When she was done, she washed up, then sat in the shade to rest and think. As she did, Albert wandered over, nickering curiously.

"Right now," she said, standing and putting on her hat. "Let's go home."

It was a fourteen-hour ride back to the cabin, and although Rose made the journey in easy stages, largely on account of Albert, she was eager to get back, and rode through the night.

The sun had barely risen the next day when she

came in sight of the A-Bar-E. She'd already made up her mind that she wasn't going to do any work that day. She would nap through the morning, then fix a cup of tea after lunch and take it up to the bluff where Muggy was buried, there to sit and stare out across the miles and daydream, as she'd done so often when she lived alone. But as the little ranch took shape, Rose began to get an uneasy feeling in the pit of her stomach, like something had gone horribly wrong in her absence. Kicking Albert in the ribs, she raced toward the cabin.

Her heart was pounding as she came around the barn and dismounted on the fly. She approached the cabin with the Smith & Wesson drawn, her senses bucking wildly. She saw smokeless chimneys, a whiskey bottle smashed against the stoop, the door standing ajar. The corral gate was open; the mules were gone. Pausing on the stoop, she took a deep, fluttery breath, then stepped inside.

Nora lay naked on her bunk, her flesh pallid, already starting to decompose. A sharp cry broke from Rose's throat, but she held herself together otherwise. Summoning up all of her strength, she forced herself to look closely for any sign of an ambush before advancing any farther.

The inside of the cabin was a shambles. Trunks and boxes lay everywhere, their contents spilled and smudged with boot prints. The cook stove had been knocked apart in an eruption of soot and ash, the shaker bar ripped loose and used as a club to crush the dangling stovepipe. The spice cabinet had been turned over and sacks of sugar, coffee, and dried fruits had been slashed open and scattered. All their glassware had been destroyed, even the tea cup and saucer Rose had given Nora for Christmas. Whoever had done this had been familiar with the rumor of Rose's secret hiding place under the water barrel, for that had been tipped aside as well, the water splashed across the floor and the tin box under it dug up and emptied.

Finally Rose turned to Nora. Perhaps it was best that way, she would later reason. Perhaps, during her methodical examination of the cabin, something inside her had been busily reconstructing that familiar wall separating reality from emotion. Whatever it was, it was working. There was very little feeling left when she holstered the Smith & Wesson and kneeled at her friend's side.

Nora's death had been violent. She'd been raped and beaten. Tiny circular blisters—dried now, yellowed—had been raised on the flesh of her cheeks and torso by burning cigarettes, and teeth marks and deep scratches scarred her breasts, shoulders, and thighs. She'd survived a nightmare, and when the terror had ended, they'd cut her throat, the wound gaping like a demented grin.

"God damn," Rose rasped, reaching out with a trembling hand to brush back the stiff, dark hair from Nora's forehead. The coldness of the flesh was disconcerting, and she quickly stood and turned away. Her eyes darted around the cabin until they lit on a wooden bucket.

She brought water from the creek and warmed it in a kettle in the fireplace, then washed Nora and dressed her in her favorite blue dress. Afterward, Rose wrapped the body in their heaviest quilt and sewed it shut with needle and thread. She would have preferred a coffin, but she knew she didn't have time to construct one.

She chose a spot under the trees along the creek for the grave, digging it deep and squaring off the corners. Then she rough-hitched Albert to the wagon and hauled Nora's body to the site, where she jumped into the grave to arrange the corpse the way she wanted it.

Rose performed these chores with the same inscrutable detachment that had served her so well the day before, while burying Wiley and Dave. It wasn't until she was near the end that her composure began to crumble. As she patted the final shovelful of earth into place, her movements became awkward, her self-control deteriorating. The gentle curve of the bit flashed in the dappled sunlight, whistling louder as Rose swung harder. She was gulping in air, yet felt as if she were suffocating. She began to pummel the grave, putting her back into it, leaving deep, clear imprints of the shovel's heel in the loose soil.

"Damn you," she choked, speaking to Nora.

"Damn you," she repeated to Wiley and Dave and Muggy.

"God damn you," she said to Shorty, her voice rising.

She slammed the grave, beat at it in a fury of rage and despair. *"Damn you!"* she screamed, bringing the shovel down maniacally. *"God damn you god damn you god damn you!"*

The rage faded abruptly, there one minute, vanished the next. She dropped to her knees, her eyes wide with guilt and shame. Then she felt something move inside her, a rippling sensation that started in her stomach and slid quickly upward, exploding past her lips. It was a sob, and it was immediately followed by another. She groaned when a third cry tore loose, a fist-size chunk of anguish hurtling upward like bile. Tumbling onto her side, Rose wrapped her arms around her stomach and drew her knees to her chest. The tears came then. Not the pooling kind that had embarrassed her so often in the past, but the real thing, slowly at first, creeping across the uncharted territory of her cheeks, then faster and freer, a salty flood that turned the dirt on her face to mud.

She tried to stop them by clamping a hand over her mouth, afraid that her body wouldn't be able physically to withstand the trauma, but her grief was too deep. It couldn't be stopped that simply. Not any more. Her precious wall had been breached; there was no turning back.

After a while she quit fighting it and the crying became easier. The tears flowed warmly and her sobs found a rhythm her body could adapt to. Eventually it stopped. When it did, she rolled onto her back to stare numbly at the interlacing branches overhead. After a few minutes, she began to cry again.

The day passed that way. In time she moved—first to a tree, then to lie in the grass in the sun, then to cross the creek and huddle against a fallen log too large to cut into firewood—crying in spurts and jags that rose and subsided and rose again. By nightfall her cheeks felt hot and chapped, her throat raw.

In darkness she got up and made her way to the cabin, but she couldn't force herself to go inside. She spent the night in the barn instead, wrapped in a smelly horse blanket. The next morning she returned to the grave to cover it with stones to keep the wolves away. Then she went up to the bluff and did the same for Muggy, not because she feared scavengers at this late date, but because it was the right thing to do. The tears had ended for good by the time she finished, the sobs retreating deep within. In their place had crept a cold, hard resolve. Albert grazed nearby, still saddled. Rose caught the horse and tightened the cinch. Then, dry-eyed and resolute, she led him to the cabin.

ROSE OF
YELLOWSTONE

Chapter Thirty-Two

Even taking into account her own shortcomings as a tracker, it didn't take Rose long to decipher the maze of prints surrounding the A-Bar-E buildings. What she found convinced her that Jed Plover and his posse had returned from their short probe toward the Bull Mountains either on the same day she'd left in pursuit of Wiley and Dave, or early the next.

Rose had already dismissed the posse as suspect. She couldn't believe Plover would sanction the kind of brutality Nora had been subjected to. She was looking for something else, and she found it behind the corral—three distinct sets of tracks facing the rails, as if the horses had been hitched there in stealth or under cover of darkness.

Two of the sets of tracks were indistinguishable to Rose's unskilled eye and could have been made by any horse in the territory. It was the third set that aroused her interest.

Indented clearly in the soft soil under the right rear hoof was the imprint of a bent horseshoe nail, the mark of a negligent blacksmith or an uncaring rider. As soon as she saw it, Rose knew that in the days ahead, that single act of slipshod workmanship would prove invaluable.

Returning to the cabin, she began a more thorough inspection. The killers had taken just about everything of value, including the deed to the ranch and Rose's marriage certificate. They'd taken Nora's costume jewelry and the pocket watch and fob Rose had purchased in Sheridan the year before. They'd taken Nora's shotgun and her little Colt Rainmaker. They'd even taken the A-Bar-E branding iron. But they hadn't taken any of the food. There was jerked beef, tins of peaches and tomatoes, and, on the floor, piles of flour, dried apples, and coffee, portions of which she was able to scoop into small cotton sacks to stuff into her saddlebags.

Although they'd taken all of the extra ammunition, Rose still had full cartridge belts—thirty-six rounds for the Smith & Wesson, thirty more for the Sharps. She also took along gloves, her sack coat, and the butcher knife she'd purchased from Two-Hats, a replacement for the clasp knife she'd ruined scraping out a grave for Wiley and Dave.

The killers' trail led her northwest over the Bulls, via the now familiar route to the horseshoe bend of the Musselshell. Although Rose stuck to the trace with a bulldog's tenacity, she was to suffer her first disappointment before she even reached the foothills.

The point at which Plover's men had turned back was easily discerned. From there on, only the killers' trail remained, established sometime after the posse's retreat. It was then, with the concentration of tracks reduced, that Rose realized she was following just two sets of prints. The third set had disappeared completely, as if the horse had taken wing.

She hauled up in dismay. She'd been so confident that all three of Nora's attackers were ahead of her that she could hardly credit what she saw. Reining off the main path, she cut back and forth through the sage, but the only prints she turned up were those of an antelope, paralleling the main trail. She stared back the way she'd come, but there was no sign of a delayed third rider, no waving flags or blaring brass band to announce that here, Rose Edwards, lay the answers you so desperately seek. There were only the gently rolling hills with their scattered, solitary junipers and busted shelves of caprock, cloaked in the bright green of spring buffalo grass.

Rose was certain three men had been involved in Nora's death. The shape and style of boot prints left in the spilled flour confirmed that. So what had happened to the third individual? Had he veered off somewhere after leaving the A-Bar-E? Or had the split occurred at the cabin itself? Who was he, and where had he gone?

Although Rose tried to convince herself that information wasn't needed yet, she knew her odds of finding the third man would be significantly diminished if she couldn't come up with at least a name.

With the tracks of Plover's posse out of the way, Rose began to make better time. She camped on top of the Bulls that night, and by noon the next day was watering her horse in the Musselshell. It produced some odd sensations to stand so calmly at the river's edge and study the various sites of importance within her view—the ridge where the Indian she'd killed had been standing, the sandy beach where Jeremy Frakes had laid in a halo of his own blood, the purling waters of the river itself, where Wiley's mount had gone under in a hail of bullets.

Yet there was more to her feelings than just the enormity of all that had happened since those days. Something had changed within herself. She wasn't the same Rose Edwards any more, and, with a touch of sadness, she recognized that she never would be again. The old Rose was dead; the new one missed her already.

Three days later, she guided Albert down the last leg of the Highwood Road to the Fort Benton ferry. It was a cool, breezy day, with a light rain falling from leaden skies, and the steep grade was slick with mud.

The weather had changed a couple of days before, when a slow-moving front pushed through from the northwest. Now the clouds hung low and the steady drizzle had saturated Rose's clothing. The temperature had dropped, as well. Last night her breath had puffed like steam from a loco-motive as she huddled over her smoky fire. Then just after dawn this morning a series of snow showers had swept across the soggy ridges, leaving behind a gray slush that hadn't melted until midday. But if June snows and teeth-chattering summer winds were unusual, they weren't unheard of, and although Rose suffered from the unexpected cold, her biggest concern was for the tracks she'd dogged all the way up from the Yellowstone. The bent-nail print had deteriorated rapidly in yesterday's rain; she'd lost it completely that morning.

It was a gamble coming into Fort Benton on nothing more than a hunch, even though the trail had been angling that way ever since leaving the Musselshell at Box Elder Creek. That was no guarantee they'd be here, of course, but the old fur trading post seemed like a logical destination.

Staring at the town from the bluff south of the river brought an unexpected smile to Rose's face. It had been a long time since she'd last visited the little high-plains hamlet stretched out along the Missouri's left bank. The town hadn't changed much in the years she'd been away, although she reckoned it soon would, what with the St. Paul, Minneapolis & Manitoba Railroad near to knocking on its front door.

At one time, Fort Benton had been a river port of some prominence, a vital link to the fur streams, mining camps, and buffalo ranges of the vast Northwest. Its pulse had kept time to the throbbing engines of steamboats plying the river between here, the Missouri's head of navigation, and the East, the cities of Kansas City and St. Louis in particular. In past years Rose had seen half a dozen or more stern- and side-wheelers tied off along the levee at any given hour during the high-water season that ran from May through August, while the bench above the river that served as one side of the town's main street had swarmed with men and draft animals moving merchandise between decks and warehouses.

Back then, a small mountain range of stiff buffalo hides had waited to be loaded aboard decks stripped of their cabins to accommodate the huge numbers of hides bound for the downriver markets. Nowadays, outgoing cargoes ran more toward wool and cattle, and the cabins had been returned for passenger traffic. But the boom days were about over for Fort Benton. Soon the Manitoba would reach the community and push on, and the town would lose its distinction as the head of navigation, becoming just another whistle stop along another railroad.

At the landing, Rose leaned from the saddle to ring a brass bell affixed to a post above the slip, letting the ferry operator know a customer was waiting. Then she sat back in hunched-shouldered misery to stare across the river at the levee, where a single, two-hundred-ton packet was moored to the bank, its engines cold, its decks slick from the rain.

Rose paid four bits to cross, and on the Fort Benton side she kicked Albert up the slippery incline to Front Street. She remembered most of the businesses she saw from when her pap had hunted out of here—T.C. Power & Bro.; I.G. Baker; Murphy and Neel. There were several hotels, including the elegant Grand Union, but Rose doubted if she could afford any of them. Besides, her first priority was to get Albert inside, out of the rain; she'd worry about her own lodging afterward.

The E. Willard Livery was just off the Mullan Road to Helena, near its junction with Front Street. Rose reined in there and swung down. Old Edgar Willard himself came to the door, one whiskered cheek bulging around a wad of tobacco, his too-large nose spidered with broken capillaries.

"My God, if it ain't Miss Rose of the Yellerstone," he brayed when he recognized her. A grin split his woolly face, broad enough to reveal a set of stained ivory uppers.

Rose smiled and nodded with a mixture of embarrassment and pleasure. She'd forgotten how loud and boisterous he could be. "Hello, Edgar," she said, genuinely pleased. She'd only called him Mr. Willard once, and that a long time ago; he'd forgiven her the trespass, but made her swear never to do it again.

Edgar laughed loud enough to rattle the rafters, then twisted at the waist and spat into the rain. "Come on in where it's dry," he bellowed, "before ya catch yer death!"

She led Albert inside, and Edgar nodded to an empty stall next to his office.

"Have that 'un, girl, if ya plan ter spend the night."

"Likely I will." She pulled the saddle off Albert's back and slung it on top of the stall's high wall, then hung the bridle off the horn and draped the saddle blanket behind it, hoping it would dry by morning. With just a hand on the gelding's jaw, she guided him into the stall, then latched the gate. There was already water in a wooden trough that served two compartments, and Edgar dumped a quart can of oats in the feed box.

"That straw's pert near fresh," he said. "He'll be warm enough. Come on inter the office, girl, and warm yerself. Ya look half froze."

"I'm feelin' half froze," she allowed, following him into a cramped, stall-size room where a small stove crackled. She backed up to it with a grateful sigh.

"If ya ain't a sight fer sore eyes," Edgar said cheerfully. "I noticed ya still got that roan hoss, too. I figure that turned out ter be a square deal, don't you?"

"He's been a loyal friend," Rose agreed. "I wouldn't trade him for a Kentucky Derby winner, even if you throwed in the jockey for boot."

Edgar guffawed. "That's the spirit, but damn iffen yer daddy didn't throw a fit over that broom-tail. Came in here the next day raisin' all kinds a hell with me fer selling it ter ya."

"Pap was some put-out, for a fact," she recalled, sniffing back a drippy nose, "though he was sportin' a put-out nature in them days."

"Still is, I'd wager. Ya want some coffee?"

"Coffee sounds good."

He brought a white, graniteware cup down from a shelf above the stove and filled it from a tin pot. Handing it to her, he winked and said: "That there cup cost me a wife, ya know?"

She paused with the cup half raised, peering at him over the rolled rim. "How do you figure that?" she asked warily.

"Ain't much ter figure. I married me a widder woman here three, four years back. Good-lookin' gal, too, hefty . . ." He held his hands out in front of his chest to indicate breasts of impossible dimensions. "Ya know?"

"It must've made walkin' a chore," Rose remarked dryly. "Did she tip over a lot?"

"Forward," Edgar replied seriously, "always forward. But ya know what? No matter how many times she fell, she never bumped her nose." He laughed loudly, then slapped his knee with the flat of his hand. "Well, mayhaps I stretched 'er a mite," he acknowledged. "She was a handsome woman, but tight. Lord, that gal was tight. We was always bickerin' over money, and not the big kind of money, either, but the little stuff . . . the penny 'n' nickel stuff. Then one day last spring a mule stepped on my cup and cracked the seam in the bottom, so I went over ter Baker's and bought me this here enamel one. Cost me ten cents more'n a reg'lar tin cup, and that was the blow-up that cooked the goose."

Rose took a sip, grinning, then held the cup to

her face so that its warmth could caress her cheeks. "She was ag'in' it, was she?"

"Heart 'n' soul. Got so mad she walked out and went ter stay with a friend, an old biddy just as tight-fisted and sour as she was. Figured I'd come fetch 'er, I guess, but I never did. Three weeks later she left town with a hardware salesman out of Chicago, but I heard he dumped her before they reached Bismarck. I say she was lucky he didn't toss her in the river with an anvil in her apron pocket."

"Now, that sounds kind of like a windy to me," Rose said.

"Well, there might 'a' been some gambling the night before that added fuel ter the flame, but it was the cup what broke the camel's hump."

Rose's smile dimmed. "Edgar, I'm lookin' for a couple of men who might've come through here a day or two ago, from the south."

"Billy Garcia and Larson Web?"

She took a deep breath, nodding. "That sounds about right."

"Saw 'em day before yesterday, but ain't seen 'em since." He gave her a shrewd look. "I'd heard ya'd given up yer wayward ways after that little set-to on the Musselshell last summer."

"It ain't necessarily what you think," she replied, although she didn't elaborate.

The conversation shifted to lesser matters after that, mostly the old days and what had become of the various men and women they'd known. Edgar told her of the town's plans for the future, assuring her that Fort Benton had no intention of rolling over and dying just because a railroad was coming up the trail.

"The ol' Manitoba's gonna be a boon for Benton," he told her. "They're talking about a waterworks plant and maybe forming an electric company as soon as next year. Plan ter build 'em a wagon bridge across the Missouri, too, for the Judith Basin trade." He became wide-eyed in the telling, as if the changes lurking just over the horizon would come rolling in like circus wagons, all a-glitter in paint and sparkle.

When Rose finished her coffee, she left Edgar to his chores and went across the street to the Triplehorn Saloon, where she ordered a beer. Conscious of her dwindling funds, she took pains to nurse her drink slowly, before moving on to the next establishment. In that way she passed what remained of the day, hoarding her change by buying beer, then making it last while she listened to the ebb and flow of conversation, keeping a constant eye on the customers who came and went. No one bothered her, although she figured they were probably curious about this woman in trousers who carried a pistol and drank like a man. If anyone suspected her identity, they made no mention of it within her hearing.

The cold drizzle strengthened into a downpour toward evening, complete with the rumble of thunder. It was into this pounding wall of water that Rose exited the Trapper's Glen Saloon and ran onto her first piece of luck. Crossing Front Street from the riverbank just down the block was a wiry half-breed dressed in a hodge-podge of Indian and white clothing. A jolt of recognition coursed through Rose when she recognized him as one of the two 'breeds who'd accompanied Larson Web that long-ago day at Two-Hats's.

"Here's opportunity," she muttered to herself, and when the half-breed reached the shelter of the covered boardwalk, she stepped out after him.

Chapter Thirty-Three

The half-breed was a block ahead, threading his way through a growing crowd of pedestrians, and Rose hurried to catch up. She feared she might lose him in the failing light, but he didn't go far. Pausing in front of a dry-goods store, he accosted a man in a business suit and received a couple of coins, offered grudgingly. Two more attempts at panhandling earned him quick rebuffs. A fourth man laughed in his face, then spat at his feet. The fifth gave him more change.

Monitoring his progress from the shelter of a recessed doorway, Rose waited impatiently, hands thrust into the soggy pockets of her light coat. By the time true dusk settled over the town, the half-breed had accumulated enough money to enter the I.G. Baker store with confidence. He emerged en minutes later carrying a parcel wrapped in brown butcher's paper. Shivering, Rose continued to follow him. He led her to a row of warehouses where activity had ceased for the day, slowing noticeably as he approached a building sitting hard on the Missouri's bank. With a furtive glance toward an office at the opposite side of the compound, he ducked through a side door and quickly shut it behind him.

Rose halted fifty yards away, but when the half-breed didn't reappear after several minutes, she pulled the collar of her coat tighter around her neck and, as inconspicuously as possible, sauntered into the freight yard after him. Cat-footing along the back wall of the warehouse, she soon found what she was looking for, an empty knothole where she could peer inside.

A single lantern illuminated the interior. The warehouse was long and narrow, a double row of columns supporting a tin roof that rattled loudly in the rain. Huge doors at either end allowed access to even the largest freight wagon. Although nearly empty, Rose could tell from the smell that its contents had come from the backs of Montana woollies. A trio of high-sided freight wagons used to haul the wool in from the shearing grounds sat, tongue to tailgate, down the center of the warehouse, and ten-foot-long canvas bags of compressed fleece, at least three feet in diameter, were stacked like cordwood in one of the middle bays.

The half-breed was sitting on the lowered tailgate

of the last wagon, slurping tomatoes from a tin can with his fingers. The lantern, hanging from a nearby spike, created a pocket of light that he alone occupied. Watching, Rose decided he was a trespasser, rather than an employee.

Backing away from the knothole, she hunkered briefly beside an empty hogshead. She was miserably cold, her fingers and toes numb as steel pipe. She knew she had to get warm soon, else risk hypothermia. Just the thought of such an ignominious death irked her beyond measure. It would have been the rudest kind of insult, she thought, to have survived the winter of '86 and '87, only to freeze to death the following summer.

Pushing to her feet, Rose slogged back through the rain to the nearest saloon, where she moved unhesitantly to a cast-iron stove still set up in the middle of the room. The heat felt good, and in no time her clothes were steaming in the warm air, the odor of horse and campfire smoke mingling unnoticed with that of a muleskinner standing next to her.

Although it was well after dark when Rose left the saloon, she had no trouble locating the warehouse or finding the knothole again. Creeping close, she peeked inside. The half-breed continued his occupancy of the lowered tailgate, curled up now in a single blanket and using his hat for a pillow. Satisfied that he was alone and probably asleep, Rose moved to the side door. Drawing her pistol, she carefully lifted the latch and stepped inside. Her nerves were tingling, but no cry of alarm challenged her. Stealthily she crossed the cavernous warehouse. The half-breed didn't stir, and her hope grew as she crept within the circle of waning lantern light. At his side, she slowly reached out to shake him awake. The appearance of a knife coming up at the edge of her vision caught her completely off guard.

"Damn," she breathed, staring at the heavy blade out of the corner of her eye, hovering just in front of her ear. Although she still gripped the Smith & Wesson, she realized belatedly that she'd allowed the muzzle to drift when she reached for the half-breed's shoulder. It was pointed more toward the tailgate than his heart, and although only inches from her target, she knew it was much too far away to believe she could cock the hammer and pull the trigger before he could flick the cutting edge of the blade across her throat.

"You shouldn't have tried to get so close," he admonished in surprisingly well-articulated English. His eyes were wary and mildly curious, but not especially threatening. He sat up, keeping the knife close to her cheek, so close she would've sworn she could feel its coolness against her flesh, even though the blade itself didn't touch her. It was a Hudson's Bay buffalo knife, huge and wickedly sharp, hefty enough to chop down a small tree, delicate enough, in the right hands, to dissect a June bug.

"I didn't think you was awake," Rose confessed.

"I've been waiting for you."

"Damn," she said again.

"It was fairly stupid of you to think I wouldn't recognize you on the street. There aren't that many women running around Montana in pants."

She tried to pull back, but he tapped her cheek warningly with the tip of his blade. "No, you stay close."

"It ain't you I'm after, if that means anything. It's your partners I'm wantin'."

"I don't have any partners."

Rose's calm evaporated in a blaze of anger. Leaning forward, she shoved the Smith & Wesson's muzzle hard against the half-breed's chest, and in the unexpectedness of the move, she was able to draw the hammer back to full cock. "I *know* you got partners," she said. "I followed 'em up here from my place on the Yellowstone."

Although it was obvious he knew he'd lost his advantage, he met her gaze evenly. "That was a neat trick, coming toward me instead of away," he said. "I didn't expect it."

"Where are they? And I want 'em both."

"Go to hell."

"I'll send you to hell if you don't answer my question."

"Do that," the half-breed taunted, nonchalantly resheathing his knife. "At least it'll be dry there."

Rose stepped back, her knuckles white as she leveled the Smith & Wesson on his forehead. "I ain't gonna ask you again."

Even then he refused a reply. She shifted the pistol to remind him it was there, but he wouldn't be intimidated. He returned her gaze without malice, a cocky half smile perched on his lips.

"Son-of-a-bitch," she grated, wheeling and stalking away. Before she could turn back a flash of steel sped past her face, followed by the thud of metal striking wood. She spun on her heels, thrusting the Smith & Wesson before her, but the half-breed was sitting calmly on the wagon's tailgate with both hands in plain sight.

"It was stupid of you to turn your back on me, too," he said.

"It was stupid of you to give up your knife," she countered. Glancing behind her, she saw the blade's tip buried at least an inch into the grub box of the next wagon, its rosewood handle still quivering. Straightening, she lowered the Smith & Wesson's hammer. "Maybe it was foolish," she allowed. "I ain't been thinkin' clearly of late."

"That's not much of an excuse. I could have as easily put that blade in your heart. Skin isn't nearly as hard to pierce as oak. Besides, I have a pistol, too." He moved his blanket aside to reveal a holstered revolver within easy reach. "I could have already shot you three or four times tonight."

"All right," Rose said testily. "You've made your point. Now what?"

"Larson Web."

Her pulse quickened. "What about him?"

"You want him and Garcia. So do I, and know where they are. I want to make a deal."

"What kind of deal?"

"Food and bullets for information."

"Food and bullets?"

"I'm out of both."

She looked doubtful. "How'd that happen?"

"I lost my outfit crossing the Missouri on the ice last spring. The damned river swallowed everything I owned except my knife and pistol and the clothes on my back. It took a good saddle horse and a pack horse and a winter's catch of pelts. I've been shearing sheep ever since, but that's no work for a proud *Métis*, so I quit. Begging handouts ain't much of a life, either."

"What do you know about Garcia and Web?"

"I know they came into town a couple of days ago and did some quiet bragging. Not to everyone, but to me, since they think I'm a friend. They told me about a woman down on the Yellowstone. Know her?"

"Nora?" Rose asked tonelessly.

"They didn't mention a name, but Garcia said it was you he was wanting. If they hadn't been feeling flighty about some posse nearby, they probably would've waited."

"Where are they now?"

"They left Fort Benton yesterday."

"Where'd they go?"

He shook his head. "For cartridges and food and your word that I get to kill Web."

"Uhn-uh, I want 'em both."

"Then go make a deal with the devil," he said indifferently.

"I got my reasons. It ain't nothin' personal against you."

"I have my reasons, too. Besides, Web didn't touch your friend. That was Garcia and another man."

Rose's grip tightened on the Smith & Wesson. "You're lyin', 'breed. Web was your friend. So was Garcia. For all I know, you was the third man. You're tryin' to trick me into followin' you out of town so's you can cut my throat."

"Web killed my brother," he returned matter-of-factly. "A couple of years ago, right after you and the Collins gang shot your way out of Two-Hats's. Web was drunk and got the idea Remon was going to pull down on him, but he wasn't. He was sitting at a table adjusting his holster so that his pistol wouldn't dig into his ribs. He didn't even know what Web was up to when he pulled his gun."

"It don't savvy that you're tellin' the truth," Rose said guardedly. "If that old man killed my brother, I'd've shot him right there."

"There wasn't much I could do without getting myself killed in the process. Web and Caldwell were close, and that damn' Mexican was thrown into the pot, too. I took my brother home to bury. When I got back, they'd disappeared. I hunted for them for a while, then gave up. I'd been trapping the Milk River country until I lost my outfit this spring."

"Gol-dang it, are you lyin' to me, 'breed?"

"Am I?"

"What's your name?"

"Jacques."

"Jacques what?"

"Jacques is all you need to know."

"Bastard. Why didn't you shoot Web the other day, if you wanted to so bad?"

"It was in a trading post . . . a white man's trading post."

"And Garcia just up and told you everything they'd done, in front of the trader and everyone?"

"Web was drinking alone at the counter and still sober. Garcia was drunk. Not so drunk he would talk to just anyone, but he still said more than he should have. We were sitting alone at a table in the corner where no one could overhear us."

Rose's shoulders slumped. "Does the old man know you're after him?"

"I don't think so. I don't think he even knows Remon was my brother. He thought we were friends, but I guess he doesn't think a *Métis* would kill to avenge a friend. Or maybe he doesn't care. He's a crazy old coot."

Although Rose still harbored plenty of doubts, she let the Smith & Wesson's muzzle dip toward the floor. Jacques slid off the tailgate and walked over until he was standing only inches away. Then he reached over her shoulder and jerked the buffalo knife free from the wagon's grub box.

"I know where they went," he said, his voice

barely a whisper, his breath warm on her face. "I want Web, but I need an outfit. How badly do you want Garcia?"

"What about a horse?"

"I have a horse. I need cartridges and food."

Rose holstered the Smith & Wesson. "All right, but I get Garcia."

"As long as it's understood that I kill Web."

It was, and, as soon as Rose told him so, they shook hands on the deal.

Chapter Thirty-Four

The rain had stopped by the time Rose led Albert outside the next morning. The sky was pale but clear in the dawn's light, and a light frost whiskered the iron bands on the water barrel.

Jacques waited nearby with a gray gelding that was the sorriest excuse for a horse Rose had ever seen, outside of a few dead ones. It was small and ewe-necked and had a long, ugly scar across its chest, the skin puffy and without hair. Proud flesh, her pap had always called such poorly healed injuries. Although it didn't necessarily handicap an animal's performance, it almost always lowered its value to a point where a seller practically had to give the animal away. That must have been a godsend for Jacques, Rose reflected as she eyed the balance of his broken-down outfit. Still having been poor most of her own life, she wasn't in any mood to lavish out sympathy.

"I hope we ain't got far to go," she said scornfully. "I ain't lettin' that jug-headed gray ride behind me on Albert, I don't care how wore-out it gets."

"This horse will be walking strong when that ancient nag of yours is sucking wind on its knees," Jacques retorted mildly.

Rose shook her head. "I had me a jack rabbit pony like that once. I was gonna put it in the kettle for a stew, but the dang' thing saved my life a couple of months ago."

"That can make a horse harder to eat," Jacques agreed. "I had a fine bay mare a few years back that brought me out of the Peace River country in the middle of a bad winter. The day I shot that horse and carved a steak out of her hip was one of the saddest of my life." He swung into the saddle, and Rose smiled in spite of herself.

They went to I.G. Baker's first and outfitted for the journey ahead. Then Jacques led her down the Mullan Road toward Helena. At first Rose thought Web and Garcia must have doubled back, but as soon as she and Jacques topped out on the plateau above town, Jacques abandoned the well-graded former military artery to angle northwest across the high plains. There was a road of sorts under them here, too, though rutted and winding.

"It's a part of the Whoop-up Trail," Jacques explained, and Rose felt a thrill of excitement.

She'd heard of the Whoop-up all her life, that nebulous, spidery route over which illegal furs and robes were smuggled south out of Canada, while whiskey and other contraband went north to stimulate the trade. This was her first time on it, however. In all his years hunting and trading out of Fort Benton, her pap had always ranged south of the Missouri, down into the Big Lonesome country.

Although it had been frosty early on and snowing only yesterday, the temperature climbed steadily. By noon it was not only warm, but humid after all the rain. Rose's shirt stuck to the flesh along her ribs, and the deer flies were troublesome for such an open country. She kept her eyes on the worn trace created by years of surreptitious wagon traffic, but didn't see anything that indicated the road had been used recently.

"Are you sure they went this way?" she asked Jacques that afternoon. They were squatted on their shanks beside the trail, eating a snack of cold biscuits and raw bacon while their horses grazed nearby.

"They went north," he replied absently.

"*North* covers a lot of territory," she reminded him.

Jacques shrugged. He'd been that way ever since they turned onto the Whoop-Up, as if his thoughts were elsewhere. Although Rose told herself it didn't matter, it still annoyed her. She could understand if he didn't trust her enough to tell her where they were headed, but she didn't see any reason for his prolonged silences. She'd spent too many years alone not to appreciate a lively conversation when the opportunity presented itself. She was tempted to broach the quiet several times, but her own natural stubbornness eventually won out, and she rode through the afternoon without a word.

Toward nightfall they came to a grove of box elder trees shading a narrow creek and unsaddled their horses. Rose kindled a fire while Jacques stood nearby looking surly. She was still nursing the flames with smaller pieces when he tossed a sack on the ground beside her.

"There's flour in there," he said brusquely. "Fix some squaw bread." He yanked her rifle from its scabbard. "I'm going hunting for some real meat. Bacon ain't fit for pilgrims."

Rose surged to her feet. "Put that rifle back," she snapped. "And you can fix your own damn' biscuits. I ain't your mam."

Jacques gave her a dismissing look. "You're the woman, ain't you?" He started to walk away.

Rose's anger boiled over in a flash. Taking a running kick, she caught the sack perfectly with her square-toed boot, lifting it in an arc to slam against Jacques's shoulder. He whirled with a snarl, but Rose had already palmed her Smith & Wesson. She pointed it at him with her thumb on the hammer, her index finger curled tautly over the trigger.

"Cook that god-damned bread yourself, you two-bit son-of-a-bitch."

"Someone should have taught you some manners when you were a filly," Jacques growled. "I'd do it myself if I had a club."

Rose cocked the Smith & Wesson. "There ought to be a club somewhere amongst these trees," she replied coolly. "Why don't you go find one, then see how far you get tryin' to teach me your manners?"

For a long moment, Jacques didn't say anything. Then he straightened, letting the Sharps hang loosely in his hands. "I think you'd shoot me, Rose of Yellowstone," he said.

"I'm tired," she allowed, "and I been pushed hard of late." She lowered the Smith & Wesson's hammer. "And you're right, I'd have shot you. Now put the damn' rifle back and fetch some more wood. I'll cook supper tonight, but, by dang, you can fix it tomorrow."

Leaning forward in her saddle, Rose scowled at the hard ground, but no matter how intently she stared, all she could make out was a tiny scuff mark in the dirt.

"How do you know it ain't them?" she asked.

"It just isn't."

"It's going in the same direction," she bluffed.

"No, it's not. Besides, Web and Garcia were riding geldings, one of them with a bent nail in its shoe. This track was made by a mare with good shoes. She's dropped a few foals in her time, too."

"How would you know that?"

453

"Mares are wider in their hips, so they can birth more easily," he replied as if speaking to a very young child. "A stallion, or even a gelding, is wider up front, for fighting. Like a man's shoulders are usually wider than a woman's, and a woman's hips are usually broader than a man's. Most grass-eaters will track the same way, the rear hoofs stepping on top of the tracks left by the front hoofs, so that the print on top is either to the inside or the outside of the print under it, depending on the sex."

"Then where the hell are the tracks?"

Jacques laughed. "Under your nose, White Eyes. Someday I'll show you how to see them."

"I don't reckon that'll be necessary," Rose replied tartly. "And don't go gettin' no notions for some-day. After I kill Garcia, I aim to go back south and find the scoundrel that helped him and Web."

"He was Indian," Jacques said casually, reining away. "Garcia called him Pine Tree."

"Pine Tree!" Rose jogged Albert alongside Jacques's gray. "Pine Tree *Manning?*"

"What?"

"Did Garcia call him Manning?"

"He called him Pine Tree."

Taking a deep breath, Rose said: "Well, I don't suppose it matters. There can't be that many roosters runnin' around with a handle like Pine Tree, white or red."

"Who's Manning?" Jacques asked.

Shorty's voice whispered in her ear from the

alley beside Broadwater and Hubbells, in Miles City: *Pine Tree's a Hill Country Texican, and they say he's handy with that Marlin rifle.*

"Just a man," Rose replied, a faraway look coming into her eyes. "Just another god-damn' man."

Rose and Jacques became friends, in spite of their best efforts not to. Jacques was an ex-buffalo runner who'd learned the trade hunting for Hudson's Bay Company. His mother was a Turtle Mountain Chippewa, his father a Scotsman who'd died while Jacques was still a boy. Jacques had received a rudimentary education at a mission school in Winnipeg, but he'd been on his own since he was fourteen. His brother Remon—a half-brother, actually—had found him about five years ago, and the two had thrown in together. The rest Rose already knew, more or less.

Jacques had garnered a lot of stories in his ramblings, but the ones Rose liked best were those he told about the Chippewas—their culture and religion, family and tribal tales passed down through the generations. During the day he would show her a few tricks about tracking—how to interpret signs she would have dismissed as meaningless beforehand, how to see what was there, plain as day, when viewed with the proper knowledge.

For her part, Rose told Jacques of growing up along the mining frontier of western Montana, and what she knew about the infamous Plummer gang that had, for the most part, all been hanged while she was still a girl. She also showed him a few of the gun tricks Sam Matthews had taught her—the behind-the-back flip, the border shift, and the road agent spin.

They crossed the border into Canada a couple of days later. Not anticipating it, Rose didn't know what to think when she spied a pile of rocks about three feet high, with a flat iron stake poking up from the middle. Riding over, she saw the words *United States* embossed on the near side, *Canada* on the other.

"What were you expecting?" Jacques asked, watching her curiously. "A red, white, and blue line painted across the prairie?"

"I wasn't expectin' nothin'," she admitted, "let alone a post stickin' up in the middle of nowhere." Far to the east she could see another cairn and stake. "Is it like that all the way across?"

"As far as I know."

She gigged her horse over the line, then whoaed. "Now I'm in a foreign country," she announced, looking left, then right. After a pause, she added: "I would have expected more."

"It ain't no more thrilling going the other way," Jacques replied, heeling his gray across the boundary after her.

Later that same day they abandoned the Whoop-up Trail for a more westerly direction. Far ahead lay a mountain range, its peaks capped with snow, its flanks black with forests. As they drew closer, they entered a land of gently rolling hills timbered with tracts of conifers, like patches on a pinto. The air was high-country crisp, the creeks icy cold and running bank to bank. In the week since they'd left Fort Benton, they hadn't seen another human being, or even much sign of one, so it was a shock to Rose when late one afternoon they topped a low saddle flanked by towering pines and Jacques pointed out a fort in the distance.

"There it is," he said tersely.

Narrowing her eyes against the bright mountain sunshine, Rose said: "There what is?"

"Harker's Fort. It used to be a straight-up trading post, but that went under when the robe trade petered out. Old Jake Harker moved to Oregon and retired. Now his place is run by whiskey peddlers who deal mostly in furs and stolen horses, although I hear the Mounties plan to shut it down soon."

Harker's Fort sat in the middle of a broad, green valley, surrounded by piney hills. A stream ran in front of the palisades, its banks grown over with groves of elm and ash and white-barked aspen. Beyond the fort grazed a herd of horses that probably numbered three thousand head—by far the largest cavvy Rose had ever seen. It was being watched over by at least a dozen men, and even from here she could see the rifles lying across their saddles.

Closer, running along both sides of the stream for

half a mile or more, was a good-size Indian village. The sight of so many lodges was startling to Rose. It was something she hadn't seen in a long time, or ever expected to see again. Many of the lodges were made of soft-tanned leather—ten- and twelve-skin teepees, brown as mud—but it was sobering to realize that over half of them were constructed of canvas, the cream-colored material standing in sharp contrast to the older, smaller, more earthen-toned lodges of an earlier generation.

Just as significant, to Rose's thinking, was the number of buckboards and small wagons parked behind lodges, where once only travois had leaned. It brought home with painful clarity the changes being wrought to this land, to a way of life that was mostly gone now.

The post itself was constructed in a style her pap would have called Kentucky, meaning it was surrounded by log walls set upright in the dark loam, sharpened on top to form notches behind which riflemen could stand in the event of an attack. Although the stockade had appeared impressive from the low rise, closer inspection revealed a post badly in need of repair. Timbers were rotting at the base, many of them leaning dangerously outward, and the wide, double gates sagged on broken hinges, locked permanently open by mats of weeds and grass.

Inside, Rose discovered more of a rough-shod community than a single trading post. At least two dozen rooms, located in several long, log dwellings backed up against the palisade walls, housed an equal number of independent traders. Wagons and two-wheeled carts were parked haphazardly around the hard-packed quadrangle, and horses and mules wandered loose with only a catch rope around their necks. Rotting hides and gnawed bones littered the ground in front of several establishments, attracting clouds of blowflies.

The men were a mixture of Indian and white, but the women were all marked by the dusky complexion and raven-black hair of their native ancestry. The place was ripe with the sights, sounds, and smells of a thriving industry, and over it all hung the pungent aroma of the element that held it together like glue—trade whiskey.

Jacques drew up in front of the largest building, what had once been the main trade room, and stepped down. Wrapping Albert's reins around the hitch rail next to Jacques's gray, Rose followed the *Métis* inside. They went to the counter and leaned into it, while a bartender ambled down the opposite side.

"*Hau*, Jacques," the bartender said.

"Brock," Jacques returned politely.

"Whiskey?"

Jacques looked at Rose, who nodded. "Two," he said.

Brock poured, then corked the jug. Jacques slid a half dollar across the bar and Brock pocketed it without making change.

"We're looking for some old friends," Jacques said, gently spinning the glass between his fingers.

"Who might that be?"

"Billy Garcia and Larson Web."

Brock furrowed his brows in thought, then shook his head. "I must be gettin' old. My thinker ain't what it used to be."

Jacques placed another four bits on the counter.

"They rode in yesterday," Brock said, "but I ain't seen 'em since last night. They were awful drunk when they left here. They might not be up yet."

"Where'd they bunk?"

"Why, I don't rightly know, hoss. They have lots of friends hereabouts. They might be passed out anywhere."

Rose slapped another 50¢ piece on the counter, and Brock scooped the pile of change into his pocket.

"Newcomers generally throw their blankets on the floor in one of the bastions until something better opens up. Not that I figure Web and Garcia will hang around that long. They never do."

"*Merci*," Jacques said, pushing away from the counter. Rose shadowed him outside, her drink untouched. They paused on the verandah, but, before they could speak, Rose spotted a pair of men approaching from her left.

"Son-of-a-bitch," she said huskily, reaching for the Smith & Wesson.

Less than twenty feet away, Billy Garcia was already pulling his pistol. "*¡Puta!*" he shouted, snapping off a shot that raked the air past her shoulder.

"Bastard," Rose returned, firing from the hip.

All hell broke loose then. Garcia dived for the shelter of a nearby water trough, while Web, caught flat-footed, seemed even more stunned to see Jacques yank free his Remington revolver and pop a cap at his brother's killer. Jacques's ball dug a long furrow in the wall at Web's side, but Rose didn't hang around to see what effect the flying bark would have on the older man. She jumped to the ground and scrambled under the porch, lead from Garcia's Colt singing around her ears.

Crabbing into the deeper shadows close to the building, Rose kept up a steady return fire, her bullets splintering the wooden trough. Through the thickening powder smoke she caught glimpses of Garcia's brown hand snaking past the edge of the trough to throw another round into the shallow crawl space.

Rose emptied the Smith & Wesson, then rolled onto her side to trip the pistol's top latch while pulling down on the barrel. As the cylinder and barrel pivoted away from the butt and hammer, she turned the pistol upside down, the empty brass tumbling free. Her fingers trembled as she dropped fresh rounds into the wheel. She kept glancing at the water trough, less than twenty feet away, but Garcia remained hidden and Rose knew, without really knowing how, that his revolver was also empty, and that he was frantically reloading.

It was there Rose held the advantage. The Smith & Wesson was quicker to reload than Garcia's Colt, which required that each empty case be punched out individually before a live round could be chambered. It wasn't much of an edge, and her own rattled nerves were working against her, but she finally closed the Smith & Wesson with a sharp, upward slap of her hand. Scurrying out from under the porch, she darted into the quadrangle, where she had a clear view of Garcia kneeling in the mud behind the trough, his fingers poised with a cartridge at the Colt's open gate.

Rose fired instinctively, then fired twice more. At least two of her bullets struck Garcia, one in the leg just above his knee, the other in his side. Howling, he lifted his Colt, but he hadn't finished reloading, and his first hammer-fall was on an empty chamber. It was his second that found a live round. Rose jerked back with a startled yelp as Garcia's bullet zinged past her jaw, tugging at her hair. Heart pounding, she scuttled back under the porch.

Things seemed to slow down after that. Curled up as far back as she could get, she cocked the Smith & Wesson and waited, but Garcia didn't show himself. Above her, the roar of gunfire between Jacques and Web had ceased. Only the gentle splashing of water from the perforated trough competed with the ringing in her ears for attention.

Rose didn't know what to make of the silence.

Was Garcia still crouched behind the trough, waiting in ambush? Or had he made his escape while she crawled back under the porch? Not knowing what else to do, she finally crept out from under the boardwalk. She'd lost her hat in the fray and her long blonde hair was plastered across her face; several strands were caught in her mouth, others menaced her eyes. She brushed the hair back with an impatient swipe, then warily approached the trough. She found Garcia still behind it, lying on his side in the mud, his chest slick with blood.

Turning, Rose saw Web lying, motionless, on the verandah. She glanced at the opposite end, where Jacques had been standing, but the porch was empty. Limping over, she discovered him sprawled head down and on his back across the wooden steps, a bullet hole above his right eye.

"Jesus Christ!" a voice exclaimed in quiet disbelief.

Looking up, Rose saw a white man in buckskins crouched at the entrance to the trade room, his eyes as wide as double eagles. Two pieces of a briarwood pipe lay on the planking beneath him, where he'd bitten the stem in half.

Others began to appear, many of them staring at Rose with the flat intensity of a predator. It was an unnerving experience, and even with the Smith & Wesson firmly in hand, she started to fear for her safety—here, where she was the stranger and Web and Garcia and Jacques had been familiar faces. She retrieved her Stetson, then limped to Albert's side. Keeping the pistol unholstered, she mounted, then reined toward the open gate. No one spoke as she gave the roan its head, but there were volumes uttered in the charged silence that followed her retreat.

Chapter Thirty-Five

Rose hauled up on the back side of the same low saddle from which she'd first viewed Harker's Fort. Although surrounded by several hundred yards of open meadow, thick pine forests walled her in on either side—well within range of the long-shooting buffalo guns so many of the ex-hunters at Harker's seemed to favor. With that in mind, she decided to abandon the route she and Jacques had used coming north and veer east, into the trees.

She began to breathe easier as soon as the forest closed in behind her. Still, she didn't slow down. The afternoon was ebbing, and she knew she'd have to stop before dark. With only the stars and a quartering moon to guide her, she couldn't risk traveling over the uncertain terrain she was encountering among the pines. In the meantime, she wanted to put as much distance as possible between her and the fort.

Oddly it was the thought of having to make camp that brought the pain in her foot to the forefront of her mind. Glancing down, her vision started to blur when she spied the blood-soaked leather of her right boot.

"Oh, Lordy," she whispered, drawing rein. "I been shot."

Carefully she slid her foot from the Mother Hubbard's stirrup to study the torn leather as best she could without dismounting. As near as she could tell, the bullet had sheared away the outer edge of her boot, paring off a small section of the upper and a larger chunk of the sole. Although the leather was stained with blood for an inch or so around the tear, she saw no evidence that the wound was still bleeding, or that it required immediate attention.

Reinserting her foot in the stirrup, she straightened with a huge sense of relief. "I don't reckon it's anything to fret over," she told Albert. "It's only a little bit bloody, and too far from my heart to kill me." But when she glanced along her back trail, her expression darkened. "Come on," she said, lifting the gelding's reins. "Let's put a few more hills between us and them yahoos back to Harker's. I ain't keen on gettin' myself Custered by a bunch of dang' whiskey peddlers."

It was almost dark when she came to a little aspen glade locked in on three sides by a deep pine forest, then sundered down the middle by a fast-flowing brook. Limping awkwardly, she pulled the saddle from Albert's back and dumped it close to the stream, then picketed the gelding on some grass below the quakies. She collected firewood in the deepening twilight, then struck a blaze with a lucifer. With the fire burning to her satisfaction, she unfurled her bedroll and sat down on top of it, then gently pried the boot off her right foot.

The pain intensified as the stiff leather slid over the injury, but eased again soon afterward. Setting the boot aside, Rose carefully peeled off her sock, then sat back in disbelief. The little toe on her right foot was gone, apparently shot off.

"I'll be damned," she murmured, unable to look away. Even though she could see a piece of bone sticking out of the mangled flesh, the wound didn't appear all that serious. She remembered her brother Luke accidentally lopping off half an inch or so from the tip of his index finger with a razor-sharp skinning knife, back in their buffalo days. Luke had cursed a blue streak for a while, but then he'd succumbed to her pap's ridicule and wrapped the stubby finger in a dirty bandanna and gone back to work. Her pap had dressed the wound that evening with a cleaner rag, but pronounced it too trifling to waste good whiskey on by sterilizing it.

Rose was forced to accept a certain degree of apathy toward her wound simply because she lacked any medical supplies to treat it properly. She didn't even have a pocket flask of whiskey with which to bathe the torn flesh.

To make matters worse, the pain was increasing with the injury's exposure to the cool night air, causing her to feel suddenly queasy. Sliding the foot as close to the fire as she dared, she lay back to collect her thoughts. Even though the injury wasn't life-threatening, she doubted if she'd be able to function very well for the next few days. Being alone intensified her anxiety, as did the fear that someone from Harker's Fort might trail her and cut her throat in the middle of the night.

Knowing she'd have to make do, Rose tugged the long tails of her shirt out of her britches and cut several inches off the bottom for a bandage. Although she didn't have any alcohol or salve, she did have a small bottle of sperm whale's oil she used to lubricate her firearms. She poured a little of that over the tail of her shirt, then wrapped it around her foot. The thick, amber-hued liquid quickly soothed the worst of the pain. Heeling off her other boot, she wiggled inside her bedroll, then pulled the blankets to her chin. Although her concern about being followed hadn't lessened, weariness soon triumphed over worry, and she slid into the dreamless sleep of the exhausted.

The sun was well up when Rose awoke the next morning. In the pines across the creek, a camp robber jay was scolding a squirrel, and a soft breeze whirred the delicate aspen leaves.

Still groggy, Rose was content to just lie there for a while, wrapped in a cocoon of warmth that was only marginally disturbed by the remote discomfort of her foot. Gradually she became aware of the incongruous sounds of a crackling fire, the low rumble of boiling water where neither fire nor roiling water had any business being. She let her head loll to the side, peering through bleary eyes at a man she at first mistook for Jacques, drinking coffee by the fire. Then, abruptly, she realized that although this man had the same dark features as her *Métis* friend, and was dressed similarly, he was a stranger, and Jacques was dead.

With a little gasp, Rose threw her blankets back and sat up. The sudden movement caused the pain of her missing toe to surge powerfully.

At the fire, the Indian watched calmly, coffee cup in hand. Rose's revolver lay by her side, but she didn't reach for it. Looking around, she saw a small cavvy of horses at the lower end of the glade. With them was a man in his late forties or early fifties, with a paunchy stomach and hair the color of steel shavings; he wore buckskins and moccasins, as did two of the three women with him. The third woman and two young children were dressed in the more diverse style of the coffee drinker, a coalescing of white and Indian influences.

"Don't be afraid," the coffee drinker said in fluent English, when Rose got around to returning his gaze. "My woman has some medicine for your foot." He glanced at the youngest of the three women, the one wearing a buckskin skirt and moccasins, but a white man's double-breasted shirt. "María," he called.

María was standing patiently beside a pack horse. At the coffee drinker's hail, she started up the incline to Rose's side, a rawhide parfleche clutched in one arm. One of the older women dismounted to join her.

"My name's Johnny Long," the coffee drinker said. Indicating the younger woman with a slight jut of the chin, he added: "That's my wife, María. I used to be called Jonathan Long Bow, but I shortened it to Johnny Long. I get along better with the whites if I don't sound too Indian. That older gent down there is María's father, Fights His Enemies. The other"—he made a motion toward the woman following María—"is Cow Elk Running. She's my mother-in-law, so I won't be speaking directly to her, as the old-timers consider that ill-mannered. The other woman, still on her horse, is Cow Elk Running's sister, Never Talks, which isn't altogether true, but close enough when Cow Elk Running is around. Cow Elk Running was born with an active tongue, and age hasn't slowed it down any."

Half a hundred questions were jumping around inside Rose's head, but the one she finally blurted sprang more from impatience than any desire for an explanation. "I thought all Indians didn't talk much. You ain't hardly shut up since I opened my eyes."

Johnny chuckled. "Now, that's a fact, but you looked so startled when you saw me sitting here, I was afraid you'd start shooting." His smile slipped a notch. "These people have been shot at enough for one lifetime."

"I ain't inclined to shoot without cause, but

things is moving along a mite brisk for my taste. What's she doing?" She meant María, who was lifting the blankets away from Rose's foot.

"You were fast asleep when we found you, so we took the liberty of peeking," Johnny explained.

Rose leaned forward to keep an eye on the proceedings. Flashing a reassuring smile, María spoke rapidly in Sioux, a language Rose recognized but was unable to follow. "What's she saying?" she demanded of Johnny.

"She says your injury isn't bad, but it'll need to be doctored or it could get worse. Best you just let her do what needs to be done. Cow Elk Running will help her if she needs it. Cow Elk Running's a healer." A look of affection came over Johnny's face when he glanced at María. "She's passing on what she knows to my wife."

"You sound proud."

"I am. I'm a Blood Blackfoot myself, but raised more white than Indian by the missionaries at Saint Peter's. I was afraid marrying a Blackfoot might hurt María's standing with her people, but times are changing. The tribes aren't nearly as clannish as they used to be."

"Her people?" Rose glanced at Fights His Enemies.

"Hunkpapa Sioux," Johnny replied laconically, then grinned at the expression that came over Rose's face. "Kind of puckers the ol' bunghole, doesn't it?"

"Sitting Bull's people," Rose breathed.

"Fights His Enemies was a good friend of Sitting Bull's, but when Bull went south in 'Eighty-One to surrender to the American soldiers, Fights His Enemies stayed in Canada. He said he'd rather starve a free man in the Grandmother's Land than as a slave on the White Father's reservation in the United States. He's almost done it a time or two, too. Starve, I mean."

At Rose's feet, María was gently probing the tender flesh of her injured foot. Cow Elk Running raided the coffee pot, pouring some over a piece of clean trade cloth and handing it to María, who began to dab carefully at the wound, washing away the dried blood.

Rose stiffened, then sucked in a lungful of air. "Hell's fire," she gritted, leaning back on her elbows.

"They have to remove a couple of bone fragments," Johnny explained, but his comment elicited only a grunt from Rose. For the next several minutes she was too busy trying to keep from hollering or passing out to care much about the cause of her hurting.

With the picking and prodding finished, Cow Elk Running brought out a small tin kettle with a rawhide lid. Pulling off the stiff hide, she dipped a finger into the gooey black mess and began slathering it over Rose's wound. Within seconds, the throbbing was cut by half.

"Hey," Rose said softly. "That ain't bad."

María spoke, Johnny interpreting. "It will

prevent the red swelling that poisons the blood,"
he said, then amended: "She means infection. She
says you're to keep salve on it for the time it
takes the moon . . ." He paused, struggling to
make the translation from Sioux to English, via
Blood Blackfoot. "She means a quarter . . . a
week. Keep this beaver dung on your foot for at
least a week." He switched to Sioux, speaking
rapidly. María replied without looking up. "Keep
it bandaged, too," Johnny said. "We'll leave some
stuff with you for that, some salve and cloth."

Rose frowned. "You . . . ah . . . you say there's
beaver dung in this concoction?"

"Not much," Johnny replied, then flashed
another quick grin. "Hardly enough to stink?"

"Shoot, I've smelled worse many a time," she
assured him.

At the lower end of the glade, Fights His
Enemies had dismounted and was addressing her
horse. Rose edged a hand toward her revolver, a
move not lost upon anyone. "I can pay for this
here beaver dung," she told Johnny.

"I doubt if he wants your horse," Johnny replied
curtly. Then his voice softened. "The old bugger
does like them, though. He's told me that when he
was younger, before the Long Knife soldiers
stole his land, he used to own forty or fifty head at
a time."

Albert whickered softly as Fights His Enemies
approached, but made no effort to evade the
gray-haired warrior's hand. Shaking her head in

reproach, Rose muttered: "It's a wonder he ain't pullin' a Sioux travois somewhere."

Fights His Enemies allowed Albert to smell the back of his hand, then stepped closer. He ran his palm along the roan's neck, then back over his withers and spine and down his croup. He examined the gelding's belly and legs and hoofs, looked into his eyes and ears, then checked his long, yellowing teeth. When he was finished, he came over to the fire and sat down just as María finished tying a fresh bandage on Rose's foot. Smiling amiably, Fights His Enemies said: "*Hau kola.*"

It was one of the few Sioux phrases Rose recognized. "Howdy," she replied.

Fights His Enemies glanced at the clean-up work his daughter was doing, then turned to Rose. As he began to speak, Johnny set his cup aside to translate. From that point on, the voice was Johnny's, but the words belonged to Fights His Enemies. "Is there much pain, little sister?"

"I've hurt worse. Hurt worse and smelled worse."

Fights His Enemies's smile widened as Johnny turned her words into Sioux. "Wounds earned in war are never painful for long. Not if the battle was honorable, the warrior brave."

"You heard about that fracas at Harker's Fort, did you?"

Fights His Enemies nodded. "It is told on the wind," he replied, which Rose figured was sufficiently vague to mean just about anything.

"What's the wind have to say about anyone following me?" she asked.

"No one follows."

She breathed a sigh of relief at that. Then, remembering her manners, she waved a hand toward the coffee pot. "Have some. They's plenty."

"Is there sugar?"

She shook her head.

"Then I will not have coffee." Fights His Enemies broke off a stem of tall grass, running it back and forth between his fingers. "I am on my way to Fort Walsh to assure the Grandmother's chief that I will not fight with the half-bloods against the red-coated Mounties, if that war comes to pass." He meant the *Métis*, Rose knew, and specifically those who had fought with Riel and Dumont during the troubles at Batoche in 1885. "But I wanted to speak with you first," Fights His Enemies continued. "I wanted to say hello one more time."

"Once more?" Rose asked, puzzled.

"Do you not know that I know you?"

"I figure I'd remember, had we met."

Fights His Enemies's eyes twinkled. "We did not meet, but I still know you. Many of my village do. We called you Sunflower Girl because of the color of your hair. Once I spied upon your father's camp for the passage of two suns, and considered stealing you so that you might become a Hunkpapa woman. I liked the way you handled the horses and mules, and cared for the hides the young men in your camp skinned so carelessly. I thought you would be happier as a Hunkpapa, but the other members of my party persuaded me to leave you with your father and brothers. We had come south from the Grandmother's Land to kill some white buffalo hunters, but my friends did not want to risk the wrath of the Grandmother's Red Coats by kidnapping a white child."

"Lordy," Rose breathed, wide-eyed. "That was over to the Square Butte country below Fort Benton, wasn't it?"

Fights His Enemies looked pleased. "You saw us?"

"No, but I sure as heck felt you. Them mules was god-awful fractious for a spell then, too. What was that . . . eight, nine years ago?"

"Yes, about that. It was after we followed Sitting Bull north into Canada, but before he surrendered."

"Yeah, I remember," Rose said, nodding.

Gathering their things, María and Cow Elk Running returned to their horses, calling to the children. Fights His Enemies's expression sobered. "You would have made a good Hunkpapa," he said. "I think maybe I should have taken you that day."

"Well, thanks just the same, but I'm used to being who I am."

"Your horse is not well," Fights His Enemies said, changing the subject.

Rose sat up straighter, her gaze going to where

Albert was watching the ponies of Fights His Enemies's family.

"He is long in the tooth, and your travels have taken much out of him," Fights His Enemies went on. "Maybe it is time you stole a younger horse and allowed this one to go free."

"I reckon times have changed for everyone," Rose replied. "Nowadays they'd hang me for stealin' a horse, rather than just steal another one for themselves, like folks used to do. That's how come I'm in all the trouble I am."

Fights His Enemies nodded gravely. "It is true, little sister, that I do not understand the values that guide the White Eyes who now come onto our lands. But listen to this story. When I was a young man, long before even the first iron horse crossed our lands along the river called the Platte, the White Eyes came like streams of ants in their white-topped wagons. They came but they did not stay, for they were bound for a land called Oregon, beyond where even the Nez Percé live. In those days the white men killed our buffalo for food and sport, and never paid for them or asked permission to hunt them. But one day an Indian, a Cheyenne, if I remember correctly, killed a *whoa-haw* . . . one of the white man's spotted cows that they use to pull their wagons . . . and the Army came and took that Cheyenne away and hung him.

"That was a bad day for the Indians, to see how the White Eyes could come onto their land and kill their buffalo, then hang a red man for shooting just one of theirs. I think that is when I started to hate the White Eyes, even though I had been friendly to them before. But also I think I knew even then that our days would be like snow in the summer, and that our time upon the plains would soon be no more. I did not know then if I would live to see that day, or if it would be a thing for my children's children to behold, but now I think I will see it, and so I mourn for my children's children as I mourn for my own children, and for myself. Yet I also mourn for some of the White Eyes, little sister. Those who I used to fight but always respected. I think they have been lied to, as well, and that their time on the plains will be short, as the Indian's is. They will suffer as the Indian has suffered, these hunters and traders, and then they will go the way of the Indian."

He stopped, and for a long time no one spoke. Finally Fights His Enemies said: "It is a bad way to die, hanging. It closes off the throat and prevents the spirit from escaping, so that the spirit is trapped inside the body to rot along with the flesh." Pushing to his feet, he tossed aside the sprig of grass he'd been fiddling with. "Perhaps you should steal a horse from the herd outside the fort that once belonged to the man named Harker. There are many good ones there, and they do not watch them too closely. It is where I would go, if I was in the mood to steal a fresh horse."

"Maybe I'll do that," Rose said, although she knew she wouldn't. Fights His Enemies knew it, too.

With a gesture from her husband, Cow Elk Running came forward with a haunch of meat and a small cloth sack. "This is from a deer my son-in-law shot last night," Fights His Enemies said. "There is also some rice traded from a Cree. It will be enough until you are able to ride again. Perhaps by then your horse will be rested."

"I thank you for your kindness," Rose said.

"May you have good hunting, Sunflower," Fights His Enemies said, then headed for his horse.

"He was more of a gentleman than I would've expected," Rose said to Johnny Long, when Fights His Enemies had moved out of earshot.

"He is," Johnny concurred. "There's no finer man, red or white, between the Athabasca and the Platte. Of course, he's got a scalp pole in his lodge that carries almost thirty pieces of hair from the White Eyes he's killed over the years. Most of them belonged to men, but a few came from white women and children."

"Ain't that the way," Rose said softly.

"It's a funny ol' world," Johnny agreed. He shook the last drops of coffee from his cup. "Good luck, Rose of Yellowstone."

His words startled her. "How'd you know I was called that?" She half expected him to reply that a grasshopper had told it to him, but he surprised her.

"Hell, everyone knows your name. You're famous. You're going to be even more famous if the Stranglers don't catch up with you too soon and hang you."

Chapter Thirty-Six

Johnny Long was right. Rose of Yellowstone was becoming a sensation, much to the chagrin of Rose Edwards, who was hurrying down a Fort Benton alley, simmering over the inconvenience of her unexpected fame.

After six days of convalescence in the forest east of Harker's Fort, she'd come south in easy stages, hoping to continue her recuperation in Fort Benton. That would be out of the question now. From the size of the crowd gathering outside the cobbler's shop where she'd had her boot repaired, she knew she'd have to hustle if she wanted to stay ahead of the rumors floating down from Canada.

Edgar Willard was sitting on a bench behind the livery, working diligently on a bottle of Anheuser-Busch beer, when Rose came around the corner. Albert stood saddled nearby, his bridle hanging off the horn. On the gelding's hoofs, new shoes shone like buffed pewter.

Propping the dark bottle on his knee, Edgar said: "I saw the crowd gatherin', so figure ya wouldn't be stayin'. I can take that saddle off, iffen I'm wrong."

"Naw, you ain't wrong," Rose said in annoyance. "You'd think them jaybirds would have jobs to go to, though."

"I expect they ain't never seen a lady shootist

before, let alone one wearin' britches. Pants don't leave much to a fella's imagination, ya know?"

"Fellas like that generally don't need much to kick off their imaginations," she replied. "I just hope my wearin' trousers and packin' a shooter was worth the bother for them. If they hadn't been there, I wouldn't've had to sneak out the back way." She pulled Shorty's old buckskin poke from her pocket. "What's the damage, Edgar?"

The old man guffawed. "Why, half of Harker's Fort is what they're sayin'."

She made a face. "That ain't funny, dang it."

"No, it ain't," he agreed. "Listen to an old man, girl. Ya need ter hightail it back ter yer ranch and pull yer head in for a spell, 'cause the grease is fixin' ter fly around here."

"What do you mean?"

"They're sayin' yer name's been moved to the top of Joe Bean's list, and that don't shine, no matter how ya polish it."

"Dang, Edgar, I ain't hurtin' them boys. What do they want to keep wavin' that list in my face for?"

He leaned forward, brows knitting. "I don't reckon it's about money no more. It ain't hardly about range or water, either. It's about image, and yer a-tarnishin' theirs plenty by hangin' onto that property ya own down there by the Yellerstone."

"Ain't Ostermann got enough? It's already ten times more'n what most folks has."

"It ain't that simple. Tell ya the truth, I ain't

sure Ostermann really wants the A-Bar-E. I ain't even sure he wants the Flyin' Egg, at least not the way someone like you'd want a place. It's prestige ol' Howie is cravin'. With yer property, he can claim all that land between the Musselshell and the Yellowstone as his own little empire, and that'd be one hell of a claim. It'd be one hell of an image, too, can he pull it off." Edgar's expression changed. "Ya got to cache, girl, 'cause ol' Howie's still hungerin' for that prestige. Wants it like a starvin' wolf wants a colt, and he'll likely get it, too, if ya don't pull yer head in like a turtle in its shell."

"It ain't my intention to cache until after I locate Pine Tree Manning," she said stubbornly.

"Manning, huh?" He stroked his whiskered jaw reflectively. "I've heard of him. Mean, they say."

"Mean or not, I aim to run him down for what he done to Nora." She bounced the buckskin poke in her hand a couple of times. "I gotta git, Edgar. What do I owe you?"

"Put yer money away, girl. I don't want it."

"I ain't no bum."

"I know ya ain't. It's just something I want ter do. Call it an investment in my future."

She frowned. "How's my not paying my tab an investment in your future?"

"Think about it." Setting his beer aside, he walked over to lift the bridle from the Mother Hubbard's horn. With Albert bitted and ready to ride, he handed the reins to Rose, his expression grave. "Best ya sleep with one eye open from here on," he advised.

"I plan to."

"I mean it. Seems like ever' other ranahan wha stables his hoss here is a-whisperin' yer name That don't bode well in my book."

"All right, Edgar, I hear you." She held out her hand and the old man shook it. "I thank you for Albert's new shoes, and wish you prosperity when the railroad comes through."

"Good luck, Rose Edwards," he replied, his voice suddenly thick with emotion. "It's been an honor knowin' ya." That said, he turned and hurried away, leaving his beer behind, unfinished.

Although Rose considered hunting down Pine Tree Manning a priority, she decided to swing past the Flying Egg on her way home to confront Howard Ostermann. She figured the Egg owner had remained hidden for too long behind his shield of money and title, and she wanted to see what he'd say when she accused him of Nora's murder. She wasn't sure what she hoped to accomplish by her action, other than to remind him that there were human beings involved at the other end of his decisions, people with names and faces and dreams of their own that would never be fulfilled now, because of blind greed. Where it went from there would be up to him, she supposed.

The thought of killing Ostermann had occurred to her more than once on the long ride down from

Canada, but she doubted if she'd have the gumption to gun down someone in cold blood, no matter how much he might deserve it. And she was pretty sure Ostermann wouldn't fight her. Not with men like Frank Caldwell on his payroll.

Taking a more southwesterly route than she would have used to go directly home, Rose passed through the Judith Basin toward the gap of the same name, at the valley's southern extremity. It was her first visit to the Basin in several years, and she was appalled by the changes she saw. At one time this had been a veritable hunter's paradise, teeming with game of every description. Now it looked like a wasteland, overgrazed, weedy, spotted with old cow chips but nary a beef in sight.

She saw plenty of ranches, though. Four on the Judith itself, plus several more back in the hills. She avoided them all, fearing that every man's hand would be against her now.

Below the Judith Gap she entered the Musselshell drainage. From there on, south and east, she was on Flying Egg land, and rode more openly. Although she figured every man's hand would be against her here, too, she was feeling fighty, and would have welcomed a good mix. But in two more days of travel she saw no one, and so approached the Musselshell feeling as prickly as a cactus patch.

Uncertain as to the location of the Flying Egg's headquarters, she took a gamble and turned downstream. As luck would have it, she came in sight of the sprawling complex of barns, sheds, and corrals shortly after sundown. Although the size of the place was impressive, Rose was more intrigued by the main house, an imposing two-story affair of log construction, with a single, towering cupola on the southwest corner and a covered verandah that ran along three sides. The area immediately surrounding the house warranted more than a passing glance. There was an irrigated polo field, complete with freshly painted goals, a well-tended yard in front of the house, and hedges the likes of which she'd never seen, trimmed in the shapes of various Rocky Mountain fauna—a grizzly bear, a mountain goat, two bison. Behind the house and to one side of a summer kitchen was an extensive kennel containing an assortment of long-legged hunting dogs.

"Dangnation," Rose muttered, eyeing the spread. "I guess it ain't such a bad deal, being the third son of a Fifth Earl."

Bats were just starting to make their appearance in the smoky light as Rose rode past the dark mansion. They darted among the cottonwoods along the river, swooping low over the water. As she came abreast of the house, the hounds set up a baying that brought forth a pair of huge mastiffs. Rose wrapped her fingers around the Smith & Wesson's hard rubber grips, her pulse accelerating, but the dogs remained obediently at their posts beside the front steps, and allowed her and Albert to pass along the lower edge of the lawn unmolested.

"Now that's something to remember," she murmured, keeping an eye on the dogs until she was a couple of hundred yards away and approaching the ranch proper—bunkhouse, equipment sheds, and the like. "I reckon I'd dang' near rather face Frank Caldwell and all his hired guns as them two," she added to Albert.

A match burst into flame in the shadows beside a small cabin across the lane from the bunkhouse, and Rose drew up. A short, bowlegged individual in a broad-brimmed hat detached himself from the dark wall and approached casually, lighting a pipe. Shaking out the match, he dropped it in the thick dust of the lane and crushed it under his heel. Tipping his head back to reveal a chiseled chin and a small, iron-gray mustache, he said: "How do you do, ma'am?"

"I'm Rose Edwards," Rose said. Although this pipe smoker with the big hat seemed polite enough, she hadn't forgotten that this was the camp of her enemy, and that it wouldn't do to let her guard down.

"I thought you might be. I'm Mason Crabb, foreman of the Crooked Bar-O-Bar." He touched the brim of his hat. "I hope you don't mind my smoking? I'd gladly put it out if you found it offensive."

"No, pipe smoke don't bother me."

From the bunkhouse came the searching notes of a guitar, played softly. It brought a smile to Crabb's shadowy features. "That Toby Joe is gonna get that instrument roped one of these days. It was painful to listen to, last year this time."

"It ain't so bad now, though I don't recognize the tune."

"The scales, he calls them. He won't play until he's run his scales a time or two. Sort of like checking your cinch before you saddle a bronc', I suppose."

Rose was giving the bowlegged foreman a thoughtful look. "You ain't hardly what I'd expected for an Egg man," she allowed.

"I'm an old cow man from the San Saba country of Texas," he replied. "I was hired this summer to manage the day-to-day operations of the Crooked Bar-O-Bar, but I don't involve myself in its politics. The last foreman did, but Mister Ostermann fired him this spring."

"You ain't no friend of Frank Caldwell, then?"

"I don't allow Mister Caldwell or his men to reside in the bunkhouse. They have rooms in the main house they can use when they're here, which isn't often. I personally have fourteen good men and one of the finest cooks in Montana under my hire, but I won't allow them to associate with gunhawks."

"I'll be danged," Rose said.

"If I could help you in some way?" Crabb encouraged gently.

"I'm lookin' for Howard Ostermann. I won't call him Mister."

Crabb hesitated. "You understand that, although I

don't involve myself or my men in activities outside the scope of running a cattle ranch, I'd consider the safety and protection of my employer to fall within the realm of my duties?"

"Is he around, Mister Crabb?"

"Mister Ostermann is away right now. I expect him back in a couple of weeks, when we'll all go to Billings to pick up the first shipment of short-horns."

"Shorthorns?"

"I don't believe I'm betraying anyone's confidence when I say he's bringing in three thousand head of shorthorns from Oregon and Washington, and another fifteen hundred from New Mexico."

Rose didn't know what to say to that. For some reason, it hadn't occurred to her how easy it might be for men like Ostermann to start over, just to go out and buy new stock.

"I suppose he's still gonna want the A-Bar-E, then, too?" she said after a while.

For the first time, Mason Crabb appeared somewhat flustered. "As I said, Mister Ostermann doesn't share his plans with me, outside of my duties as foreman."

"Yeah," she said dryly, her esteem for the grizzled old-timer withering. "Well, it's easier that way, I reckon."

Crabb's lips thinned under his mustache. "Perhaps you'd better leave, Missus Edwards. Unless I could supply you with some supper . . . something to take along."

"Is Caldwell or any of his men around?"

"Not at present."

"What about a Pine Tree Manning?"

Crabb hesitated, then lowered his voice. "Manning was here about three weeks ago, delivering some documents to Mister Ostermann. He returned south immediately. That's all I can tell you."

Rose swore softly. "I bet it was the deed," she said.

"I beg your pardon?"

"Them documents . . . I'll bet they was the papers Manning and his pards stole off my property the day they killed Nora Alder. I'd been wondering what they wanted 'em for. I guess I should've known."

Gently Crabb said: "I think it's time you left."

"I'll go, but you tell Ostermann I was here. Tell him I ain't forgot who my real enemy is, and that, one of these days, I'll be back. Tell him that him and me has got some unfinished business to 'tend to."

"Is that a threat, Missus Edwards?"

"Yeah, Crabb, that's a threat." She pulled her horse around without waiting for a reply. Judging from the agitated manner in which Mason Crabb's jaw was working in the shadows of his hat, she suspected it would have been taken as one, anyway. Giving Albert a nudge with her heels, she rode off into the night.

Reaching home, she discovered that either Caldwell's men or Joe Bean's had not been idle in their efforts to drive her off. Piled in the center of the yard, stacked in and under the remains of her wagon, were the ashes and débris that had once been the furnishings of home and barn.

Virtually nothing had been spared. Tools from the barn, harness, even the pitchfork had been tossed on top of the chests, crates, table, and spice cabinet from the house. Rose was so stunned she felt half sick. All that remained was the cabin with its two built-in bunks, the empty barn and lean-to, and the corral and water trough.

Letting Albert wander loose, she sat down on the stoop and just stared. It wasn't until she glanced toward the lightning-struck pine above Muggy's grave that she noticed a man sitting his horse there, silhouetted as sharp as a steel etching against the blue Montana sky. Startled, she jumped to her feet, but stopped when it dawned on her that whoever it was had had ample opportunity to slip away undetected. Or shoot her, depending on his frame of mind or place of employment. Moving away from the cabin, she waited until the solitary figure realized he'd been spotted and rode down the slope to the yard. He hauled up about twenty feet away.

"Was this your doin'?" Rose demanded.

Joe Bean shook his head. "I would suspect Caldwell's men, although I have no proof."

"No, I didn't figure you would."

He glanced at the rubble surrounding the charred, sagging wagon. "I judge this was a symbolic gesture," he said. "A statement of ownership."

"Ownership!"

"My guess is that they left the cabin and barn unfired because they hope to use this place as a line camp, but the rest . . ." He shrugged. "They mean to have it, Rose. There's nothing you can do to stop them."

"I can fight 'em. Maybe a bullet through Howard Ostermann's skull would slow 'em down."

"Killing Ostermann would only afford the rest of them a legitimate excuse to hang you. Howard Ostermann might be your particular thorn, but he's hardly the whole bush."

"Joe, they're gonna hang me anyway, they catch me."

He nodded morosely, his gaze flitting once more to the pile of blackened lumber. "They took your branding iron, didn't they?"

"How'd you know that?"

"It would be their way, something they've done before. They'll brand some of their calves with it as proof that you're as incorrigible as they've claimed. They'll get a federal marshal out to verify it, but he won't stay to see it through. At least he never has."

"Those sons-a-bitches," she said. "Those dirty, rotten . . ." She laughed then, shaking her head. "Well, it don't matter. I was on their list long before I helped Wiley and Shorty run them Crow ponies up to Two-Hats's. I reckon I was on their list as soon as they saw that crick yonder and decided they wanted it for themselves."

"It's not just the Cattlemen's Association you're at odds with, Rose. There are other organizations involved. I'd venture that Web, Garcia, and Manning were working for one of the smaller alliances."

"You know what them three did to Nora?"

"I know what I've heard. Pine Tree quit me some time ago, but he wasn't a Caldwell man, either. This bunch"—he indicated the wreckage at the wagon—"may not even be in operation any more. It has the earmarks of a one-job deal. I don't know who orchestrated it, but I do know Howard Ostermann was involved, even while Caldwell and his men, who work strictly for Ostermann, weren't. I have it on good authority that Caldwell's group has been . . . occupied . . . farther west."

"Christ, Joe, what kind of mess have you boys created?"

"A rather large one, I'm afraid. Most of the smaller syndicates are fairly loosely organized. Many seem to be splinter groups, dissatisfied with the direction the larger Association is taking, yet unwilling to give up their membership in it."

She felt her anger growing. "What about you, Joe? How many innocent men have you strung up since all this begun?"

His face flushed red. "That's an ugly accusation."

"Hangin's an ugly business."

"I've helped bring an end to horse stealing and cattle rustling. I'm not ashamed of that."

"What was Nora's crime?"

"I won't dignify that with a reply. You know who killed Nora."

"I don't know who ordered it. Do you? Do you know who ordered me 'n' Nora killed, our stuff burned?"

Joe's composure was beginning to crumble. "You're mistaking honesty for a poor man's privilege and a rich man's deficit. What I've done has been honest enough. Can you say the same?"

"I ain't never in my life claimed to be no angel, nor have I always been honest, at least not accordin' to the letter of the law. But I've always been honorable and aboveboard with folks, and never stole from no one just to get rich or get my way. Them that know me, trust me, and them that say I'm a killer or a thief, it's because they don't know the whole of it, or want to. What Ostermann's doin' is wrong, Joe. It's underhanded and unethical, and, was there justice in this land instead of the damned law that can get all tangled up in words, it'd be them run outta their homes, instead of me gettin' run outta mine."

"You can whine all day about justice and the law and it won't get you anywhere. Time moves forward, Rose. You either go with it or get left behind."

"I'd rather get left behind than throw in with that bunch."

He snorted. "Who are you to sit in judgment of men who have brought prosperity to this land?

You, who helped destroy the buffalo and the wolf and the Indian?"

"Sure, I've done things I ain't proud of, or that ain't turned out the way I'd hoped they would, but I never run over nobody to do it. I got along with them that was here first, and done it on their terms, too, rather than try and force them to live on mine.

"I ain't denyin' I lived a hunter's life while it lasted, but it was shared on equal terms with the red man, and I'll tell you this, it wasn't me nor mine who fought so hard to put the Indians on reservations, or paid the bounty on wolves. It was them you're workin' for, Joe . . . the Ostermanns and old man Frakes of the world . . . who ruined what we had and loved, then had the audacity to call it progress and prosperity."

"Rose, I swear I'd like to . . ." They glared at one another for almost a full minute, until Joe suddenly looked away. In a voice unfamiliar to her, he said: "Maybe you're right. About some of it, anyway. I used to think I *was* serving a greater cause. But lately . . . it seems like I'm just . . . serving."

"You could quit," she said, her anger gone.

He smiled dismissingly. "So could you." Loosening the strap on his pommel bag, he pulled out a handful of coin-size globs. Riding closer, he dropped them into her hand. "I found these under the wagon," he explained.

Rose's throat constricted when she recognized the half-melted objects. "These was the buttons off a ridin' skirt Nora gave me for Christmas last year," she said. "I never wore it because I always thought it was too pretty for chorin'. I wish now that I had."

"I found these, too." He pulled her spurs from the bag, the ones she'd purchased in Sheridan, with the bronze hearts affixed to the outside of each shank. The spurs had come through the fire in better condition than the buttons, and were undamaged save for a layer of baked-on grime and curled straps.

"I regret taking them," Joe said. "I suppose I had some notion of keeping them as mementos, but I should've known you'd come back." He straightened and cleared his throat, his eyes hardening. "You need to be more vigilant, Rose. Had I been so inclined, I could have easily picked you off from the bluff while you were strolling around the yard."

She nodded, knowing the moment of clemency between them had passed, that Joe Bean was a Regulator again, she a wanted woman. "I reckon you could've," she agreed.

"When I see you again . . ." He didn't finish the sentence, or need to. When they met again, it would be as enemies. There was no other way. "Good bye, Rose."

"So long, Joe."

He reined away, riding toward the gap in the bluffs that would take him down to the Yellowstone. But Rose didn't watch him leave. Something else had caught her eye—a spot of tawny yellow, far to the east. Staring at it, she felt her eyes mist over. "You ornery old devil," she said affectionately to the distant buckskin, then added fiercely: "You stay free, you hear? Don't you ever let 'em put a rope over your neck again . . . and, by damn, I'll try to do the same."

Chapter Thirty-Seven

Rose went to Billings next. It was out of her way, but she had obligations there she couldn't ignore.

It was midafternoon when she reached town, and although she looked as she passed the Jepson & Lane Livery, she didn't see any activity at her pap's cross-tie shack behind the corrals. She would need to see him before she left, but she wasn't looking forward to it.

Her first stop was Sutherland's Mercantile, near the center of town. The store was housed in an old-fashioned wooden-framed building, complete with false front and covered boardwalk. She hitched her horse to the rail, then climbed the steps to the store. It was a warm, lazy day, and the scent of cheeses, spicy meats, leather, tobacco products, grains, and kerosene met her at the door like a faithful dog.

Herman Sutherland was a tall, handsome man in his early sixties, with a full head of soft gray hair and a kindly smile. He was waiting on a customer when Rose walked in, but he gave her a smile and a brief wave of recognition when he saw her.

Rose waited beside the pickle barrel until he was free. After calling into a back room for his wife to watch the counter, Sutherland motioned for Rose to follow him to a small desk in the corner. Pulling out a cane-bottomed chair, he invited her to sit, then settled onto a wooden swivel chair at his desk and spun it around to face her.

"You all right?" he asked, inclining his head toward her patched boot. "You are limping, I noticed."

"It ain't nothin'," she assured him.

"I would remind you there is a doctor in town. Two, in fact. I prefer Paus, across the street."

"Thanks, but it's already been looked at." She didn't add that the attending physician had been wearing moccasins, and that her ministrations had been supervised by the first wife of one of Sitting Bull's more noteworthy Hunkpapa captains.

"So, if not a doctor, then your account?" Sutherland ventured.

"I was hopin' we could settle up," Rose acknowledged.

Sutherland pulled a ledger from the top drawer of his desk and flipped it open, paging slowly backward until he came to the A-Bar-E entry from the preceding year. On a separate sheet of paper, he tabulated the interest, double-checked the figures, then looked up questioningly. "One hundred, twenty-two dollars? That is agreeable with your figures?"

"To tell you the truth, I ain't tallied it, but I trust

you." She looked out the front window at the hills south of town, already shading to tan. She would miss this land. It was a big, wide-open country, hard on even the strongest of hearts, but she couldn't imagine anything—anywhere—comparing favorably. Taking a deep breath, she said: "Plain and simple, I just ain't got the money, Mister Sutherland. I reckon you've heard what's been goin' on?"

He nodded. "Even the dirtiest secrets reaches the public's ears eventually."

"They burned me out again, too."

"I have heard."

"I ain't got nothin' no more except my horse and gear and that land, and I ain't keen on givin' up my horse. I reckon Howard Ostermann's won this pot, at least as far as drivin' me off my place, but he don't own the land yet, and I'd like to see that he doesn't get it. Would you take it, Mister Sutherland, if I signed it over, and consider my debt clear?"

Sutherland's eyes widened. "Your *land!*" he exclaimed. "For the debt?"

"The deed was stolen, but it's registered in Bozeman and ought to be on the books in Helena, too. I ain't sure how all that works."

"No," Sutherland protested. "No, no, no, Missus Edwards. That is not even a poor business decision. That is an absurd one, through and through. You mustn't even consider it."

"Time's short. I'd rather you got that property,

but sure as heck someone's gonna, because I can't keep it. Not any more."

The shopkeeper's expression relaxed. "What kind of a man do you take me for, Missus Edwards, that you think I would accept your ranch under such circumstances, and for such a piddling debt?"

"It's all I got. What ain't been stolen has been burned."

"I will tell you what I think, what I have been thinking for some time. I will buy your land and run my own cattle, if you are sure you want to sell."

"I ain't got much choice," she stated glumly.

"I think," Sutherland admitted, "that you are right, although it saddens me to say so. Even to me, word comes that Rose Edwards's name has risen to the top of the Regulators' list. Who these people are who put names on lists, I don't know, but I think you do, and I think the list is real. Too many people have died for that list not to be real. So now your name is at the top, and I don't think you can stay unless you wish to die, and that, I fear, would happen pretty quick. They would bury you out there, where no one would find you. It would have to be out there, is what Mama and I think. To bury you where your grave could be found, your death mourned, would cause too much embarrassment." He shrugged apologetically. "Forgive my bluntness."

"Naw, it weren't blunt," Rose lied, feeling tight-chested all of a sudden. "I just hadn't considered it like that before. It makes sense, though. I don't reckon fellas like Howard Ostermann or Maxwell Frakes would look too kindly on something like that smudgin' up their reputations."

"No, they wouldn't," Sutherland agreed. "So I think . . . Mama and I . . . that the thing for you to do is to sell your property and go away. Far enough away that Howard Ostermann or Maxwell Frakes or any of those people who make lists won't ever be afraid of you again. But hear this, Missus Edwards, and believe me. It does not matter who you sell your property to. It does not have to be me. But it should be sold so that the money is yours to take with you, wherever you go."

"Well, I ain't goin' nowhere right off, but if you're of a mind to buy the A-Bar-E and wouldn't consider it a burden, I'd sure like to sell it. I don't know what you'd call fair, but Ostermann offered me a thousand dollars for the place last winter."

Sutherland's lip twitched in contempt. "Missus Edwards, Howard Ostermann offered to steal your land, not buy it. How many acres do you own, exactly?"

"The deed said six hundred and forty, although it ain't been surveyed."

"Then not even two dollars an acre did he offer. I am a businessman, Missus Edwards, not a thief. I know the value of your land, especially its water. Whoever owns the A-Bar-E *controls* five thousand additional acres, and *that* is worth considerably more than one thousand dollars, don't you think?"

"What'd you have in mind?" Rose asked cautiously.

"For the land you have title to, I will offer five dollars an acre." He turned over the piece of paper he'd tallied her bill on and scratched out some figures. "What is that for a section, say . . . three thousand . . . two hundred." He looked up. "Would that be satisfactory, Missus Edwards . . . three thousand and two hundred dollars?"

"Holy smokes," Rose squeaked. "Are you sure?"

He smiled. "Yes, I am sure, if that is suitable with you."

"Mister Sutherland, that suitables me to a T. Have you got that kind of money on hand?"

The storekeeper's smile disappeared. "No, I would have to raise it, and that will take time. Three weeks, perhaps a month." A frown creased his forehead. "You can wait that long?"

"Not here in Billings, but I aim to hang around Montana for a spell."

"Listen to me, you should leave this country. I will say it again . . . if you stay, they will kill you."

"I got unfinished business, Mister Sutherland. I ain't goin' nowhere until I've seen it through."

"Your mind is made up, then?"

"Yes, sir."

"You intend to fight?"

"Uhn-huh."

"Then I am glad. May God forgive me, I am glad." He glanced around the store, shared a look and a nod with his wife, then motioned for Rose to follow him to the counter. "Come," he said. "I will show you something."

She followed him down the counter, he behind it, she in front. Midway, he stopped and reached underneath, bringing out a short-barreled Merwin Hulbert revolver in a sturdy shoulder holster, plus two boxes of .45 cartridges.

"This I got on trade a couple of weeks ago," he explained, setting it before her. "Mama and I talked about saving it for you. We knew you would come back . . . if you were able."

But Rose was already shaking her head. "I appreciate the offer, but I'm short on cash and long on debt as it is. I can't afford another pistol."

"No, you misunderstand. I am giving this to you. A gift."

She shook her head again.

"Please," Sutherland said. "This is important. To me, this is important." He took a deep breath, as if collecting his thoughts. "Listen, I want to tell you something. What you do when you fight these men, men like Ostermann, Frakes, it is against the law. We all know that. But it is right, too. It is fighting an injustice that masquerades as law. Maybe there is a better way, I don't know. I don't know how the poor can fight unjustness when men like Ostermann and Frakes hold so much sway with their expensive attorneys.

"I am a coward, Missus Edwards, but I'm not a fool. I see what is going on. We all do. But I am too old, too scared. I have a wife, children, a business, home, friends, a position in the community. All these things I have, and I know that to stand up to these people is to risk losing everything. So I am a coward, and when Ostermann or Frakes come into my store, I bob my head like a good little peasant and say . . . 'Yes, Mister Ostermann,' or 'Yes, Mister Frakes, what can I do for you today?'

"But let me tell you something, it does not feel so good to be a coward. Not at night, in bed, when my wife lies sleeping. Others feel as I do. I know this because I talk to them. But they are also afraid . . . to lose their businesses, their places in the community. They are afraid to band together, yet they are even more afraid to stand alone.

"We are not a rich people, Missus Edwards, those of us who own the small businesses, the little farms, but still we have something we do not want to lose, that becomes precious to us because it is so vulnerable. I think maybe that is why so often it falls to the poorest among us, to those who have nothing left to lose, to fight our battles."

He pushed the Merwin Hulbert, its holster and cartridges, across the counter. "You take this. Maybe it will save your life someday. If it does, then it will have been worth it to me. And remember also what I said about the others. You are Rose of Yellowstone now, and Rose of Yellowstone should not be afraid to ask for help from a small rancher or homesteader, or a small businessman. She should not be afraid to ask for help from any man who sweats at his labor, because they will know, and they will give what they can.

"Meanwhile, you go and do what you have to do, and I will not ask what that is. When you come back, I will have the money and the papers for the A-Bar-E drawn up and ready to sign. How does that sound?"

Slowly Rose closed her hand over the Merwin Hulbert, but in her heart there was no pride, and on her tongue there was only bitterness, as if she'd swallowed something sour. "I reckon that sounds all right, Mister Sutherland," she said, but thought: *You ain't so different from Frakes or Ostermann, not in the long haul.*

"Herman," Herman Sutherland said expansively. "You call me Herman from now on. You don't be calling me 'Mister' no more."

She nodded, but his words echoed in her mind: *Those who have nothing left to lose.*

Sutherland daubed his eyes with the hem of his apron. Down the counter, his wife wiped hers with a handkerchief. Rose stared woodenly out the front door. Pulling himself together, Herman said: "You will need some supplies, too, no?"

"I could use a few. Food, cartridges for my rifle and pistol." She hesitated. "And one other thing. I want a ridin' skirt. You know what that is?"

"Why, certainly," Sutherland replied, looking surprised and pleased at the same time. "I have several right back here." He motioned toward an aisle brimming on both sides with stacks of board-stiff overalls and scratchy wool shirts. At the far end was a dressmaker's wire-framed dummy, fitted with a bright purple riding skirt and matching vest. "Mama," Herman called to his wife, "you would help Missus Edwards pick out some new clothes, wouldn't you?"

"Of course," Mama Sutherland replied. She came down the outside of the counter, snagging Rose by the elbow as she passed. "Come, we will fit you like a proper young horsewoman."

She did, too. Although Rose was hoping for a skirt in the same shade of green as the one Nora had given her for Christmas, she had to settle for blue corduroy, instead. While she was at it, she added a new blouse of soft lavender and a light beige jacket, trimmed in a compatible shade of blue to match her skirt—all to replace the man's shirt, vest, and trousers she'd worn since the day Jed Plover showed up at her garden.

She slipped into the Merwin Hulbert's shoulder rig, and with Mama Sutherland's help, adjusted it so that it rode comfortably out of sight beneath her left arm. She left her old clothes piled on the dressing room floor. Returning to the counter, she found that Herman had already put together a sack of supplies.

Taking in her outfit, he nodded approvingly. "Very good. A woman should wear woman's clothing, don't you think? Mama, don't you agree that a woman should wear woman's clothing?"

Mama did indeed agree, voicing several of the

more important reasons, all of which seemed to hinge upon a woman's aspiration to ensnare a man in matrimony. It was an argument Rose had strong feelings about, having once been ensnared herself, but she kept her opinions to herself as she signed Herman's credit slip. With the Sutherlands' well wishes snapping at her heels like a feisty terrier, she beat a hasty retreat for the door.

Outside, she tied the sack of supplies behind the cantle, then stepped into the saddle. Keeping Albert to a walk, she returned to Jepson & Lane's. Turning into the alley beside the livery, she was unprepared for the sight that greeted her—her pap sitting on an empty fruit crate in front of his shack, as unkempt as any bum.

Rose could tell at a glance that Daniel Ames had fallen off the wagon. His clothes were filthy, his neck and jaw stiff with stubble; his long gray hair hung about his face in greasy strands, and even from the alley, Rose could see that his hands were trembling. It made her heart sink to see him that way. Pulling up beside the last corral, she reluctantly dismounted.

Daniel Ames didn't look up until she came over, and even then his bloodshot eyes had to struggle for focus. Squinting into the westering sun, he said: "What happened to your foot?"

The question caught her off guard. Even sober, her pap wasn't known for his concern for others. "I got shot," she replied.

"By who?"

"Billy Garcia."

"You shoot him back?"

She hesitated, then said: "I reckon I did."

His voice turned gruff. "Ain't no reckoning to it. Either you shot him or you didn't."

Sighing, Rose said: "Yeah, I shot him. I killed him, but not because of my toe."

Daniel sniffed and nodded, then leaned back against the splintery wall of his shack. "Doesn't matter what the reason, it just saves me the trouble of doing it for you."

Wrinkling her nose, she said: "I can smell you from here. What happened?"

He laughed hoarsely. "I been puking my guts out is what happened. Got it all over me. I can barely stand myself."

"You ought to go down to the river and wash yourself. There ain't no call for this." But her scolding brought only a quick wiggling of Daniel's eyebrows, signaling a potential mood shift.

"Don't be telling me what to do," he said in a threatening tone. "How'd you get a Mexican mad enough to shoot you?"

Rose shrugged and wandered over to a clump of grass upwind of her father's position. She sank down, cross-legged, and picked up a couple of small railroad cinders that she bounced in her hand like dice. "It's a long story," she said.

"Then you'd best not tell it. I'd just forget, the shape I'm in."

"Why'd you start drinkin' ag'in? I thought you was huntin'."

A menacing look came over Daniel's face, and Rose tensed in case she had to make a run for it. Instead her father's reply almost bowled her over. "That worthless shit of a brother of yours stole my rifle."

"*Brother!* Who?"

"Luke."

She sat up straighter. "Luke's here?"

"No, god dammit. If he was, I'd still have my rifle."

"But he was here?"

Looking away, her pap growled something unintelligible. Then he said: "They let the little bastard outta prison. I guess they let him out. Maybe he broke out. He didn't say. He showed up last spring and bummed food off me for a week, then stole my rifle and hopped a westbound freight for Oregon. Gone to look for his brothers, I figure." He wagged his head. "Now all my kids have turned against me."

That was her cue, Rose would realize later. Her place to jump in and reassure her father that no one had turned against him—she, least of all—and that they all loved him dearly. But her thoughts had taken a different track, and she missed it completely. "Did he ask about me?" she said.

Daniel gave her an irritated look. "Nope, not once."

She nodded and blinked, and her eyes started

to tear up despite her resolve not to lower her guard. Her pap's vision had sharpened during their conversation, though, and he spotted her misery instantly. Grinning wolfishly, he said: "Turned against you, too, didn't he? How's it feel, missy?"

"Just shut up," she said, unmindful of the consequences.

But her pap had lost interest in Luke. He was watching Rose shrewdly, one eye narrowed. "Got yourself in a hell of a fix with that Cattlemen's Association, didn't you?"

"It ain't nothing I can't handle."

"I don't see why you have to be feuding with those people, anyway. You're pretty enough to've married one."

She gave him a startled look. "I don't reckon pretty is reason enough to throw my life away. I'd sooner marry a snake than a remittance man and I'd probably feel safer with my back turned."

"You'd have been better off with a remittance man than Muggy, I'll tell you that. I always did regret the way he took advantage of you. You should've had an easier life, Kitten."

"Easier ain't always better," she replied.

"You'd think differently if you'd lived through some of the hard times I have. Why don't you go fix me some breakfast? There's beans in back, maybe a little slow elk if it ain't gone to rot."

Rose shook her head. Getting to her feet, she said: "It's suppertime. You ought to take a gander at the sun on occasion, if you're too drunk to hear the roosters crowin' at dawn."

"Was there a rooster handy, I'd have fried chicken instead of tough beef. You know a skinny-assed kid named Bud Tracer?"

"Never heard of him."

"He said he knows you. Acted put out by it, too."

"Being put out with me don't cull the herd down much any more."

"He was hinting around about Muggy's gold."

"Muggy's gold!" She laughed, shaking her head. "That's the first I've heard of that old rumor in nearly a year. Did you tell him it weren't true?"

Daniel gave his daughter a sly look.

"You son-of-a-bitch," she said wearily.

Anger sparked in his eyes, then ebbed under Rose's scornful stare. "I told him you didn't have it," he admitted finally. "You could tell the damn' fool didn't believe me."

"Well, maybe it was that mansion behind you that tipped your hand." She turned toward her horse. "I wouldn't worry about skinny-assed kids dumb enough to think I'm sitting on a pile of gold," she added over her shoulder. "Sooner or later, even the idjits'll figure it out."

"Where are you going?" Daniel called.

"I'm looking for a fella named Pine Tree Manning." She paused, reins in hand. "You wouldn't know him, would you?"

"Heard of him. He the one who killed Nora Alder?"

"One of 'em." She mounted, then sat there a moment, staring at her father, who'd refused to rise. He looked frail, she thought, old and worn-out, as if the loss of the Remington-Hepburn rifle and the life he'd lived with it had somehow shrunk his body as well as his soul. "You gonna be all right, Pap?" she asked, pity twisting in her breast at last.

"I've been fine so far, ain't I?"

"I could send for you, once I resettle."

"Resettle?" He looked momentarily perplexed.

"I gotta leave Montana pretty quick. I was thinkin' I'd go west to the coast and see the ocean, then maybe south. Somewhere where the winters ain't so long."

"*I* ain't going nowhere. It ain't me everyone wants to lynch."

Rose nodded, knowing then that her visit was finished, as was a relationship that had haunted her since childhood. It struck her as odd, though, that she felt neither sadness nor regret at this final parting, and made her wonder if it hadn't been over for a long time, and that maybe she was just now realizing it. "Good bye, Pap," she said.

"Ain't you gonna fix me some breakfast?"

"No, you can fix your own breakfast from here on. It'll do you good." She reined away, riding back up the alley at a walk. On the street she turned east, kicking Albert into a shuffling trot.

Chapter Thirty-Eight

Rose quit the Miles City road shortly after leaving Billings, following the old Coulson to Fort Custer route as far as the northern boundary of the Crow Reservation. There she abandoned the road altogether to cut across country.

Although she'd never had any trouble with the Absarokas—or Sparrow Hawk People, as the Crows referred to themselves—she knew things could get a little dicey for outsiders on the reservation. Game was scarce, and bellies went consistently empty. Annuities promised under treaties either didn't show up or were so horribly misrepresented when they did arrive that they proved useless for the jobs at hand. Crooked agents became rich; honest ones chafed with frustration and disheartenment, while the tribes grew more and more sullen at what they considered a long list of broken promises by the Great White Father in Washington.

Nor could Rose forget the ambush Wiley, Shorty, and Billy Garcia had tripped against the Crows right after she'd thrown in with them. Although she hadn't been involved in the fight itself, she doubted if that would cut much ice with the Absarokas. So it was for that reason, as much as any, that she decided to take to the hills.

Bird flight, it was roughly a hundred miles from

Billings to Sheridan. On a good horse she could've made the trip in two days. It took four on Albert, and Rose was limping badly by the time she came in sight of the tiny burg. The roan had lost his footing on the long climb out of the Yellowstone Valley and come up tender in his shoulder, forcing Rose to walk a good portion of the way.

Sheridan was a rough compass point rather than an actual destination, and she skirted wide around the town to avoid being seen. She knew only one person in Wyoming well enough to approach for the kind of information she needed, although she wasn't sure how she'd be received. The last time she'd seen Fred Baylor, he'd been riding south out of the Bull Mountains with a bullet hole in his leg from her pistol. She could only hope it would be as Lew Parker had speculated, that Fred and his wife Della would both be so grateful for Rose's interference that they'd forgive her on sight.

Rose's right foot was throbbing past her ankle by the time she led Albert into the Baylor yard. Fred was sitting on a bench in front of the cabin, repairing a bridle. He looked up when his hounds started barking, then set his work aside. With the ruckus caused by the dogs, Della came to the door, carrying a toddler on her hip. Stopping some distance away, Rose nodded a cautious howdy.

"Come on in!" Fred called. "You're welcome here."

"All things considered, I wasn't sure," Rose admitted, limping into the yard.

Her confession brought a grin to Fred's face. "You've nothing to worry about, Rose." He turned to Della. "Hon, warm up some of that stew we had for supper last night."

"I can't stay," Rose interjected quickly.

"You can have a bite to eat, can't you?"

She hesitated, then said: "Well, maybe a bite."

Fred's gaze shifted to Albert, and his smile disappeared. "Is that the horse you were riding last year?"

"Uhn-huh."

"I didn't recognize him. There's not much roan left, is there?"

Rose backed off a couple of paces for a better view. It was true that age had bleached most of the color from Albert's hair, but the sight that jolted her worse was his gauntness. In her single-minded pursuit of Nora's killers, she had lost track of the changes overtaking the aging gelding on their trek to Canada and back. Seeing them with such clarity now alarmed her. "Well, we've covered a heap of country this summer," she said guiltily. "I reckon it's taken its toll."

"He's favoring his right shoulder, too," Fred said, heading for the corral. "Wait here," he added. "Della'll have some grub ready in a minute. I won't be gone long." He slapped a saddle on a bay, then loped south into a fringe of timber.

Uncertainly Rose pulled the Mother Hubbard from Albert's back, then found a currycomb in the Baylors' tack room and started working on the gelding's coat. She was just finishing when Della returned carrying a wooden bowl and a clunky earthenware glass filled with fresh milk.

"You can eat inside, if you'd like," the younger woman offered shyly.

"I reckon I ought not," Rose replied, accepting the bowl and glass. "I'm mighty dusty."

Pushing a strand of ash-blonde hair out of her eyes, Della said: "Dust is the least of my worries. It's stinky inside, is all. The baby's just getting over the scours."

"I saw her when I rode up. She's a pretty little thing."

Della flashed her a quick look of gratitude. "I could bring her out when you're done," she said tentatively.

"Why, I'd like that," Rose replied. "It's been a spell since I been around anything that teeny." After an awkward pause, she dug into her food. The stew was expertly seasoned, and there was a fist-size chunk of coarse bread on the rim of the bowl for sopping. Eyeing the place as she ate, seeing past the hard-panned yard and cobbled-together sheds to what might be, she said: "You 'n' Fred's got a nice spread here, Della."

"It ain't like some for fancy, but Fred has his plans. He figures to hang on, build up what we lost last winter. Them of us that lived in more sheltered spots did better than those who built in the open."

"Winter played heck above the Yellowstone," Rose said, then recited some of the stories she'd heard, including the one about the Helena legislator who was urging ranchers to import Tibetan yaks to better withstand Montana's harsh winters. She finished her stew about the same time she finished a joke she'd heard in a Fort Benton saloon about yak's milk and Indian whiskey, and returned the bowl and spoon fairly polished.

"You want some more?" Della asked.

"Naw, I'm full up. It was good, though." She licked her fingers clean, then dried them on the seat of her riding skirt. Della took the dishes inside. After a moment, Rose followed as far as the door.

The place hadn't changed since her brief hold-over here last year. The walls were hewed logs, painted white, the floor dirt, although swept clean and recently sprinkled to keep the dust down. An iron bed sat in a rear corner, a crib and pallet beside it for the kids; a tall wardrobe and a washstand completed the sleeping quarters. The dining area consisted of a parson's table with benches on either side, a Hoosier cabinet with tin-lined bins for flour and such, and an early model Atlantic and Pacific cast-iron stove with a warmer built into the over-head pipe.

The Baylors' oldest child, Chad, sat in a rocker in front of the stone fireplace, studying a small, paperbound book on veterinarian care. Rose could tell at a glance he was too young to read, but he seemed content to study the drawings and graphs.

At the crib, Della had straightened with a wiggling bundle in her arms. Coming over to the patch of sunlight that spilled through the front door, she brushed back a corner of the blanket. "She's squabby," she warned. "She's tired after feeling so poorly."

"Why, sure she is. I won't keep her but a minute."

Keeping her eyes on the baby, Della said: "I . . . wanted to thank you for what you done last year." Shifting the baby, drawing Rose's attention back to it, she added: "We named her Rosalie, in honor of the woman who saved her daddy's life, but we call her Little Rose."

Rose blinked rapidly. "You . . . ah . . . you named your baby after me?"

Nodding, Della said: "Would you like to hold her?"

"Naw, I'd better not." She laughed nervously and looked away, then brought her eyes back to the slowly churning limbs under the quilt. "Yeah, I reckon I would, if you don't mind." Della placed the child in her arms, then stepped back. Staring at the tiny face, Rose felt tears building at the corners of her eyes, spilling down her cheeks as they rarely did since she'd left her own childhood behind. "She's just about as pretty as they come, ain't she?" she said quietly.

There were tears in Della's eyes, too. "She takes after her father, I think."

Rose looked up, bawling silently but unable to wipe the tears away for the child in her arms. "Della, them stories about me 'n' your pap, they weren't none of them true. Not a one."

"I know," Della said. "My father . . . he ain't a good man. It took him not coming in for Jeremy's funeral for me to realize that, although I think now I'd been working on seeing it for some time. You making Fred come on home like you did, for the reason you did, that got me to thinking. It made me realize you wasn't the monster my mama thought you was. I believe you, Rose, and I'm sorry for the grief my family's caused you."

Rose caught her breath, the tears coming faster. "That means a bunch, Della, you believin' me. That means a whole bunch."

Smiling past her own tears, Della said: "My father hasn't visited us once since Fred and I were married. Now they say he's deathly ill, but he won't let me come to care for him unless I renounce my marriage and get a divorce."

"Lordy," Rose whispered.

Della wiped her eyes. "It doesn't matter. If I don't have a father, at least I have Fred and Chad and Little Rose." She paused, looking almost embarrassed. "You can't stay, Rose. Not in Wyoming or Montana. They'll kill you if you do."

"So I been hearin'." There was the clop of hoofs out front, and she knew Fred had returned. Glancing down, she saw that the tears she'd shed had dripped onto the little one's wraps. "Shoot," she said, laughing and crying at the same time. "I got your blanket all salted up." Della laughed, too, reaching for her daughter. Handing her over, Rose said: "She sure is a sweetie. I hope she grows up in better times than these."

"She will," Della said fiercely. "She has to. These big ranchers can't run without reins forever. Sooner or later they'll have to be stopped. If enough people . . . if enough people would just do what you're doin' and fight back, instead of always waitin' for someone else to do something . . . I don't know. I don't know what's needed."

After a moment, Rose said—"I don't either, Della."—and left the cabin. She hauled up short when she saw Fred throwing her saddle atop a dark sorrel stallion with perky ears.

The horse was short-coupled and stocky, chiseled with muscle; he had flaring nostrils, intelligent eyes, and a thin, crooked blaze. Before she could protest, Fred said: "No, you don't. You saved my life that day, Rose, keeping me away from the Musselshell. You gave me the gift of seeing my little girl, and maybe being able to watch her and her brother grow up to have young ones of their own."

"Fred, that's a dang' fine horse. You need to hang onto him, put him to stud."

"We've already got some good foals out of him. Besides, it's already decided. Me 'n' Della weren't sure you'd ever come back, but we'd been hearing about your troubles and wanted to have him ready, just in case. He's a four-year-old and rambunctious, but I've seen you ride. You can handle him as well as any bronco artist." He glanced at his wife. "Della, fetch that bill of sale, would you?" He got an apologetic look on his face. "I went ahead and wrote one out, in case you showed up on the run and couldn't tarry."

"That's near about the situation," Rose admitted. "Truth is, I'm lookin' for Pine Tree Manning. I'm thinkin' he might've been with Jed Plover's posse a few weeks ago."

"He was," Fred said. "He didn't come back with Plover, though. I heard he went to Miles City."

"Miles City, huh?"

"That was a couple weeks ago."

"It's still the latest word I've heard on him since leavin' the Musselshell."

Della returned with a sheet of paper and a pencil. Using the outside bench as a writing pad, Fred inscribed his name across the bottom of the page, then added the date in the lower right-hand corner. Stepping back, he offered the pencil to Rose. "You can read it if you'd like, see if you think it's an adequate description of the horse."

"I, ah . . ." Rose scanned the page but it was all in script, as foreign to her as Chinese. There were two bold Xs at the bottom, however, and Fred had signed his name beside the first one. Bending over the bench, she scrawled, **ROSE EDWARDS** beside the second in rough, blocky letters—that sole literary talent the result of many a lonely winter's evening spent painfully extracting the individual characters from a Bloomingdale Brothers catalog. When she finished, she folded the document and shoved it into her pocket. "I reckon that'll do just fine," she said. "I just hope you don't come to regret your decision."

"We won't. You can leave that roan here if you'd like. I'll look after him until you come back, or until he gets too old to forage for himself. I won't sell him, and I won't let the wolves get him if I can help it. I'll promise you that."

Fred's words struck her like a hard jab. Until that moment it hadn't occurred to her that her acceptance of the sorrel would mean the end of a trail she and Albert had followed together since Rose was little more than a sprout herself.

"I . . . ah . . ." She started to look at the skinny roan, then quickly averted her eyes. "His name's Albert," she said, accepting the sorrel's reins. "I don't know why I ever come to call him that, but it's been his handle ever since . . ." She moved around to the sorrel's side, straightening the reins above the stallion's thick neck. "He could use some rest, and good grass'll fatten him up again in no time. He's been a good ol' boy." Realizing she was speaking more to herself than to Fred, she abruptly shut up. Hooking a toe in the stirrup, she swung into the Mother Hubbard's seat. The stallion threw his head up and attempted a few choppy crow hops, but Rose brought him around and back with a minimum of effort.

"He'll be a handful for a while," Fred predicted, "but he'll settle down with a steady hand."

"He's full of fire, all right. I feel like I'm sittin'

on top of a cannon and can hear the fuse burnin', but ain't sure which way the dang' thing's pointed."

The Baylors laughed. Even Little Rose gurgled happily. But Rose's insides were twisted in anguish for the worn-out gelding she was leaving behind. She dared not look at him. Even a glance, she feared, would rip her apart. "I gotta git," she said, "but I thank you for the horse and food. I'll bring him back after I find Manning."

Fred nodded, but it was clear he didn't expect to see her or the horse again.

"Be careful," Della said, but Rose was losing control and didn't attempt a response. She slapped her spurs against the sorrel's ribs, and the horse took off with a squeal. He settled into a run far swifter than anything Rose had ever experienced aboard Albert. The wind created by the stallion's passage was so stout that it blew the tears off her cheeks and back across her ears. But it was a long time, a very long time, before it dried them completely.

Chapter Thirty-Nine

Rose didn't find Pine Tree Manning in Miles City, although the leggy ex-Texan had been there recently, leaving only after he'd gunned down Gene Sidwell in a fight some said was fair, but others argued was as rigged as a back-alley shell game.

She heard the story first from Tom, the Silver Star bartender, but before the day was out she picked up two additional versions of the shoot-out, which had occurred behind Russell's Roller Skating Rink on the east side of town. Although all three stories agreed on the major points—diverging only in areas of motive and who had fired the first shot—Rose deemed Tom's account the most accurate.

"We'd all heard about Nora, even before Manning showed up," Tom confided, "but no one knew for sure who'd done it until Manning started dropping hints. Nothing outright, but enough to let the boys know, if you catch my drift."

"He was braggin' on it?" Rose asked incredulously.

"In a roundabout way. Nobody ciphered it at the time, but we figure now he was baiting Gene."

"How?"

"There was a big community dance at Russell's about three weeks ago, on a Saturday night. Fiddlin' John Johnson and the Bismarck Boys had come in by rail all the way from Dakota Territory to play, so there was quite a crowd. Well, you know how those affairs go. All proper and polite up front, but jugs and gamblin' aplenty out back, where a lot of the smaller ranchers and home-steaders were camped. That's where Gene and Manning tangled. They had some words, then Gene shoved Manning, and Manning grabbed his rifle and shot Gene dead." Tom shook his head. "I didn't see it myself, but Sparky Osgood did, and he said Gene went for his pistol as soon as Manning reached for his lever gun, but that Gene never stood a chance. I'd heard Manning could handle that Marlin like a pistol. I guess that's what he did that night.

"Anyway, the law was sent for, but by the time it showed up some Association cowboys were claiming Manning had acted in self-defense and had no choice but to fire, even though Sparky and a whole bunch of others eye-witnessed the shooting and said otherwise. Well, you know how the law works when it comes to Association matters. They didn't even walk Manning to jail, although he was told to get, which he did."

"Which way'd he go?"

"East, they say. Maybe Glendive."

"What about Lew Parker?"

"Lew was working late that night for one of the stores, unloading boxcars down at the N.P. siding. He didn't hear about the shooting until a couple hours after it happened. He was around the next day for the funeral, but I haven't seen him since."

"You figure he went after Manning?"

"Or Manning went after him."

"No!"

Tom nodded. "That's what some of the boys are speculating . . . that one of these days some fly fisherman is gonna catch more than he bargained for."

"What about Lew's gear, his horse and all?"

"He'd sold just about everything. Lew and

Gene had fallen on hard times after their trapping venture last winter. Oh, they went on a spree for a while when they first got in, like men'll do, but when they settled down to look for gainful employment, there wasn't any to be had. A lot of boys are out of work right now, what with so many of the smaller outfits going under."

Rose's shoulders slumped. "This can't be let to happen, Tom. They're pickin' us off one by one, either drivin' us out or buryin' us."

"These are desperate times, Rose. Even the big boys are hurting this year."

She turned to stare out the batwing doors, at a sky gone hazy with the growing heat of early July. "They can afford it better'n we can," she said softly.

"That ain't the way they see it."

"No," she admitted. "I reckon it ain't."

"Are you all right, Rose?" Tom asked.

She nodded and pushed away from the bar. "Yeah," she said. "Yeah, gol-dang it, I'm gonna be fine . . . one way or the other."

It was early evening when Rose knocked at Alice's kitchen door. Callie opened it.

"I figured you'd be along sooner or later," she said with unexpected curtness.

Taken aback, Rose replied: "I can stop by tomorrow, if you're busy."

"No, I ain't busy." She opened the door wide. "Come on in, before someone takes a shot at you."

Rose removed her hat as she entered the roomy kitchen. "I just come by to say howdy," she said.

Closing the door, Callie made a brief, snorty sound, like a startled deer. "Howdy, or good bye?"

"Howdy," Rose repeated, puzzled by her friend's coolness.

Callie stared hard for a moment, then her features softened. "You ain't quite figured that out yet, have you?"

"You mad at me, Callie?"

"Yeah, sugar, I am. I'm so mad at you I could spit hornets." She pulled the younger woman into her arms. "Child, child, what have you got yourself into?"

Rose allowed herself to relax. "Trouble, I guess," she said, her voice muffled against the black woman's soft shoulder.

"A peck of it, I'd say." Callie loosened her grip, pushing Rose away. "Sit down," she said, moving to the stove. "You had supper yet?"

"Had me a bite down to the Bull's Head."

"Would you like some tea? I've kept a pot warm." She brought down a cup and a tin container of Earl Grey from a shelf above the sink. Spooning the tea into a silver egg, she set it in the bottom of the cup, then poured hot water over it from a cast-iron kettle on the stove. "Eben'll be sorry he missed you."

"Where's he at?"

"Eben got himself a job on a ranch down by Powderville, digging post holes." Callie replaced the kettle, then picked up a cup of coffee that had been warming on the stove and sat down opposite Rose.

"Somebody must be powerful lazy if they ain't got enough gumption to dig their own post holes," Rose opined, gently lifting and lowering the egg on its thin silver chain. "Either that or they figure to put in one heck of a corral."

"Oh, it'll be big, once they get it done. It's what they call a drift fence. Gonna run it thirty miles, east to west."

"Thirty miles! Lordy."

Callie nodded as if to affirm Rose's reaction. "Folks are dead set against letting what happened last winter happen again. Lot of the bigger outfits are putting up fences to keep their cows from drifting too far in a blizzard. They're bringing in haying machines and building stock sheds like they had a snapper turtle clamped to their butts. Folks say in another five years, Montana'll be fenced in solid, as full of red barns and cow pastures as a country lane in Pennsylvania. A body won't be able to go no place then, unless they take a road."

Rose hadn't thought her spirits could sink any lower, but she discovered there was still a little drop left. It must have shown.

"You feeling poorly, sugar?"

"Just tired."

"You look like you've been wrung through a wringer, sure enough. When was the last time you slept in a bed?"

Rose counted backward in her mind, then hazarded: "Late May or early June, I figure."

"There's an empty bed upstairs. Soon as you finish your tea, we'll march up there and put you in it."

Rose recalled the last time she'd stayed at Alice's, and how Callie and the girls had taken her under their wings. That seemed like a long time ago now, and not just in years. "I reckon not," she said quietly.

Callie took a deep breath, then let it go, smiling her warm, sad smile. "No, Rose Edwards doesn't need folks to be looking out for her no more, does she?"

Averting her eyes, Rose's attention was captured by a contraption bolted to the wall beside the parlor door—ear and mouthpiece hanging from a wooden box, a pair of domed bells sitting side-by-side on top, black, insulated lines running everywhere like arteries. "I'll be damned," she said. "Is that what I think it is?"

"It is, and as fool a notion as any I ever saw. It gets used, though. Thing'll ring two, three times a week sometimes." She gave Rose a shrewd look. "You want to talk on it?"

"Me? Who would I talk at?" Remembering how she'd begged Shorty to let her talk on a telephone made her cringe now. Lord, but she'd been naïve.

"You could call Miss Doris," Callie suggested. "Order yourself a new dress."

"No," Rose said flatly.

Callie's expression changed. "How many men have you killed, child?"

The question caught her off guard. "None but three. Why?"

"Three? I would've thought a dozen, to hear folks talk."

"Folks talk too much. It gets to be a habit for some of them. The truth is three, but only one I regret. An Indian I shot over on the Musselshell, right after I throwed in with Shorty and Wiley. He surprised me 'n' Jimmy Frakes while the others was away. I guess he figured he was gonna be one rich redskin, with Jimmy scalped and maybe me, too, and a passel of good Crow ponies on top of it, but I cooked that dream with a Forty-Four from my Sharps. I didn't have much choice, but I still wish I hadn't had to've done it."

"It ain't often we get the choices we want," Callie agreed.

"It ain't that I feel bad about it, so much," Rose mused. "It's just that it wasn't as personal for me as the others was. With that redskin, it was the suddenness of it I always found troubling."

"Is Wiley Collins dead? First we'd heard he was, then lately some have said he ain't. About a month ago a Powder River waddy came through saying Wiley had been sighted in Wyoming, up to his old tricks again."

"He's dead," Rose said bluntly. "Him and Davey Merritt both. I buried 'em myself."

"Oh, my," Callie said, touching her lips with her fingers. "And Shorty Tibbs?"

"I buried him, too."

Reaching out, Callie placed a pudgy hand atop Rose's sun-browned lean one. "You ever tell Shorty about that young 'un you nearly had?"

"No, I never did. To tell you the truth, I never really figured out what I felt for Shorty. Some of the time I was as smitten with him as any pigtailed gal after her teacher, but it seems like the rest of the time I wanted to carve out his gizzard with a dull knife. But I never told him about that baby. I still ain't made up my mind whether I should've or not."

"If you didn't, then I'd say you made up your mind just fine," Callie replied. She pulled her hand away. "Men don't need to know everything. Most of them have already got swollen heads, knowing just what little they do."

Rose smiled and straightened, shoving back from the table. Her tea was cooled, nearly gone; she swallowed the last of it in a single gulp.

"You in that big a hurry to go kill that Manning fella?" Callie asked.

"It's on my mind."

"You ought to stay the night, at least."

Rose stood, holding her hat against her leg. "I thank you, Callie. For the tea, but mostly for all you've done for me. You've been a good friend, better than I'll ever be able to return."

"Killing Manning won't bring Nora back. It

won't get you off the Association's list or make your life any easier."

"On the day I buried Wiley and Dave, I asked a fella how far a body had to let 'em push her around before she fought back. On the day I buried Nora, I found the answer to that question. I reckon there are some things worth fightin' for. Worth dyin' for, too, if that's what it comes to."

"I was born a free child in Ohio," Callie said. "I never knew the bonds of slavery that so many others did. But free wasn't much for a black woman, not even in the North. The things I put up with every day, every blessed day . . . well, they grew a powerful anger in me. Especially when I was young. But I gave up that anger once I got older and saw what a constant mad could do to folks. I didn't want to grow old and gray and wrinkled with mad, so I gave it up. Ain't no reason you can't do the same."

Rose moved toward the door. "It ain't even mad so much, not any more. It's just something I gotta see through."

"Walk away from it," Callie said, rising after her. "It's not too late to start over."

"If I walk away now, something inside me is gonna wrinkle up bad, Callie. Like it did when I was livin' with my pap and Muggy, and maybe even Shorty, some. It ain't a thing I can rightly explain, but I know it when I feel it, and, when I feel it, it hurts something awful. It gets so a body can just stand so much of that kind of pain, then I reckon you have to either do something about it or go ahead and let your soul die."

She put her hand on the door's cool, porcelain knob. "Nora used to say you had to learn to roll with the punches, but lately it seems that once you start rollin', nobody wants to let you stop. They just keep on punchin'."

The sound of narrow, rubber-tired wheels, the kind used on better carriages, came to them through the open kitchen window, interrupting their conversation. The vehicle rolled around behind the house and creaked to a halt. A horse snuffled and stomped its hoofs in agitation. Callie stared at the wall as if she could see through it, listening sharply. Rose watched her closely, ready to take her cue from the larger woman's reaction.

"Now, who could that be?" Callie asked softly.

Occasionally a cowboy or hunter would tie up out front, but most men didn't approach Alice's until after they'd stabled their horses and had a drink or two. Few men wealthy enough to afford a carriage would risk humiliating themselves by parking it outside a parlor house. Not even after dark.

"Rose Edwards! I know you're in there. Come out here . . . right now! Come out and . . . face your sins, before I . . . come in and . . . drag you . . . out!"

It was a plucky threat for such a frail voice, Rose thought, broken as it was by wheezing gasps. Standing beside the table, Callie's eyes widened.

"You slip out the front door, sugar," she urged. "Maybe he won't hear you."

Rose loosened the Smith & Wesson in its holster. "No, my horse is this way." She twisted the knob and yanked open the door. With her hand on the pistol, she stepped outside and quickly to one side, out of the kitchen's light.

The carriage had stopped about thirty feet away, a polished black surrey with its leather top folded down. A bearded man in denim trousers and a flannel shirt handled the lines, but it was the creature in back who caught Rose's eye. In the reflective light of a pair of kerosene running lamps, the passenger looked more dead than alive. The skin was stretched tight across his face, and his hands reminded her of bleached parchment shrunken over a framework of fragile bones. Thin wattles connecting chin to neck suggested a fuller, more powerful figure in the not-too-distant past. Even his clothing appeared to have been tailored for a man several sizes larger, and the silk-banded Homburg atop his head looked like it would slide off if he turned too abruptly. The overall effect was of a turkey vulture dressed in a man's suit, the image chilling.

Warming the vulture's lap was a sleigh robe of buffalo, but, as Rose approached the edge of the stoop, it was flipped back to expose a double-barreled shotgun. He brought the muzzles up to cover her, but even that small exertion seemed to wind him.

"I've been . . . waiting for you. I knew you'd . . . come, that I'd get . . . my chance."

"Who the hell are you?" Rose demanded.

His lips quivering with indignation, he began to struggle with one of the shotgun's stiff hammers.

"Aw, Christ," Rose breathed.

"Careful," Callie warned from the door. "I expect he's been demented by some disease."

"It's Frakes," Rose said hollowly. "Maxwell Frakes. Lord, I didn't even recognize him."

Callie gasped. "It's the cancer," she said. "Pearl told me he'd come to town to see the doctor for it, but, blessed be, it's turned him into a ha'nt."

In the surrey, the old man finally gave up trying to cock the shotgun. He fell back against the seat a thin line of drool running down his chin, glistening in the lamplight. "Bodine," he gasped. "Shoot . . . her."

The driver looked around helplessly. "I ain't gonna shoot a woman, Mister Frakes."

"Damn you, kill . . . her!"

"No, sir, I won't." He glanced at Rose, embarrassed.

"You sorry old buzzard," Rose said, coming down off the stoop and striding angrily to the surrey's side.

"Here, now," Bodine said, looking suddenly worried. "He's a sick old man."

"He was a sick old man long before the cancer bit him," Rose said. "But don't worry, I ain't gonna hurt him, although I ought to." She put a foot on the iron step pad and leaned part way into the carriage.

"Help," Frakes squawked.

"Shut up," Rose snapped, jerking the shotgun from his grasp. His skin was so thin that, as one of the hammer spurs slid across his palm, the flesh ripped like cheap paper. Frakes shrieked at the sudden spurt of blood, his eyes wide as silver dollars.

Rose stepped back and opened the breech, extracting a pair of shiny brass ten-gauge shells that she tossed into the darkness behind the car. Then she flung the shotgun as far as she could in the opposite direction.

Frakes glared at her, clutching his bleeding hand to his chest, but he had no words—neither threat nor promise—with which to attack her.

"I hope you rot in hell, you god-damned cadaver in a hat," Rose said. Whirling, she stalked to the Baylor horse, hitched to one of the clothesline poles.

"You took . . . my children," the old man screeched, his voice like fingernails on slate.

Rose mounted, her face set hard as stone. But she didn't reply. She knew the truth. More important, so did Frakes. Tapping the sorrel's ribs with the sides of her stirrups, she rode out of the yard. It would only be later that she would recall with regret that she'd failed to say a final good bye to Callie.

Chapter Forty

East of Miles City wasn't a whole lot different from west of it, other than that it was a country Rose had never visited before. She followed the Bismarck road past the mouth of the Powder River, but when that little-used freighters' route—the Northern Pacific had rendered it virtually obsolete by now—veered more directly eastward, she abandoned it for a rutted trail hugging the Yellowstone's right bank.

It was about seventy-five miles from Miles City to Glendive, a trip Rose made on the Baylor horse in less than twenty-four hours. Although such a distance covered in such a short period of time was hardly unique, she doubted if there were many horses that could have done it with the same high level of energy as the sorrel. The stallion's endurance was impressive, even a little awe-inspiring.

Glendive sat at the bottom of a kettle-like valley, right on the river. Rose knew from word along the Owlhoot that the town had suffered its share of problems with rustlers and Regulators alike, but her bitterness had grown complete in the days since leaving Albert with Fred and Della, her heart scabbing over like the dark, scaly residue that continued to flake off her toe whenever she removed her sock. In this new temperament, she had little empathy for the innocents of Glendive.

She was guiding her horse toward one of the saloons on Main Street when a voice hailed her from a nearby building. Rose wheeled the sorrel, her hand dropping to the Smith & Wesson, but she could discern no threat in the manner of the heavy-set bald man standing in the doorway of a tiny saddle shop, a knee-length leather apron mounded over his round belly. He had curly red hair, a ruddy complexion, and a smile that seemed genuine, if a little nervous. Cautiously she let her hand fall away from the pistol. "What do you want?" she demanded.

"I'm Axel Carrington. I doubt if you remember me."

She heeled the sorrel closer. "Nope," she said, after a second look. "Where'd we meet?"

"Above a little town called Rosebud, a couple years back. Me and some trail pards took it upon ourselves to relieve you of the gold we was certain you were carrying, but you got the drop on us."

"I'll be damned," Rose said. "I remember that. You was travelin' with a colored cowboy and a skinny kid that needed his face washed."

Axel nodded sheepishly. "I've felt ashamed about that ever since."

She glanced at the shop behind him, a sign above the door proclaiming: *GLENDIVE SADDLERY, A. CARRINGTON, PROP.* "It looks like you went honest," she said.

"I wasn't cut out for an outlaw's life."

"You got off to a poor start, for a fact."

"I have a corral out back. You're welcome to use it if you want. Truth is, I'd kind of like to buy you a drink or a meal or something. I figure most folks would've shot us for what we tried that day. It always impressed me that you didn't."

She nearly refused, until it occurred to her that she was looking for some specific information, the kind a local citizen might be leery of parting with to a stranger. Dismounting, she said— "All right."—then led her horse down the alley between the saddlery and a tinsmith's shop.

She stripped her gear from the stallion's back and turned him into the corral. As she did, she took note of an empty woodshed nearby, and thought that, if nothing better turned up, she'd sleep there tonight. After seeing to hay and water, she walked back to the street just as Axel emerged from his shop, having exchanged his apron for a herringbone suit coat and bowler hat. A *CLOSED* sign was propped in the window.

Walking down the street, Rose couldn't help noticing how anxious the burly saddlemaker seemed. She didn't know whether it was on account of her being a woman or her growing reputation as a shootist, but she found it annoying. It was to ease her own irritation more than Axel's discomfort that, when he reached for a chair in the Cattleman's Café to pull it out for her, she chose another and seated herself.

Axel seemed to breathe a sigh of relief as he

quickly sank into the chair across from her. A stout woman with gray hair appeared to take their orders. When she was gone, Rose got down to business.

"You know a bird named Pine Tree Manning?"

Axel nodded. "Uhn-huh."

According to Axel, Manning had been in Glendive as recently as ten days ago, and was well-known in the area. Although a suspected participant in several lynchings from the previous summer, the law had left him alone. He'd moved on more than a week ago, Axel said, but no one seemed to know where.

"Was you inclined to guess, which direction might you suggest?" Rose pressed.

"I couldn't begin to say. You might poke around some of the saloons, although I'd be suspicious of anything I learned there."

Rose leaned back in her chair. "I've been huntin' that rooster for some weeks, and this is as close as I've gotten. I'd hate to lose him now."

"He was employed by the Cattlemen's Association for a while, although I've heard he's gone independent."

The waitress returned bearing platters of steak, potatoes, and black-eyed peas, with bread, butter, jam, and cups of coffee on the side. Rose and Axel dug in with the concentration of people who'd gone hungry more than once in their lives, and didn't speak again until they had finished.

On the street afterward, Axel fired up a long

black cigar that, even upwind, brought a grimace to Rose's face. "Dang, Axel, I've smelled dead things that didn't stink that bad."

"I get 'em for a penny apiece," he replied defensively. "A saddler can't be choosy."

But Rose had already turned her attention elsewhere. Looking west toward the setting sun, she recalled something her pap had said. "What was the name of that skinny fella you was ridin' with the day you tried to waylay me?"

"Bud?"

"Yeah, Bud. Did he have a last name?"

"Probably, but he never mentioned it. We didn't ride together long, and he was touchy. The Nigra's name was Charlie Sims. I liked Charlie fine, but I was glad to see Bud go his own way after we reached Miles City."

Rose nodded. She'd only known Jacques by his first name, too—that was just the way it happened sometimes. "I reckon I ought to get about my business," she said.

"Will you be staying in Glendive?"

"Not if Manning ain't around. I'll mosey through a couple of saloons tonight, but if I don't turn up something new, I'll head on over to the Little Missouri country."

"I wish I could've been more help."

"You've been help enough." She shoved a hand toward him. "Thanks for the meal, and for the use of the corral."

Axel accepted her hand solemnly. "Were you to

stay, I'd see about courting you," he said with a trace of hopefulness.

Jed Plover had expressed a similar desire, Rose recalled, but she hadn't put much stock in his words, either. "That'd be something to study on, was I stayin'," she replied. "But I ain't."

He withdrew his hand. "Good luck, Rose."

"Good luck to you, too," she said, already walking away.

She went to the Empire Saloon first, where she'd been headed when Axel diverted her. Her optimism was low as she entered the long, narrow building, but she'd barely started her first beer when the general conversation of the room shifted to the news that a fresh spate of rustling had flared up near Fort Peck, on the Missouri. Word in the Empire that night was that an Association man by the name of Dietrich had been bushwhacked by cattle thieves west of the fort, and that hired guns were descending on the area like buzzards on a dead horse. Although no mention was made of Manning, Rose considered Fort Peck a promising lead, and certainly better than drifting aimlessly up and down the Little Mo.

She left the saloon without taking time to finish her beer. Although tired, she wanted to check over her gear while there was still some light left, that way, she'd be ready to leave first thing in the morning. To her surprise, she found that the sorrel had been freshly groomed in her absence, his hoofs cleaned, mane and tail combed. An unfamiliar saddle sat on its horn beside her own. It was a lighter rig than her old Mother Hubbard, and although it looked used enough to be broken in and comfortable, it was in noticeably better condition than her old hulk.

Axel was sitting on the steps behind his shop, whittling on a piece of stove wood. He was silent a moment, giving her time to contemplate the new rig. Then he said: "That old saddle of yours must weigh close to sixty pounds. The other one there is lighter by twenty, at least. It'll make a difference over the long haul, and I'm guessing that's what you've got ahead of you."

Stiffening, Rose said: "I thank you for the offer, but I can't afford a new saddle."

"It ain't for sale. I'm giving it to you. That sorrel's a strong horse, but the kind of riding you'll be doing would take the starch out of the best animal."

"No," Rose replied stubbornly. "I'm obliged for the meal, but this is too much."

Axel tossed his stick aside, then folded his knife. His words came hesitantly, as if dredged from parts of himself he didn't probe too often. "The thing is, I appreciate what you're doing. I remember the way Pine Tree Manning used to walk the streets of Glendive like some kind of king, lording it over the rest of us. Truth is, it'd suit me just fine if someone knocked him down a peg or two."

Rose remembered Herman Sutherland's similar

views, and how after a while the sentiment had grown distasteful. What right, she wondered with sudden indignation, did men like Herman or Axel have to share in her quest, no matter how peripherally? Did they think a monetary contribution made on the sly could make them legitimate participants? That in not standing up to be heard, but clandestinely patting the backs of those who did, did they believe they were equally deserving of whatever accolades the risk takers might eventually reap—assuming the risk takers didn't lose everything in the end?

Rose had owed Herman Sutherland money, and there had been a slim but tenable connection to the Baylors, but she didn't owe Axel Carrington a damned thing.

"No," she said bluntly, picking up the Mother Hubbard and heading for the gate. "I like my old rig, and, if you want to pull somebody's pegs, do it yourself."

Earlier she'd contemplated spending the night in Axel's woodshed, but now she was determined to move on before full dark. There would be plenty of places along the Yellowstone to pitch her bedroll.

With her eyes on the sorrel, Rose couldn't have said later what it was that alerted her to trouble. Certainly it wasn't the stallion, whose attention was riveted on a string of mares with colts, grazing on a hillside some distance away. Nor was it Axel, who was behind her and silent. Perhaps it was some sixth sense, some delicate sharpening of perception a person picked up naturally in times of jeopardy. All she knew was that, without thought, she suddenly dropped her saddle and spun in a crouch, palming the Smith & Wesson as she did.

Unlike when she'd pulled down on John Stroudmire, this time the pistol slid free quickly and smoothly. She cocked and fired in as fluid a motion as any she'd ever seen from Sam Matthews or Wiley Collins, her bullet smacking into the corner molding of the tin shop next door, shearing off a piece of wood beside the head of the gunman who'd been hiding there among the weeds, taking aim with a revolver.

The gunman swore and fell back, his shot going wide. Rose fired into the cover of weeds a second time, more for effect than any hope of a solid hit. Then she started running, wanting a better position for her third shot, an uncluttered view. In all the chaos, she didn't even see the second gunman.

The other shooter was lurking in an irrigation ditch behind the corral, about sixty yards away. He opened up with a small-bore carbine even as the echo of Rose's second shot bounced off the bluffs behind the town. Had it not been for the lattice-work of corral posts and poles, he might have dropped her with his first round. Had he been a better shot, he would have hit her anyway. Instead his bullet struck one of the gateposts, causing the sorrel to squeal and take off pitching.

With nowhere else to go, Rose dived for the dirt.

Rolling swiftly over the hardpan, she came even with the rear of the tin shop just as the sloping shoulders of the first gunman ducked around the far corner. She almost fired anyway, but held up at the last instant. Scrambling to her feet, she raced toward the empty woodshed. Her heart was thumping wildly as she tried to keep an eye on both the weed-lined ditch and the rear of the tin shop, but no shot followed her into the shelter of the open-faced hut, where she ducked behind a large, squat chopping block.

Rose broke open the Smith & Wesson and flicked out the empties with her thumbnail, then replaced them with fresh rounds and snapped the hinged cylinder closed. The whole process took only seconds. From the saddle shop, Axel called: "Rose? Are you all right? Rose?"

She squirmed to a side wall and put her eye to a crack between two planks that offered a view of the irrigation ditch. It looked deserted, as far as she could tell in the deepening twilight. On hands and knees, she quickly crawled to the other two walls, but saw no evidence that her attackers were still around. From the saddle shop, Axel continued to call her name.

Cautiously Rose got to her feet and moved to the broad entrance of the shed. The sounds of a crowd gathering on the street out front began to drift over the rear lot. From it came a new voice, louder and more authoritative, calling for Axel, demanding an explanation.

"Rose!" Axel exclaimed as she stepped clear of the shed. He slipped out the back door of his shop toting a single-barreled shotgun. Rose lifted the Smith & Wesson—it was already cocked—and Axel jerked to a stop. "Rose?" he gulped.

"Put it down, Axel."

He looked uncomprehendingly at the shotgun. When Rose repeated her command, he stooped to obey. "I only wanted to help," he explained, straightening. But she already knew that. She just didn't care.

In the alley between the saddle shop and the tinsmith, curiosity seekers were warily advancing. "Axel?" someone called. "Where you at, boy?"

"Back here," Axel replied. "Someone send for the sheriff."

But the sheriff was already there. Entering the rear lot at the head of a small crowd, he quickly swung a short-barreled revolver toward Rose, its silver plating flashing in the dusk. "Drop your pistol," he ordered.

"Son-of-a-bitch," Rose grated.

Darkness had fallen completely by the time the Glendive sheriff finished his lantern-light inspection of the back lot. Sitting beside Axel on the rear steps of his shop, Rose chafed at the delay. She knew that whatever chance she might have ad to examine the tracks for herself had been lost with the light and the sheriff's heavy-booted canvassing. She was pretty sure the sheriff knew that, too. Approaching Rose with grave solemnity, he assured her that he would initiate a thorough investigation in the morning, and not rest until the perpetrators were either caught or he was satisfied that they'd left town.

"If they're around, I'll find 'em," he promised just before he left.

But Rose had reached the limits of her patience, and went over to retrieve the Mother Hubbard. Axel followed her to the corral, peering through the rails while she saddled her horse. "You're leaving?" he asked.

"Figured I would. I got my doubts them shooters hung around any longer than it took to fork a bronc'. Was it me, I'd go lay out in the hills and wait for me to come along at first light."

"They wouldn't know which direction you'd take."

She considered telling him about Fort Peck and the trouble brewing up there, then decided against it. "I figure they'll know," was all she said.

She pulled the gate open and led the sorrel through it. Hooking a toe in the stirrup, she heaved herself wearily into the saddle.

"You need to rest," Axel said.

He had a point, Rose knew. She'd been on the go for better than thirty-six hours, and had covered more than seventy-five miles in that time. But after what had happened tonight, she knew she needed to push on. It wasn't just her and Manning any longer. Joe Bean's Regulators were going to start closing in pretty soon, too.

Staring at the saddlemaker, she said: "You got a good start here, Axel. Likely you'll make something fine out of it if you don't wander off the trail again."

He nodded. "I don't plan to."

If there was anything more to say, Rose couldn't think of it. Reining her horse around, she rode down the alley to the street, then turned west toward the Yellowstone.

<u>Chapter Forty-One</u>

Rose crossed the Yellowstone in the dark about a half mile below the town, hoping to lose herself in the wide-open spaces to the north. She made a fireless camp around midnight, and awoke the next morning feeling frosty and unpliable. Shoving aside her blankets, she sat up to discover that the splotch of green that was the town of Glendive was still visible, no more than seven or eight miles away. The sight perturbed her, for she'd hoped to have left the burg behind during the night. Stomping into her boots, she quickly readied the sorrel.

It was on a final, backward glance just before pulling out that movement far below caught her eye. Swinging around, she squinted into the distance. She wished she had a pair of field glasses like Wiley used to carry; with them, she might have identified the two horsemen prowling the slopes below her. Still, she figured the odds were good that these were her ambushers from the night before. Or if not, then others like them.

"I wouldn't be a bit surprised if they brought in six or eight hardcases," she told the sorrel.

There was no response from the horse, whose gaze was fixed to the southwest, nostrils flared as he tested the wind. Following his line of sight, Rose saw a trio of mustangs grazing on a ridge a couple of miles away, foals playing at their sides. With a scowl, she pulled the stallion around. "You 'n' Wiley would've made a fine pair," she groused. "He couldn't tell the difference between his pecker and his brain, either."

Staying close to the winding coulées that tracked the low hump of the Big Sheep Mountains to the west, Rose made her way to the top of the divide separating the drainages of the Yellowstone and Missouri Rivers. She crossed over late in the morning, then dropped down to a creek where she pulled the saddle from her horse and picketed him on grass above a still pool. Keeping her rifle with her, she hiked up the bank to a box elder tree, then settled down with a clear view of her back trail.

She sat that way for an hour while the sorrel grazed and rested. When she finally moved on, the horsemen she'd observed that morning hadn't appeared. Rose was beginning to think that she'd maybe misjudged their intentions, but as she climbed an old buffalo trail away from the stream, a prickly sensation skittered across the back of her neck. She glanced over her shoulder just in time to see a man on foot ducking into a coulée several hundred yards away. Hauling up, she reached for the Sharps, but when she looked again, the slope was empty, without even a puff of dust to mark her stalker's point of disappearance.

"Dang," she murmured, letting her hand fall away from the rifle. It gave her a chill to think that in another few minutes he might have crept within range for his light carbine. "I was watchin' for horses," she confessed to the sorrel. "It didn't even cross my mind that they might try to sneak up tippy-toed."

She gave the stallion a taste of her fire-smudged spurs, and for the next hour they fairly flew over the land, making their way steadily northward. She kept a sharp watch over her shoulder, but her attackers never showed themselves, and it began to occur to Rose that, despite two failed attempts so far, they were probably pretty good at what they did—more cautious than timid—and that sooner or later they'd corner her if she didn't find some way to ditch them for good.

It was another twenty-four hours to Fort Peck, what with the roughness of the terrain between the Glendive crossing and the old fur trading post that now served as a sub-agency for the vast Sioux and Assiniboine Reservation headquartered two days ride to the east, at Poplar. For the first time since leaving the Baylors, the sorrel was beginning to show signs of strain, even breaking into a sweat on the second day. His interest in his surroundings waned, too, although he did manage a curious whicker late in the afternoon when a band of mustangs passed over a ridge to the south.

It was still light when Rose came in sight of the sub-agency on the Missouri's northern shore, but she didn't go in. She figured the Army might have a partial troop stationed there for emergencies, and, even under the best of circumstances, she'd never been comfortable around soldiers. In the past few weeks, coming to understand how men like Ostermann worked, Rose's distrust of authority had deepened. She wouldn't put it past either Ostermann or the Association to have conjured up some kind of federal charge against her. Although a local lawdog of the ilk she'd encountered in Glendive didn't overly intimidate her, Rose reckoned the Army would be a different animal altogether.

At dusk she rode down to the river to look for a ferry. What she found instead, and just as good in her opinion, was an Indian woman getting ready to row back across the Missouri with several buckets of early chokecherries that she'd picked for a green-cherry jam. The woman had a skiff, and Rose paid her a nickel to haul her and her gear across the river while she towed the sorrel on the end of her picket rope.

"He's a splashy swimmer," Rose confided to the woman as she clambered on board, recalling the soaking she'd taken while crossing the Yellowstone at Glendive. "At least this way I'll stay dry."

"As long as he does not try to climb into the boat," the woman replied. She was Rose's age or a few years older, round-faced and chunky, pretty with her long, dark hair and quick smile. She was the wife of one of the traders who had an establishment just outside the walls of the post—a questionably legal operation that was tolerated only because Congress hadn't yet ratified an official boundary for the reserve. She spoke fair English due to her marriage, although speaking English was a trait more and more of Montana's Indians seemed to be picking up in recent years.

"If he gets close, I'll help on the oars," Rose promised.

"If he gets close, you must hit him over the head with one," the Indian woman replied. "He would capsize the boat if he tried to get in, and I cannot swim."

But the stallion swam the river like an old pro, shaking himself off afterward as if proud of his accomplishment. The Indian woman took her time gathering her berry buckets, while Rose saddled the horse. They walked up the bank together, not speaking until they reached the flat above the river. Here the woman asked with an Indian's bluntness: "Where is your man?"

"I ain't got one."

"You are *cante tinzawin* then, a warrior woman?"

Rose looked away uncomfortably. "I hadn't

much considered it that way before," she admitted. "I ain't sure I like the sound of it, to tell you the truth."

"You are Sunflower Girl, who rides the warrior's path against the spotted buffalo men, the cattle-men."

Sunflower Girl. It was the name Fights His Enemies had used, back below Harker's Fort. "How'd you know I was called that?"

"Everyone knows Sunflower Girl and her red horse." She glanced at the darker sorrel, her expression sorrowful. "Time is like the circle that never stops."

Rose nodded grudgingly. "He wore out on me down in Wyoming."

"This is a good horse, too? A warrior's horse?" She smiled.

"He's strong, for a fact," Rose acknowledged. "I reckon good is a matter of opinion."

"Not fast?"

"No, he's fast enough. He just ain't much of a conversationalist, is my complaint." She stepped into the saddle, her leg dragging on the bedroll.

"You are tired, Sunflower Girl?"

Rose hesitated, then said: "You know what they call me? My other name?"

The woman nodded. "But you are Sunflower Girl to my people. My name is Little Swan. I am wife of Long Hair Douglas."

"The trader?"

"Yes. My man is away now, receiving pelts from

the Grandmother's children who come south to trade."

A grin flitted across Rose's face. She suspected Little Swan's husband would be none too pleased to learn how cavalierly his wife was passing along information about his trading for furs smuggled in from Canada, although, in Little Swan's defense, Rose doubted if an international boundary meant much to a people whose own borders had once followed the courses of rivers and mountain ranges, rather than arrow-straight lines staked out with stone cairns and iron pikes.

"You'd best not tell too many people what your husband's up to," Rose advised. "White man's law is a funny thing."

Little Swan looked puzzled. "Funny?"

"Strange."

Little Swan nodded. Strange was a concept she seemed to understand in regard to the white race. "Yes, it is true that my man does not like for me to speak of these things, but are not your enemies my enemies?"

That was a new thought, especially recalling her sentiments during the Sioux wars. Yet after some reflection, Rose tentatively agreed. "I reckon that's true, at least part way."

"Yes, I think it is true. You make war on the spotted buffalo men, and that is a good thing. Even the old ones agree. But now you are tired, hungry?"

Rose exhaled slowly. "Yeah, I'm bushed."

"Come with me. Tonight you will eat in the lodge of my mother, Yellow Rock Woman, and my brother will care for your horse. Tomorrow you may go, before the colonel's spies hear of you, and the colonel's lieutenant comes to see for himself that you are here. But tonight you will be safe, and you will eat well."

Rose glanced behind her. In the diminishing light the Missouri lay like a dull pewter sheet, its surface rippled with undertows. Yet as broad and deep as it might be, she knew it wouldn't stop her pursuers. It would hardly slow them down.

"Someone follows?" Little Swan guessed.

"Likely. Two men, I figure. They've been doggin' me for a couple of days now, although they ain't been overly enthusiastic about it."

"A successful hunter takes his time, is that not true?"

Rose nodded morosely. The same thought had occurred to her.

"Come," Little Swan repeated firmly. "These hunters will not find their prey tonight."

She led Rose east, away from the post, to a treeless plain perhaps a mile away. Here, scattered haphazardly across the flattened grass like Chinese lanterns, were twenty or more canvas teepees, glowing softly from the fires within. As the two women entered the village, Rose dismounted to walk at Little Swan's side. Growling dogs emerged from the shadows, and here and there Rose spied a solitary human, frozen in whatever late chore they had been about. But there were no playing children or outside fires around which families sat and talked and laughed—scenes Rose remembered well from when she'd accompanied her pap on his trading expeditions out of Fort Benton.

"What's goin' on?" she asked.

Little Swan gave her a questioning look.

"It's awful quiet."

Little Swan's lips drew taut. "It is not good to laugh when your enemies are near, is it?"

"The soldiers?"

"Even though we have made peace with the Long Knives, it does not yet feel like peace."

Rose nodded. That was a concept *she* understood.

Stopping outside a nondescript lodge about midway through the village, Little Swan called out in Sioux. A moment later an older woman in buckskins stepped out of the low, oval door. She eyed Rose silently, then glanced at Little Swan.

"This is my mother," Little Swan said, then switched to Sioux. Her mother spoke. Little Swan replied, then turned to Rose. "This is Yellow Rock Woman. You will sleep in her lodge tonight. I must return to the trading post, where my husband's second wife waits. She will worry that I drowned if I do not return soon."

"You ain't stayin'?" Rose asked in alarm.

"No, but my younger sister will be here, as will my brother, who has seen ten summers. Both speak the white man's tongue well. They will translate all that needs be said."

Rose nodded dubiously. Despite Little Swan's assurances, she felt uneasy.

Yellow Rock Woman spoke into the teepee and a girl of fifteen or so, then a boy Rose took to be Little Swan's brother, exited the lodge. Yellow Rock Woman spoke briefly to the girl, who hurried off.

"She will tell Old Man Bull of your visit," Little Swan explained. "He is chief here, and will want to speak with you. My brother is Young Wolf, but the soldiers call him Robby. He will take care of your horse." Readjusting her grip on the buckets, Little Swan started to walk away.

"Hey!" Rose called after her.

Little Swan turned expectantly.

"Uh . . . thanks. I just wanted to say thanks."

"Trust Old Man Bull. He will know what to do." Flashing a quick smile, Little Swan added: "All will be right." Then she walked away, disappearing into the shadows.

Yellow Rock Woman spoke to the boy, who sullenly took the sorrel's reins and led him away, allowing Rose only enough time to slide the Sharps from its scabbard. When Yellow Rock Woman motioned toward the lodge, Rose muttered—"What the heck."—and stooped to enter.

In all her years on the frontier, Rose had never been inside an occupied teepee. Not even when her pap had traded among the Piegans for buffalo robes had she dared explore the Indian culture too closely, for fear of violating some tribal custom.

But she knew plenty of men who had embraced the lifestyle, and she'd learned a passel just listening to their stories. She knew, for instance, to move to the left upon entering the lodge, as was proper for a woman, and to stay behind the two middle-aged women already seated there, rather than pass between them and the fire.

Rose took her place just to the right of the spot facing the teepee's door, close to the tiny, ceremonial lodge altar—in this case a flat, painted stone about the size of a loaf of bread—that the family used for daily prayers. Tucking her legs modestly under her and to one side while keeping her knees together, she opened the Sharp's breech to finger the long brass cartridge from its chamber. Sliding the shell into an empty loop on her belt, she removed that and her revolver belt and placed them behind her, out of the way. It was a gesture of respect and trust, although she kept the Merwin Hulbert holstered under her left arm, hidden by her jacket. Rose figured that even if Yellow Rock Woman noticed the short gun, she would under-stand, and not be so impolite as to make a fuss about it.

Seating herself on Rose's right, Yellow Rock Woman reached for a white, enamelware bowl and a spoon made from the horn of a buffalo. A cast-iron kettle sat at the edge of the fire on three stubby legs, containing a stew of meat and wild vegetables. Dishing up a serving, the older woman passed it and the spoon to Rose.

"Lordy, that looks good," Rose murmured as she accepted the bowl. She glanced at Yellow Rock Woman. "Thankee, ma'am."

Yellow Rock Woman's answer was in Sioux, for which Rose had no reply other than a polite nod. After an uncertain pause, she began to eat, and soon her rapid progress brought knowing smiles to the faces of the three Indian women.

By the time Rose finished her first bowl, Little Swan's younger sister had returned. Her name was Beth, and one of her first utterances was to declare her love for a young shavetail stationed at the sub-agency, a West Point man about which her family had yet to learn.

"His name is James," Beth gushed with a teen-ager's bubbly exuberance, "and we're to be married as soon as he's transferred back East. He's hoping for a post in one of the larger cities on the coast. Oh, I'd love New York, although Boston or Philadelphia would be nearly as good."

"What do you know about them places?" Rose asked.

"James has visited all of them, and he's told me everything. So has Missus Canby, at the mission school. She lived in New York City, and I'm her star pupil."

"Why don't you and your soldier beau get married here?" Rose asked, although she figured she already knew the answer to that.

"There's too much prejudice here," the young woman replied by rote. "Even the redskins would have a fit. They can't seem to understand the Army just wants to help them."

Rose didn't know how to respond to such a blunt and, to her mind, misguided statement. To her relief, she didn't have to. Beth was quickly off on a tangent covering several somewhat vague perceptions of the Catholic, Protestant, and Methodist principles regarding interracial marriage.

Rose had still been middling hungry when Beth returned, but she quickly lost her appetite with the young woman's incessant jabber. She finally set her bowl aside—empty, though hardly licked clean in a manner to show her recognition of the difficulty in procuring food, and her appreciation for their sharing what they had—and tactfully declined when Yellow Rock Woman inquired by sign if she wanted more. It was during a brief pause in Beth's second-hand assessment of New York's theater district that Rose managed to ask the girl what name her mother called her.

Making a face, she replied: "Sweet Grass, but my real name is Beth, short for Elizabeth."

"Uhn-huh," Rose murmured. There was a sound from outside, then the rustle of canvas as the flap was lifted away from the door. Young Wolf— Robby, to the soldiers—dumped Rose's saddle just inside the entrance, then swiftly darted from view before his mother could stop him.

Giggling, Beth said: "Robby thinks it's beneath a man's dignity to carry a woman's burden, especially her saddle."

"Shoot, I could've carried it," Rose said, irritated with herself for not having thought of it.

"Don't be silly," Beth replied. "It does him good to see what his new life will be like."

Rose studied the girl quietly. "It don't seem to be doin' him much good so far," she said finally.

Affecting a pouty expression, Beth said: "Oh well, you're just a dumb frontier girl. James says that in proper society, it's the man's place to labor, the woman's to live elegantly. James promises we'll have servants."

"Men or women?"

The question momentarily stumped the young girl, then her face lit up with inspiration. "Irish," she proclaimed.

Yellow Rock Woman spoke firmly and Beth abruptly fell silent. It made Rose wonder if Little Swan had been mistaken about her mother's command of English, or if perhaps the older woman had observed Rose's annoyance through her facial expression. Then she heard the clop of approaching hoofs, and realized it was neither.

Tensing up, Rose cast a wary eye toward the sloping wall of the lodge. The horses stopped about ten yards away, followed by a brief, masculine discourse in Sioux among the riders. Rose glanced at Yellow Rock Woman, but the older woman smiled reassuringly and patted Rose's knee. After a few minutes the hoofs—Rose figured they accounted for at least four horses—moved away at a trot. Seconds later she heard the whisper of moccasins outside. Then the door was swept aside and a creviced male face the color of stained cherry wood peered inside. He spoke gently to Yellow Rock Woman, who quickly bid him welcome. Stepping inside, he moved around to the right and sat down across from Rose. He was a fine figure of a man—tall and wiry, dressed in smoked buck-skins, his long, steel-gray hair braided, then wrapped in strips of otter fur.

Despite her tender years and obvious contempt for things Indian, Beth's voice took on a note of respect when she introduced the visitor as Old Man Bull, a tribal chief of some importance and the Sioux's primary negotiator with the soldiers. "He wishes to speak with you," Beth added, eyes cast toward the fire.

"Sure," Rose said. "Tell him howdy."

Old Man Bull smiled reciprocally when Beth translated Rose's greeting into Hunkpapa. He beamed and nodded, and, had Rose been uninitiated to frontier mannerisms, she might have considered him a buffoon for his exaggerated motions. But she knew he only meant to speak clearly, that his every intent be fully understood, and so she waited civilly as he completed a visual inspection of her that was thorough but in no way sexual. After a time he spoke, and Beth translated as Johnny Long had done for Fights His Enemies, her young woman's voice soon fading into the background of Rose's mind until the words belonged to Old Man Bull.

"You have come far, Sunflower Girl. For several moons now my people have heard of your troubles with the spotted buffalo men who wish to drive you from your land, as the Long Knives drove the Lakota from theirs. But your battles were fought on the Elk River, that which the whites call the Yellowstone. Now you are here, and I am curious."

Briefly Rose told him about the tall rifleman known as Pine Tree Manning, of what he'd done, and her wish to kill him for it. No one appeared surprised or upset. Retribution was a strong thread within the fabric of Lakota society, understood and accepted. But Old Man Bull had other questions, and Rose soon came to realize that he knew more about Western policies than she would have suspected.

Although he queried her further about Manning and her problems with the cattlemen, he quickly moved on to more germane matters, those that might eventually affect his own people. He wanted to know especially about drift fences, several of which were going up around the reservation. He understood what they were, but seemed unable to grasp the logic behind them. After a time, Rose began to suspect he was searching for a deeper meaning, one that didn't exist on such a fundamental issue as profit and loss. She could sense his genuine fear, though, when he spoke of the consequences of partitioning off the land as if it were pieces of butchered venison that could be divvied out among friends.

Finally they were finished. If Old Man Bull's curiosity hadn't been sated, he'd at least grown weary of the process. Before leaving he repeated Little Swan's promise that she would be safe in Yellow Rock Woman's lodge for the night.

"Tomorrow the colonel's spies will fly to him like sparrows with the news that the white warrior woman has come to the land of the Lakota, but these spies have assured me this knowledge will not reach the colonel's ears until the sun rises. With their words, I make this promise."

"I thank you and Yellow Rock Woman and Little Swan, and all those who've helped me here tonight," Rose said solemnly. "But know, also, that I don't intend to bring trouble to your village. Tomorrow, with the sun's first light, I'll be on my way."

Old Man Bull nodded graciously, but Rose thought she detected a trace of relief in his expression. She didn't blame him. The Indian wars were still fresh in the minds of too many people, both red and white. Harboring someone of her reputation would not bode well in the eyes of the Fort Peck sub-agent.

Pushing to his feet, Old Man Bull said: "I wish you success in your hunt, daughter, for in your victory there is hope for all."

"And in my failure?"

He smiled gently. "In your failure only a little will be lost. It is in the failure of those who love something but will not fight for it that the greatest loss occurs. You have battled well, and in that you have won, so that it does not matter if in the end you lose."

Rose was still mulling that one over long after the old chief had gone. It was only later, in her blankets staring at the dying embers of the fire, that she realized tears were trickling down her cheeks.

Chapter Forty-Two

The sorrel was waiting outside Yellow Rock Woman's lodge the next morning when Rose exited the teepee. Young Wolf—she refused to use the Christian name the soldiers had given him—had curried the stallion's coat thoroughly, combing out his mane and tail until he fairly sparkled. As a parting gesture, the young Sioux had fastened a swallow's feather to the horse's mane, tying it behind the trimmed bridle path where it would flutter in the wind. It represented fleetness and agility, Beth explained contemptuously as the boy stalked haughtily away.

Eyeing Young Wolf's retreating form, Rose said: "I noticed your pap didn't come home last night."

An involuntary gasp escaped Beth's lips. Edging backward, she said: "I have to go. James is leading a patrol up Porcupine Creek today, and I want to watch him leave the post."

"Beth, I'm sorry," Rose said, but the young

woman was already turning away, her stride lengthening.

Starting to run, she called: "James looks ever so gallant, riding his fine chestnut!"

"Beth!" Rose shouted, but the girl was already racing toward the post, the hem of her skirt hiked high above her knees. Watching, Rose wondered what Beth's future would truly be like, once her dashing James was transferred away from the isolation of northeastern Montana.

Yellow Rock Woman came out of the lodge carrying Rose's saddle. Rose moved to intercept her, but Yellow Rock Woman laughed and twisted away.

"You should let her do it," a voice said from behind. Turning, Rose saw Little Swan coming from the direction of Old Man Bull's lodge. She wore a white woman's dress of cotton paisley, with dainty, square-toed shoes. "It is a woman's job, is it not?" she added.

"If it is, what's that make me?" Rose asked glumly as Yellow Rock Woman lugged the saddle to the stallion's side.

"*Cante tinzawin*," Little Swan said. "Brave-hearted woman." She shifted a white cotton sack in her hand, letting it bounce against her leg. "I have brought food and . . . other things."

"You didn't have to do that. You and your mam's done a bunch already."

"You have far to travel to catch the man called Pine Tree."

Cocking a brow, Rose said: "Did Old Man Bull tell you that?"

"He told me the man you seek is in the town called Piñon."

"Piñon!"

Little Swan looked puzzled by Rose's reaction. "This that I tell you is a bad thing?"

"Naw, it's just that I'd heard he was around Fort Peck. I was hopin' to flush him somewhere close by. Piñon, shoot, that's clean over on the other side of the Musselshell." The thought of the huge circle she'd ridden brought a grimace to her face. "I wasn't all that far from Piñon comin' back from Canada some weeks ago. Had I known, I could have waited for him there and saved myself a passel of ridin'."

"Why did you think he was here?"

Rose told her about the man named Dietrich, killed by rustlers, and the rumor of trouble about to descend on the area. Little Swan was smiling before she finished.

"This man, Dietrich, was killed almost a moon past, at a ranch west of here, off the reservation, where the soldiers go to drink whiskey. There are women there who the soldiers share, and it is said that Dietrich, who many times came into my husband's post to trade, tried to take a woman away from a soldier. Dietrich was found the next day with his head crushed. The soldier had witnesses and was not charged in the Long Knives' court-martial."

"He wasn't an Association man, then?"

"He was a fur trader sometimes, but mostly he drank bad whiskey and made the women of my village uncomfortable with his eyes. It is agreed among the soldiers and the Lakota alike that his death is a good thing for both races."

With the sorrel ready, Yellow Rock Woman took the sack of food from Little Swan's hand and fastened it behind Rose's bedroll.

"You figure Old Man Bull's right about Piñon?" Rose asked.

"Old Man Bull would not have said it if it was not true," Little Swan replied.

Rose sighed, but she already believed Little Swan, and she trusted Old Man Bull. "Well, Piñon it is, then," she said, accepting the sorrel's reins from Yellow Rock Woman and stepping into the saddle. She gave the older woman a brief smile. "Tell your mam I'm obliged for her kindness," she said to Little Swan. "Yours, too."

"My mother can see your gratitude, but I will tell her, anyway."

Rose gave the two women—mother and daughter —a short salute, then reined away. She didn't look back to see if Little Swan or Yellow Rock Woman would wave. She figured it would be too much to expect if they did, and too keen a disappointment if they didn't.

Rose nooned that day on a sandy spit along the Missouri. Taking a seat on a sun-bleached log, she opened the sack Little Swan had prepared and began rummaging through it. She found strips of jerky tied in a bundle, half a loaf of hard bread, and a jar of last year's gooseberry jam. At the very bottom she discovered a pair of tiny pelts stretched on willow hoops. Mystified, she drew the hides into the light.

"Sweet Jesus!" she cried, falling backward off the log and scuttling away. She didn't stop until her left hand splashed into the cool waters of the river. On the sand beside the log lay a pair of scalps, the bone-white flesh still moist from the skull.

"Christ!" Rose hissed, then fell onto her back, breathing hard. "Son-of-a-bitch."

Staring at the blue cap of the sky, she knew that Old Man Bull's promise from the night before—his reiteration of Little Swan's assurance that everything would be all right—had come true. At least as far as the old warrior had been able to guarantee it. The men who'd attempted her assassination in Glendive, then followed her west across the Big Lonesome to the banks of the Missouri, would never bother her again.

Rose raised Piñon on the fourth day after leaving the Fort Peck reservation. It was midafternoon, and she was pleased with the time she'd made, even as she was aware of the heavy toll it had taken on the Baylor horse. Even the best animal needed more rest and feed than Rose had allowed the sorrel on their journey across the rugged Missouri River terrain, and she was feeling guilty as she sought out a stable and made arrangements for the stallion's care.

Afterward, she moseyed up the street with the Sharps and saddlebags over her shoulder, her bedroll tucked under one arm. She was looking for a hotel where she could get a room for the night and stow her gear, but hadn't gone two blocks when she came to an abrupt stop. Standing in the middle of the boardwalk, oblivious to the peevish glances of other pedestrians as they squeezed past her, she stared across the street at the Yellow Rose Saloon and Hotel and knew. In her heart, she knew.

Shifting the rifle and saddlebags to her left arm, Rose loosened the Smith & Wesson in its holster, then did the same with the Merwin Hulbert. After that she started across the street, dodging through the brisk traffic without really seeing it. Although conflicting emotions were clamoring for her attention, she ignored them all as she climbed the wooden steps to the saloon. Her gaze darted swiftly as she entered the building, but Manning was nowhere to be seen.

The saloon's interior was dim but pleasantly cool, the large room crowded for that time of day. A knot of gamblers was clustered around a faro table at the rear of the room like iron shavings on a magnet; a roulette wheel against the front wall held a similar group enthralled. At the far end of the bar, nearest the stairs that led to the second floor, eight or ten cowboys were whooping and hollering and having a grand old time, all of them young and boyish and gaudily dressed.

Moving to a relatively empty section of the bar, Rose ordered a beer, then asked permission to leave her stuff behind the counter.

"Sure," the bartender said. He took her bedroll and saddlebags and placed them on a shelf out of the way, but when he glanced at her rifle, she shook her head.

"I'll hang onto this."

Returning with her beer, he said: "We've got a couple of empty rooms upstairs, if you're interested." He grinned suggestively.

Cold-shouldering the innuendo, Rose said: "How many of them rooms is rented out?"

"One's all we'd need."

She shook her head impatiently, knowing he hadn't yet caught the drift of her questioning. "I'm lookin' for a man," she said, complicating the issue further.

The bartender's smile stretched toward his sideburns. "I've never had any complaints."

"God dammit, I'm lookin' for Pine Tree Manning. Do you know who he is?" The smirk vanished, but, when he didn't snap a reply or tell her to go to hell, Rose knew she'd finally cornered his attention. "I figured as much," she said softly, reading his answer in his expression. "Which room is he in?"

"I don't know what you're talking about."

He started to move away, but Rose reached

across the bar and grabbed his sleeve. "Do you know who I am?"

"I do now."

"Is Manning upstairs?"

He glanced toward the stairs leading to the second floor, then growled: "All right, but don't tell him who told you, understand?"

She let go of his shirt. "You've got a deal."

Chuckling harshly, he said: "I've got a deal with a dead woman."

"Which room?"

"Number Two. Top of the stairs, first door on the left."

Rose lowered the Sharps' breech to double check the load. There was a round already chambered. Not so long ago she would have kept the rifle empty until she wanted to use it, but her life had changed radically, and an empty gun now was no better than a stick.

She headed for the stairs, only peripherally aware of the bartender hurrying down the back of the bar to pass along word that Rose of Yellowstone was in town. It wouldn't be more than a couple of minutes before the entire lower floor knew she was there. Those who knew Pine Tree Manning might guess her intentions, but few would note the slim stranger with the hawk-like nose who entered the saloon just as she started up the stairs. Fewer still would attach any significance to his furtive climb after her, once she'd disappeared around the corner at the top.

Chapter Forty-Three

Rose paused on the upper landing, staring down a long, narrow hall with three rooms on either side, a window at the far end for ventilation. A parrot-green runner muffled the heel thud of her boots as she moved toward room Number Two. Pausing in front of the door, she thumbed back the Sharps' big side-hammer, then stepped forward and slammed her boot into the wood beside the knob.

The door sprang open, crashing into the wall and embedding the knob there, offering her a clear view of the room's interior. Pine Tree Manning sat, cross-legged in his underwear in the middle of an unmade bed, the fabled .40-60 Marlin lying atop the wrinkled sheet at his side. Part of a deck of cards was cradled in his left hand, the rest were fanned out before him in a game of solitaire. He looked up in surprise as the door was hurled inward, momentarily frozen as his eyes met hers across the room.

Rose had no need to gloat, no desire to remind him of the crime that had brought death to his door. She fired from the hip, and the Sharps' heavy slug drove him into the headboard. The playing cards still in his hand flew toward the ceiling like flushed quail, raining back around his head and across his lap.

A woman screamed and bolted from a chair

beside the bed. She had curly red hair and was naked save for a pair of vertically striped red and white stockings that came up midway on her white thighs. She stopped dead in her tracks when Rose leaped inside. Switching the Sharps to her left hand, Rose palmed the Smith & Wesson with her right. Dutch Weinhart—he who had participated in the lynching of Wiley Collins and Dirty-Nosed Dave Merritt back under the Crazy Mountains—was standing at the window smoking a cigar. He wore pants and boots but no shirt, and his suspenders hung off his shoulders. His gun belt lay coiled on a nearby table; he was already reaching for it.

"Dutch, don't!" Rose cried, but Weinhart had no intention of obeying, and, as the bearded killer's fingers wrapped around the pistol's grips, Rose wondered why she'd even offered him the opportunity. She squeezed the Smith & Wesson's trigger, and Dutch howled and grabbed his side. Then he spun toward her, flinging the holster away as he brought his pistol up and around.

Calmly, as though everything was happening in slow motion, Rose fired twice more. Both bullets struck Dutch squarely in the chest, and he staggered backward with a startled expression on his face, crashing through the window with the cigar clamped firmly between his teeth.

Shards of broken glass were still rattling off the sill when the red-headed woman made her break. Spotting the charge from the corner of her eye,

Rose reacted instinctively, clubbing the hooker with the Smith & Wesson's barrel as she tried to dodge past, turning toward the door as she did. The woman fell like a snow-white otter into an emerald pool, but, although Rose regretted her action, there was no time to dwell on it. Lifting the Smith & Wesson, she fired again—fired even as Pine Tree Manning started to peel away from the headboard, dead but not yet fallen; even as the red-haired woman began her skid across the harsh, time-worn green carpet; even as the sound of falling window glass continued to ring throughout the room.

At the door, a slim man with a hooked nose sagged against the jamb, his free hand clawing at his shirt just below his sternum, where Rose's bullet had struck him. His finger tightened convulsively on the trigger of his Colt and the pistol spat smoke and lead toward the floor. Below its muzzle, the red-headed woman jumped as his bullet struck her in the neck. She cried out and reached for the corner post of the bed as if to pull herself away, but her strength failed before she could reach it and her arm dropped limply to the floor.

Across the hall, Dutch Weinhart's old pard, Ted Keyes, burst out of room Number One with his pistol drawn. But Keyes lacked the killer's instinct that guided men like Manning and Weinhart. His eyes widened at the sight of the stranger crumbled on the floor, fear rushed into them when he looked at the dead hooker beside the bed, and finally they rose to where Pine Tree Manning lay sprawled across the mattress with both arms hanging off the side, and a tiny sound, like the far-off screeching of a locomotive's brakes, escaped his lips. Rose pointed the Smith & Wesson at Keyes's chest, and for perhaps a full five seconds, neither of them moved. Then Keyes darted down the hall quick as a cat, so swift, in fact, that Rose missed her chance to snap off a shot.

"Son-of-a-bitch," she hissed, leaping to the door. She eased past the jamb, but Keyes was beyond contemplating an ambush. He was fleeing madly, his boots pounding the stairs as he made his way to the ground floor. Rose reached the upper landing just in time to see him ram through the batwing doors to the street beyond. She started to go after him, then stopped when she recognized the futility of trying to overtake someone so completely consumed with flight. Her shoulders sagged. "Son-of-a-bitch," she repeated, but slower this time, with resignation.

In the main room, the saloon's patrons were staring at her in a combination of stunned silence and morbid fascination. Some were half hiding behind tables or the bar or other customers. The games of chance—faro and roulette—were forgotten, the chuck-a-luck cage stilled. At the near end of the bar the drunken cowboys were gazing upward like round-eyed puppies halted in the middle of their play. No one spoke or moved. Then a murmur like a soughing breeze stirred somewhere near the bar and spread rapidly. A voice rose above it, awed: "God *damn!*"

With a whoop, the bartender shouted: "There she is, boys, the genuine article! Rose of Yellowstone, right here in the Yellow Rose Saloon!"

At the rear of the room, someone started to applaud. A couple of men tittered nervously. Then Rose lifted the Smith & Wesson and pointed it at the clapper. He stopped, the color draining from his face. Silence once again settled over the room. To the applauder—a bearded miner in a red-checked vest—Rose said: "I want you to go down to the Piñon Livery and tell 'em to saddle my horse. It's the sorrel stallion that was just brought in. You reckon you can handle that?"

The man swallowed loud enough that even Rose heard him, then quickly bobbed his head.

"Git," she said, and he hurried out the door. Looking at the bartender, Rose said: "You'd best come upstairs."

Nodding mutely, he followed her up to room Number Two. A fair-size contingent of gawkers crowded his heels.

The stranger lay where he'd fallen. Sliding a toe under his shoulder, Rose rolled him onto his back. She recognized him as one of the men who'd accompanied Howard Ostermann on his visit to the A-Bar-E last winter.

"Know him?" she asked the pale-faced bartender.

"His name's Jared White. He worked for . . ." He shut up.

"I know who he worked for," Rose said flatly. She stepped over him, into the room, but the bartender remained at the door.

"Christ," he croaked, looking at the dead hooker.

She lay in a fetal position, her cheek resting in a pool of her own blood. She was older than Rose had at first thought—maybe thirty or thirty-five. Her stockings were askew, worn thin at the knees and toes and heels, the red stripes bleeding into the white from too many washings.

With her gaze on the dead prostitute, caught innocently in the crossfire of Ostermann's range war, Rose said: "Who is she?"

The bartender shook his head. "Nobody. She wasn't nobody."

"No," Rose said tautly. "She was somebody, dammit. To someone, she was somebody. What the hell's the matter with people that they think some count and others don't?"

The bartender shrugged uncomfortably, and Rose realized he didn't understand the question. Not the way she meant it. "Her name's Sally Mayfield," he said. "That's all I know. She's only been here a couple weeks."

"Well, it don't matter how long she was here," Rose said. She pulled Shorty's buckskin poke from her jacket pocket and withdrew all the cash she had—nearly $11—and shoved it into the barkeep's hand. "I want you to see that she gets a proper burial, and I mean done right. You don't, and I'll come lookin' for you."

"Sure," he said. "I can do that."

"Put up a good marker, too. Oak or hickory, with her name and all the right dates. I don't want some cheap pine cross that's gonna fall apart in a couple of years."

"All right."

She gave him a menacing look. "I ain't dead," she reminded him.

The statement seemed to confuse him. "Ah . . . huh?"

"Downstairs a while ago, you said you had a deal with a dead woman, but I ain't dead."

"No," he agreed, "you aren't."

Nodding toward the money sitting in his hand, she said: "I'll be back to check on Sally's grave." Then she shoved past him, into the hall.

The gawkers moved respectfully out of her way, several of them flattening themselves against the wall. Rose headed for the stairs, reloading as she went. As the empties fell willy-nilly across the hall runner, she was aware of a flurry of movement behind her as men scrambled for the spent cartridges—souvenirs to display on their mantles or store away in empty cigar boxes.

Downstairs, Rose retrieved her gear from behind the bar, then walked outside where the miner in the red-checked vest was waiting with the sorrel. He licked nervously at his lips as Rose came down the steps, his eyes darting involuntarily to the twisted lump that was Dutch Weinhart, lying in the street amid shards of broken glass. He said:

"I . . . ah . . . didn't know whether you wanted me to bring the horse here or leave it, or . . ."

She brushed past him without comment and tied her saddlebags and bedroll in place. After resheathing her rifle, she stepped into the saddle and reined away, heeling the horse into a trot.

She passed the local law on her way out of town, a burly man wearing a shiny badge, prominently displayed. He was heading for the Yellow Rose Saloon at a brisk pace, carrying a double-barreled shotgun under one arm. Although he scowled as she jogged past, he didn't slow down or call for her to stop.

Five minutes later, she was free of town, urging the sorrel into a canter. Ahead lay the Judith Mountains. Her plan was to skirt them on the east as she made her way in as straight a line as possible to Ostermann's Crooked Bar-O-Bar, and her long-delayed confrontation with the Flying Egg's pompous owner.

Chapter Forty-Four

Rose pushed hard until nightfall, even though it took a lot out of both her and the stallion. Dismounting beside a narrow, treeless creek, she pulled the saddle from the horse's back and picketed him downstream. Then she came back and unrolled her blankets and crawled inside. As tired as she was, sleep refused her. She'd been exhausted long before reaching Piñon, worn ragged by the drawn-out chase, the poor diet, the sporadic rest. But Manning was dead now. The incentive that had fueled her long pursuit was depleted. With it, suddenly, had gone both energy and will. She was not just tired, she felt physically ill, as if she might throw up or pass out if she didn't stop soon.

What made her exhaustion even worse was the knowledge that the battle wasn't over, not yet. As tired as she was, as sickened as she'd become of the whole ordeal, she understood all too well that even though her mission was completed, the war still raged. It would continue until either Howard Ostermann had his way—legal title to the A-Bar-E—or until one or the other of them was dead.

Even as Rose considered the many gains Ostermann's death would afford not just her, but so many others, she knew any reprieve would be short-lived. Joe Bean had assured her of that. Ostermann might be her personal nemesis, but he was still just one of many, a bit player in a production that spanned the Northwest.

In the meantime, the law would soon be after her for the killings of Manning and Weinhart and the Flying Egg gunman, and in all probability, someone would tag the death of Sally Mayfield on her as well.

Had it not been for Ostermann and the Yellowstone Basin Cattlemen's Association's undesirables list, Rose might have stayed and taken her chances with a jury trial. But she knew the influence of the territory's ranch owners was woven throughout the local judicial system. Her odds for a fair trial would be slim, this close to the Flying Egg. No, she'd have to run now. She'd have to quit this land she loved so dearly and never return. She supposed she'd known that the day she offered her property to Herman Sutherland.

Rose felt better the next morning, though still somewhat draggy. But she was afraid to linger, even for breakfast. Saddling up, she forged ahead.

The strain of the journey was beginning to tell on the sorrel. His eyes were sunken, his flanks gaunt. As Rose took stock of the big stallion's condition, she knew she'd made the right choice when she left Albert behind. There was no way the aging roan could have withstood the rigors of the past two weeks.

She continued south in easy stages, stopping often to rest and allow the sorrel to graze. She watched her back trail all that first day but saw no sign of pursuit. Entering her second day out of Piñon, she began to relax.

It was late that same day that she topped a high, rocky ridge and discovered the Flying Egg headquarters sprawled below her like a miniature city. Whoaing, she let her gaze sweep the maze of corrals and outbuildings. The main house, surrounded by a broad yard and flower gardens, was set apart from the rest of the spread by a couple of hundred yards of open range.

Seen from this vantage point, her view unobstructed by the cottonwoods along the Musselshell that had shielded much of the ranch on her first visit, Rose found the size of the place even more intimidating than she remembered. The longer she looked, the angrier she became. It didn't seem right that someone who already had so much should be able to cause the harm Ostermann had, yet remain so distanced from the consequences of his greed. She'd met the man only once, on a cold winter's day almost eight months before, and had spoken with him for barely fifteen minutes, yet he'd taken away friends, cost her the land she loved, the territory she considered home. Could she turn the other cheek to that? She'd killed Garcia and Manning for what they'd done to Nora. Did Howard Ostermann merit any less?

"What about it?" Rose asked the sorrel. "Does this jasper deserve any better than Manning?"

The stallion's ears were perked forward, nostrils distended as he studied the array of barns and sheds, the paddocks where groomed and grain-fed horses with pedigreed bloodlines stood listlessly in the summer's heat. The kennels behind the house reminded Rose of the mastiffs she'd seen on her first visit, and she pulled the Sharps and laid it across the pommel of her saddle. Giving the sorrel a tap with the side of her stirrups, she said: "No opinion, huh? Well, let's go say howdy, anyway."

Rose approached the corrals and outbuildings first, figuring whoever was about would be hard at work, but, as she drew closer, she began to detect an emptiness to the place, an air of desertion. She assumed a lot of the hands would be out looking after the shorthorns Ostermann had had shipped in to replenish his range, but she expected a few waddies to be around. No outfit the size of the Crooked Bar-O-Bar could afford to leave its buildings unattended for long. There were always corrals to mend, roofs to patch, penned livestock that needed feed and water.

And in the case of the Flying Egg, there was the polo field and the lawn surrounding the main house to irrigate and mow.

Pulling up in front of the bunkhouse, Rose raised a call that no one answered. Riding over to a nearby barn, she peered inside without dismounting. "This is feelin' a mite shudder-some," she confided to the sorrel, but the stallion's attention was riveted on a large lot near the river where a band of yearlings ran.

She reined toward the main house, where a thread of smoke curled above the dark slate roof of a summer kitchen. Although she kept a wary eye peeled for the mastiffs, and cocked the Sharps as an added precaution, she saw no sign of the huge, slick-coated beasts.

Circling to the rear of the house, she grew even more puzzled when she realized the kennels where Ostermann had kept his hounds were empty, the pine-framed wire gates left carelessly open. Looking around, she began to notice other signs of neglect, as well. Weeds peeked out from among the flowers in the beds fronting the verandah, and the rose bushes and waist-high topiaries of leafed wildlife—grizzly bear and bison and mountain goat—drooped in the high plains heat.

She pulled up in front of the small summer kitchen behind the main house just as a middle-aged Indian woman exited the building. The woman paused when she saw Rose, but no flicker of emotion crossed her face. She stood silently in front of the kitchen door in a simple cotton dress, her hands dusted with flour, her dark eyes patient, waiting.

"Howdy," Rose said.

There was no reply.

"I'm lookin' for Ostermann." A pause. "Howard Ostermann, your boss." After another brief silence, she said: "You savvy English?"

The woman stood as if carved from stone. Rose was trying to frame the question in sign when a screen door creaked open on the rear porch of the main house and a lanky blond man stepped into full view, a toothpick canted jauntily from the corner of his mouth. Before the door could slap shut, two others had appeared.

"God damn," Rose said huskily, sliding her finger around the trigger of the still-cocked Sharps.

"Hello, Rose," Frank Caldwell said with a familiar smirk.

Chapter Forty-Five

"She isn't very talkative," Caldwell continued, advancing to the edge of the porch. Casting a sidelong glance at the Indian woman, he added: "She is handy, though, in more ways than one."

Making no effort to disguise her feelings, Rose said: "I'd kind of gotten used to not thinkin' about you, Frank. Now here you are, poppin' up again like a bad smell."

Caldwell put his hand on the brass buckle of his gun belt, subtly drawing attention to the twin Colts holstered there. Although Rose didn't at first recognize the skinny, roughly dressed fellow on his left, the one on his right was Ted Keyes. Meeting Keyes's sullen stare, Rose grinned boldly. "Don't I know you?" she mocked. "Turn around, so's I can see your back."

Keyes flushed, glowering.

Chuckling, Caldwell said: "Now, Rose, quit picking on the boy."

The statement seemed so out of character that not only did Keyes look surprised by it, but it brought a guffaw from the gunman on Caldwell's left. Rose glanced at him, her gaze lingering.

"Dammit, Frank," Keyes growled.

But Caldwell's smile had vanished. "If you'd done your part in Piñon, this mess would be finished by now."

"That ain't true," Keyes objected, but Rose could hear the defeat in his voice.

Her gaze went back to the third gunman, as if drawn there. Then it came to her, and she laughed. "Well, I'll be damned . . . little Bud."

"That was a long time ago," the slim gunman replied coolly. "I won't be surrendering my pistol today."

"I saw your old pard over in Glendive a while back. Axel Carrington. He's doin' real well for himself, which is more than I can say for you, if you're ridin' for Frank Caldwell."

"I don't give a hoot what that potbellied nose-picker's doing," Bud replied. He moved his hand back to touch the grips of a nickeled revolver. "I don't give a damn what you think, either."

"Was that you pesterin' my pap last spring, lookin' for Muggy's gold?" she asked. Her eyes narrowed. "I'll bet it was you who tried to dig up Muggy's grave last year, too, wasn't it?"

Although Bud refused a reply, Rose figured the look on his face was answer enough. Grimly she turned to Caldwell. "Where's Ostermann?"

"What's your business with him?"

"Personal," she replied, a trace of sarcasm coming into her voice.

"Sure it is, but I'm curious. Did you come to kill him?"

From Caldwell's question, Rose knew her answer wouldn't matter. "He ain't here, is he?"

"Is that why you came?" Caldwell persisted. "To kill Howard Ostermann?"

She was quiet a moment, thinking. Then she shook her head. "I don't know, Frank, and that's the God's honest truth. I know I wanted to look him in the eye one last time, let him know that I knew who he was, what he was. I wanted him to know that I saw him the way he sees himself, late at night when he's alone with his thoughts, and that, despite what he tells himself, maybe even what his friends tell him, the world still sees him for what he is. I reckon that ain't much for me to crow about, but it looks like that's all I'm gonna get."

Caldwell laughed. "I wish he was here. It was always fun to watch his face when someone called his bluff."

"Where'd he go?"

Still grinning, Caldwell said: "He's on his way back to England."

"What!"

"He's calling it an extended vacation, but he took his best polo horses and all his hunting dogs. He nearly gutted the house of his favorite trinkets, too. My guess is that Montana has seen the last of Howard Ostermann, and that the Egg will be taken over by some English corporation that'll send a prissy little bookkeeper out to run the place from an office."

Rose leaned back in her saddle. Of all the scenarios that had run through her mind on the ride down from Piñon, none had included the possibility that Ostermann might cut his pin and run.

"Then it's over?" she asked, hardly daring to believe that it might be, that with Ostermann gone, things could return to normal.

"No," Caldwell said, the old, hard edge returning to his voice. "Not for you. It'll never be over for you. Not in Montana. If Ostermann doesn't want your property, then that prissy little bookkeeper will."

"The sons-a-bitches," Rose said softly, bitterly.

"There's something else," Caldwell said. "Something you need to understand. *I* have to eliminate you now. Not for Ostermann, but for myself. People are saying I can't do it, that Rose of Yellowstone is too much of a match for Frank Caldwell. They're laying wagers against me in Billings and Miles City at two to one odds. If I don't disprove those nay-sayers, if you don't disappear, I'll be finished on the northern ranges."

Rose nodded. She understood. "It's a fact a gunman's reputation is a fragile thing," she commented. "Once the myth gets shattered, the man is sure to follow."

"Then you understand how it has to be?"

There was more to Caldwell's question than met the ear, Rose knew, and it alerted her to what was coming next. Her finger tightened on the Sharps' trigger. "I'm sorry to hear that, Frank," she said.

Later, it would bring her some small measure

of consolation to know that, even before she'd finished speaking, Caldwell and Bud were reaching for their guns. Not that it would have altered her own response if they hadn't, for, as soon as Caldwell announced his intent, Rose knew she'd have to kill him first, drop him before he could even get his hands on one of his pistols, if that was possible. So it was with the same breath that she confessed her regrets, as the two gunmen began their own moves, that Rose let the muzzle of the still-cocked Sharps swing abruptly toward Caldwell.

She was quicker by a hair, the Sharps' blast slamming Caldwell into the side of the house, the bullet going all the way through his chest to chew a hole in the log wall behind him. Then she jabbed her spurs hard against the sorrel's ribs, the stallion squealing and jumping even as Rose let the Sharps fall. Bud had already fired once and missed. Now he was darting out of the way of the sorrel's flashing hoofs, bringing his pistol around for a second shot. Rose's throat went dry as the horse leaped toward the porch. She knew she wasn't going to be fast enough to palm her Smith & Wesson before the angry youth fired his second round at almost pointblank range.

Bud's Colt seemed to explode in Rose's face, so loud she thought the noise would surely unhorse her, even if the bullet didn't. But his slug clipped her saddle horn first, the hard wood and thick leather deflecting the bullet however slightly. She felt a sharp burn across her side that was like a hot poker laid against her ribs, but she kept her seat. Even as the stallion landed on the porch with a thunder of stamping hoofs, she kept her seat.

Bringing the Smith & Wesson around, Rose fired intuitively. Bud cried out and tumbled off the porch. Then the sorrel nearly lost his footing on the tractionless planks. His rear hoofs skidded out, and he would have gone down if he hadn't come up hard against the side of the house. Rose grunted as her leg and shoulder were rammed into the logs. She almost lost the Smith & Wesson. It jumped in her hand like a trout leaping clear of an icy mountain stream, then dropped neatly back in place.

As the sorrel struggled for its footing, Rose twisted in the saddle to snap a shot at Keyes. She needn't have bothered. Keyes stood twenty feet away, his pistol drawn but pointed toward the porch, his eyes wide with fright. He didn't move when Rose fired, and only flinched pathetically as her bullet zinged past his ear.

Bud's was a grittier mettle, however. Rose spotted him in the yard, struggling awkwardly to his feet. His left thigh was bloody where her bullet had laid open the flesh. He lurched after his pistol, lying several yards away, the nickel plating glinting in the sunlight. Her next shot struck the Colt just behind the barrel, bouncing the pistol into the air and knocking the cylinder half out of its frame. Only then did Bud stop.

The sorrel got its hoofs under it at the same time and came to a trembling, splay-legged halt on the porch, facing outward. Keyes hadn't moved, but the front of his trousers were dark where he'd urinated himself. Bud was breathing hard, glaring at Rose with a hatred that had been born on the day he and Axel and a black cowboy named Charlie Sims had tried to rob her above the Yellowstone.

At the summer kitchen's door, the Indian woman stood as before, stoic and unaffected.

Puffing hard herself, Rose said to Bud: "That was some for slick, switchin' places like we done, you on the ground now and me up here. I doubt we could do that again if we tried."

"If you're going to shoot me, get it done," he replied harshly. "I won't waste words with someone I intend to kill."

"Well, you got fire in your craw, all right, but I ain't keen on killin' you if I don't have to."

"You'll have to," he promised. "Caldwell was a fool and Keyes is a coward, but I won't make the same mistakes they did."

"You ain't makin' this easy," Rose reprimanded. "You ought to shut up before you back me into a corner I can't get out of." Glancing at his leg, she added: "You've been shot, if you ain't noticed."

But Bud remained true to his word and refused to answer. Rose didn't know what to do. She didn't want to kill him, but she was afraid that, if she didn't, he'd force her hand. It was the Indian woman who came to her rescue. As she moved away from the kitchen's shadow, all eyes turned toward her. She picked up the Sharps, then climbed onto the porch and handed it to Rose. Still without speaking, she jutted her chin toward the ridge where Rose had stopped earlier to study the Flying Egg's layout. Coming over its crest at a gallop was a trio of horsemen, kicking up clouds of dust that swirled behind them like flapping banners. Rose shook her head in exasperation, but didn't figure there was any need to speculate about their business.

Booting the Sharps, she said: "Listen, Bud, there ain't no reason we gotta go around shootin' at one another. You just let me slide outta this territory, quiet-like, and I'll be one less burr under your saddle blanket."

Bud glared daggers but didn't reply. Keyes also remained silent, but Rose had already dismissed him. Nodding her thanks to the Indian woman, she gave the sorrel a gentle tap with her stirrups. Snorting his displeasure, the stallion gingerly approached the edge of the porch, then stretched for the long step down to solid ground. With *terra firma* under his hoofs once more, the sorrel's old, cocky personality returned full bloom. Keeping a tight rein on the horse and her pistol on Bud, Rose glanced toward the rise. Although the approaching horsemen were still too far away to recognize, she knew who they were. Or at least she knew who their leader was. Every man and woman sat a horse differently, and she'd known Joe Bean too many years not to know it was he who rode at the van of the three Regulators.

Chapter Forty-Six

After crossing the Musselshell, Rose kicked the sorrel into a run. Joe Bean and his men were still half a mile behind, but she could tell by the fleetness of their ponies that they were riding fresher mounts than her own.

Coming to a well-defined trail that led south, the direction she wanted to go, Rose swung onto it. Far ahead were the northern slopes of the Bull Mountains, and, with her gaze on those distant heights, she suddenly knew what she wanted to do. She wanted to go home. She wanted to lay her hands on the cool log walls of the cabin she and Nora had built together. She wanted to slake her thirst in the cold waters of the creek, then wander through the garden to see how the pumpkins and corn were faring. And lastly, she wanted to stand on the high bluff that overlooked the valley of the Yellowstone and stare out as she had so many times before and wonder, however briefly, what the future held for her.

She wanted to say good bye to Nora, too, but strangely, she was more eager to talk to Muggy. She'd judged him harshly for his death and the grief his gambling had brought her, but time had dulled the sharpest edges of her feelings. He was still a scoundrel in her mind and probably always would be, but she'd come to see him in a different light recently. If Muggy had been a rogue, he'd at least been up front about it, and hadn't tried to hide his true colors behind a façade of pursed-lip propriety. And quite unexpectedly he'd caused her to recognize the worth of her own hard-scrabble existence. She'd once considered herself less than others because of her poverty and lack of education, but she saw now that she'd been wrong. She was a good woman, and neither poverty nor riches or an outlaw's reputation would take that away from her.

There had been a time in her life when a trek such as this—returning home for a final visit, a last good bye—would have wracked her with guilt and grief, but she experienced neither today. She thought there might even be a trace of joy in the prospect of going back. She hadn't thought she would ever see the place again. Now she figured there was a chance she might, as long as she could stay ahead of Joe and his men.

Rose had a good lead, and she played it for all it was worth. She kept the sorrel at a lope for most of what remained of the day, only pulling back to a jog or a walk for short stints, before spurring into a canter once more. Sweat soon darkened the stallion's chest and shoulders, foaming up along the cinch to blow back over the legs of her riding skirt. His breathing was becoming labored, too, although not yet dangerously so. Had it been earlier in the day she might have fretted, but the afternoon was waning, the sun already slipping below the horizon.

Nightfall slowed her, forcing her to a jog, then a walk. Finally she was obliged to dismount and lead the flagging stallion on foot, picking her way cautiously until an anemic quarter moon came up a couple of hours before midnight.

The country became noticeably more rugged as they climbed toward the top of the Bulls. Scattered groves of pine—trees largely absent along the more easterly route she normally followed—further blocked what little light the moon gave up, so that she was never sure what her next step would encounter. She feared rattlesnakes and precipices, but was more afraid of what lay behind her.

It was after midnight when she reached the summit. Dawn found her among the rocky foothills, tired but no longer exhausted. She'd passed the point where she didn't think she could take another forward step somewhere on the descent. She knew now that she'd be able to go as far as needed, to face whatever this new day might bring.

When the light had strengthened, she led the sorrel behind a screen of scrubby pines, then climbed a nearby knob where she had an unobstructed view of the surrounding country. There was no sign of the three Regulators, no hint at all of another human being in all that vast expanse. It was as if she alone rode the hills south of the Bulls.

Rose didn't trust it for a minute. Hurrying back to the sorrel, she swung into the saddle. "We're gonna push on a spell," she told her weary mount. "We'll have breakfast down the trail, but we won't tarry even then. I got me an uneasy feelin' this mornin'."

It was another hour to a narrow runnel winding out of some lichen-covered boulders. A pool not much bigger around than Billy Garcia's sombrero held enough water for the sorrel, with half a dozen places upstream where Rose could satisfy her own thirst. Afterward, she checked the wound received in yesterday's battle, relieved to find that it was nothing more than a scratch across her ribs.

"I've seen my pap cut himself worse than this shavin'," she observed to the sorrel.

Keeping the stallion's reins in hand, Rose finished off the last of the food Little Swan had prepared. Then she draped the reins over a nearby limb and went to the brook for another drink. As she bent forward, a shot rang out, the bullet smacking into the dirt less than a foot away.

"Damn!" Rose exclaimed, scrambling across the tiny stream on hands and toes. She ducked behind a boulder just as a second shot kicked up a geyser of water. She slid the Smith & Wesson from its holster but didn't bother cocking it. She'd already spotted the cloud of powder smoke that marked her assailant's position some two hundred yards away, and knew her .38 would never reach that far. She glanced longingly at the sorrel, less than twenty feet away, but dared not make an attempt to reach it, or the rifle booted under the saddle's off-side stirrup.

A voice hailed from the distance. At first Rose

thought it was directed at her. Then she realized it came from behind her attacker, and was meant for him.

"Don't shoot!" the voice ordered.

"I've got her nailed down tight," her assailant replied distantly. "Hurry up!"

"Don't shoot, dammit! Joe wants her alive," the farther voice called.

"But I've got her cornered!" her attacker repeated in frustration.

His dismay brought a taut smile to Rose's lips. She'd needed an edge, no matter how slim. She figured this might well be the only one she'd get.

Pushing to her feet, she sprinted for the sorrel. Already skittish from all the gunfire, the horse spooked and jerked his reins loose as soon as Rose surged from cover; he might have bolted if she hadn't called for him to stop in that no-nonsense tone she normally reserved for when he was acting up around other horses. A third round from her attacker inadvertently helped when it kicked up a cloud of dust in front of the nervously prancing stallion, causing him to hesitate just long enough for Rose to grab the reins.

Then the horse was running, breaking through the scrub with Rose clinging desperately to the chipped saddle horn. She got her feet under her just as her attacker opened up in earnest. Racing alongside, she gave a jump and made a flying leap—what the old-timers called a pony express mount—by letting the sorrel's momentum help catapult her leg over the cantle, landing her squarely in the Mother Hubbard's cradle. Bending low until the stallion's mane snapped in her face like tiny whips, she raked the horse's ribs with her spurs.

They were about four hundred yards away when the sorrel stumbled and nearly went down among some rocks. Rose tensed to jump, but the horse caught its stride and stretched out like a thoroughbred, the swallow's feather Young Wolf had fastened to its mane dancing in the wind. The shots of her attacker began to fade out. Leaning forward, Rose whispered encouragement into the stallion's ear, assuring him that nothing could catch them now.

It was noon when Rose reached the cabin. She half expected to find a Flying Egg brand on it somewhere—line riders in the house or Flying Egg cattle bedded down along the creek—but the place appeared pretty much as she'd left it, right down to the charred remains of the A-Bar-E's furnishings in the front yard. Only the wind had been along to smooth over the ashes.

Rose supposed there was little to cheer about as she hiked into the yard, the sorrel gimping awkwardly after her. The stallion's right rear fetlock was swollen, hot to the touch above the spot where the ambusher's bullet had struck the hoof. Although the wound would heal, Rose knew it would take time. Until then, riding the sorrel was out of the question. She might use a horse hard out of necessity, just as she pushed herself from time to time, but she would never knowingly risk ruining an animal for her own greed. Not even if that greed was for her life.

"Well, I reckon this is the end of the trail for us, big fella," she told the sorrel as she pulled off the Mother Hubbard. She stripped the bridle but left the swallow's feather, then stepped back to look the horse in the eye. "You did good, in spite of your randy ways. Had things turned out differently, we might've made a fine team, you 'n' me."

The horse returned her gaze unblinkingly, head up, ears perked forward as if in concentration.

"Dang it, don't start listenin' to me now. I've been talkin' your ears off ever since we left Fred and Della's, waitin' for you to make some kind of reply."

The horse whickered softly, his rubbery lips fluttering.

"See, I knew you was capable of holdin' a conversation," she said, grinning. "Now I'm gonna . . ."

"Rose!"

She started, turning to the barn. Joe Bean stood in its entrance, pistol in hand. Behind him was a pair of lathered horses, and she knew instantly what he'd done. It had been a neat trick, she had to admit, confiscating one of his men's mounts and coming on to the A-Bar-E the long way around. By switching off from one horse to the other, he'd been able to make better time than the three of them could have done together—better time than Rose could have made on the sorrel, even without the stallion having been clipped in the hoof—yet his men could easily follow along on one horse if they took their time. It also explained where Joe had been that morning, when his men had ambushed her at the stream.

Moving clear of the barn, Joe said: "This is the end of the line, Rose. Drop your gun belt."

She stared back in indecision, flexing her fingers. Before she could make up her mind, her attention was drawn to the creek near Nora's grave, where a patch of color had moved. At first she thought it was a bear, a large silvertip perhaps, coming onto the plains in search of food, but the shading was wrong, the shape confusing in the brush below the spring. Then her pulse quickened and she said, under her breath: "No . . ." Tears sprang to her eyes. "It can't be."

But it was. After breaking free of the brush, Albert shifted his course toward her. Blinking back tears, Rose went to meet him.

"Stay where you are," Joe ordered, but she ignored him. "I'll shoot," he added.

Rose stopped, but only because the roan had broken into a trot. A smile lit up her face even as the tears spilled across her cheeks, and she thought: *Now I'm gonna bawl like some love-sick gal, and Joe'll hang me with puffy red eyes.*

It didn't matter. Not any more. She had come

home, and although she'd thought nothing could beat that, something had. Her friend was here. Her old pard who had comforted her during her gangling teenage years, who had listened to her and been there for her when her pap and brothers and Muggy never were.

As the aging gelding slowed to a walk, Rose went to meet him. Albert pressed his graying forehead against her chest and pushed gently into her. Rose scratched his bridle path. She wanted to tell him how much she'd missed him, and how leaving him behind had turned her cold inside, but the words wouldn't come. Finally she squeezed her eyes shut, content to scratch the rangy gelding behind his ears, raising a fine dust.

Was I gonna live, she thought fiercely, *I'd trim that mane close, and get them burrs outta his tail.*

"Rose," Joe said gently. He stood barely a dozen feet away.

Swallowing hard, she said: "You must think I'm the biggest kind of baby." Then she noticed that his eyes were also misty, and added: "Maybe we both are."

"You were always fond of that horse."

"He's the best friend I ever had."

"Why didn't you leave when you had the opportunity?"

"Let me go now. I got nothin' holdin' me here any more."

"It's too late. You're wanted by the law."

"Whose law?"

"It doesn't matter who owns it. You're a wanted woman, and you're still on top of the cattlemen's list. That's Ostermann's gift to you. That and a price on your head that will never go away."

"You figurin' to collect it, are you?"

"No, I won't take you in."

"Then you aim to leave me hangin' in a tree as a message to others, like you done to Sam Matthews and them boys at the mouth of the box cañon, and Wiley and Dave?" Her eyes darted involuntarily to the old, lightning-scarred pine where vigilantes had strung up Muggy so long ago.

Joe shook his head. "No, I'll see that you're buried properly. I promise you that. I'll bury you beside Muggy, if you'd like."

"It ain't him so much as I was always partial to the view from up there."

Joe made a motion with his revolver. "You'd best drop your shooter, Rose."

She did as she was told, then moved away from Albert. Joe was pulling some pigging string from his pocket and shaking it out. She knew he intended to bind her wrists with it, the way they'd done Muggy.

"Come here," he said.

"You ain't gonna wait for your pards to catch up?"

"No, they're a crude lot and would only make this harder. We'll settle it before they get here, for old times' sake."

"You don't have to do this."

He looked up, his expression suddenly furious.

"It's too damn' late for that," he rasped, his face turning dark with anger, the prim and proper man he had become in his association with the big cattle outfits peeling away like dried mud. "I all but begged you to get outta this territory so it wouldn't come to this. Don't you dare start pleading for your life now."

"I ain't pleadin'," she said, taken aback by the rawness of his voice, the quick, savage breaths he was taking to control his temper. It made her realize just how difficult this was going to be for him, and she wondered if he'd have the where-withal to see it through in Regulator style—which meant hanging—or if he'd weaken in the end and shoot her down, quick-like, to get it over with. "I admire your pluck, Joe," she said, her voice all of a sudden shaky with emotion. "I always said you was no quitter. No matter how difficult the task, I'd tell folks . . ."

"Shut up," he said in a ragged voice, then repeated his command for her to come closer.

Keeping her gaze on his pistol, she walked toward him, stopping again only a few feet away. Her pulse was thundering in her ears. "Joe," she said. "There's something I forgot to tell you."

"What's that?"

"I got me a little hide-out gun under my left arm."

He leveled the Colt between her eyes, cocking it. "I need you to pull that piece slow, Rose, real slow."

She lifted the lapel of her jacket to reveal the Merwin Hulbert, then cautiously slid it from its holster, the moment so charged Rose thought surely one of them would have a stroke.

"Hand it here," he said, reaching for the stubby pistol with his free hand. As he did, the Colt's muzzle shifted slightly away.

"Joe," she whispered.

He froze, his gaze locked with hers; the Colt's aim was still to the side, somewhat lowered now. "Yes, Rose?"

She was holding the revolver toward him butt first, her forefinger curved through the trigger guard just like Sam Matthews had taught her. She paused uncertainly. Then a reckless grin split her face and she said: "Have I ever showed you my road agent spin?"

About the Author

Michael Zimmer grew up on a small Colorado horse ranch, and began to break and train horses for spending money while still in high school. An American history enthusiast from a very early age, he has done extensive research on the Old West. His personal library contains over two thousand volumes covering that area west of the Mississippi from the late 1700s to the early decades of the 20th Century. In addition to perusing first-hand accounts from the period, Zimmer is also a firm believer in field interpretation. He's made it a point to master many of the skills used by our forefathers, and can start a campfire with flint and steel, gather, prepare, and survive on natural foods found in the wilderness, and has built and slept in shelters as diverse as bark lodges and snow caves. He has done horseback treks using 19th Century tack, gear, and guidelines. *Michael* Zimmer is the author of twelve previous novels. His work has been praised by *Library Journal*, *Historical Novel Society*, and *Publishers Weekly* among others. Zimmer's *City of Rocks* (Five Star, 2012) was chosen by *Booklist* as one of the top ten Western novels of 2012, the reviewer saying of the first-person narrator that "at times we can hear the wistfulness in his voice, the bittersweet memory of a time when he and the country were raw, young, and full of hope and promise. A stirring tale, well told." Zimmer now resides in Utah with his wife Vanessa, and two dogs. His website is www.michael-zimmer.com.

Center Point Large Print
600 Brooks Road / PO Box 1
Thorndike, ME 04986-0001 USA

(207) 568-3717

US & Canada:
1 800 929-9108
www.centerpointlargeprint.com